November Sunshine

By

Annie Billups

DEDICATION

To my mother, Annie—your quiet strength, boundless love, and enduring spirit have been a guiding light in my life. Everything I am, I owe in part to you.

And to my husband, Timothy—my steadfast anchor through every season. Your unwavering support, gentle wisdom, and the deep friendship you shared with my mother have meant more than words can say.

With all my love and gratitude,

Judi Billups Ripley and family.

ACKNOWLEDGMENTS

This book is more than a story—it is a tribute, a memory, and a promise kept.

To my mother, Annie Billups—your voice is as strong on the page as it was in life. Though you are no longer here, your words endure, and through them, so does your spirit. Thank you for the wisdom, the grit, and the beauty you left behind.

To my late husband, Timothy—thank you for being my anchor in life, and for always honoring my mother with the kindness and friendship she cherished. I carry your love with me in every step of this journey.

To my children and family—thank you for standing beside me, for encouraging me to see this book through, and for understanding the weight and wonder of preserving our family's story.

To the readers, thank you for holding this story in your hands and in your hearts. May it stir compassion, spark reflection, and shine a light on lives often left in the shadows.

With deep love and gratitude,

Judi Billups Ripley.

ABOUT THE AUTHOR

Annie Billups was born in Reading, Pennsylvania. She was an only child and an avid reader and artist.

She married and became a minister's wife, giving birth to a son and adopting a daughter: two grandchildren, three great-grandchildren, and one great-great-grandchild.

During the years, she had many jobs, working for the defense department during WWII, going to Hollywood, and working for Republic Studios. It also included being an English teacher for twenty-seven years, a professor, an editor of a newspaper, and working for the girls' club. She learned that she was a Quaker and practiced as such in her later years.

She was a beautiful person who cared for everyone.

Table of Contents

NOVEMBER SUNSHINE BEFORE

Laws, I can still see 'em now, just the way they looked them dark-haired like their Paw, an' scruffy, an' there was twelve of 'em. Twelve boys. They was dressed like the tail-end leavin's of somebody's ragbag, an' they stood all squashed in a bunch, scarce darin' to breathe lest someone might take notice of 'em an shoot 'em away. Most of 'em had stood like this before, waitin' for their Maw to finish birthin' another baby. I know, 'cause I'm the one what helped their Maw, Ella Mae, with all her babies.

Anyways, bein' a midwife, which I be, folks call me in whenever a woman gets near her birthin' time. An' that's why I was there in the Mudi's cabin lookin' at them twelve boys. Lem, first-born, the only one who was fair-haired like his Maw, had come and fetched me cause it was beginnin' to look like their Maw was comin' on to her time. Soon's I got there, I set Sam'l, Ella Mae's man, to hangin' up a blanket by the bed to give her some space away from watchin' eyes. Lord knows, I could tell right off that she was in a bad way, an' needed all the help she could get. Once Sam'l got the blanket up, I went back in there with poor, frail Ella Mae to see what I could do to help her.

Ella Mae was really bad off an' didn't hardly know me. She was moanin' and makin' hurtin' sounds as would break your heart. She was turnin' an' twistin' on that bed like she was wont to die. There weren't much I could do for her but to hold her hand real tight and let her try to give me some of the pain that was pullin' at her so.

Kneelin' there by that bed with Ella Mae holdin' on to me for dear life, I couldn't help but remember how it'd been before. Sam'l had sent for me, same as always, an' I came a hurryin' over to their cabin. There weren't as many boys then, but

1

whatever of 'em there was, they was standin' as close as they dared, waitin' to see what would happen. An' not too long after I got there, Ella Mae would set to groanin' an' pretty soon the baby would pop out. I'd cover Ella Mae an' wipe off the baby some, an' then Sam'l would come pokin' around the blanket to see what kind of a lookin' boy she'd up an' give 'im this time.

He always counted on it bein' a boy. I don't think he ever give a thought to havin' anythin' else.

Anyways, once he'd seen that the baby was fit an' had his tiny little pecker all right, Sam'l would step out from behind the blanket with his pigeon chest all puffed out. Then he'd beller to anybody within hearin', "A boy, I done it again!"

Then, with Sam'l so pleased an' happy, the boys would feel happy, too. See, they always knew they could get by with stuffin' off their chores a bit when their Paw was in such good spirits an' so damn proud of himself. It wasn't until the birthin' before last that things didn't seem to go as easy as usual. After that one, her terith had got itself born, and Ella Mae got to where she just seemed to be barely draggin' herself around. Didn't seem able to do for herself an' her family like she'd always done before. An' that sure didn't sit well with Sam'l. He got crankler, a wet rooster, an' was quick to whomp the closest behind with his big, rough hand.

It didn't seem right that Ella Mae should have more babies after all that. But Sam'l was a pig-headed man about what he figgered was a wife's duty, an' sure enough, she started makin' another baby 'fore too long. She dragged herself around with her belly gettin' bigger an' bigger until folks thought sure she'd drop. But not Ella Mae. She just kept on goin' an' sure as shoot in Sam'l sent for me sayin' it was her time again.

I tell you, it near broke my heart to see Ella Mae. She was so peaked an' tired lookin' an' her eyes was full of hurt an' sad.

2

She didn't look at all like a woman's 'sposed to look when she's bring' a new little one into the world.

Well, somehow that baby got itself torn, and after I cleaned it up, I laid the baby next to Ella Mae on the bed. She pulled the little one up to her breast an' he started suckin' away like he knowed what to do all along.

But it had been too much for Ella Mae. Her milk had dried up on that little mite sucked an' fretted an' made mewly sounds, but couldn't get a drop.

I finally took Sam'l aside an' told him to go down to the neighbors who kept a cow, an' ask 'em for some milk for the new baby. Sam'l stamped off in a huff mutterin' to himself that "She done it a-purpose!"

The neighbor lady, Mrs. Sappington, was real nice an' sent word up with Sam'l that if he'd send one of the boys down each mornin' she'd send up fresh milk for the baby an' some extra for the little boys, too. So, they managed.

Lookin' at Ella Mae now, so thin an' worn out with tryin' to birth another son for Sam'l, I just couldn't help thinkin' how hard life can be sometimes.

Ella Mae an' I went way back. She was a hill woman through an' through. She never complained that the cabin Sam'l had made 'em was far too small for their big brood. An' she carried water from the nearest spring an' used her wood stove to heat it an' cook, an' warm the place just like we all do here in the hills, far as I know, she never asked for much, neither. Once she said, soundin' real sad, that she wished Sam'l would stop givin' her babies.

But she didn't really 'spect he would. There's not much to do after a full day of workin' your land an' mendin' tools an' such like. Most of the men hereabouts look forward to tiddlin'

3

around with their woman come nightime. Figger it's their right. An Ella Mae had grown up knowin' what would be 'spected of her when Sam'l up an' spoke for her.

Ella Mae an' Sam'l weren't the only ones with a passel of kids. Lots of the folks here in the hills are given to big families. They need 'em. It takes a lot of hands to scrabble up enough earth to make a garden to grow beans an' such. An' if you're lucky, some of the young-uns turn out to be good at fishin' or huntin' an' that helps make enough food.

So, Ella Mae was just doin' what was 'spected of her.

I remember back to when the Preacher, all dressed in his black preachin' suit and shirt, and two of the members of the Freewill Baptist Church down in the valley came to see Sam'l. They drove the Preacher's old car up the twisty, rocky road as far as it would go when the car just couldn't go no farther, they got out and put some big rocks behind the wheels so it wouldn't roll downhill whilst they were busy. I was over at the Mudd's helpin' Ella Mae with the last baby, an' I seen one of the men look up the hill an' shake his head. Then the preacher reached out an' sort of patted him on the back, an' they all took real deep breaths an' started climbin'.

At first, they all three tried to walk straight up like they weren't payin' any mind to the steep mountain they was climbin'. But the climb got to 'em an' by the time they reached the Mudd's cabin, it was all they could do to haul themselves up the steps to the porch. Two of the men sort of collapsed on the old bedsprings that had been rustin' away on the porch for as long as I can remember. One of the men brushed at the springs like he was seein' if any rust would come off on his clothes. He seemed to give up when his hand came away all covered with bits of rust an' dirt. The Preacher, though, seemed to think it would be safer to sit on the top step, which he did.

4

Sam'l seemed puzzled about why they'd come. He knew, though, that when folks came by your place, you were bound to treat 'em nice. So, he hurried inside the cabin an' came back out carryin' a jug of his latest squeezins. He handed it around, real proud-like. For just a bit, the Preacher looked longingly at that jug an' reached out a hand. Then he pulled his hand back an' shook his head, kind of sorrowful. The two men sittin' on the springs sure looked disappointed when he did that. But they did what he done an' shook their heads, too. Sam'l just looked at 'em like he was tryin' to figger things out. Then he tipped up the jug an' let the liquid run down his throat.

"Well?" he asked after he wiped his mouth on the back of his hand. It was clear he was waitin' to see what'd brought 'em up the mountain. When nobody said nothin', he finally asked, "What brings you folks up here?"

The two men who'd come with the preacher looked like their shirt collar was too tight. They fidgeted an' waited for the Preacher to speak. Then the Preacher looked like he was wishin' he was somewhere else an' stood up. He brushed off his suit and sighed. At first, I thought he was gettin' ready to preach.

"Well, Mr. Mudd," he said, soundin' like he was just gettin' started.

"Sam'l! Just looked at him, not makin' a sound."

"Hm, well," the Preacher went on, "It's just that we the Freewill Baptist Church, that is, have been glad… on many occasions… to help out when you sent down to the ladies for… um… baby clothes. But…" he stopped, look in' like he didn't know quite how to go on. "We can't help but notice that you're… unemployed… an' yet you an' your wife keep on havin' babies quite regular."

"All boys!" Sam'l said, soundin' real proud.

5

"Yes, I know," the Preacher said, noddin' his head. Lord knows, from what I've heard, he loves them four daughters of his, an' folks in the valley said they seemed happy enough. But you could tell that when he looked at this scruffy, toothless mountain man who had managed to get himself twelve sons, that maybe he thought things just didn't seem quite fair. "Well, as I said," he went on, "we can't help but notice…"

Sam'l cut in then. He was proud of the envy of some of the men around him who seemed to breed nothin' but girls. "It's all in the way you lay her…" he started to explain, soundin' real satisfied with himself.

"Uh, that's fine, Mr. Mudd, that's fine," the Preacher broke in, lookin' a little pink around the neck. "I'm sure you must know what you're doin', but it's just that the folks in the church… the members…well, they asked me, that is, to come up here and talk with you." He drizzled off to a stop.

Sam'l looked at the Preacher, his face all scrunched up from tryin' to understand. "Talk with me? What about?" he asked.

"Well," the Preacher took a deep breath and blurted out, "we want to ask you… suggest… that you think about limiting the number of… babies."

Sam'l didn't bat an eye, and the Preacher hurried on.

"That is, we'd like to ask you and your wife to think about not havin' so many babies… that is… since you seem to have a hard time… uh… providin' for them." He sort of ran out of breath and stopped talkin' then.

Well. It was plain to see that all this had caught Sam'l purely by surprise. He sat down on the edge of the porch and just looked up at the Preacher. His mouth was hangin' open wide enough to show them toothless gums of his. Finally, after seemin' to give it some deep thought, Sam'l reached up and scratched his grubby chin. Then he stood up slow, makin' himself as tall as he could. He faced the Preacher with a prideful look on his face.

"Well, Preacher," he said, soundin' just like he'd been thinkin' this over for a long time. "It's this away," he went on, takin' a few steps away and then turnin' to face the three visitors. "You see, I can't read, and I can't write. Ain't got none of them radios an I'm too old to get me a job in town." He stopped for a minute, smilin' at the men like a grown-up smiles when he's talkin' to a child that hasn't got much smarts. "So," he said, talkin' real slow like he hoped they'd understand, "you can see...I gotta do SOMEthing to piddle away the time!"

"Well," the Preacher looked plum beat. Then he just turned and started walkin' down the path towards his car. The other two men watched for a bit, then they both got up off the springs and followed the Preacher down the hill. None of 'em looked back at Sam'l.

Afterwards, the oldest Mudd boys would talk about the time the Preacher and the two men came to see their Paw. That is, they talked about it when they was out of Sam'ls hearin'. They weren't just sure what it all meant, but when the oldest one, Lem, was sent down to the church to ask for another bundle of baby things for this last baby, he told me he sure as hell wished he didn't have to go.

So now, as their Maw struggled with this latest Mudd tryin' to get itself born, it was like the weight of all the world was pressin' down on them boys and makin' 'em almost afraid to breathe.

I knelt there by Ella Mae's bed just holdin' on to her hand, I watched her twist and turn in torment just wishin' there was somethin' I could do to help. She looked up at me, and her face was so filled with pain that it made tears come to my eyes. It wasn't right that she should have to suffer so; it just wasn't

7

right. And then her body went into a terrible twistin' and Ella Mae commenced moanin'. I had to turn away from her face, cause I knew the baby was gettin' itself born and it needed all my help.

Then, as that little baby came fightin' to get out, it made a thin, mewly cry that would have sent shivers down the back of an angel, Sam'l came bargin' in behind the blanket to see what was happenin' and look for his newest offspring. I motioned towards the baby and said, "It's a girl." He acted like he never heard me, just stood, rock still, watchin' the life drainin' out of Ella Mae and me unable to stop it.

And that's how she went, quiet, uncomplainin' an' gentle.

Sam'l finally turned, heavy-like, and pushed the blanket back.

"She's gone," he told the waitin' boys in a voice that sounded flat and empty. When the boys didn't seem to get what he was tellin' them, he waved his hand towards the bed and shouted, "Your maw's dead! She's done, left me to raise the whole passel of you all alone. He turned his back on Ella Mae and never even looked at the baby. He bent down, like an old man, and picked up his Jug. Then he went out to the porch, lettin' the door flop behind him, not carin' that it didn't latch an came to rest half open, half shut.

The boys sort of bunched up together, scared and confused. I tugged the hangin' blanket back and started settin' things to rights. I wiped off the baby and wrapped it in a piece of soft flannel that Ella Mae'd fixed before her time.

Then I took the baby and laid it in Lem's hands. I told him, "Here, you hold your sister an I'll clean up your Maw so you can say your goodbyes to her."

Then I did what I could to maxke Ella Mae look better. I was plum filled with a terrible sadness lookin' down on that husk of a woman. It hurt to remember that she had once been young an' alive an' filled with dreams an' hopes an such. She'd lived to see nothin' but poverty an' hard work an' bein' held down. I couldn't do a thing to make the life she'd lived any better, but I did all I could to make her look proud in death. I hunted through the cupboard in the corner of the room until I found her very best things. Then I washed an' dressed her an' combed her hair all soft an' spread it out on the pilla'. I sent one of the boys out to fetch me a bunch of wild flowers. When he came back, I tucked one in her hair an' put the others in her hand. They made the air around Ella Mae smell sweet and fresh.

I could hear the boys talkin' on the other side of the hangin' blanket.

"She said that we got a sister", one of the boys said out loud.

"Reckon so," Lem answered.

I looked out then, an' saw one of the younger boys reach out his hand real slow an' pull back the worn flannel cover wrapped around the baby. Without a sound, all twelve pairs of eyes followed his hand as he pushed the cover away, showin' the baby all naked.

"I'll be dipped," one of the smaller boys breathed. "So that's what a girl looks like!"

They must have sensed that I was watchin' because Lem flicked the cover back into place. But I could see that most of 'em was tuckin' what they'd just seen away in their minds someplace so they could take it out later an' mull it over.

"What's her name?" one of the boys asked.

"How the hell should I know?" snapped the one next to him.

9

Without a word, the older boys looked at each other. Then Lem went over to the door an' stood there a moment.

"What'd you name her, Paw? he finally asked.

Without even lookin' up Sam'l brushed his hand in the air as though he had nothin' to do with it.

"I was fixin' to call the new one Jacob," he said, soundin' real put out an' resentful. "Ain't got no giri's name in mind." He was quiet for a bit, broodin', then the bitterness got mixed in with the hootch he was driving in an' his voice sounded thick. "Nothin' I want less than a puky girl baby that killed her Maw! If you want her to have a name, you give her one."

Lem just stood there a moment, then he turned an' walked real slow back to his brothers.

He says, "We can name her if we want," he told them.

"Lem, you're the eldest an' you're holdin' her. I think you oughta name her," one of the brothers said. The others all started noddin' an' lookin' relieved.

"Well then, Lem said, lookin' down with a look of somethin' like tenderness on his face as he studied the sleepin' baby I'll do it, I'll name her, I'll name her. He looked out the window, lost in thought for a bit. Then he turned towards his brothers, smilin' "It's a passable nice day for this time of year," he said, "An' the sun's shinin' I think I'll name her November Sunshine."

He finished, soundin' satisfied as he said the name out loud.

There wasn't time to find out what the brothers thought of the name Lem had picked because just about then, I was done with Ella Mae.

She looked right peaceful an' at rest when I finished an' went out to tell the boys. "Your Maw was a good woman, an' don't you forget it. Not many women could put up with what she put up with an' still be a good woman. But she was. I pulled back the blanket, then an' told'em, "Best you go see her now an say your goodbyes. Your Maw is all cleaned up an' laid out. Just keep in mind that it's the last time you'll ever get to see her, so whatever you want to remember about her, you'd best get it in mind now."

The boys were real quiet an shy-actin' as they shuffled behind the blanket to where Ella Mae lay. They stood bumpin' each other by the bed an' stared down at the silent form that had once been their Maw.

"Ain't she never comin' back?" the littlest one asked, soundin' real choked up an' ready to cry. His older brother cuffed him on the head an looked at him scornful-like. The little one began to bite his lower lip, tryin' to keep back the tears that pushed in back of his eyes. You could tell it was hard for him to keep them from spillin' out. The brother who had cuffed him suddenly moved closer. Then he put his arm around his little brother's shoulder an' pulled him close. He turned his eyes away as the tears began to trickle down the little boy's dirty, worried face.

After he'd looked at his Maw for a bit, Lem looked around the cabin. I looked at it too, then, tryin' to see it like it must look to Lem.

That cabin. There was little enough in it to make life easier or more pleasant. Everythin' had the look of being dirty, used, an' all worn out.

Lem turned an' looked at his brothers, then. Like he was tryin' to see them in a different way from the way he was used to. They were a pretty scruffy-looking bunch. Most of 'em was skinny and dirty, an' they looked pretty bad around the head

11

where their paw had hacked off their hair every now and then. When someone's hair got long enough so it hung over his eyes and he couldn't see right, Sam'l would yell, "Here, boy!" Then he'd whack at their hair with his rusty old scissors. They never looked very good after, but at least they could see.

After Lem studied his brothers for a bit, he turned to look at Sam'l. He was still sittin' on the porch drinkin' from his jug. Sometimes when he'd been pretty heavy into the corn likker an' was sweatin' up a storm, he was pretty hard to take. I mean, he really smelled. When he got too bad, Ella Mae would start naggin' in her gentle way till he took himself off to the creek and washed proper. She'd usually send one of the boys down to the creek after him to sneak his dirty clothes away so he wouldn't put 'em right back on an' start stinkin' again.

For a while after Ella Mae'd gotten him to wash up, Sam'l be touchy as an old bear. I heard him yellin' once, "Ain't a man got the right to be the way he wants to be in his own place?" But the kids had all gotten used to his way by now and learned to stay away from him. They knew that in a day or two their Paw'd be over his mad an' life would be back to usual. The only difference was that Sam'l would smell better for a time.

Sam'l. You could tell, just by lookin', that Sam'l was just an older version of all the boys. Someday they'd probably all have the same look about 'em that Sam'l had. Except Lem, maybe. Lem was as tall as Sam'l already. But there was somethin' different, somethin' gentler about him. It was in his eyes.

He had Ella Mae's soft, kind eyes.

No matter what them kids ate, they never seemed to put on weight. Only belly was Sam'l's, and that came from drinkin' too much of his own shine.

12

There was nothin' soft about Sam'l. Nothin' gentle. You just had to look at him to know that here was a short, skinny banty rooster who'd scrap over anything that didn't suit him. I used to wonder, before, if Lem'd end up, after all, like his Paw. But seein' him with that skinny little baby, I knew he wouldn't. I was glad he seemed to have at least a little of his Maw in 'im.

Ella Mae. The only touch of gentleness in that cabin had come from her. An' now, what had made life in that grubby little place tolerable lay limp an' still, like some old rag doll nobody wanted. She was so wasted away that she scarcely made a mound under the bedcovers.

Then I looked at the new little baby. It was still wrapped in that old flannel, lyin' tiny in the crook of Lem's arm, feelin' the beat of Lem's heart, feelin' safe. The baby was too young yet to know the different kinds of hunger that can starve a soul an' waste a body. The kind of hunger that had helped kill Ella Mae.

"Lord," I prayed in my heart, "please keep that little one safe as long as you can."

The birth of a girl into the Mudd family didn't really change things very much. November Sunshine did just what her brothers had done. She hung on to a thread of life, somehow, an' survived.

After their Maw was laid away, I showed Lem how to manage with the baby. I tore up an old sheet into squares an' showed the older boys how to fold diapers. The boys didn't seem to mind puttin' the things on in November, but they sure did hate to take the messy ones off her.

"Hey, Lem!" one of 'em would yell. "She's done pooped an I ain't gonna touch it.

Then Lem would stop whatever he was doin' and clean November up some, and put on a fresh diaper. He and his brothers finally worked it all out. If Lem would take care of the poopy ones, they'd take care of all the rest.

It worked out pretty good.

I got hold of some rubber nipples from a woman up the hill who'd stopped havin' babies some time ago. I showed the boys how to put milk in a bottle an' then stick a nipple on it. It was lucky the neighbor's cow was fresh an' they had more milk than they needed. They sent up all the milk Lem needed for the baby. When one of the boys would give November a bottle, she'd hang on to it like her life depended on it. An she'd suck and suck until every drop of milk was gone.

"God! Ain't she the hungry one!" one of the boys said one day. She'd sucked her way clear through her whole bottle without stoppin'. The boys felt real proud that she was thrivin' so. I stopped by the Mudd's cabin every couple of days or so to make sure things were goin' right.

When the weather got cooler, November began needin' somethin' more than diapers to wear. I helped Lem hunt through the latest box of cast-offs from the Freewill Baptist ladies. We found a few things that would do.

All in all, things went along pretty smooth for five or six months. One of the boys noticed that she'd cut a tooth when she latched onto his finger an' wouldn't let go. After he'd cussed at 'er and pried 'er jaws apart, he pulled out his finger an' studied it. Nothin' would do, he had to show everybody what a big dent her tooth'd made.

"I'll be dinged!" he said. "Ain't that somethin'?"

I figgered it was 'bout time to fix up a sugar tit for November to suck on. An' it turned out, too, that she was real happy when she had a piece of hard old cornbread to chew on.

Seemed like no time at all, with November growin' like a weed, that it was about time to start gettin' her to quit wettin' her pants. I told Lem what to do.

So, Lem had his brothers take turns takin' off November's diapers an holdin' her on a big old cookin' pot that Lem had found for the purpose.

It took a long time an' a lot of holdin' her on the pot to get the idea into that little girl's head. She seemed to like the feel of a warm, wet diaper next to 'er. But, bit by bit, she began to catch on to the idea of the pot.

When she was a year old, November took her first step. No one would rightly have noticed if she hadn't tripped an fallen over the old houn' dog, Jacob. Jacob, though, started howlin' and set up such a racket that everybody stopped and looked to see what had upset Jacob so.

"Hey!" Caleb, the littlest brother, yelled, real pleased an' surprised. "Look what she's gone an' done!. She's started walkin'." He hauled November to her feet, tryin' to sweet talk her into doin' it again. Bein' around someone smaller than he was sure made Caleb feel bigger an' more Important. So, he'd taken it on hisself to watch an' report on November Sunshine. It didn't seem like a chore to him. It was somethin' he liked doin'.

Anyway, everybody got around November coaxin' her to come to one or the other an show what she could do.

"Here, Sunshine, come get this piece of biscuit. I'll dip it in 'lasses if you come an' get it."

Now, November may not have known all the words, but she sure did know what a piece of biscuit dipped in 'lasses was. Darned if she didn't step right out on those skinny little legs an' reach for the goody in her brother's hand.

"Hot damn!" he said as she took two full steps before fall flat on her behind on the cabin floor "Did you see that?" he asked, built her up so she could grab the biscuit he held out to her.

"I guess she's growin' up," Lem said, shakin' his head. There was a pleased look on his face. He looked a bit proud, too.

Sam'l had more or less washed his hands of November. He wanted nothin' to do with a girl-baby. More an' more the little girl was in Lem's hands while Sam'l went his own way

At First, Lem'd been sore about havin' November sorta dumped on 'im. But in spite of the extra work an everythin', November got to be real important to Lem. She'd follow him with her big, shiny eyes just poppin' out of her tiny face, watchin' everythin' he did. It was easy to tell the sun rose an' set in Lem as far as November was concerned.

November Sunshine made a warm spot right under Lem's heart. He got to lovin' 'hr more'n anybody in the whole world. He made up his mind that somehow he was goin' to make life better for November than it had been for her Maw. She was that special to him.

Life in the West Virginia mountains was all Lem knew. Things didn't change much way back in the hills, an' when November was born in 1948, things weren't very different from what they had been back as far as Lem could remember. Once he'd gotten to talk with a soldier passin' through on his way back to Kentucky. He'd told Lem about how he'd gone away from the hills to fight in the war. Lem was only about ten then an' didn't know how to ask questions very well. He did ask the soldier, though, why he'd gone off to fight. But the soldier, who'd been raggedy and tired, said it wasn' pleasant to talk about, an' he'd just as soon forget it. Before he'd gone on his way, though, he'd taken time to tell Lem a little about how things were outside the mountains. What he'd told Lem had boggled his mind an' plum scared him. But it did set Lem to thinkin' about things that'd never seen in his mind before.

Now that he had November Sunshine to think about, Lem wished he'd paid more attention to what the soldier had said. Maybe there was some things he could've learned that would have made it better for November. Sometimes, Lam felt real bad that he didn't know more.

The Women's Guild of the Freewill Baptist Church spent quite a lot of time discussing the youngest Mudd. One of the ladies in the Church Guild called me in as a midwife when the town doctor was sick. They never called themselves women like the rest of us, they always liked to be called ladies. Anyway, she told me about it. She said they had discussed their duty an talked it over an' over, but nothin' much ever came of it.

Once in awhile a couple of the ladies would get themselves all done up in their good church clothes an' make the long trip up the hill. They didn't do much on those visits, but I guess they felt that at least they'd done SOMEthing. I think it was just that if they came up here once in a while, their consciences didn't bother 'em so much about leavin' little November Sunshine to be raised in what they called "such a heathen fashion".

Some of the Guild ladies came to visit the woman I was tendin' while I was still there. Even though I was workin' in the kitchen, I could hear what they said.

"It's plain that her father, Sam'l, doesn't pay any mind to the little girl," one of them said. She'd just been up the hill to the Mudd's. "He never even bothered to come around while we were there," she said. "Seems to me he might at least've come by to say thank you for the clothes and concern."

The other ladies had agreed with her. Then one of 'em said, "Now, now, ladies, we mustn't forget that what we do for that poor little girl is only our Christian duty." The other ladies all chimed in with, "True, true," an' things like that.

It's just like doin' foreign missionary work right here in West Virginia, one of the ladies said. She sounded real pleased about the idea. Then I heard 'er sigh and say, "Surely does make a body feel good!"

Well, in spite of bein' considered a foreign mission, November Sunshine did right well. She grew an' got older. She lived through learning to pee in the pot. She lived through a diet of green beans an' cornbread an' not enough meat. She didn't seem to notice or care that her clothes were raggedy an' didn't really fit. She tagged after Lem every chance she got.

Lem was her Paw, an' Maw, an' God all rolled up into one.

When she fell down an' skinned her knees or got bit by a bee, it was Lem she'd run to. If lightnin' flashed around the cabin or early snow silenced the world outside, it was Lem's lap she'd head for. She'd climb up onto his knees an' throw her little arms as far around 'im as they'd go. Then she'd hang on for dear life until he made everythin' better for her.

As she grew older an' taller, it was from Lem she learned what she needed to know. She learned about takin' care of herself out in the woods and not lettin' herself get lost. She learned how to look for berries an' honey an even how to catch a catfish down in the creek. She learned all kinds of things a mountain child needs to know.

All in all, November Sunshine did just what her brothers had done. She hung on to a scrap of life an' survived.

ME NOVEMBER SUNSHINE

Somethin' scary an' hurtful kept pullin' at me to wake up. I made myself lie real still, scarce darin' to breathe lest the pain might get worse. I kept my eyes tight closed, tryin' to hang on to that safe grey softness that comes just before you let go an' wake up.

Lyin' there, I could feel the lumps in my mattress an' the way the old blanket scratched at my skin. I made myself keep thinkin' about those things an thinkin' about 'em real hard. If I didn't open my eyes, an if I didn't give in to whatever was hurtin' me, maybe that awful pain would go away.

I was just 12 back then. But tellin' you about it now makes it seem just as clear as though it all happened only a little bit ago, I can still remember that shaky feelin' I got every time the pain let up a little bit. It was like I was torn between glad it wasn't so bad an' scared that it would come back worse'n ever.

But, anyway, to get on with my tellin'.

Lyin' there, I knew just what I'd see when I opened my eyes. Wasn't much, but it was a part of my goin' to sleep an my wakin' up every day. It was what I was used to. It was safe. I knew I'd open my eyes an see the boards in the cabin wall, old an' grey an some of 'em still rough, like when they were first put up there. Where the window was set in the wall there was a chink just under it where the wood had been broken. Sometimes, when the wind was swishin' round the cabin, it made a kind of moanin' sound through that hole, it sounded real mournful and sad. I decided to try an do somethin' about it. So, I set to goin' through a parcel of old clothes sent up by the Freewill Baptist ladies. I found a red an' white window curtain in the box. It was a little faded, but it looked kinda pretty, so I tacked it up. It hung real nice an' bright there at the window. Lyin' there with my eyes closed an listenin' to the breeze moanin' through that chink, I knew that the red an' white curtain was movin gentle like in the air comin' through the hole. It made somethin' nice to think about.

I lay there real quiet an' started to feel better.

I began to wonder if I'd just dreamed about that pain, was it just a part of some late-sleep bogey dream?

Real slow an' careful, I began to let myself breathe full again, air goin' way down inside. Bit by bit, I made my arms relax. I hadn't noticed how tight I was holdin' myself until I started to let go. Then I reached out with one hand an' pulled my cover closer over my shoulders. Now that the pain was gone, I felt all wrung out an' shivery.

I tried to pull myself back into the safe world of sleep.

But then, sudden' as a mountain thunderstorm, it was there again. The pain. Like pokin', fiery fingers, it was, twistin' an pushin' an clawin' at the Inside of me. I jerked my knees up so hard that I banged one of 'em against my chin. Never in my whole life had I felt anythin' like that pain inside of me.

All I could do was to hold myself tight an' hope it would go away.

After what seemed like an awful long time, the pain began to let up again. I lay there, shakin' an scared, tastin' blood where I'd bit my lip in the worst of it, an wonderin' what was happenin' to me.

I remembered back to when Old Clara, the woman who'd midwifed me, had come to tell Paw that she was leavin' the hills. She'd said she was g'tting' too old for midwifin' anymore an; was goin' off to live with her sister. She had a place in Ashland, Kentucky. I was about eight years old then, and Old Clara was just about the only woman I knew. I didn't know much in those days, but I sure cared about Old Clara. She'd done her best to help me with my growin' up, especially after Lem got up an' married an' built him an' his wife a cabin over the mountain from Paw's. Every now an' then Old Clara'd stop by our cabin an' sorta look in on me. She'd get me off alone somewheres an' ask me how I be. I'd save up all kinds of questions to ask Old Clara, an' I was always glad to see her comin' up our path. I remember how sad I felt the time she told me that she was movin' to Kentucky to live with her sister. I sure felt lonely.

I just didn't know how I could manage with both Lem an Old Clara gone.

Before Old Clara left, she said there was wlots of things I needed to know about becomin' a woman, an what weighed most on her mind was that she wouldn't be around to tell me when it was time.

Lyin' there hopin' the pain was gone for good, I wondered if now was the time she'd meant.

Bit by bit, I made myself let go, tryin' not to move more than I must.

I opened my eyes real slow. Early mornin' light was comin' in through the old red an' white curtain, an' I could hear the soft sounds of the woods-things comin' awake outside. The bit of wind that was blowin' in the chink was movin' the old black-walnut tree outside, too. It was makin' soft swishy sounds where it brushed against the cabin wall.

I always liked those sounds when I was real little an' still sleepin' in the room with the boys. I used to tell myself that the big old tree was sort of watchin' over me, an' as long as that tree was there, I was safe.

I'd never told my brothers about my fancies 'cause I knew they already were shakin' their heads about what to do with me. They finally figured somethin' out one day. With Lem married an gone an' my next two brothers run off to find work in Ohio, the cabin wasn't so crowded anymore, an' one of my brothers, Amos, got an idea. Amos was the oldest brother left at home, an' the others looked up to him like they all used to look to Lem. Well, Amos came into the cabin carryin' some old boards one day, an' the oldest boys set to with hammers an' nails. When I asked 'em what they were doin' they just smiled at me sort of smug-like an' said, "Wait an' see!"

What they did was build a wall across the far corner of the kitchen.

Then they moved my cot behind it, right next to the window.

"Why'd you do that?" I asked 'em.

"You're gettin' too old to sleep with us anymore," Amos said in that scratchy voice of his that had gotten 'most as deep as Paw's.

"Why?"

But I didn't get any answer. I'd wished then for Lem of Old Clara to ask.

That first night in my own little cubby-hole, I felt awful alone. I was scared to tell my brothers that I was afraid to sleep by myself, so I tried to keep from snuffin'. I lay there feelin' all alone an' scared, wonderin' why they didn't want nothin' to do with me anymore. I pulled my cover as high as I could an tried not to make any noise with my cryin'. I listened an' listened for the sound of the old black-walnut tree. But the night was still an' dark, an' the tree didn't offer me any comfort at all. After a long time, I guess I just cried myself to sleep.

In the mornin', when I woke up, my pilla' was still damp from the tears.

But that seemed long ago. Now, lying in that bed, waitin' to see if the pain was gone for good, I could hear the murmur of the old black-walnut tree, an' I felt some better.

I swung my legs real slow over the side of my cot an stood up.

Oh my God! The bed cover where I had been lyin' was all a smeary messi. The old flannel nightdress that had been my mother's was stuck to my body an' soaked with blood!

Inside my head, somethin' was screamin', "What's wrong with me? What did I do wrong? Am I dyin'?"

I tried not to be so scared. I told myself, I gotta think, I gotta think, over an' over. But nothin' came to mind. I pulled the cover tighter around me where I stood, cold an' scared, starin' at my cot. I tried real hard to sort things out.

For the past couple of days, I'd had a real gnarly feelin' in the pit of my stomach. I figured it had somethin' to do with eatin' the left-over ham hock that had set on the table overnight. I learned early on not to eat much leftover food because it often made a half-sick feelin' in my stomach. But the ham hock had been so good! It wasn't often that we got meat other than sow-belly, an' we had all eaten until we were full. Then, next mornin' when I woke up hungry, I'd seen what was left of the ham hock sittin' there on the plate where it was left on the table. I just couldn't stop myself. I chewed on that old bone until it was clean an' shiny in its bareness.

Then my stomach began to ache.

An it had ached off an' on all day an some of the next day, too.

23

"No more left-over meat I'd told myself, figurin' that was to be the end of it.

But it wasn't. The pains had kept gettin' worse an I wished I were back in the big room with my brothers. I'd wished it was like when Lem was still livin' in the cabin an I could go to him with my questions. I wanted to ask what about the pains an' have him say, "Oh, you're just off your feet, November."

My other brothers would have teased me an' said, "Don't make such a pig outta yourself an' you won't get such a stomach ache!"

Then things would have been all right.

But Lem an' Paw hadn't gotten along very good for quite a while before Lem up an' married an went away. Paw'd taken out his mad on the next two older brothers till they'd got their fill of it an gone away, too.

Now I mostly had Caleb to talk to, but he wasn't all that much older'n I was, an' I didn't figger he'd have the answers I needed. I'd never been very close to my other brothers. They mostly weren't around the place very much.

They all had jobs off somewhere. Three of 'em worked at Miller's sawmill an' two of 'em cut wood for the White Lumber Company that was clearin' the woods an settin' up strip minin' on the hills a piece. The rest of my brothers got work scratches as scratch can, wherever they could find them.

About the only other brother, besides Caleb, who seemed to pay me any mind, was Viticus. Viticus was about sixteen or seventeen then. He was easy goin' like. Paw'd get mad at Viticus, real mad. He'd yell, "You ain't worth a goddam, Viticus! You're too soft, just like your Maw was!"

It had been Maw's way to name him Leviticus, a name she'd found in her Mam's old Bible. I guess that name had been a sore spot with Paw right from the first, an' he seemed to still be takin' it out on Viticus. He seemed to be takin' quite a bit out on Viticus lately, an' I was afraid Viticus would be the next one to go.

More an' more lately, Viticus seemed to have his thoughts somewhere else. I just didn't seem to be able to find the nerve to break in on 'em.

I knew that Viticus an Paw weren't gettin' along too good. Viticus was stayin' away from the cabin more an' more, an leavin' some of his chores for the other brothers to do. When Viticus would come in late, Paw would stamp an' snort an' sometimes even make like he was goin' to hit him. Paw'd mutter somethin' about how Viticus had best watch himself or he'd send him off to Bergoo to live with cousins who worked in the coal mines there. Paw khew Viticus purely hated the idea of workin' in the mines away from the sunshine an' fresh air. Viticus wouldn't answer Paw, he'd just turn his back an' get busy doin' whatever it was he was 'sposed to be doin'.

By an' by, the whole thing would blow over, an' Paw'd calm down until the next time Viticus came in late.

I was the only one who knew why Viticus was comin' in late.

He was stoppin' by at the Hinton's who lived way up the next holler. The Hintons had a passel of kids, an' the oldest girl was named Sara.

Sara Hinton an Viticus had taken a shine to each other.

When I first became aware of Sara. I mean... when I first REALLY saw her, I was about nine or so. It was after Old Clara'd moved away an I'd gone off into the woods to be by myself an' sort of feel sad. This girl an an older woman had gone by on the path down to the valley, an I could hear them talkin'. That's how I knew her name was Sara. The older woman had called her that, an she'd called the older woman Ma. Anyways, the first time I saw Sara, I thought she was awful fat. It didn't cross my mind that she was only fat in certain places.

Then it wasn't until about a year ago that I was out in the woods alone an' saw Sara off by herself. She seemed to be gatherin' berries, an' I stayed real quiet an' just watched. I didn't know how old she was cause her face was young-lookin'. But what I'd first thought was fat, full, round hips that sort of sashayed when she moved. What I couldn't help starin' at was the biggest, roundest bosom I'd ever seen. Clara'd told me womenfolk called them things bosoms. I already knew somethin' about bosoms, though, cause Old Clara had one an' when she held me to her now an again, I could feel 'em. Really soft an' warm. When I went off with Paw to Lem's marryin', I'd seen other grown women an some of them had pretty big bosoms, too. But I'd never seen anythin' at all like Sara's!

Sara must have been hard-put to button her blouse up all the way. At least that's what I figgered for she had left the top buttons open, an' you could see those big soft, round white things pushin' up as though they wanted to get outside her clothes. Watchin' as she bent over to pick some berries, I figured that a bosom like hers must be kind of a nuisance, gettin' in the way all the time.

Then one day, not too long after, I was cuttin' through the woods, takin' a shortcut home from berry-pickin' myself, an' I came across Viticus an Sara off by theirselves in the woods. Viticus was kissin' Sara like I'd never seen anyone kiss before. There wasn't much of that kind of stuff in our family, an' I wondered where Viticus had learned to do what he was doin'.

He had his left arm around Sara's shoulders an' his head was bent down so's their lips were pressed tight together. I was worried about her bein' able to breathe, but it didn't seem to bother her none.

Sara had her arms around Viticus's neck an' was hangin' on like she was drownin' an' he was the only one who could save her. All the buttons on her blouse were open, an Viticus was moanin' an feelin' of 'er an pressin' hisself against 'er an' sort of roochin' around.

Somethin' in me wanted to go on watchin', but seein' them together like that had made me feel kind of funny, so I sneaked away before they found out I was anyways nearby.

What I had seen bothered me, so I went off to my favorite place in the woods an sat down on the big rock where I always went to think. It was at the edge of a quiet little wood-pool that not many folks seemed to know about. It was the best place I knew to go to work things out of my mind.

I could tell someone had been to the wood-pool before me 'cause some of the ferns were mashed down. I'd noticed before that someone else was coming' to the pool. But after I looked around real careful, I could tell whoever'd been there had gone. I didn't like to think that anyone else knew about my special place, but as long as they weren't there now, I guessed it was all right.

I settled down on a rock an' thought about Sara.

I thought back over what I'd seen. At first it had sorta turned my stomach seein' Viticus pawin' her like that an all. But when I studied back over it in my mind, I had to think they had certainly seemed to be enjoying themselves.

I was sure mixed up.

I looked down at myself. Really looked, I mean. I always knew that I was made different from my brothers. There wasn't much I didn't know about the way their bodies were made an all. But I hadn't thought much about it. It was just the way things were. When you share a small cabin an' a privy with nothin' but menfolk from the time you're born, there aren't many secrets. Sometimes I used to feel little cheated because when we were out in the fields or the woods gatherin' wood for the stove, they could run off behind a tree an' pee without makin' a mess. I always had to loosen the pin that held my drawers up an' squat down behind a tree an make a big thing out of not getting my clothes wet. Then I'd have to scrounge around an find a couple of big leaves to wipe myself off before I could pull my drawers back into place. It sure seemed to me that it must be a whole lot easier to be a boy then a girl.

Sittin' there on the rock after watchin' Viticus an Sara, my thoughts kinda felt bothersome. I thought about how Sara had looked. I yanked off my shirt an' leaned way over the pool to get a good look at myself. I sure didn't look anythin' like Sara. Where she was round an' soft, I was flat an' skinny. I looked at my hair hangin' down around my face. It was long an' yeller an' hung stringy-like down over my shoulders. But for the rest of me, I might just as well have been a boy. I looked at myself real good, ponderin'. It was the first time I'd ever really...you know...looked at myself. I tried to push the flesh on my chest into a bosom like Sara's, but there wasn't enough there to do anything. My eyes looked too big for my face, too. I was sure sorry lookin'.

I tried to tell myself I didn't care how I looked an' yanked my shirt back on. Who wanted some boy pawin' you all up, anyways?

Just then, a fresh spell of pain tore into my rememberin'. I fell back onto my cot, holding myself tight, tryin' to squeeze out the hurt. I stopped thinkin' about Sara an Viticus an just gave in to the pain. I'd never felt nothin' so bad. It was pullin' an twistin' my insides an it near took my breath away. When the pain finally let up a bit, I felt scared that it might start all over again.

Then I began to notice wakin-up sounds from my brothers' room. They'd soon be gettin' up an' one of 'em was bound to come lookin' for me to help do breakfast chores.

The thought of my brothers seein' the bloody mess I'd made scared the daylights out of me an gave me the strength to move. I got up as quiet as I could an' pulled both the bed covers off the bed an dropped them on the floor. Then I skinned my nightdress off an' bundled it in with the covers. I got into my regular clothes as fast as I could, an' hurried out of the cabin, carryin' the bundle with me.

It didn't take me long to reach the creek an find my big flat rock by the pool. I began to wash the sheets in the water, rubbin' them against the rocks time an' time again until all the stains were washed away. Then I spread the covers over some low bushes so they'd dry. It didn't take as long to get the stains out of the nightdress because the material was so old an' worn that it was real thin. When the nightdress looked clean, I spread it over another bush. I headed back to the cabin, hopin' I could slip in before anyone noticed I was gone.

As I turned to walk back up the hill, I began to feel a warm stickiness between my legs. Each step caused the stickiness to get more an' more bothersome. I hated the way it made me feel, dirty. When I finally reached the cabin, I could hear the sounds a houseful of men-folks makes, an' I suddenly felt real shy about havin' anyone see me. So, I crawled into the shadows behind the privy an' leaned against the old wooden outhouse wall, makin' myself as small as I could.

I could hear Paw inside the house, grumblin' somethin' about, "Where the hell's that November?"

There was the bang of the door as someone came outside and yelled, "November, November! Where are you, November?" It was Caleb's voice, and I wanted to answer him, but I didn't dare. I stayed behind the privy, hidin', even when Timothy, my middle brother, came to use the seat. I tried to hold my breath, afraid that he would find me hidin' in the shadows an' be mad.

But he finished what he had come for, an' I could hear him yankin' his pants back into place. Then I heard the clump of his boots as he went back towards the house.

At last, the sounds at the house died out as all the men-folks went their different ways. I thought it was safe to come out then. I crept back into the cabin an' ducked behind the wall that hid my cot. I scrunched down an pulled the old cardboard box out from under the cot an' started pawing through the things in it. Caleb called it my "pretty box", but mostly it was full of worn-out clothes an' things that didn't fit. It took me a while till I finally found a dress that someone from the Freewill Baptist Church had finished with. It wasn't much, but it looked like it might do. It was worn and small, but it was clean. I figured I could make do with it. Fast as I could, I stripped off my stained dress an tugged the newer one into place. I was feelin' scared an in a hurry, but I dug through the box again, huntin' some soft old rags. I didn't know just what it was I could do with 'em, but I was pleasured when I found an old towel that had been worn smooth an' soft over the years. I rolled it tight an' Jammed it up between my legs. Next, I tore a long strip off an old worn-out sheet, an' fixed myself a kind of diaper to hold the rag bundle in place.

That made me feel a little safer. I hurried out of the cabin an' back to the creek. I scrubbed an' scrubbed until my bloody dress was clean. Then I spread it out over another bush.

For the first time since those awful pains an' the bleedin' had started, I felt like I could draw a deep breath. I looked at my washin'. No tell-tale stains were showin'. I began to feel a little better.

I sure wished I knew what was happenin' to me, but I didn't feel like I could go to any of my brothers about it. There just wasn't anybody I could talk to.

Years back, when I was just real little, some of the women from the Freewill Baptist Church down the valley had come by. I remember hearin' one of them ask, "What do men folks know about raisin' a girl?"

"Nothin'!" one of the other women had answered her, soundin' kind of put out about it. "It'll be a miracle if she grows up knowin' she's a girl!"

They kind of giggled, then. They didn't know I could hear 'em talkin'. It seems the women had gotten all pooped out climbin' the hill to our place an were sittin' on the porch, waitin' to get their breath back. One of 'em said, "We oughta do somethin'," an I could hear her shift her bottom where she was sittin' on the old bedsprings. "Seems to me we ought to do our Christian duty by that child," she had said, an then she gave a big sigh like she hoped she wouldn't have to do anything much at all.

From where I was sittin' in the cool shadows under the porch, I could hear someone else chime in, "You're 'zactly right? What she needs is for somebody to take her into their home an' give her a good Christian upbringin'!"

That scared me. I didn't want to live in a house with strangers. I didn't know for sure what a Christian upbringin' was, but it sounded bad, an' I didn't want any part of it.

My Oliver hasn't been at all well, one of the women said. "Otherwise, I'd be gladder to take her in with me."

"And I've got my husband's problem to think of," another woman said. "I can never tell when his problem is likely to act up." It wasn't until much later when I heard Paw an' Lem talkin' that I learned that the man's problem was drinkin' too much of that stuff my Paw sold in jugs.

But in time the women stopped makin' excuses for not takin' me in, an' one of 'em said, "As Christian ladies we've got to do SOMEthing."

Then they all seemed to talk at once an got up an' went off without having seen me hidin' under the porch at all. A couple of days later, the husband of one of the women came puffin' up the mountain with a big paper bag full of old clothes. The man told Paw, "The Women's Guild sent it," an as he handed it over, he said they'd be sendin' more now an again.

I figgered that's what they meant by doing SOMEthing.

At first Paw's hackles were raised by what the man said. "Who the hell's he think he is to be givin' his throw-away stuff to my kids?" Paw bellered. But some of the older boys told 'im the stuff might come in handy, so he shut up about it.

An me? I was just glad I didn't have to go off an' live with none of 'em an have to have a Christian upbringin'. Sounded like such a thing might be a bit uncomfortable.

But every now and again, I'd think that it sure would have been comfortin' to have one of them Baptist women to talk to about what was happenin' to me as I was growin' up.

I sat on the rock an' looked around at the quiet woods. It made you feel good just to be there. An I wondered, how come the whole world looked so peaceful outside while inside I was all chewed up an' worried. I felt more lonely than I'd ever felt, an' looked to see if any of the grass was mashed down like the last time. I did find one patch that looked like someone had

32

walked on it not too long ago, an' I almost found myself wishin' whoever it was might come this way again.

There was a place on the rock where the sun was makin' a warm spot, an' I put my head down, restin' it on my arm on the soft green moss. I felt all wrung out with all the worryin' an all, an' it was soothin' to be lyin' there so.

Bit by bit, thoughts started comin' to my head an I lay back an' just let 'em come. I hadn't ever really done much thinkin' about how I lived an all. There'd always been somethin' to eat an' somethin' to cover myself with, an' a place to lay my head at night. Paw said that's all anyone could ask for. It had always seemed enough.

Now though, things were changin' an' I didn't know what was happenin'. It was scary. It wasn't like the bad dreams that my brothers could always seem to chase away by doin' somethin' silly to make me laugh. This was different. This was... well... It was real.

When I was little an' Lem was still livin' in the cabin with us, whenever somethin' bad happened to me, he'd pick me up in his arms an hold me. The first time he did it, I thought he was lookin' for bugs like our Paw would do every now an' then after the ladies from the Freewill Baptist Church had been up to "look in" on us. They always seemed to remind him of what they called his "fatherly duties". Anyways, after they'd been up, he'd grab us one at a time an' look behind our ears an' through our hair an' sort of sniff at us. "You stink!" he'd roar at one of the boys, and backhand him off towards the creek to wash up.

But when Lem picked me up, it was different. He'd found me cryin' where I'd fallen an' twisted my foot. Then he'd gotten a funny look on his face, an picked me up an held me close. He'd held me for quite a long time, pattin' my back an sayin', "It's gonna be all right, November Sunshine. Just you wait."

"It's gonna be all right." I didn't know quite what he meant, but it made me feel good, an' I was sad when in a little bit he put me down.

I wasn't much given to self-pity. I'd found out early on that it don't do you no good to feel sorry for yourself. My brothers sure didn't like to see me all tearin' up an actin' like the end of the world. I found out that they had enough worries of their own to do 'em. They had no time for mine. But just the same, I couldn't keep the tears from crowdin' up when I thought back over how good an safe I'd always felt with Lem an I remember how kind Old Clara used to be, too. Thinkin' of both of them gone, I was just filled up an runnin' over with sadness. Tears pushed their way down my face; an' I didn't do a thing to stop 'em.

I'd just never felt so alone, sobbin' away there in the woods all by myself.

Then a twig snapped nearby, an' I sat up, so startled that I nearly fell off the rock.

"Are you all right?" a soft voice asked me. I stared at the woman who was watchin' me. I couldn't remember ever seein' her before. It came to me that she must be the person who had mashed down the grass there in the woods.

But who was she?

Where'd she come from?

There wasn't any way of knowin', then, how much she was goin' to change my life.

ANSALU WILLIAMS

You know, thinkin' back, I don't rightly know what happened next. Part of me was real put off at seein' a stranger, but still, I wasn't all that surprised after seein' the mashed down grass an' ferns when I came to the woods-pool earlier on. One thing I'd learned from my brothers was that if things are mashed down in the woods, somethin' alive had to do the mashin. So, when I saw this strange woman just standin' there an lookin' at me, I knew right off she'd been there before.

But the funny thing was, even though I'd never seen her before, there wasn't nothin' at all about her to make me scared. Not even a little bit. She had a real easy look about her.

So, I just sat there looking right back.

She looked like she belonged there by the pool in the woods. You know how sometimes things just seem right? She was real different from anybody I'd ever seen before. The dress she had on looked awful, long an' like it was worn to the nub. It took me a bit before I figured out that it wasn't her dress bein' so long that made her look so, it was that she was awful short. She didn't look anywhere near as tall as me an' my brothers. An' her skirt hung so full it covered her all up. Made her look like an old rag doll, the Baptist Freewill Ladies had put in their box once. Even though it was kinda faded when I got it, I'd loved that doll to pieces. It was so soft an' nice to the feel.

The stranger looked like she might be soft and nice, too.

"I'm sorry," she said then, an' I had the feelin' she said it before, but I was so busy studyin' her I hadn't heard. "I didn't mean to scare you none," she said, smilin' a bit so her face looked friendly. "I saw you was upset an I figured that I might be able to help."

35

I hadn't meant to stare at her. Old Clara told me once that starin' at folks wasn't nice, so I stood up, meanin' to be polite. But when I stood up, it made me take more notice of what she had on her head. She was wearin' somethin' wrapped round an' round it so that her hair was all covered up. It wasn't like anythin' I'd ever seen, an' I couldn't help myself starin' again.

It came to me that I was like some big ol' bird perched on that rock just starin' at some little bit of a thing it was waitin' to pounce on. As fast as I could, I let myself slide right down off the rock, so I was standin' beside her on the ground.

"I didn't mean to be starin'," I told her, "It's just I never saw a livin' soul but the woods animals here by the pool before. I guess you took me by surprise."

She just waved her hand in the air as if my starin' wasn't much to talk about. "Well, what I asked was if I could be of any help. She had a real nice look about her when she talked. Like she cared. I liked the way she sounded when she talked. Like what I figured a mother would sound like if a body had one.

"Peers, to me, you got things pretty well in hand, now, though," she said. Then she made like she was goin' to walk off.

Somethin' inside of me made me reach out an' take hold of her arm. "Uh, I well...I... Don't go sort of blurted itself out.

"I don't mean to pry or butt in," she said, holdin' off.

"You ain't, honest!" I said, not lettin' go of her arm. I didn't know how to tell her just how bad I needed someone friendly to talk to. "It's just that I've got...a problem. I came here to try to figure it out," I let go of her arm, hopin' she wouldn't turn an' go away. "I often come here to be by myself an try an' puzzle things out," I told her.

"An I came bargin' in an' scattered your thinkin'," she said, shakin' her head as if to say she was sorry. "But you see," she went on, "I'm pretty new to this part of the mountains an' when I was just takin' a sort of look around one day, I came on this here pool." She waved her hand at the pool like she was wantin' me to see it with her eyes. "It seemed so friendly an invitin', I knew it was just the kinda place my Will would have liked." She turned away from me just a bit like her voice was caught in her throat. Then she turned back, somethin' glistenin' in her eyes as she said, "So I just made myself free an came back here to sort of bring Will close again."

I didn't say anythin'. It felt so good just to have this kind woman talkin' to me that I didn't want to do anythin' to spoil it. Inside, I was filled with as many questions as the night sky has stars, but I didn't dare ask a single one of 'em lest I shy her off. Instead, I sat down on the bank of the little pond an made room for her to sit beside me. She nodded an' sort of folded herself onto the grass next to me. Without sayin' anythin, she reached out a rough-worn hand an picked up a little round pebble. She dropped it straight down into the pond, an' watched it disappear as it fell down through the water. Then she pointed to the spreadin' rings.

"It always amazes me how a plain old pebble fallin into the water can make so many circles an each one of 'em's perfect," she said, real soft. "An," she went on, pickin' up two more pebbles an droppin' them both into the pond together, "when you drop two pebbles in at the same time, they both make circles. She watched the ripplin' water for a few moments. Then she looked at me an' asked, "Did you notice that the circles run into each other? Each one spreads out till it touches the other circles?" She seemed to think about that a bit. "I guess it's sort of like people," she went on. "When we talk to each other, our circles spread out an we take each other in."

Then she sighed an settled herself more comfortably to talk.

"Where're you from?" I asked her.

"Lots of places," she answered. "Work took my Will an me all over West Virginia an' Kentucky. Now, though, I'm livin' in what folks call the Old Walker Place by Little Creek."

I looked at her real Interested. One of my brothers had come home one day with the news that someone had moved into the Walker cabin. It had stood empty as long as I could remember. He said whoever had moved in had done a right smart of fixin' an sprucin' up the place. I had wanted to go over an see for myself, but the cabin is a good way off, an' Paw wasn't much for my goin' off like that. Anyways, it just wouldn't've been right. Hill folk are private people, an' we don't push ourselves in nowhere 'less we're invited. It's just not right.

"Is... uh... is Will your man?" I asked, not sure just how far you can go talkin' to a stranger like this.

"You mean, is Will my husband?" she asked.

When I nodded, she shook her head.

"He was," she said real low. For a moment, a deep sadness made her whole face look sad an' lonely. As she sat there, quiet, all the wrinkles on her face seemed to run downhill an' give her a mournful look. Then she shook herself an' started talkin' in a soft, faraway voice. "This was meant to be such a good place for my Will an me," she said, soundin' sad. She was quiet a bit, an' I almost thought she had said all she was aimin' to. But then she went on, her voice soundin' stronger an' more cheerful as she talked. "My Will an me came here so's he could work as a guard at the Boswell mines," she said. "Will got taken with the Black Lung back in Kentucky," she explained. "You must know about Black Lung," she went on, "Most miners get it sooner or later. They get their lungs so full of black coal dust that fresh air ain't got nowhere to go. Gets 'em so they can't hardly breathe. Anyway, my Will got taken with Black Lung back in Kentucky, an they said he wasn't fit to work underground no more an' laid 'im off. We didn't know what to do. Then a drummer came by sellin' things an' said as how he'd heard the Boswell mine was hirin' guards for their mines. It's somethin' new. I guess some gov'ment man told 'em they's got to do it. Anyways, my Will an me sold off what we could an' packed the rest an came here. But Will got real sick soon after we got here an' died before he ever got to work even once at the Boswell mine." She gave a big sigh, then just looked into the pool like her thoughts were somewheres else.

"With him dyin' like that an all," she said after a bit, "there wasn't anythin' for me to do but stay on. I didn't have enough money left after puttin' him away to move on."

I must have looked like I pitied her or somethin' because she sat up real straight an' said, "But it's goin' to be all right. I already found myself a Job takin' in washin'. I plan to make ends meet thataway."

I looked at her real close. She might be awful small an' wear strange clothes, but she sure gave off a feelin' of strength.

"Ain't you got nobody at all?" I asked.

"Nary a one," she answered.

"Oh," I burst out before I could stop myself. "If you want someone to be your friend, it'd make me mighty proud if I could... If I could be it." An' then a lump came up in my throat at havin' spoke so bold, an' I couldn't say any more for fear I'd already said too much.

At first, she looked surprised, an' then a big, happy smile spread all over her face. "Say now," she said, lookin' pleased. "That's just about as nice an offer as I've ever had. Always before I'd had Will to help me make my way with new people. When there are two of you, it's ever so much easier to get to know new folks. People don't seem as easy with one person alone."

Then she stood up, smoothin' that grey dress over her roundness, an turned to face me. "Since we're plannin' to be friends, if you'd care to walk a place with me, I'd be proud to have you see my home. I just baked some bread an' I still have a jar or two of my plum preserves that I brought along from our last place."

Her Invitation swelled up inside of me so big that I felt like I ought to fly up into the air an' swoop an' glide like butterflies do when they get all excited. In my whole life, I had never, never been asked into anybody's home. Like comp'ny. Paw had fetched me along when he was deliverin' his jugs of white lightnin', but that was just so I could help carry. But now someone had invited me an' was goin' to share her fresh bakin' an' plum preserves with me. I stumbled to my feet in a hurryso, she wouldn't change her mind an go off without me.

An' then, gettin' to my feet, I remembered my problem as I felt the bundle of rags shiftin' tween my legs. I sat down again, real fast, touchin' myself just to make sure that I wasn't makin' another mess.

"Somethin' wrong?" she asked me in a quiet voice that made me know she'd seen what I did.

"No, yes!" I answered, stammerin' with shame. There's somethin' wrong with me. Dreadful wrong. An I ain't got no one to talk to about it."

"What about your ma?"

"Ain't got one. She died when I was born, I told her.

"Well, haven't you got an older sister or someone to talk to?" she asked. There was a worried look on her face.

"No ma'am. All's I got is brothers. Twelve of 'em. An some of 'em have already left home," I explained. "Oh, an there's my Paw, too," I added in a hurry, ashamed that I had almost forgotten to mention him. He was always around, but he never had much to do with me, an' I had learned early on not to count on him for anythin'".

She stood studyin' me for a bit. Then she said in a nice, easy voice, "Well, girl, my name's Ansalu. Ansalu Malvern Williams, but you'd can just call me Ansalu. An I think we'd best get on to my place an do some talkin'."

She turned, an' I began to follow her. Then she stopped an turned back to me. "What do they call you, girl?" she asked.

"November Sunshine. November Sunshine Mudd," I told her.

She seemed to chew that over in her mind a bit, nodded, an went back to leadin' the way.

We went through a part of the woods that I didn't know very well. It wasn't very long, though, til she motioned to a snug little cabin up ahead.

"That's it," she said, soundin' a bit proud. "It ain't much, but it's all I've got. Then she smiled shyly like an' said, "You'll be my first real comp'ny, November. Folks have come to fetch their washin', but that doesn't count as comp'ny. You be the first."

My pride gave me a nice warm feelin' an' I hurried, feelin' happy right after her up the steps an into the little cabin.

I stopped inside the door an' looked around. From outside, the old wooden cabin hadn't looked that much different from the one I lived in. But once I got inside, I was in a different world. I took a quick look around tryin' to take it all in at once. Then I let my eyes slide back slow, enjoyin' all the things there was to see. The windows had soft white curtains of some kind of material that had been washed an ironed real careful. They hung cool an' crisp lookin' an made the whole place look special. On the wooden floor was a big rag rug, the likes of which I had never seen except in a picture. There'd been an old magazine at the bottom of a box of things from the Freewill Baptist ladies, an' it was full of pictures. I kept that magazine in my pretty box an looked at it till the pages all shredded up, an' it finally fell apart. Then Paw found me lookin' at it an' used it to start up the fire.

"What you want with that, girl?" he'd yelled at me. "Just a wishin' book for things you ain't never gonna havel." He'd stormed 'round the cabin a bit an' then finally forgot about it. But I hadn't. One of the pictures in the magazine showed a real nice room in a little house. An on the floor was a rug made just like the one on Ansalu Williams' floor. We had a scrappy little old rag rug on the floor in front of the pot-bellied stove where the littlest kids used to sit on cold nights to keep warm. But this rug, this rug on Ansalu's floor, was almost as big as the whole room an' it was thick an' warm-lookin' an made of all kinds of colored cloth. It made me think of a rainbow. I felt kind of nervous to be standin' on anythin' so fine, an' I looked at Ansalu to make sure it was all right an I wasn't doin' wrong.

She laughed a funny little laugh, an' said, "Don't fear to step on this rug. November. It was made to be stood on. You're standin' on all the bits an' pieces of my life."

That worried me some, an' I looked for a bit of bare floor to stand on.

"Oh, I didn't mean to worry you none, November, I just have a way of talkin' that has to be got used to," Ansalu said. "But I made this rug out of all the bits of cloth that my mother saved from my early-on clothes, an' I put in some bits of my own, too. There are a lot of memories braided into that rug, November, it pleases me to stop an' think about 'em." She looked at the rug for a bit an then pointed to a piece of bright green cloth woven into the rug in such a way that it blended with the deep blue next to it. "See that green bit there?" she asked me. When I nodded, she said, "That was from my very first store-bought dress."

She smiled a bit to herself, an' motioned me to sit down on a chair.

"My Grandma Willis lived with us for a year or so before she died. Every night she used to tell me about a beautiful dress she had seen in a store winda' in Madison when her paw took her there with him. He had to go into a store to buy some new tools to do his carpenterin' an' my Grandma got to go along as a special treat for her birthday. Well, he left her to stand outside the store an' just eat up that dress with her eyes while he dickered for his tools. Then he took her home with him. He'd bought her a big stick of sugar candy to suck on all the way home. Bein's her birthday an all.

"It was a long time ago, but she said she'd never forget the way that green dress looked just standin' there in that store window." Ansalu paused a bit. "Then after she died, my Grandma, I mean," she went on, "my Maw found a little tin box tucked in with her things. There was a note in the box sayin' that she meant me to have what was in it. An do you know what else the note said?"

I shook my head 'cause of course I didn't have any idea what Ansalu's Grandma might have put in it for her.

She said "I was to use what was in the box to go an' buy me the prettiest green store-bought dress I could find!" Ansalu shook her head with the wonder of that memory. "There were two silver dollars an' a little pile of change in that box. She must have been savin' whatever money came her way for a long, long time."

I got down on the floor an knelt on the rug, reachin' out to feel the softness of the bright green cloth. "It's so softl," I said, almost whisperin'. I'd never felt anythin' like it before.

"Velvet," Ansalu said, noddin' her head. "That's what it's called, velvet." She smiled at my pleasure an went on to tell me how her Paw an' Maw had gotten her all cleaned up an taken her real proud into town where there was a store so big it had a part of it for just the clothes women wore. Ansalu said it was a department store. Then she had to explain what she meant by department. I had a hard time Imaginin' a store just filled with things like dresses an' clothes that people came to buy.

"Well," she said, "I wore that dress till it started to fall apart around me. I wore it to every church social an weddin' an baptism around. My, I did feel fine when I wore that dress. An It made my Maw an' Paw proud, too. I'd been teased a lot about bein' so little an all, but when I wore that green velvet dress, I knew I was the envy of every other girl around."

She turned her attention away from the dress an' the rug, an went over to her work space where she did her cookin'. Then she busted herself for a bit, tellin' me just to "Set an relax," when I moved to help her. In a few minutes, she brought over the prettiest white plate with sprigs of roses all over it. An on that plate were slices of her freshly-baked bread, all spread with butter an' jam an lookin' like nothin' I'd ever seen before.

I felt awkward tryin' to hold the glass of iced tea she gave me an take a piece of bread at the same time. I was awful afraid I'd spill somethin' on that rag rug. Ansalu noticed me strugglin' an' said, "What's wrong with me? Let's you an' me sit at the table where we can eat an' talk in comfort."

After I had eaten two pieces of that bread an' plum jam, I started to reach for a third piece. Then, lest I seem not to have any manners, I pulled my hand back.

"Help yourself, November," Ansalu urged me, nudgin' the plate closer to my hand. "I enjoy eatin' so much more when I have someone to share it with," she said. "You'll be doin' me a favor if you'll eat another piece or two. I can't put it away once it's been spread."

So, I did, thinkin' to myself that this was sure a day I'd remember.

"Care to tell me what 'tis that's botherin' you, November?" she asked me after a bit, smilin' to show she wasn't just pryin'.

"Well," I started, but I couldn't go on. How do you go about tellin' your private worries to someone else? What if tellin' her about my bleeding made her turn against me? I wasn't used to sharin' my ideas with anybody, an' deep inside, I was worried about what I'd do if she laughed at me or got mad.

She leaned over an touched my hand. "It's all right, child," she said real soft an easy. "I don't mean to pry. But sometimes it helps to bring things out in the open. Sometimes the things we worry an' fret so about sort of melt away when there is someone else to help you see the shape of 'em."

So, without quite knowin' how, I found myself pourin' out all my worries about the awful thing that was happenin' to me. Ansalu listened, not sayin' a thing. She was listenin' as though what I was sayin' was real important to 'er.

"I just don't know what's wrong with me," I finished, scared an' relieved to have it all said.

Ansalu sat back in 'er chair an' patted my hand in a comfortin' way.

"My, my, November," she said, shakin' her head. "That Paw of yours didn't do you any favors, did he?"

"Favors?" I asked.

45

"I'm sorry," she said, shakin' her head. "I don't mean to talk him down. I just think he should've told you or had someone else tell you about what's happenin' to you. You're becomin' a woman, November."

"Is that bad?" I asked, not sure I wanted her to tell me, but knowin' I needed to ask.

"No, it's not bad, it's natch'ral. All that gnarlin' in your stomach is just your insides gettin' you ready to be a woman," she told me gently. "And since no one else has told you a thing about it, I 'spose I'd best tell you what to expect an what to do about it."

An' for the next hour or so, Ansalu Williams told me all the things I never knew about makin' babies an growin' up an' gettin' a big bosom like Sara had.

I sat an' pondered about what she had just told me, and went over it in my head while Ansalu made us some fresh tea.

"I don't think I'll like that," I finally blurted out, embarrassed to look her in the eyes. "I... mean, the part about makin' babies an all."

"Oh, it'll be all right when the time comes," she told me. I figured she sure didn't know me very well if she thought so. "But now you got to learn how to take care of yourself when you have the curse," she said, plushin' back her chair an going to a cupboard along the wall.

"Why do they call it the curse?" I asked.

She just looked at me. "There's lots of folks who say it was a curse put on Eve way back when she tempted Adam to eat the forbidden fruit."

"What's the forbidden fruit?" I asked her. I like fruit real well an' when the season is right, I go berryin' an gatherin' blackberries an' thimble berries an' raspberries by the bucketful. Sometimes I can find a place where there are wild grapes or mulberries, too, an then I'll sit with my pail full of fruit an' have a feast before I go back to the cabin. This forbidden fruit thing worried me. "Nobody ever told me about some fruit bein' forbidden," I told her.

Ansalu got a funny look an' then bit by bit 'er face crinkled up until she broke out in a laugh that scrinched her eyes up into nothin'. She laughed an' laughed, an' I sat there wonderin' what I'd said that was so funny.

"I'm sorry, November," she said by an' by, wipin' her eyes with the hem of her dress. "I'm not meanin' to poke fun at you, it's just that you sort of took me by surprise an' I don't get much chance to laugh these days." Then she seemed to gather herself together an went on. "It's easy to see that no one at your house ever told you ANYthing! Law, child, don't you know the story of Adam an' Eve that's in the Holy Bible?"

I felt ashamed when I had to admit that I'd heard of Adam an' Eve, but I wasn't rightly sure who they were.

We sat together there at the Williams' table an' Ansalu told me all kinds of things she figgered I ought to know. She told me more than I really wanted to know, an' more than my head could hold. Things started runnin' into each other, an' it got hard to keep the ideas apart. But I could sure see where she meant well. I just let her go on talkin'. After a bit, I noticed that the sun had gone clear across the sky an' it was fixin' on towards gettin' dark. I told Ansalu that I had to go, but I purely did appreciate her takin' time to tell me all those things. She said she was glad to do it, an' now she felt we were gettin' to be friends, it made her feel good.

She said she wouldn't feel so much like a stranger in the hills no more. When I was gettin' ready to leave, Ansalu wrapped up what was left of the loaf of bread an' said I should take it along an add it to whatever was cookin' for supper. I figgered the boys would be mighty pleased when they each got a slice of Ansalu's good fresh bread. No one in our family had learned how to make real good bread yet, an' you can get awful tired of hard, dry cornbread.

"Hey, girl, where the hell you been?" Paw yelled at me as soon as I came in the door. I was carryin' the little package with the bread in it, but he didn't give me no time to explain. He just grabbed that package from me an threw it in the corner. Then he motioned for me to come stand by him. I didn't want to. Paw had some tall, skinny, stranger standin' by his side, an' I wanted to be let be. But Paw shot me a mean look, so I went an' stood by him.

The stranger seemed kinda nervous an' shifted from one foot to the other. His dark eyes looked shy. I thought that was funny if he'd just come to buy some of Paw's white lightnin'. No need to be scared about that.

I turned my head a bit so I could see the man without him seein' me lookin'. He looked kind of familiar, dark hair an all, but it was a bit till I could place him. Then I remembered that I'd seen him goin' an comin' a couple of times. But he lived up the hill a way, and I didn't rightly know who he was.

I remembered the first time I saw him; he was walkin' up the hill real slow carryin' a hoe. My brother Edson was there an' he saw 'im, too. He said the man went down to the valley most every day an did odd jobs for people. Said that he didn't know his name, just that folks called him Odd. For his manner of workin', I guessed. But the man hadn't paid us no mind, so I never paid him none, either. Later on, I'd come across him once in the woods when I was out pickin' up kindlin' for the fire. He had been standin' so still amongst the trees that I hadn't noticed him at first. When I looked up from pickin' up some kindlin' and saw him there. I had acted like a ninny an let out a terrible yell, an went peltin' off through the woods. Worst was, I dropped all my kind in an knew Paw'd raise sand about it. Which he did.

An' now here the man was, standin' in our cabin, an' my Paw was lookin' at him with a real strange, pleased look on his face.

The man, Odd, wasn't really lookin' at anybody, though. He kept lookin' at the walls an' the floor an' the stove an' whatever. Once he caught me lookin at 'im an' he got redder'n a beet! It was sure hard to tell what manner of a man he was to be so skittery. But it sure wasn't nothin' to me. No skin off my nose.

The only thing I needed to worry about was what Paw might have cooked up for me. Every now an' then he'd put me up to deliverin' his white lightnin' so he wouldn't have to do it. Specially if the batch hadn't turned out so good. Paw hated it when people complained about his lightnin'. Said it made him feel real bad. So, he sent me, figgerin' folks wouldn't be so likely to fuss at me or not pay if I was collectin'.

I guessed Odd had come to complain, an' Paw was gonna make me go get him a jug from under the cabin where he always kept his best squeezin's. He called those hidden jugs his insurance.

Anyways, Odd was standin' there shiftin' from one foot to the other a hundred times or so. I just stood there waitin' for Paw to tell me whatever it was he had on his mind.

"Well, there she is, Odd," my Paw said to him, jerkin' his head in my direction. "What d'ya say?"

I wondered what on earth Paw was thinkin' to say somethin' like that. I could see that it made Odd feel funny, too. He started shiftin' feet faster'n ever, an lookin' up, down every which way.

49

When he felt my eyes on him, Odd turned away an' mumbled somethin' to Paw. I saw Paw look at him real disgusted like, an then he stamped out of the room. Odd turned to me an' sorta mumbled, "What do folks call you, girl?"

I told him my name, but he didn't really seem to notice. Just looked at me like I had somethin' dirty all over my face.

Then Odd went out the door, an I could hear his feet crossin' our porch. In a little bit, I could see him out the winda', walkin' fast as he could up the hill towards his cabin. He wasn't carryin' none of Paws' jugs, so I couldn't figger just what it was that had brought him to our cabin.

When Paw came back, he was crankler than usual. He yelled at me for every little thing, an' I had to bite my lip to keep from cryin'. He got me so upset that when I was puttin' the beans on the table, I let go the edge of the bowl with one hand an' the beans slopped all over the table an' the bread.

"You ain't worth the space you take up!" Paw yelled at me then. As I ran out of the room, I heard him yellin' after me, "No wonder Odd didn't want ya!"

That didn't make much sense to me then, but I figgered I'd best keep out of Paw's way for a bit. I knew he'd get riled up at one of my brothers if I weren't around.

After that, I managed to sneak off an' visit Ansalu every now an' then. She sure was a source of comfort to me. She told me lots of things that she thought I needed to know, too. An she showed me how to make good cornbread. That's when Paw quit fussin' at me goin' over to see Ansalu. At first, he said it wasn't natural that a grown-up woman would want me to come visit. An he complained that I wouldn't get my chores done if I was runnin' off all the time. But just about the time my cornbread came out nearly as good as Ansalu's, Paw said he guessed a visit now an' then wouldn't hurt things none.

"Iffen she can teach you how to cookso your vittles are bettern' what we feed the dawgs, then for Gawd's sake, go see her!" was the way he put it.

Spring went into summer an' summer went into fall. What had happened when Odd came by sort of slipped my mind.

Until one day I came in from bein' over to Ansalu's an found Odd there in the cabin again. Paw'd been watchin' for me.

"Come here, November," he snapped at me as soon as I got into the cabin. I went over to him, wonderin' what it was all about this time.

"Well," he said to Odd, "there she is."

Odd just looked at me. I noticed he wasn't shiftin' from foot to foot like last time an' wondered what he an' Paw were up to.

"How old are you, girl?" he asked me. He didn't yell like Paw did, but I had a feelin' he wasn't settled inside hisself for some reason.

I didn't answer him at first, tryin' to puzzle him out a bit.

"Well, November, can't you hear him askin' you how old you are?" Paw bellered at me. "Well, tell him!"

"I'm almost thirteen," I said, wonderin' why it mattered to this man.

"She's still awful young," Odd said, turnin' away from me an facin' Paw.

"She'll get older!" Paw said.

"But, thirteen?" Odd said as though he was askin' somethin' else.

51

"What's wrong with thirteen?" Paw demanded. "She's most a woman. Knows how to cook an' fix things around a house as good as any grown woman."

They just stood there, Paw glarin' at me like I'd done somethin' wrong, an Odd lookin' away from me an beginnin' to shift from foot to foot again. I wished I could run away an' hide. Somethin' about the way they were actin made me feel awful strange.

"O.K." Odd finally said. I watched Paw's face light up like it did when he found out that a batch of 'shine had turned out extra good an' he could make the men folks pay more for it.

"Pack your things, girl," Paw said.

"What?" Things weren't makin' sense to me just then.

"I said," Paw repeated in a real tight voice, "get your things together. You're goin' home with Odd here."

I looked at Odd for some sign that Paw was makin' a joke or somethin'. But he wouldn't look me in the face. He just looked away an' fidgeted an' sort of turned his head. While I looked at him, I saw he rubbed his hand real hard over his chin an' then shook his head like he was tryin' to clear it.

"Maybe it's not such a good idea," he began in a slow, nervous way.

"A man's word is as good as the law," Paw yelled, stampin' his foot on the floor. "Ain't you ready yet, November?" he growled at me, an' I ran into my cubby-hole to hide.

I sat on the edge of my cot. I didn't quite know what to do. Did Paw mean it, really mean it? Was I to pack my things?

"What's takin' you so long, girl? You ain't got but a few things. Hurry it up, Odd, don't want to spend all night gettin' home."

52

Then I knew he meant what he'd said. With an awful scared feeling, I started putting the few things I had into a neat pile. Then I ripped a narrow edge off my bedcover an' tied it around the little bundle. My things made a pitiful small package, but that wasn't what worried me. What really worried me an made my stomach knot up was wonderin' what Paw....an Odd had in mind.

I sat on the edge of my cot an held on with both hands as though it was rockin' an' I might fall off. I held on to that cot for dear life, an all the time there was this awful worry buzzin' around in my head.

I was scared. I didn't know anything at all about Odd. He was a stranger, but Paw said he'd come to take me away. I didn't even know where he was takin' me or why.

All I knew was that I was purely scared, so scared I felt like I was goin' to die. So scared, I was afraid I wouldn't.

CHANGES

I didn't die.

But sittin' there in my cubby hole with my eyes scrunched tight closed an holdin' on to the edge of my cot, I wished I would. Not knowin' what was ahead was scarier than anythin' I could remember. Somehow, I just couldn't make my hands let go of the side of my cot, no matter how hard I tried. Then I heard Caleb whisperin' to me.

"November... November Sunshine, you gotta listen to me."

When I heard his voice, my eyes popped open an' my hands let go of their hangin' onto my cot. I looked up at Caleb's worried face an' whispered back.

"What is it, Caleb?"

"I'm sorry, November, awful sorry, but I couldn't stop him," he said, leanin' close to my ear so no one else could hear.

"Stop, Paw, what, Caleb?" I asked, hangin' on to his arm like I'd been hangin' onto my cot before.

Caleb looked back over his shoulder to make sure Paw hadn't seen him slip in to talk to me. I could see he was so upset there were tears pushin' at his eyes. "It ain't right, November, an' I tried to tell Paw so..."

"What the hell's keepin' you girl?" Paw's voice broke in, an' Caleb shot me one more sad look an' bolted out of the room.

I didn't know what it was Caleb had been wantin' to say to me, but I could tell from the sound of Paw's voice that I'd best be movin', now.

When I came outta my cubby hole, I found Paw an Odd sittin' at our old table. There was a jug sittin' on it. Paw's hand was strokin' the outside of the Jug an' he seemed to be enjoyin' himself.

My brothers were standin' in a bunch off to the side. They all had funny looks on their faces. None of 'em said a word to me. Caleb had sorta of hidden himself back of some of the others. I felt awful alone.

It was like everyone was waitin' for somethin'.

Then Paw hoisted his jug an took a big swaller. He wiped his mouth with the back of his hand an gave the jug to Odd.

"Here, a fella's gotta have a drink on a deal".

Odd took the jug, but looked like he didn't much want to. He looked at me kinda funny an' then looked back at Paw. Then he tipped the jug on his shoulder an' drank some of Paw's lightnin'. He couldn't have swallered much because he tipped the jug right back down. But it seemed to satisfy Paw.

"We got us a deal!" Paw said, slappin' his leg an soundin' happier than I'd heard him in a long time. Odd was lookin' at me with a funny look on his face, an' when Paw saw him, he leaned over an' said, "She ain't much now, Odd, but when she gets herself all filled out, she'll do all right."

Then Odd stood up an turned to face me. "Get your things, woman," he said. "We'd best be goin'."

I looked at Paw again hopin' he wasn't really gonna make me go off like this. I felt awful strange. Odd had called me 'woman Nobody'd ever done that before.

I sure didn't feel like a woman. I didn't feel like I was grown at all. The little bundle of my belongins' wasn't very big, but I hung on to it for dear life. It was all I had to hang on to.

"Want another swaller?" Paw asked, offerin the jug to Odd again.

Odd just shook his head an' motioned me out the door.

Nobody said a word to me an' I wondered if this was what a funeral was like. Couldn't be no worse.

We went out of the cabin an started up the mountain at a pretty good clip. Odd in front an me followin' with my little bundle of things, I was glad for the fadin' sunlight. It made me need to look real close where I was steppin' an sorta kept my mind off what was happenin.

It wasn't all that far up the mountain to where Odd lived. A cabin came into sight before I was ready to face bein' there. All the way up the hill, I'd tried to make myself think of good things, nice things. Ever since I was just a little girl, I'd come to know that I could only think of one thing at a time. So, I'd figgered out that if I crammed my head with good things to think about, there just wouldn't be no room left to think about the bad.

It had almost worked, too.

Anyways, here we were at Odd's cabin, an' he was motionin' me in while he stopped to pick up a couple of pieces of wood for his stove.

Before I went in, I turned to look down the mountain the way we had come. I could just barely make out the smoke risin' from what had to be our chimney. I had never really thought much about where I lived, but when I saw that smoke, I got so homesick I almost burst into tears. I tried to tell myself I'd be goin' back home soon. But even then, somethin' in me knew different.

I walked as slow as I could into Odd's cabin.

Law, what a mess!

Even with all of us Mudd's livin' in our little cabin an fallin' over each other because it was too crowded, it never looked as bad as this one did. Odd's cabin even smelled bad.

As he came in carryin' the wood he saw me lookin' at his place. I guess he didn't much like the look on my face because he just dropped the wood near the stove an turned to me, fierce like.

"Well, what did you expect with no woman on the place?"

I didn't have any answer.

He just stood there lookin' at me for a bit like he was darin' me to say somethin'. I tried to look back at him, but I couldn't. I just looked at the floor.

Finally, I called up all my courage an' asked, "Don't you ever try to neaten things up?"

He looked at me like I was somethin' that just crawled out from under a rock. "Hell no! That's a woman's work! Why do you think I made that deal with your Paw to get you up here?"

I looked around the cabin again. One thing was sure: I had a lot of work ahead of me. Strange enough, though, that made me feel some better. At least now I could figger why I was here. I was here to clean up Odd's cabin. I was here to get rid of this mess. I wasn't scared of hard work. It had been not knowin' what was comin' that'd scared me.

Feelin' some better about things I began to wonder just what the deal was Paw an Odd had made for me. I remembered when Paw sold off our sow's last shot. I'd felt bad to think of that little pig bein' sold off, but Paw had said, "Business is business. Ain't no place in business to have feelin's about what

57

you sell." He'd always been one to make out real good on a deal.

I wondered what kinda deal he'd made for me. I thought about the way he'd been in a hurry to get Odd to take a drink an' seal it, an' I figgered he must've done pretty good.

Thinkin' that Paw had made a deal about me sure gave me a bad feelin' I wasn't just one of his shoats to trade off. I was his blood kin, but it just didn't seem right that Paw had made some kind of deal about me. An he hadn't even told me about it! I guessed I'd have to do some real ponderin' about it. I couldn't let myself dwell on it now, though, or I'd burst into tears an make a fool of myself.

Oh God, I looked around the strange, messy cabin an felt like a great big foot was squashin' me down.

"Can I see the rest of the cabin?" I asked Odd.

"If you want," he said. "Ain't much else," he added, motionin' to the big room in which we stood.

I grabbed the chance to be doin' somethin' an took my time. I walked around the cabin pretendin' to be lookin' at things.

Odd had been makin' a bit of noise tendin' to the fire, but now he was quiet. I felt his eyes on my back an made myself turn around.

"Uh, did you make this table?" 1 asked him, just to break into the quiet that sort of seemed to swaller me up.

"Yep," he answered. "Made everythin' you see." I didn't know what to do next, an' it come to me I was still hangin' on to my little bundle.

Odd looked at me for a bit, standin' there hangin' onto that bundle, "You goin' to hold on to that thing all night?" he asked.

"I... I don't know where to put it," I finally answered, thinkin' how little an' scared my voice sounded.

"Put it on the floor under the bed," he said, wavin' his hand in the direction of the only bed in the cabin.

I wondered if he was plannin' to give me the bed, where was he goin' to sleep? I didn't dare ask him, though, so I just bent down an put my bundle of things under it.

When I stood up again, he said to me, soundin' like he'd waited long enough. "When you gonna fix supper?"

I looked at his, s'prised. "Why... I..."

"Come on, woman. That's what you're here for. I been eatin' my own cookin' long enough, an' your Paw says you do a passable job of cookin."

It came to me then that I was gonna do more than clean Odd's cabin. He wanted me to cook for him, too. I thought about that for a moment an I guessed I could do it. At least I'd keep myself busy. But I wondered when I'd get to go home again.

"Umm, I was wonderin'. How long is this deal you an' Paw made for?"

Odd gave me a sharp look.

"Didn't you Paw tell you nothin' about it?"

I shook my head no.

"Damn!" he muttered to himself. "He said you knew all about it an' was agreeable."

"All about what?"

"Get me a cup of coffee an get yourself one, too," he added, lookin' at me kinda strange.

I poked around a cupboard on the wall, but I couldn't find but two cups.

Both of 'em had thick brown stuff at the bottom like they'd been that way for a long time. Then I looked for a bucket of water but couldn't find one.

"Give 'em here," Odd said, reachin' for the cups. Then he made a swipe at one of the cups with his shirt tail an' set it on the table while he wiped out the other one. I got the old enamel pot off the back of the stove an' poured both cups full of thick, black coffee.

It looked awful. An, when I tasted it, it tasted awful, too.

Odd drank his like he was used to it. Then he turned to me like he'd just thought of somethin'. "Hey, woman, can you make passable coffee?"

I shook my head yes.

He looked at me an' a smile broke out over his face. "Is that a fact?" he said, but not like he was askin' me at all. Made that fresh yesterday, an it's been sittin' on the stove keepin' warm ever since. Tastes like hell, though. Can't figger what I'm doin' wrong to it." He turned to me again. "You're sure you know how to make coffee?"

I nodded. "I make it for the menfolks at home," I told him.

"Good," he said, an' then just sat there thinkin'.

"Bout that deal," he said, lookin' straight at me. "Your Paw an me made a deal for you to be my...woman."

"You mean to clean an' cook for you?" I held my breath till he answered.

"Partly," he said, soundin' firm in his answerin'. "You know what it means to be a man's woman?"

There wasn't any way I could answer him.

"God, you're not real smart, are you?" he said, soundin' almost mad at me.

"An you're awful skinny, too," he added, lookin' real careful at me. I wondered if he could tell how much I was shakin' inside. Then he leaned back in his chair as though he was thinkin'. "Well, your Paw told me I'd be the first. So, I guess I should have expected it. With a sigh, he stood up an made as if to go outside.

I couldn't hold it in any longer. "The first what? I don't know what you're talkin' about," I said, fightin' tears so they wouldn't show in my voice. Somehow, I didn't want this man standin' there in his messy cabin to know how bad I felt.

"Your Paw an me made a trade. I needed a woman, an' he wanted my Steven's rifle. I had two rifles, an' your Paw said his'n wasn't fit to shoot no more, so he wanted one of mine. He's been offerin' to trade you for the rifle for a long time. I finally took him up on it."

I felt like I'd been hit. It took my breath away an I felt my mouth fall open, but I couldn't find the strength to close it. All I could do was stare at Odd. I waited for him to tell me it was some kind of stupid joke or somethin'.

But he didn't.

He just stood there an looked at me like he figured Paw had got the best of the bargain.

"But... I'm... I'm a PERSON! You can't just up an' trade people like you trade an ax or a pig or a bushel of potatoes!" I burst out.

"We done it," Odd said like it was all cut an' dried an' done.

Which it was.

Odd just shrugged his shoulders an' went on outside. In a little bit, I heard what I figured was the privy' door bang an I knew where he'd gone.

I sat down on the edge of the bed like my knees wouldn't hold me no more.

This must have been what Caleb was tryin' to tell me back at our cabin. Everybody must've known but me. Paw figgered I was just a thing to be traded. All I was worth was an old rifle.

Right then, I felt so low I wanted to die.

After a bit, Odd came back in the cabin carryin' a couple more pieces of wood for the fire. He threw a chunk or two in the stove. Then he damped it for the night an turned to me.

"Gettin' too late to fix supper. Figger we can eat what cornbread's left from before. You can fix a good meal in the mornin'." Then he went to an old cupboard in the corner an fetched a burned an' battered pan. Sittin' in the pan when he handed it to me was some of the sorriest lookin' cornbread I ever did see. I looked at Odd to make sure this was to be my supper. From the look on his face, I knew it was. By the time, I had broken off a piece for myself, Odd was back with a pitcherful of buttermilk. I looked around for glasses, but there weren't any. So, I went to the door an' dumped out what was left of that awful coffee an' tried to wipe the cup out with an old rag I found on the sink. I wasn't sure the rag was very clean either, but by then I guessed it didn't matter much anyway.

That was some supper. You know, Old Clara used to say every cloud has a silver linin'. For some reason, I thought about that then. I sure couldn't see a silver linin' to this cloud. I went to eat that cornbread an' drink that warm buttermilk, an' it nearly choked me. I was so mixed up inside that I just knew I couldn't make it go down. I tried a bite or two so Odd wouldn't get mad at me, but there was no way I could eat any more'n that. I guess the silver linin' was that Odd didn't seem to notice when I quit tryin'.

While I was sittin' there pretendin' to chew, Odd said, "Your Paw is gettin' ready to get him another woman to take care of things around his cabin. Some widder woman he knows up Hollis way."

I was surprised to hear that. Paw had never let on that he was lookin' aroun' for another woman. I wondered what all he'd been up to, an howcome he never said nothin' about it?

Odd went on, "Your Paw said it never does work out for two women to share the same cook-stove. Said it never did, an' it never would."

"Oh," was all I could manage to say. I felt like someone had pumped all the air out of me. I felt that weak. I sure wish I had Ansalu there to help me out of this.

I just sat there, waitin' to see what would happen. Odd finally got up an' threw one more chunk of wood on the fire. Then he went an shut the cabin door an turned down the wick so the lamp went out. The room was real dark then, with only the glow from the stove to light it up. It took me a bit till my eyes got used to the dark an I could see.

Odd went over to the bed. While I watched, he took off his shirt. Then he took off his shoes and dropped his drawers. He stretched out on the bed an' just lay there. I stood real still, scarce darin' to breathe. I tried to remember all the things

Ansalu had told me. What I could remember near to made me sick.

"Come on, woman. Time to get to bed."

"But… but that bed's not very big," I said.

"Don't need to be," he answered, soundin' short. "What's takin' you so long?"

"I haven't been out to the privvy," I told him.

"Oh, for Lord's saker," he snapped. "Light the lamp an' take it with you. You'll never know where you're goin' in the dark."

So, I got a burnin' twig from the stove and lit the lamp. I was real careful not to look at Odd lyin' in the bed waitin' for me. Then I went outside an found the privvy an sat down on the seat to think. There had to be some way out of this mess, an' there sure wasn't anyone else but me to find it. I thought an I thought an then I remembered about the day I met Ansalu, an some of the things she'd told me. I figgered out what I could do.

I hurried up an used the privvy an went back into the cabin. Then I turned the wick down on the lamp again, an sat down on the floor by the stove.

"What the hell are you doin' over there?" Odd asked soundin' put out.

"I'm sorry, Odd, but I got the curse."

"You what?" he bellered, sittin' up in bed. "That means what I think it means?"

"Yes, I guess so," I answered him.

He heaved a sigh that must have come all the way from his feet. Then he reached down an' started pullin' on his pants an got up off the bed.

He didn't say a word. Just got up, took the top quilt off the bed, an went over near the stove where I was sittin'. He made himself a place to lie on the floor an rolled himself up in the cover. He curled up with his back to me an' lay there real still, I just sat where I was for a long time. After a while, I heard him begin to snore. Then I walked real quiet over to the bed an' smoothed the cover out. I sat down real easy on the edge of the bed tryin' not to make any noise an' bother Odd. Next, I used my left foot to pry off my right shoe. Then I pried off my left one an' lay down on the bed, still in my clothes, I held myself real stiff an' tight. I didn't aim to go to sleep. I figgered to lie there an' try to work some way out of this awful pickle I was in.

But Odd was right, the bed was comfortable. An I guess bein' so tired an upset had worn me down because in spite of everythin', I drifted off to sleep.

Next thing I knew, I smelled bacon fryin' an' the sun was streamin' in the window.

It took me a bit to figure out where I was an all. When it came to me what had happened, I began to feel awful sorry for myself. I lay there real still, tryin' not to move, just keepin' my eyes scrunched up tight so Odd would think I was still asleep. An I started talkin' to myself inside my head. Inside, I hollered an' cussed an' wished somethin' awful would happen to Paw for doin' this to me. But outside, I didn't move, not even a little bit.

Finally, when I was all worn out with fightin' in my head, I let my eyes open an sneaked a look around. Odd had his back to me while he was workin' over the stove. Looked at this way, he didn't scare me, so I thought about some of the other men

65

in the hills that Paw could have traded me to, an' I reckoned that there could be worse.

I'd bide my time an see how things turned out. Meanwhile, I'd try to keep myself busy an out of Odd's way as much as I could.

I didn't even let myself think about what I'd do about the bed part when it came time for me to tell him the curse was over an' done. And I didn't dare even think about what I'd do when I REALLY got the curse.

"Hey, you awake?" Odd called from the stove. I guess I must've moved around on the bed or somethin'.

"Yep," I answered, sittin' up an puttin' on my shoes.

Odd was quiet for a bit, turnin' the bacon, an then he said, "Won't do you no good to be mad about bein' here," he said.

I didn't answer, just got up an' smoothed out the bedcover. Then I straightened up an' just stood there by the bed. Neither of us said a word, an' I just went on standin' there. I figured I'd act kind of quiet an' not talk an' not eat an get even a little bit for bein' traded off like some old pig or somethin'.

I stood there, an Odd didn't say anythin' either. He finally fished all the bacon out of the pan an put it on a plate. He took the fryin' pan over to the door an made like he was goin' to throw the bacon grease out.

"Don't do that!" I yelled without meanin' to. The smell of that bacon fryin' an seein' that plate full of crisp, thick-cut bacon did me in. My stomach didn't care if I HAD planned not to talk or eat. All my stomach knew was that it hadn't had any supper to speak of the night before, an' it was mighty empty. I couldn't let him throw away that good hot bacon fat without fryin' at least a couple of pieces of bread in it.

"Here," I said, takin' the pan out of Odd's hands. I went back to the stove an put the pan on it. Then I went to the cupboard an' hunted out a loaf of bread. The only loaf I found was hard as a rock. But for bacon bread that didn't matter, so I called to Odd, "Come an' cut a couple pieces of this loaf."

Without sayin' anythin' Odd did just that an handed me about six pieces of bread. I plopped two or three slices into the bacon grease that was spittin' hot by now, an turned to find Odd watchin' me.

"What you up to?" he asked.

I told him I was makin' bacon bread to eat with the bacon, an' he just nodded his head like that sounded good to him.

"Are you gonna make the coffee or not?" he asked me, pointin' at the big old pot.

"You got any eggs?" I asked him.

"One or two," he answered. "What do you want the eggs for?"

"Best way to settle the coffee grounds at the bottom of the pot is to put an egg in with "em".

"You must be joshin' me," Odd said.

But I just went right on an' started makin' the coffee. Odd had brought in a bucketful of fresh water. So, first, I rinsed out all that thick black stuff he had left in the big old enamel pot. I wiped it out real good with a rag I found in the cupboard. Then I put a couple of dipperfuls of fresh water from the bucket into the pot. Odd showed me where he kept the coffee, an' I threw two handfuls or so into the water, put on the top, and set the pot next to the fryin' bacon bread on the stove.

"When do you put in the egg?" he asked.

"When it's bolled up real good," I told him.

After the coffee was ready an' the bacon bread had fried up nice an' brown, we sat down at the table. All the time I was fixin' the coffee I tried to settle my mind on what to do. But I was so busy fixin' food an' so hungry waitin' for it, my mind just never did settle down to thinkin'.

While the coffee was cookin' an' the bread was fryin', I had set to clearin' off the table so we could sit there an' eat. When I got the table cleared off, I got the rag I'd used before an' wiped off the table. I was surprised at how pretty the wood looked when it was all cleaned off like that.

By now, the cabin was full of awful good smells. It only took a minute to break the egg into the coffee pot and settle the grounds.

I set the plate of bacon on the table an put the bread on another plate. I put that on the table, too. I had to do a lot of huntin' to find two more dishes for us to eat off of. Just about everythin' Odd owned seemed to be sittin' dirty somewhere. I finally took the two dirty cups an' rinsed them out. Then I put Odd's an' my plates an' the two cups on the table. I went back over to the cupboard an' rustled around in it for a bit. Then I came up with two bone-handled forks. The tines on my fork were bent. His weren't.

There wasn't nothin' else to do but pour the coffee an' sit down.

Odd forked a couple of pieces of bacon an' bread onto his plate and shoved the plate over towards me.

I thought again about my idea not to eat an knew I'd have to find some other way to make Odd feel bad. I was hungry.

You know, I didn't mean to like anything at all about this sorry business, but it did seem nice to have a whole table for just two people an' not to have to grab for your food lest you end up without any. I was so used to being jostled by one brother or another that it was hard to make myself slow down an' not bolt my food.

It was so quiet an' the food tasted so good I just kept eatin'. Then I started to feel guilty for enjoyin' the food so much.

I finally got to where I couldn't take another bite.

I looked up at Odd, then, an' saw him watchin' me. "Are you done eatin'?"

I asked him. He said he was, so I jumped up an' started gatherin' things together. while I was collectin' all the dirty dishes from around the place an heatin' water to wash 'em in, Odd just sat there an' watched.

He didn't say anythin', just watched.

When I was bout finished with the dishes, he spoke. "Your Paw was right; you're a good worker an' a passable cook." Then he went out of the cabin.

I felt a little more comfortable with him gone.

Soon as I finished the dishes, I looked around. It came to me that nearly everythin' else in the place needed washin', too.

It was easy to see my work was cut out for me, I thought.

I heard some choppin' noises outside. In a little bit, Odd came in carryin' wood for the stove. "Since you're new, I figured I'd bring you in some wood," he told me. "By the way," he told me I knew bringin' in the wood was goin' to be part of my chores from here on in.

I tried not to pay much mind to Odd an' just went about my work for the rest of the day. Odd had to show me where the spring was so I could get more water, but mostly I managed things pretty well for myself.

Well, I finally made it through that first day. Let me tell you, by the time I was done reddin' up after supper, I was so tired I ached all over. I dropped down on that bed, too tired to care where Odd put himself.

When I woke up early in the mornin', I saw Odd sleepin' over by the fire, same as he'd done the night before.

Well, I thought, maybe things won't be too bad.

It went on that way for four or five days. I dropped, bone tired, into the bed each night, an Odd slept on the floor by the stove. After the first day, he went off somewhere to do whatever job he had for that day, an' left me to work around the cabin by myself. Bit by bit, the cabin was beginnin' to look a sight better. I had washed up just about everythin' that could be washed up. I'd started cleanin' the windows even though that seemed a pretty hopeless kind of job.

Odd never said anythin' about my work. He just looked around each night an seemed to notice what I'd done, but he didn't say nothin' about it. I was used to Paw, so that part of it didn't bother me too much. Paw always figured the inside of a cabin was women's work. The outside was man's work. I never could figure out how it was the woman had to go outside to get wood an' water. But, in the hills, a woman learns not to argue with a man unless she wants to get backhanded. An' I didn't.

Anyway, I was surprised one evenin' when Odd came an' stood in front of me with his hands on his hips like he meant business.

"Are you all right?" he asked.

I told him I guessed I was.

"That ain't what I mean!" he snapped.

The awful thing was, when I went to the privvy that mornin', I found that my time for the curse had come an' I really did have it. But when I told Odd I still had the curse, he gave me an awful, dark look.

He went outside then, without sayin' a thing, but I knew he wasn't happy with what I'd said.

Right about then, I'd have given my right arm to talk to Ansalul. There were lots of things I needed to talk to her about. I was gettin' plum worried about what to do next. Up to now Odd had been patient an believin'. But I had the awful feelin' that it wasn't goin' to last much longer. An I had seen enough about Odd to know that he wasn't a man to take bein' fooled very easy. I hated to think what would happen if he found out I'd been storyin' him at first about the curse.

So, the next day, I set about makin' a real good meal for Odd. It was hard to put things together because he didn't have much in his cupboard. But I figured out that I could make hotcakes and boil up some sugar to make syrup. So, when Odd came for his evenin' meal, he found the table fresh washed an' laid out. I had found some wild flowers not too far from the cabin, an' cleaned out an old jar I found on the trash heap out back. Then I'd put the flowers in the jar an' set them in the middle of the table on top of a clean homespun towel I'd found stuck away in a corner of the cupboard. I put the two plates that came closest to matchin' on the table an' laid a fork on the table by each one. I'd even straightened the tines of Odd's forks so they looked real good an' would be easier to eat with.

When I stood back an' looked, I figgered I'd done my best. I hoped it would soften Odd up some. I wanted somethin'.

I wanted Odd to let me go see Ansalu Williams.

The hotcakes turned out fair. Odd poured lots of syrup over them an' ate seven. Then he looked at me an' said, "I ain't had hotcakes for a long time." He didn't say they were good or not, though.

"I'd like to go across the mountain tomorrow an' see someone," I told him while he was drinkin' his coffee an seemin' to be in a good mood. "It's a friend, a woman who lives here in the hills."

"Why do you want to go see her?" he asked me, soundin' suspicious.

"Ain't you got enough to keep you busy?"

My heart sank. "Yes, I got enough to do. It's just... just that I don't have anybody to talk to..."

"Don't need to talk if you're tendin' to your own knittin'," he said.

"But, I WANT someone to talk with," I tried to explain. "I need someone to have a woman talk with."

Odd seemed to mull over what I'd said. Then he nodded slowly. "Well, I remember how my Maw used to say she'd give anythin' to have another woman to talk with. My Paw said she was crazy. What did women have to talk about? Maybe he was right, maybe he was wrong. But I got you awful young, so maybe it is best you do find a woman somewhere to talk with. Maybe."

I was caught off balance, I was so pleased! I'd figured Odd to get mad at my askin', an' here he was, sayin' maybe I could go. I didn't want to take a chance on spoillin' that maybe, so I just stood there with my mouth closed.

He seemed to mull things over in his mind, then he said, "You can go."

"Just this once, though. An don't you get any funny ideas about runnin' away or anythin' like that," he said, soundin' fierce.

You know, lookin' back, it seems funny, but I never once thought about runnin' away. It was almost as though I was caught in a trap like they use to catch wild critters. I had to wait to see what the trapper planned to do with me. I didn't seem to have any power over myself or any choice about what happened.

But I tried to cheer myself up. It was settled. I could go see Ansalu. At least this once, Odd was goin' to let me go see my friend. I felt a smile startin' somewhere near my heart an' spreadin' through my whole body.

"Hey, November, what kind of talk you plannin' to do?" Odd asked.

"Why um..." I thought quickly, "Just some housekeepin' things I need to know. You know, I never ran a whole house before an' there's a lot I need to ask about."

"Like what?"

"Well, like dryin' herbs an' puttin' up fruit when it's ripe an' things like that."

He seemed to think about that an' nodded his head. "Makes sense," he said shortly an' stooped to put some more wood on the fire.

"Make some extra cornbread for breakfast, "Vember, then I can eat what's left over for my noon meal. Then he added, "An' start the beans for supper before you go, or we'll be all night waitin' for 'em to cook."

I promised I'd do everythin' he asked, an' he seemed to consider the matter closed. He turned an' left the cabin without another word. I was left to myself to plan things out.

My head was full of plans for goin' to see Ansalu. I'd thought about it so often in my mind that I knew just what I wanted to do. I'd get up real early if I was goin' to make cornbread for breakfast. It would take a lot of stokin' to get the fire in the cookstove hot enough to bake so early, but I'd do it. An, I thought I'd bring in all the wood I'd need right now so it would be right handy for the mornin'.

For the rest of that day, I was busy heatin' water to wash out my dress an' puttin' the cabin to rights so there wouldn't be nothin' Odd could find wrong. I sure didn't want him to fuss at me an' make me stay home from Ansalu's.

FRIENDSHIP

I was scared when I knocked at Ansalu's door. What if she wasn't there? She didn't even know I was comin'. Or worse yet, what if she didn't want to see me? I'd done my best to make myself look nice an' clean. I'd washed my clothes and took a bath in a big old tub I'd found out back of Odd's privvy an even put some mint leaves in the water to make myself smell good. There wasn't any mirror in the cabin, but I'd tried to fix my long hair into one big braid goin' down my back. On the way over to Ansalu's I'd stopped an picked a little piece of fern an' tucked it in the braid to make it look pretty. I knew I wasn't much to look at, but I did the best I could with what I had.

But what if she didn't like me no more?

"November Sunshine," she cried openin' the door an findin' me on her doorstep. Just one look at her warm, welcomin' smile set my mind at rest. She wanted to see me, she really did. My heart stopped poundin' so hard.

I followed her into the cabin, feelin' happy an lookin' around with pleasure at the room that always made me feel so good.

"Here," I said, puttin' a little package into her hands. "It's cornbread. I had an extra lot of buttermilk, so I made extra bread this mornin'."

She opened the package an' sniffed at the bread. "Umm," she said, sniffin' again. "I've been out of buttermilk for quite a spell an' sure have missed havin' cornbread! You must've got up before the sun to get this baked to bring along!" She smiled at me real big an' then turned towards her stove an moved the tea kettle over the fire. "I'll make us some tea in a few minutes, an' we can eat the cornbread right away. She turned towards me an' said, "I haven't seen you in a long while, November."

She stood real still then, an looked at me close. "Is everythin' all right with you?"

I thought about all that had happened since I saw her last an didn't know where to start tellin'. "I got a lot to tell you, Ansalu, but it'll be best to wait til we're drinkin' our tea, if you don't mind."

She smiled an' shook her head. "Don't mind a bit." Then she turned back to her cupboard an seemed to be huntin' somethin'. "Do you like apple butter, November?" she asked.

I told her I sure did. Even though I hadn't had it very often, I could remember its tart sweetness with pleasure an' sure hoped the question meant I was goin' to get some shortly.

"You know, November, it's funny, but I was just thinkin' about you an wonderin' when I'd see you again. An' here you are!" she said, gigglin' like a young girl an makin' me laugh, too. "Are you on your way someplace else, or did you come all this way just to see me special?"

"Oh, I came to see you!" I told her. "I really need to get some answers to things, Ansalu." I thought a moment an went on, "Seems I'm always askin' you 'bout somethin', aren't I?"

Ansalu just smiled. She didn't say anythin' until she had put plates an' cups on the table. Then she got the jar she'd brought from the cupboard an put a spoon on the table by it. The jar was full of dark apple butter, an' it just made my mouth water to think of puttin' it on that cornbread.

"I'll pour the tea, November," she said pointin' towards the stove, "An' you can cut up the cornbread so we can eat it while we drink the tea."

For the next few minutes, we were busy spreading the cornbread with a thick layer of apple butter an eatin' it an drinkin' Ansalu's good hot yarb tea.

I guess I came as close then, in those quiet shared moments, to being really, truly happy as I'd ever been. Life with Paw an' my brothers in the Mudd cabin seemed so far away. But, thinkin' of my home an' Paw an what had happened in my life brought me back real quick to the reason I had come to see Ansalu.

"Ansalu," I started, an' then stopped. I wasn't sure whether it was best to jump right in an ask what was on my mind, or to sort of lead up to it gradual. "It's about Odd," I finally blurted out.

Ansalu stopped chewin' an looked at me with a blank look on her face.

"Odd?" she repeated, makin' it sound like a question.

"Yep," I said, "It's well...I don't know what to do."

Then it came to me that Ansalu didn't know a thing about what had happened to me an didn't have any idea in the world about who Odd was. She didn't even know about what Paw had done with me or about my comin' to live in Odd's cabin. The last time I'd seen her, I was still at home, tryin' to take care of all the menfolks in my family.

I stopped in wonder. Was that only a few weeks ago? I felt as though it was a whole world away.

"Best start from the beginnin', November," she said gently, fillin' up my tea cup as full as it would go. "I know somethin's eatin' at you, but till you tell me, I won't know beans about it."

So, doin' my best to tell the story straight an' not let my voice shake, I told Ansalu about what had happened. I told her how, when I'd come home from her place the first time, Odd was there. Then he'd gone away, an' I hadn't thought any more about it. It was almost a year later when I'd come home an' found I'm there again. When I came to the part about Paw tradin' me off to Odd for a Steven's rifle, she made an angry sound an sat bolt upright in her chair.

"Well, I never!" she snapped, settin' her tea cup down so hard I was afraid she'd crack it. But when I stopped talkin' she just motioned for me to go on.

I finally got to the part where I'd found only one bed in Odd's cabin, an' then Ansalu broke in.

"What on earth did you do then, child?" she asked, peerin' into my face with a look of worry in her eyes.

"I remembered what you told me, Ansalu," I said, "an I told 'Im I had the curse."

Ansalu burst out laughin' an laughed so hard an' long that I got over bein' afraid she'd be disgusted with me for what I was tellin' her.

"Good for you, November!" she laughed, clappin' her hands together. Then she stopped laughin' an looked at me close again. "But that was nearly two weeks ago, November. You can't be still tellin' him you got the curse."

I sighed, knowin' that I'd stretched the truth with Odd an afraid that even Ansalu wouldn't think it was a right thing to do. "Well, Ansalu, just about the time he was thinkin' I should be over the curse, I really got it."

She just looked at me.

"I really DO have the curse now, Ansalu."

She sighed. "I hear you, girl, I hear you," she said, lookin' like she was doin' some hard thinkin'. "I'm afraid you've sort of backed yourself into a corner, November, an we're goin' to have to see what you can do about it."

After sittin' there thinkin' for a few minutes, Ansalu turned to me real serious-like. "You know, November, you're in luck that your Paw seems to have traded you off to a man who didn't have much luck with women. Else, he could have made things purely miserable for you. But even though it's plain to see he hasn't been around women very much, you know as well as I do that you can't go on havin' the curse forever."

I nodded. I sure knew that I had to do somethin' pretty soon.

"Let's see, November. Seems to me you were twelve when we first got to know each other by the woods pool. She looked at me real thoughtfully. "So, that means you're 'bout thirteen now, don't it?" I nodded. "Well," she sighed so hard then that her whole body seemed to puff up with air, "I guess there's only one thing you CAN do."

I sat there holdin' my breath waitin' to see what she'd say.

"November, I know you're still mighty young for it, but there's plenty of girls here in the hills who have had to do it younger. I guess you're goin' to have to start fillin' a woman's duties."

I must have made some kind of sound because she took my hand in hers an' just held on to it hard. "Can't see any other way out of it, November. You're goin' on fourteen now, an most men think that's plenty old enough. Odd's goin' to expect...things… of you, November. He won't be patient much longer."

"But," I cried, "I don't mind doin' his cookin' an cleanin'. After doin' for all the menfolks at home, doin' for one is plum easy.

Specially, now that I got his cabin all set to rights. I really don't mind doin' for him at all, Ansalul."

Ansalu looked at me in a pityin' sort of way. "November," she said real firm like, "that's not what I meant at all, an' you know it."

I sat there feelin' like the weight of the whole mountain had settled on my shoulders. I couldn't ever remember feelin' so bad, not even when I'd been so sick an' scared on the day my curse had first started.

"What've I gotta do?" I finally asked.

"Well, November," Ansalu said, "I'll do my best to help you out. But mostly it's gonna be up to you. Movin' around like I've done, I come to find out that the only person you can really count on is yourself."

"What do you mean?" I asked her.

"I mean, November, you just got to take life the way it comes along an make do."

"Make do?" I repeated as though just sayin' the words out loud would give me the answers I needed.

"Yep, November. The secret of stayin' alive is to learn to make do."

Sometimes life gives a person somethin' easy to live with, but it's been my 'xperience that more likely than not, life hands out some pretty rough times." She looked out the window for a bit. Then she turned back to me. "Makin' do I s...well, it's learnin' that it's not what happens to you, it's what you do about it that counts."

I sat there thinkin' about what she'd just said. There was a lot to learn.

"How do you learn to make do?" I managed to ask.

"Well, makin' do is just sort of usin' your common sense. Like for instance, you've worked hard an' raised some nice greens in your garden. Let's say your mouth is waterin' for a good mess of fresh greens, but your neighbor's chicken gets in an' scratches up all your greens."

I didn't understand. "But what does that have to do with makin' do?"

"It's easy, November. You just forget about havin' greens an' make chicken stew."

I thought I was beginnin' to see what she meant.

"For Instance," she said, droppin' her voice a bit even though there was no one to hear what we said, "Take this turban I'm wearin'." She tilted her head so I could get a better look at the one she had on that day. "These turbans I wear are made do."

I guess I looked puzzled cause she laughed a little an' patted her turban in a right proud way.

"I never told anyone else about my turbans 'cept Will, til now," she said, real solemn. "But I'm gonna tell you. You see, November, I wanted to look real good for some big doin's back when Will an I used to live near Charleston. So, I saved up my money an bought myself one of those home permanents." She looked at my face as I tried to understand. "A permanent is somethin' you can put on your hair an' it makes it all curly. An' the reason they call it permanent is because it doesn't wash out for a long time. A home permanent is one you can give to yourself right in your own home. You don't have to go nowhere to get it done." When she saw I was follerin' what she was sayin' she went on.

81

"So, I gave myself a permanent, tryin' to make myself look real good. But life was ready for one of its surprises. I must've done somethin' wrong with that permanent, somethin' real wrong. Don't you know, in the mornin' when I took the cloth off my head an unwrapped all them little curlers expectin' to look real pretty, all my hair came right off with the curlers!"

I let out a little cry, thinkin' how awful she must've felt.

"It's true, November. I was as bald as a pumpkin an' every bit as shiny." She looked at me with a funny smile on her face. "You can imagine what an awful state I was in then?" She shook her head, a bit sad, rememberin'. "So, there I was, faced with big doin's an' my head lookin' like a baby's rear end. I didn't even have time to cry. First off, I went an' hunted my old mirror an looked at myself just to make sure. There wasn't any mistake. Then I wanted to die or hide forever. But I knew Will was countin' on me an' I had to figger out somethin'". She smiled at me like I had helped her in some way.

"What'd you do?" I started to ask. An' then it came to me!

"I can see you've already figgered it out!" she said, noddin' at me.

"You're right. That's when I started wearin' turbans. Will's mother had given me a piece of real pretty blue silk that I was savin' for somethin' special. Well, I decided this was about as special as it could ever be. So, I tried out different ways to wrap my head. Then Will told me about a rich lady he saw one time up in Charleston. He said she had somethin' tied around her head like the men in that far-off country, India. He said he saw a magazine in the mine foreman's house with color pictures of India in it. An he told me how they had their heads wrapped up an helped me til I got the hang of doin' it to myself. He even showed me how to pin my mother's cameo brooch on the place where the cloth is held together."

82

I looked at Ansalu, shorter'n anybody I knew but holdin' herself as Lall an proud as can be.

"You made do!" I said.

"I made do," she agreed. Then she chuckled an' said, "An would you believe, November, some of the ladies at the doin's admired my new hat. I never let on a thing, an' Will an me laughed a lot of times over my fancy getup."

"Oh, Ansalu," I sighed, crossin' to her chair an stoopin' to hug her shoulders. I'll just never learn to make do like you can!"

"Nonsense, child! Don't ever talk like that or you'll lose the battle before it's even half started!" She motioned me to sit down again, an turned to me, all serious an' solemn. "What we have to do is help you figure out how to make do."

"You mean, with Odd an all?"

"Yep." She paused a minute an looked at me hard. "Do you know what it is he'll be expectin' of you, November?"

I just shook my head an' thought a bit. "I guess he'll be expectin' me to go on doin' the cookin' an cleanin' an such like."

Ansalu shook her head sadly. "That's only part of it, November. He's goin' to want you to share his bed."

"But it works out fine the way it is now, Ansalu," I protested.

"Honestly, November, this bein' raised with nothin' but menfolks around hasn't got you ready for anythin'!" She sighed an rolled her eyes up towards the cellin'. Then she looked back at me. "Ain't you ever seen a boy you liked?"

I was taken aback by her question. "Sure, Ansalu, I like most of my brothers."

"Well," she said, shakin' her head, "I guess we're goin' to have to go through the whole thing. "Then she sat me down an told me to listen good.

She started in by tellin' me that most girls my age had already seen some boy, not a brother, they wanted to be friends with. An she told me my body would sort of let me know when the right one came along. Except that Odd was already there. I'd best get used to the idea, she told me, that Odd was the one I'd have to make do with.

Then she looked at me real hard, all over. "It looks to me, November," she said, "Like you're startin' to fill out some, but it's clear you got a long way to go. So maybe Odd might take it kind of easy on you at first, bein's he's your first, an all. But, November, a man gets...certain hungers... an' it ain't in his nature to take it easy. He feels he's got to do somethin' about 'em." She looked at me with a question on her face. "Do you know what I'm talkin' about?"

I told her I didn't.

Ansalu sighed even deeper this time. "Well, looks like we're goin' to have to start from scratch on this man-woman stuff just like we did about the curse."

"You mean there's more to it than you already told me?" I asked.

She looked at me an' shook her head. "You're only at the beginnin', girl," she said. "I guess you'd best listen pretty hard to what I got to tell you."

I sat there gettin' more shook up all the while she told me about how men get excited about women's bodles an touchin' them an all. An I couldn't help remember about Viticus an' the way he was feelin' Sara's bosom an' roochin' around. It made me feel real awful cause I didn't much like the idea of someone feelin' me up that way an' roochin' all over me. An, anyhow, I didn't have a bosom like Sara's an' the whole thing was beginnin' to turn my stomach. Then Ansalu got to the place about what happens to a man when he gets excited an what he does about it.

"You mean he's gonna stick that thing in me?" I yelled, jumpin' clear up out of my chair, I was so upset.

Ansalu just nodded.

"Oh no, he's not!" I yelled back at her. "I'm not goin' to let 'im do it!"

"November Sunshine," Ansalu began an I could hear the patience in her voice as she tried to calm me down. "You're a girl, and there's not much you can do about it. And men are the way they are. All men seem to be the same, no matter where you go, an' they expect the same thing of a woman. Seems to me you're a peck better off stayin' where you are an learnin' to get along with the man you got." She leaned closer to make her point. "Didn't he leave you alone when you first came to his cabin? Doesn't he treat you decent?"

I thought about it. She was right. I shook my head, agreein' with her.

"Well then, November, you'd best learn to make do with what you've got. You learn to please Odd all right, an' you won't have to worry about all the other men in the world who might not treat you so nice."

She left me alone to think about what she'd said an went over to the kitchen counter where she filled the kettle for more tea. I didn't like the choices I had. Didn't seem like they were real choices. Then she came back an' stood by my chair. She laid one hand real gentle on my shoulder an' sort of patted my head with the other. "It ain't always easy bein' a woman,

November," she said, "but if you learn to sort of let yourself ride with it, you can make out all right!"

I felt a sigh startin' way down at my toes an workin' its way through my whole body. When it finally worked its way out, I felt tears startin' down my cheek. I brushed the tears away an sat up straight as I could. I'd never liked it when my brothers had called me a cry-baby, an' I thought of what they'd say if they saw me cryin' now.

"Just tell me what to do," I said real low, not able to look Ansalu in the eyes. I didn't want to see her pity.

Well, she told me all right! An she even gave me a little jar of some cream she said would be real good to use so I wouldn't get too sore. I was sure glad Ansalu was there to tell me, an' I blessed her for the kind way she went about it. The whole thing sorta sickened me an made me feel like a prize pig somebody was gettin' ready to sell at the fair an' was fixin' it all up so it would bring the best price.

That afternoon, I walked real slow on my way home from Ansalu's. I had a lot to think about an' worry over in my mind. I wondered if I'd ever get to feel the way Sara seemed to feel when Viticus was pawin' her. The whole Idea of lyin' with a man an doin' those things made me feel dirty just to think about. But I was mindful of what Ansalu had told me, an' I made up my mind to do the best I could. Like I said, I didn't think I had much choice.

I was busy thinkin' an walking slow, mullin' over stuff over in my mind.

"It's about time you got back," Odd yelled when he saw me comin' up the path. "I put in a hard day sawin' wood down at the Washbon's an' when I got home I found you ain't even started my suppert!" He sounded put out, so I didn't say anythin'. I just hurried as fast as I could to stoke up the fire an' set the beans on. I kept busy til supper was ready.

After he'd eaten his fill of supper, I asked him.

"You mad at me?"

He just looked at me kinda surprised. Then he got a funny look on his face an' shrugged his shoulders. "Not really. It's just that you wasn't here..."

He stopped talkin' an looked away.

I had a funny feelin' that in some way he'd missed my bein' there when he came home. An' for some reason, that made me feel kinder towards him an all. I looked at Odd thinkin' there was a lot about him I didn't know.

After we finished eatin' I took a long time reddin' things up. All the words that Ansalu had used were jostlin' aroun' in my head, an' I was dreadin' what I knew was ahead.

When I finally finished everythin' I could think of to do, Odd came an' stood in front of me like before, "You must be all right now," he told me.

Didn't ask.

I looked at him, standin' there. It was easy to see that he was a man who didn't mean to be put off. He didn't look mean, an yet he sure didn't look mousy. I guess I hadn't really looked at Odd like that before. He had a way of settin' his two feet on the floor that I had already learned meant he wasn't gonna budge an inch. He had his feet like that, now. He didn't look at all like that man who had shifted from one foot to another the day he come to get me at Paw's.

At first, I wished I could lie an tell him I wasn't all right, but from what Ansalu had said, he'd keep pesterin' me until I let him do it. An it might go better for me if I faced up to the way things were an got it over with.

"I'm...all right," I told him.

"Bout time," he said, bendin' over to untie his shoes. He had a funny look on his face, almost like he wasn't real sure of himself, either. Somehow seein' that look gave me a little more self-confidence. I got out the little jar of cream Ansalu had given me an slipped out to the privvy. After I'd tended to emptyin' myself, I put some cream on my fingers an' rubbed it gentle into my private part. I was surprised how good it felt when my fingers rubbed back an' forth rubbin' in that cream. I remembered playin' with myself when I was scared as a little girl. But back then I didn't have cream an' had to spit on my finger to make it slide back an' forth.

I sure hoped Odd wouldn't be rough an' hurt me a lot.

I came back into the cabin an took off my shoes an' my dress. Then I thought what Ansalu had told me, an' I took off my slip an' stood there in my cotton drawers. Odd was pretendin' to be busy stokin' up the fire for the night, but I felt him sneak a look at me. He didn't seem too pleased. Finally, I dropped my drawers on the floor an got into bed as fast as I could. The bed felt cold, an' I rubbed at the goose bumps that popped up all over my bare skin. Odd looked at the goose-bumps an' said, "They're almost as big as your titties," an blew out the lamp.

I was glad for the darkness to hide my shame.

"Move over," he growled, an' I felt him get into bed next to me. I lay real still. Then I felt him reachin' for me an pushin' an pullin' at me. He started movin' around an gruntin' an crawlin' all over me. I just sort of closed my mind off an' waited for the whole thing to be over.

I didn't know I was cryin' until he pushed me away an' hollered at me.

"For God's sake, November, you ain't no good at all! And then he snatched the top cover off the bed an dragged it over to where he had been sleepin' before. He flopped down on the floor an' commenced thumpin' an bumpin' around under the cover all by himself. An' then he let out a big sigh an rolled over with his back to me. I knew what he'd done to himself because I'd seen my brothers do it. But I didn't figure he should be doin' it after he'd been in bed with me. At least not from what Ansalu had said, I felt just awful, an' I buried my face in the old feather pillow an tried to swaller my sobs so he wouldn't hear them an' be even madder at me.

Somehow, that night passed, though I don't think I ever fell asleep.

In the first light of mornin' I got out of bed as quiet as I could an grabbed my clothes. I took a panful of water an' a rag outside with me an washed an rubbed my body all over as though I aimed to rub the skin right off. I finally gave up ever hopin' to feel clean again. I put on my clothes.

Odd woke up when I was stokin' the fire in the stove. But he didn't say a word about what had happened. I just went ahead an made the coffee an' put biscuits in to bake. He went outside an used the privvy an washed up at the pump. Then he came in an sat down at the table an poured himself some coffee. I put a plateful of hot biscuits down in front of him an' he took one an' commenced chewin'.

Finally, he looked up like he was just now noticin' me.

"I'm goin' down to Webster Springs an' work for the Washbon's today," he told me in a flat voice. "I'll take some of these biscuits along for my noon meal," he said, motionin' towards the plateful sittin' on the table.

I felt a bit nervous an' waited for him to say somethin' about what had happened in bed the night before. But he didn't say a word. If I hadn't known it had, I'd have thought it didn't happen.

I didn't know which was worse-his not talkin' about what had happened or havin' him mention it an tell me again how awful I was. So, I just kept my mouth shut an' hoped he'd hurry up an' leave for work.

He wrapped three or four biscuits in his big red bandanna, an' left without another word.

I sat down, plum gave out, at the table. My head felt heavy an I leaned it on my hands. I wished Ansalu was here. I didn't know what I had done wrong. but it was sure easy to see that Odd hadn't got any pleasure out of me last night. I thought about Sara an Viticus an' their moanin' an touchin' an' I knew that Odd hadn't got the same kind of feelin's from all that floppin' around that Viticus got from Sara.

I felt just awful.

Was it goin' to be like this all the rest of my life?

MAKIN' DO

For the next couple of days, I felt like I was walkin' on eggs. You know how it is, sometimes you're afraid to put all your weight down for fear the earth'll open an' swaller you all up. Well, that's just how I felt with the way things were goin' with Odd. In some way, I was just waitin' an waitin' for somethin' an didn't quite know what.

Odd just went 'bout his business an didn't talk to me any more'n he had to. He'd eat his supper an' fuss around a bit. Come nighttime, he'd sorta look at me outta the corner of his eyes. Then he'd mumble somethin' I couldn't make out but didn't dare ask him to repeat, an' grab one of the covers off the bed. He'd settle himself in the corner near the stove, hump around some, an' finally go to sleep.

All that time I'd just stay sittin' at the table. I'd sit there so still like I was froze to the chair, until I was sure he was asleep. When I could hear his breathin' gettin' that slow, regular in an out to it, I'd take off my dress an shoes an' slip into bed.

It was quiet an all, but I wasn't easy in my mind. I knew things were just sort of ridin' along like a stick float down the creek. Not doin' nothin' about nothin' except lettin' itself move along. Trouble was, I knew that sooner or later that stick was bound to get itself caught on a rock or a mud bank or somethin'.

An' sure enough, one night I knew the way we we're livin' had got itself caught onto a rock or somethin'. Odd didn't say nothin' at all whilst we were eatin' supper, but he kept lookin' at me like he had a lot to say an' he hardly touched his vittles at all.

Right after supper was done, Odd pushed back his chair an stood up, lookin' at me in a way that let me know he'd made

91

up his mind about somethin' in a real tight voice he said, "Get yourself ready, woman."

An I knew what he meant.

I took my little jar of cream an went out to the privvy. I took as long as I could emptyin' myself out an all. I sat there on the hole a lot longer than I needed to. I guess down inside I was hopin' he'd fall asleep waitin' for me.

But it didn't work out that way.

When I came back into the cabin, there he was, plump in the middle of the bed.

"Take off your clothes," he told me.

I blew out the lamp and did what he told me.

He was reachin' an grabbin' for me as soon as I hit the bed. Odd pushed an' pulled till I thought my body would plain give out. But it wasn't no good. He just got all over sweat an I could tell by the way he was rubbin' himself against me that it wasn't at all like Ansalu had said it should be.

Nothin' happened.

Finally, Odd threw himself back on his side of the bed. He lay there for a little bit, an' I could tell he was lookin' at me in the dark. I was glad I couldn't really see his face.

Then he started swearin' an got out of the bed, takin' the top cover with him like he'd done before.

That was the last time he got in bed with me for a while. It left me feelin' real funny about it. Part of me was sayin' to myself, be glad he's leavin' you alone. But the other part of me was sayin' this ain't the way things are s'posed to between a man an' a woman.

An I had the awful feelin' that whatever was wrong was all my fault.

I didn't figure I'd ever understand about livin' with a man. That way, I mean.

Then my brother Caleb came to see me.

I hadn't seen Caleb in an awful long time. Seein' him now walkin' up the path to Odd's cabin, I knew I'd forgot how near a man he was. I guess livin' with him day in an' day out at home, I'd just looked at him as a brother, not as another person. Now I looked, an' I sure liked what I saw.

"November, November Sunshine! You in there?" he called as he got within hallin' distance.

"Calebi," I yelled back, flingin' myself out of the cabin an' down the steps.

Back in Paw's cabin we weren't much given to huggin', but soon's I got within grabbin' distance, I threw my arms around Caleb an' hugged him like I'd never let go. I nearly bowled him over! An' it felt real good the way he grabbed me back an' started laughin'.

"Careful there, girl," he said, "you're like to roll us both down the hill hangin' on so tight."

I grabbed his hand, then, an' hurried him into the cabin. "Set an have a bite, I offered. I got to admit that it made me proud to invite Caleb to break bread in my own place. Well, it was really Odd's place, but I was carin' for it.

In Paw's cabin, we never had visitors except men who came there to get a jug or two of Paw's lightnin'. An' Paw's cabin was always such a mess with all of us livin' in it, that nobody ever stayed around long enough to be sociable.

93

But here, now, with just Odd an me to do for, it was real easy to keep things lookin' nice now that I'd got everythin' cleaned up pretty good. The cabin was still full of the good smell of fresh cornbread loaves when it's just been baked.

Caleb looked around real Interested. "This looks real nice, November," he said. I could tell by his face he was surprised to find it so. "You got things fixed up real good."

His words made me feel fine, an' I hurried to fix a fresh pot of coffee. I wish I'd had time to ask Ansalu how she made the yarb tea she fixed when I went to her cabin. I told myself the next time I went over there, I'd have to remember to ask her. But for now, coffee'd have to do.

Anyways, while the coffee was comin' to a boil, I fixed a plate with big chunks of cornbread. I didn't have any apple butter, but Odd had brought in some comb honey, an' that always tasted good on cornbread. I scooped some of the comb outa the big pan he'd put it in, an put the honey on another plate with a spoon for dippin'. While I was doin' that, I snitched a piece of the comb to chew on. Caleb was watchin' me, an' he came over an' broke off a piece of the comb to chew, too.

"Always did think honeycomb was one of the best things in the world to chew on," he said.

Paw had never liked us chewin' honeycomb, though. He said we got everythin' so sticky that he couldn't get his jugs fit to hand over to nobody.

After we chewed a bit an' just looked at each other smilin' kinda silly an' happy, I licked the last of the sticky sweetness off my fingers, an asked, "What brings you here, Caleb?"

"I've been wantin' to come for a long time, November," he said. "I felt bad after Paw sent you off with Odd an I told Paw so." He smiled kinda funny an' shook his head. "Got whomped real good for my pains, too!"

I could just picture what must've happened. It made me feel sad, but still, I was pleased that Caleb had cared enough to say it.

"Things are changin' at home, November," Caleb said. He thought a bit an' then said, "Paw's brought in another woman to take Maw's place." He peered into my face to see how I was takin' the news.

"How do the others feel about it?" I asked.

"Well, most of us can hardly remember Maw," Caleb said. "An they're just glad to have someone to do the cookin'. None of us ever did get the hang of it, an' Lula, that's her name, is a right smart cook."

"I'm glad, Caleb. But what about Paw?" I wanted to ask if Paw ever mentioned me, but I guess I was afraid of hearin' the answer. So instead, I asked, "How's he now that he's got himself a woman again?"

"Oh, he's a lot easier to live with now that he's got a woman under his roof. Says it ain't so much havin' someone to sleep with as just not havin' to fret about cookin' an cleanin' an all that stuff."

I had to laugh a little at the idea of Paw ever worryin' about cookin' an cleanin' an such things. Those things'd never bothered him at all. They'd either gotten done or they hadn't, it hadn't never concerned him none. Caleb saw my face an' laughed with me, knowin' what was on my mind without my even havin' to say it.

Then the coffee boiled up an I set things on the table an' told Caleb to pull his chair up. We sat down an' I poured him a cup of fresh coffee an pushed the plate of cornbread within his reach.

We sat so for a little bit, an' it felt nice an comfortin'.

Then Caleb began actin' fidgety, an' I knew he had somethin' on his mind.

"How...how are things tween you an Odd, November?" he finally asked.

I shrugged. "All right," I said, "Everythin' is all right."

Musta been somethin' in the way I sounded when I said it, cause Caleb looked at me real sharp.

"You're changin', November," he said.

"How you mean, Caleb?" I asked.

He looked at me a little sheepish and asked, "Don't you go down to the flat rock an' study yourself none?"

I started a bit when he asked me that. I had sort of forgotten about the flat rock an' how I used to go there every time I could.

"No, I guess I'm mostly too busy to slip away like that anymore," I told him. "By the time I get the mornin' fire stoked up an' bread baked an all that, it's time to start the beans an' jowl or whatever else for Odd's supper. An there's always wood an' water to be brought in an things like that to do." I thought a bit. "I guess I maybe sorta forgot the rock an' the wood-pool. It's so much quieter here than at home that I just keep busy an do my work. My thinkin' sort've comes natural whilst I'm workin'."

Then I thought a bit. "What was it you figgered I'd see down at the rock, Caleb?"

Caleb shook his head. "It's just that I guess I was 'sprised a bit at how you're becomin' a woman, November."

I knew he meant my breasts, which had begun to pooch out so much in front that my dress pulled tight over 'em. I'd sorta tried not to notice, just like I'd tried not to notice how Odd's privates had sorta swelled up when he had last climbed into bed with me.

Not noticin' meant I didn't have to deal with what it meant.

Now, with Caleb callin' it to my attention like he had, I guessed I'd have to deal with it. I felt myself sighin'.

"Does...does Odd...use you too hard?" Caleb asked, worry showin' in his eyes.

I felt some guilty rememberin' how I'd fallen Odd somehow. I could remember Odd flingin' himself outa the bed an yellin' that I wasn't no good. I couldn't bring myself to admit that to Caleb, though. I wanted him to think good of me.

"Well," Caleb said, lettin' his eyes slide away from my face.

"What is it, Caleb," I asked, wantin' to know.

"Well, it's just that there's some talk about Odd stoppin' by the Widder Morton's cabin more'n he oughta."

"The Widder Morton?" I asked, feelin' stupid. All's I ever heard about the Widder Morton was that her man had died several years before.

"Uh," Caleb seemed uncomfortable tellin' me, but he went on. "Paw used to go see the Widder Morton every now an' then, November. At least til he took up with Lula."

"But why?" I asked.

Caleb fidgeted some. "Well, November, that's how the Widder Morton......gets along. You know how she makes her money."

I didn't get the hang of what Caleb was sayin' an' I guess I'd looked at him real stupid, for he went on.

"On, November, you're livin' with a man, you oughta know what a man needs an all."

I had a sudden feelin' in the pit of my stomach that made me half sick. "You mean she lies with 'em?" My mind was boggled at the thought of a woman choosin' to lie with a man who wasn't even hers.

An' then I took in what Caleb had said. I thought of Paw goin' to see such a woman to take care of his needs. I'd never thought of Paw havin' that kind of need before. Just never thought.

Suddenly, I thought about what else Caleb had said.

Odd was goin' to see the Widder Morton! That's why he was leavin' me alone! The Widder Morton was takin' care of Odd's needs. I'd just been so glad to be left alone, I hadn't given nothin' else a thought. All I was good for was to wash an' clean an' cook an' take care of his cabin. Shame washed over me so I wished I could run an' hide somewhere.

I couldn't bring myself to look at Caleb, dreadin' that he should know how bad I'd done at bein' a woman.

"Are you all right, November?" he asked, leanin' across the table an touchin' my hand to get my attention.

"I'm all right, Caleb," I told him, my voice comin' out in little more than a whisper. "I'm all right. But inside, I knew I wasn't.

Caleb looked at me a moment an then he shook his head, seemin' to be satisfied with gettin' what was on his mind out in the open.

Then I'd best be gettin' back, November. Paw, don't know I came all this way to see you. He'd be madder than a wet hen because he thinks I'm out fellin' trees for firewood. But if I hurry, he'll never know I came by here."

I jumped up an' threw my arms around this brother who had been as good as anyone to me after Lem had married an' gone. I loved him an it hurt a bit inside to think he was goin' back home an' I mightn't see him again for a long piece.

It was strange, though, I was kinda relieved he was goin'. He'd given me a lot to think about, an' I needed time to be alone an ponder about it. What he'd told me about Odd an the Widder Morton didn't sit real good. I told myself I was glad that Odd was seein' the Widder an leavin' me alone. Only, it didn't make me feel glad. I wasn't sure just how it made me feel.

"Can you come again?" I asked Caleb as I walked him to the door.

"I'll try to find a way," he promised. Then he kinda waved his hand an' hurried out of the cabin an' down the path towards where he'd come from.

I was sorry to see him go. I thought about a lot of things while I waited for Odd to come home to supper. I thought about how I'd come to be there in the first place. Thinkin' back to Odd tradin' his rifle for me gave me a lot to think about an' sort of made me feel better in a funny kind of way. After all, since Odd had got me by tradin' an' I hadn't a thing to say about it, then I guessed maybe I didn't have to feel ashamed or bad or anythin' because things hadn't worked out so good. About Odd an me in bed, I mean.

99

Thinkin' that way cheered me up some.

An' then I thought about Odd goin' to see the Widder Morton, what all that meant, an' I didn't like the way that made me feel at all. Though I didn't know exactly how that made me feel. I was mixed up for sure.

Anyway, when Odd came in from work, he was real quiet. I took special pains to fix his supper real nice on the table. I kept passin' food to him and urgin' him to help himself. Whenever I'd look up, I'd find him studyin' me. He'd turn away real fast, but I knew he was doin' it. He didn't say a word, though, til he asked me to pass him more potatoes. Then his voice was real low, an' he looked away when I faced him. It puzzled me.

After supper was over, Odd went outside. I suppose he was goin' to use the privvy. I got busy an' washed up the dishes an' set water on the stove to heat by mornin'. Wash day.

In a little bit, Odd came back in, carryin' some wood, an dropped it on the floor within easy reachin' distance of the stove. Even though he'd told me early on that gettin' in the wood was my job, he always brought enough in so that I hardly ever had to. Never said anything about it, just did it. Well, after he dropped the wood, he sort of fidgeted around a bit. Then he came over an' stood watchin' me wipe off the table.

"November," he said, speakin' so low I could hardly make out what he was sayin', "you don't need to worry. I ain't goin' to bother you...that way... no more," his face looked real strange. Sorta sad. Then he bedded himself down on the floor near the stove, an turned his back to me.

He was real quiet. I didn't know what to think, so I put out the light an went to bed myself. Just before I worried myself to sleep, I wished I could go to the woods pool again like I used to. An' then I told myself I would find time to go. Just thinkin' it made me feel some better.

In the mornin' it was just like before. Odd ate his breakfast without hardly speakin' a word to me. I'd been noticin' lately that he was keepin' himself shaved real good. His hair was lookin' better, too. For the Widder Morton, I figured, but he'd gotten so he didn't even look at me lest he really had to.

Soon as Odd went off to whatever job was waitin' for him, I washed up the dishes an headed off towards the quiet place in the woods, hopin' I hadn't forgotten how to get there.

It was plain to see that nobody had come in a long time to the big flat rock besides the creek. The bushes an' weeds were all grown up, an' it took me a while to make a path. After I cleared off a space on the rock, I sat down an' just sort of soaked up the quiet. The peace an' beauty of the woods were comfortin', an' I lay back for a bit to listen to the soft sounds the water made.

I decided I wouldn't wait such a long time to come here again.

I lay there thinkin' back to the time Paw had traded me off to Odd without ever a by-your-leave or anythin'. I'd been mad, then, but mostly I'd been hurt. An afraid I sort of poked around that feelin' like you poke your tongue at a hurtin' tooth to see just how much it hurts. I was surprised to find I didn't mind bein' traded as much as I had. Didn't mean I thought Paw had done right, but I just didn't mind as much.

Then I decided I'd best look into the pool an see how much it was I had changed since Caleb saw me last. I got to my knees an' leaned way out over the still water to look at my reflection. I didn't mind about Odd not havin' any mirrors in the cabin. I knew I was tall an' skinny an didn't think it mattered much how I looked. That's why I hadn't even bothered much when my dress got so tight over my front. Law knows, there wasn't nobody to see me cept'n Odd.

But when I saw myself reflected in the water, I set back on my heels.

I looked different. My face had filled out an' was a lot fuller than it had been. I reckoned eatin' with just the two of us, I'd taken to eatin' more an doin' it slower, an' now the bones didn't show like they did before. I leaned back over the pool again an pulled my hair back so I could see myself better.

I was kinda pleased that I looked older. Somehow, I felt like the changes that were takin' place inside were showin' here on my face, outside.

It wasn't a bad feelin'.

I let go my hair, an instead of hangin' like Old Yeller string around my face the way it always had, now it hung all fluffy an' reminded me of the feathery stuff that comes out of milkweeds in early fall. It fell around my face real nice in a way that pleasured me an made me glad to see.

Then I leaned over farther so I could see the rest of me. I wasn't set for what I saw. I'd known my dress was tight over my bosom, but I hadn't figured that it pulled so tight a person could see me so clear. A person could see the roundness an' fullness real easy through that thin old dress, an' I pulled it off, droppin' it on the rock next to me. Then I leaned back over the water an' looked at my reflection in the pool. I wasn't as full an' round as Sara, but now that I'd pulled off my tight dress, the swellin' softness drew my mind an I couldn't take my eyes away. I watched my reflection as my hand, almost without my mind tellin' it to, slid up over my belly an' gently moved over the roundness, feelin' its softness an' gently playin' with the pink part of my breast until I felt it harden an' push back against my fingers.

I felt strange an' shivvery an excited. Somethin' inside of me, way down, was stirrin' an makin' itself known.

Feelin' like I was peekin' at somethin' private, somethin' I shouldn't need to know, I turned away an' reached for my dress. Tryin' not to think about those changes takin' place in my body, I pulled on my dress. I was breathin' fast like I'd been runnin' hard, an' my heart was all shivvery inside. I was afraid that if anyone saw me now, my face would tell 'em real plain how I was feelin' inside.

I slid down off the rock, turnin' my face towards the way I must go back to Odd's cabin.

One thing for sure, I told myself, I needed a new dress. I needed a dress that was big enough to cover me right. This one was hardly decent anymore.

Suddenly, I felt shy. I didn't want Odd to see me in this dress with my breasts showin' so plain. Then I remembered how strange he'd been with me lately, an' I wondered if this was part of it.

Thinkin' about all that, I knew I needed a new dress real bad. I just wondered how I'd ever get it.

I was still wonderin' as I turned an' started back towards the cabin.

WILSON'S SPRINGS

I set myself to take extra pains with supper some evenin's later. I even put some wildflowers in a jar on the table. I'd come to find that when things look nice, what you're eatin' is apt to taste better. So, I did the best I could to make things look nice.

Odd didn't say much; he never did. I could see him takin' it all in, though, an' his face looked like it was all but ready to smile a bit. He seemed to mellow out a little more as he sat an ate. He finally looked up at me an' said, "I ate enough. Your bread was more'n passable tonight."

That was the first time he ever said anythin' nice like that about my cookin' an' I looked at him real close to see for sure if he meant it. He did.

That cheered me up an I figgered now was as good a time as any to ask about gettin' a new dress.

"Odd, I... I got a favor to ask," I said, havin' a hard time to make the words sound like it wasn't anythin' too special.

He looked up at me from where he was pickin' out a piece of wood to whittle from the pile he'd brought in. He stopped what he was doin' an just looked at me with an old piece of apple wood still in his hand.

"You do?" he asked, soundin' surprised.

"Yep, Odd, I do," I said, tryin' to sound natural. I hadn't said much to him since Caleb visited an told me about the Widder Morton an Odd goin' to see her. I still hadn't made up my mind just how learnin' that made me feel, but it didn't change the fact that I needed a new dress none.

True, just like he promised, Odd hadn't bothered me with wantin' to do all that bumpin' an roochin' anymore. Just plain left me alone. I figured I knew why, though, with him seein' the Widder Morton an all. But that didn't mean he'd figure he'd ought to buy me a new dress.

"Odd", I said, "It's about my dress." I stopped talkin' as he looked at me real close, feelin' sort of shamed when his eyes lingered on how tight the dress was over my bosom. But I just crossed my arms over my chest an' waited for him to say somethin'. I meant to get me a new dress even if I had to get to pesterin' Odd an gettin' him mad at me.

"Odd, it ain't fittin' for me to wear this dress no more," I finally got the words out.

He didn't say anythin' for a bit, then he asked, "What's wrong with it? it ain't got no big holes an' it covers you."

"Yes, but it's too tight!" I told him, standin' with my arms crossed my bosom to hide myself.

"It don't matter, nobody's goin' to see you nohow," he said, "'ceptin me, an' I don't care." Then he stamped out of the room, an' I knew he figured the matter was closed.

"That ain't right, Odd!" I burst out, talkin' loud so he could hear me out on the porch where he was standin'. "When you traded me from my Paw, I'm sure he meant for you to clothe me decent."

Odd poked his head back into the cabin. "What you got in mind, November?" he asked.

"I need a dress. It don't have to be nothin' fancy, just somethin' that fits decent," I told 'im.

"I'll study on it," he said, an went on back out the door. Halfway out he turned an' looked at me again. "You meanin' this?" he asked.

His question caught me off short an I couldn't answer. I just stood there an' nodded my head like a ninny.

He went on outside then, an' I set myself to reddin' up the kitchen. After a bit, Odd came back in an looked at me for a bit. "You can go with me tomorrow," he said.

He took me so by surprise that I didn't rightly know what to say then. I just stood an looked at him.

"That's settled, then, I'm goin' to town tomorrow to saw up some wood for Mr. Washbon. He already owes me for what I sawed up last week, so I reckon there ought to be more'n enough money to buy flour an' grits an' stuff. You can come along and get you a dress."

"You mean you want me to go to Wilson's Springs?" I asked. The easy way Odd had said I should go along, near took my breath away.

"Yep," he said, turnin' the wood over an over in his hands to see where best to start whittlin'.

"But... but, Odd, I can't go to Wilson's Springs, I'd only been there once an' that was when I was little an' just helpin' Paw to carry his likker to some of the folks who wanted to buy. The whole idea of goin' to Wilson's Springs pure scared me.

"Why can't you go?" he asked me.

"I... I don't know about towns. I don't know how to act, an' I don't have but this one dress to wear."

"Hold up there, November," Odd said, still lookin' at the wood an beginnin' to sharpen his knife blade by rubbin' it back an' forth over the bark. "There ain't nothin' to argue or fret about. The only way to get you a dress is to take you to town an' buy you one." He took his first lick with the knife an' smiled at the easy way it cut into the wood. "Look at that." he said, "Cuts like a new blade!"

From the way he went to work on that piece of apple wood, sendin' chips flyin' this way an' that onto that old wooden floor, I knew he wasn't of no mind to hear any more about my not wantin' to go to Wilson's Springs with him in the mornin'.

I gave a sigh that felt like it came all the way up from the bottom of my feet. Didn't help me get ready to go, but it made me feel a little better. My head purely reeled with excitement. Part of me was kinda scared about goin' down the mountain to Wilson's Springs, but the rest of me was all pleased about gettin' a new dress. I didn't know just how to feel. A store-bought dress at that!

I'd never had a brand-new dress that was bought just for me in my whole life. Never!

I hurried through my chores an' heated water to bathe in. Odd noticed me gettin' ready to take a bath an' said, "I swear, November, you're out to make yourself sick washin' yourself as much as you do. It's enough to wear a body down!"

I didn't answer him at all. I knew he didn't take much to bathin', he'd told me his Paw said bathin' made a man sickly. But I wanted to be clean if I was to go into a department store an' pick out a new dress. I just went ahead as calm as I could an tied a line near the stove where I hung a bed-cover so I could take my bath in private.

I filled the big old boiler tub full of water soon's it got hot, an' looked to see if Odd was still busy whittlin'. He was, so I skinned outta my clothes an into the tub. It did feel good!

We didn't have store-bought soap an' it was hard to lather up the lye soap I'd made, but I rubbed an rubbed an got myself so clean my skin got all pink an' shiny. When I felt clean enough,

I used a pitcher of water to rinse off with, an wrapped a piece of old comforter around me to dry me on. Then I put my dress an underdrawers into the tub an gave them a good scrubbin', too. When they looked a sight better, I took down the blanket I'd hung on the line. Then I spread my dress an' drawers out real careful on the line, smoothin' 'em out best I could, an' left 'em to dry in the heat of the stove.

I wanted to be the best I could, tomorrow.

Then I got myself into bed an' tried to go to sleep as fast as I could.

I woke up real early next mornin'. I made an extra batch of cornbread an' wrapped it in a fresh plece of cloth. I didn't know much about towns, but I knew that Odd an me'd have to eat no matter where we were, an' I wanted to be ready.

Odd didn't say much, but I saw him studyin' me every now an' then. I was havin' real trouble tryin' not to act scared, but I was managin' pretty well. He looked like he was tryin' to say somethin' an havin' a hard time gettin' out the words. Finally, he managed.

"Seems to me you'd best have some of them new underdrawers to wear under it if you're goin to get a new dress, November."

"Oh, Odd!" I cried, surprised. I hadn't dared hope for so much. "I'd really like that."

He nodded his head as though to say, "That's that, then."

When I got ready to go, I could see Odd had been ready for a bit an' was just waitin' for me. I didn't want to cause him to be angry or anythin', so I hurried an' said, "I'm all ready, Odd."

He motioned for me to follow an we started out of the cabin an' down the path. I was so excited I kept steppin' on his heels.

"For Pete's sake!" he finally bellowed, comin' to a halt an turnin' around to face me. "I can't go much faster, November, so you'll just have to settle down an' walk on your own heels."

He sounded mad when he said that, but I could see a twinkle in his eyes that I'd never seen there before. It gave me a pause. I wondered if Odd knew how to laugh. I couldn't remember ever hearin' him do it. So now I wondered if he was tryin' to be funny. Sorta makin' a joke?

I followed him, walkin' real careful to not step on his heels, for a good long way down the mountain. It was real pretty along the way, but I was gettin' so excited an all that I couldn't really enjoy it. By an' by, Odd stopped on a bluff an' pointed ahead. He motioned down the valley, there were lots of buildin's sittin' in what looked to be little rows.

"That's Wilson's Springs," he said, startin' to walk again.

"I forgot it was so big," I told him. I felt torn between wantin' to see the town an gettin' a new dress an all that, an feelin' so scared about it all that I wished I was back in the safety of Odd's cabin.

I guess I must have pulled back a bit, cause Odd turned an' waited for me to catch up. He didn't say nothin', just nodded for me to follow an' started down the path again.

It wasn't long after that we got to town. It looked even bigger than it had from the bluff, an' I figured it was best to let Odd lead wherever it was we were goin'.

We finally came to a stop in front of a big buildin' that had two stories to it. There was a sign on the store, too. I couldn't read, but Odd had said we were goin' to Washbon's Department Store, an' I figured this must be it. There was a great big glass window in the front, an standin' inside the window were real-lookin' dummies wearin' the nicest dresses

I'd ever seen. Scattered around on the floor of the window were shoes an' men's shirts an' pants, an all kinds of things.

I remembered Ansalu tellin' me about her Grandma standin' an lookin' into just such a store window an seein' that green dress she wanted so bad. I could sure imagine how that must've been. There was almost too much for a body to take in at once. It would take a lot of lookin' at each thing to do it up right an see it all.

I was sort of lost in the window when I felt Odd tuggin' on my arm.

"C'mon, November, you're standin' there lookin' stupid. No sense callin' tention to yourself." He hurried into the store. It was plain he wanted me to follow.

A young man saw us comin' an came over. Then he sort of looked down his nose at Odd an' said, "If you came to do the rest of the sawin' you should have come to the back door. The front is for customers."

Odd got that stubborn look on his face an' said, "Today's different. I want to talk to your Paw."

The man looked surprised at first, but covered it up by actin' real polite an sayin', "I'll go get him."

I watched him walkin' off. I'd never seen a man who looked like that up close before. He was dressed just as good as the men in that magazine I used to study over an' over. His clothes were all just so, an' he had on the whitest shirt I'd ever seen. Even his shoes looked new an' shiny, too.

"Who's that?" I whispered to Odd.

Odd turned an' looked kind of annoyed at me. "That's Junior, Junior Washbon, November," he said. "His Paw owns this store."

I couldn't imagine ownin' a store such as this, an' I tried to take it all in, admirin' one thing after another.

Finally, Junior Washbon came back, followed by a man who looked like he might just own the whole world. The older man walked up to Odd an' started talkin' to him. Junior Washbon sort of put himself between the men an me an' stared at me like I'd never been looked at before. He slid his eyes over me in such a way that he made me feel like he could see right through my clothes. I tried to make myself shrink down a bit, but it didn't work. I wanted to push past him an' stand beside Odd, but I figured that might make Odd mad. I just stayed where I was an tried not to pay any notice to Junior Washbon.

In a little bit, Odd walked over an' stood in front of me.

Mr. Washbon says you can pick out any dress you want, November, an then he an me will figure things out.

I could tell Odd was proud to be able to tell me that, but before I got a chance to say anythin', Junior Washbon piped up. "I'll help her find a dress," he said, just as cool as you please. Then he took me by the arm an led me over to a rack that was just full of all kinds of dresses.

Well, I was caught halfway tween heaven an' hell! The heaven part was thinkin' that I could look at those dresses an' touch any one of 'em I had a mind to. But the hell part was knowin' that Junior Washbon was goin' to watch me do it. He made me feel fidgety.

Then Odd came over an asked, "Find one you set your mind to yet, November?"

I figgered he was just tryin' to sound like he knew his way around an' was used to buyin' things in a department store. But it rattled me all the same. So, I stepped up real big an' pointed to an awful pretty green dress an' said, "I like that one."

"But that's just a cheap cotton..." Junior Washbon started to say, till Odd stopped him.

"If that's the one she wants, then that's the one she gets," he said in a way that made even Junior Washbon shut up.

"What size do you wear?" Junior Washbon asked me, runnin' his eyes all over me again.

"I don't know," I said real low, feelin' kind of stupid.

"Then I guess you'd better try one or two on for size," he said, reachin' for the dress I'd picked an' two others. He led me to a little bitty room made by hangin' curtains, an' pointed inside. "There's the dressin' room," he said, an hung the dresses on a hook on the wall.

I stood there a minute, not sure what to do. Then I saw that one whole side of the little room was a mirror, an' I stepped back from it. I turned my back on it. Seein' myself like that made me skittery.

Then I pulled the curtain across the openin' an closed myself away from everybody. I still didn't feel right about takin' my dress off in a public place that way, but I didn't know how else to see if the dresses fit. I poked my head outside the curtain an' whispered to Odd, "Hold the curtain shut!"

I could see where his hand was holdin' the curtain shut tight, so I hurried out of my dress an into the green dress I'd picked out. I guess I picked the green one because it reminded me of how Ansalu'd told me about her Grandma an' how she'd got her green dress. I wanted a green dress, too. An after I pulled it down over my head an felt its newness, I turned to look at myself in the mirror.

112

I looked awful. That dress, that pretty green dress, was awful sorry lookin' on me. It was way too big an' hung down on me like an old gunny sack. Seein' myself in it sure made me feel awful. I'd wanted to look so nice.

Then I looked at the two other dresses Junior Washbon picked out an' saw that they looked to be a lot smaller. I couldn't decide which one to try on first. But one of 'em was green, too, so I reached for that one. It was a soft green, just like leaves when they first open in spring.

It didn't take me a minute to put that one on an' turn to face the mirror. It had a good feel to it. An when I looked an' saw myself in the mirror, I could hardly believe what I saw. The dress fit like it had been made for me. An there were flowers in the material that made it look so bright an' cheery I wished I'd never have to take it off.

"Can we look now, November?" Odd called in through the curtain.

I tugged the curtain back an' stood facin' the men. Odd got kinda a half-smile, an' I thought he looked almost proud to be seein' me so. "That looks fitten, November, that'll do," he said, an there was no way you could miss that he was proud to be sayin' it. He turned to Junior Washbon an' said, "We'll take that one."

I looked at Junior Washbon. What I saw in his face caught me off short. I'd never had a man look at me that way before. He looked at me like he could eat me up with a spoon, an' for just a little bit I let myself enjoy that feelin', glad that I was lookin' nice.

Then I saw his eyes, an what I saw there shook me, an' I drew back. There was a boldness in his eyes that made me turn away, feelin' like I needed fresh air, needed not to see.

I turned to Odd feelin' strange an' confused.

Before I could say anythin' an older man an' a real pretty young lady came into the store. The young lady looked like the ladies in the pictures in that magazine I used to have. She looked like she could just reach out an' have anythin' in the whole world if she wanted it.

They both stopped still an' looked around. Then the young lady saw Junior Washbon an hurried over.

"Hello, Junior!" she said, puttin' her hand on his arm like it belonged there. It was plain to see she had some rights to him. I watched as she sort of pulled him away so she could say somethin' to him in private. I couldn't hear what she said, but he smiled an' nodded, an then she turned an' walked away. After she'd gone off a bit, she sort of half turned back an' waggled her fingers at him. I thought it looked kind of silly, but must be Junior Washbon liked it because he was smilin' real big when he came back to Odd an me.

I watched that young lady 'til she an' the older man went plum out of sight.

I sighed real big. She was everythin' I ever wanted to be. She was real pretty an' her hair was short an' fixed up like you could tell she'd had help fixin' it. An she walked like she knew everythin' there was to know. I thought of the beautiful light blue dress she'd been wearin' an' the soft way it had swished around her body when she walked. Then I looked down again at the green cotton dress with the flowers on it. The one I was wearin'. I felt sad because I could see for the first time that it was a cheap, poorly made thing. I knew I'd never feel so special in it again.

"I'd best get this dress off," I said quietly to Odd. "This dress will do just fine. If you say I can have it, I'll be much obliged."

Odd went off to make arrangements with Old Mr. Washbon, an I pulled the curtain on the changin' place. It didn't take but a minute to slip that dress off an put on my old one. I tried not to look in the mirror while I was doin' it, but I couldn't help seein' myself in my old dress. What a sorry thing I was to look at!

When I opened the curtain again, there stood Junior Washbon, leanin' against the edge of the openin', just lookin' an lookin' at me.

"I'll see about gettin' your dress wrapped up for you," he said, reachin' out to take the dress from me. An' then, instead of takin' the dress, I felt his fingers takin' ahold of mine under the cloth where no one could see. I tried to slip my fingers away from his, but he just held on real tight, his eyes lookin' straight at me. He didn't say a word or move or anythin'. Just stood there holdin' on to my hand an lookin' into my eyes. I was awful glad when Odd came back towards us. Junior Washbon let go then, an' walked away just like nothin' had happened. My mind was so mixed up; I wondered if I had just made up the whole thing.

When Junior Washbon came back with my dress all wrapped up in a package, I kept my hands down at my sides, an' he had to hand the package to Odd.

"You mind goin' back to the cabin alone?" Odd asked me. "I've got some work to do for Mr. Washbon."

"No, that's all right. I'll get on up the mountain," I said an' started away.

"I've got about six-seven hours work," Odd called after me, an' I turned to face him. "You're sure you're all right?"

"Yep, as long as it's still light," I told him. Then I remembered. "Thank you for the dress," I said, tryin' not to see Junior Washbon in his fine clothes just standin' there next to him.

I hurried outside an' stood at the corner waitin' to cross when I heard a voice speakin' softly near my ear.

"That's a mighty long walk for a young woman to have to take alone," it said, an' I didn't need to turn around to know it was Junior Washbon.

I turned to face him an' tried to look as cool an uppity as the young lady in the store had. "Oh, I don't mind at all. In fact, I'm not goin' very far. I'm stoppin' in to visit a friend," I said, wishin' it were true and I had somewhere to go an' hide. I hoped he didn't know I was lyin'. I never did take to lyin' very easy.

He seemed kind of taken aback an' then held me back with his hand on my wrist.

"It's all right this time," he said, "but you'll be seein' more of me. Count on it," he added, lettin' go of my arm quick so I was nearly pulled off balance.

I hurried back the way Odd had brought me an' hardly dared even take time to look around. From what I had seen of Wilson's Springs, I figured I was best off stayin' in the hills. There wasn't no way I'd ever feel comfortable or belong in a place like Wilson's Springs. I walked with my head down, gettin' to the hill path as fast as ever I could.

Once I was back on the hill an walkin' upwards, I began to feel a little better. I looked around as I walked, takin' in the quiet of the hills an feelin' safer now that I was close in with trees an' bushes like I was used to.

I climbed a long time, never stoppin' to look back or get my breath or anythin'. An' then I remembered what I'd said to

Junior Washbon about stoppin' in to see a friend. Why couldn't I?The thought of seein' Ansalu an bein' able to tell her what had happened made me feel so much better, I smiled to myself even though there wasn't a soul around to see.

It didn't take me long to get to the path that led up the other side of the hill to Ansalu's. I knew I couldn't stay long if I was to get back to the cabin before Odd got there. But I was glad to be goin' to see Ansalu. She knew about things an' people an' the way they act. She seemed to have an awful lot of knowin' stored up inside her. The kind of things I needed to learn.

Well, I walked as fast as I could, an' it wasn't but about an hour till I come up on Ansalu's cabin. She was out workin' some earth in back of the cabin an didn't see me at first. When I found her, she had her skirts hitched up an' sort of knotted at the waist. The turban on her head was sittin' kind of crooked, too. But she looked mighty fine to me.

When Ansalu finally saw me comin' up her path, she dropped the hoe she'd been usin' an hurried down to give me a big hug.

"What a wonder!" she cried, "I was gettin' awful tired of turnin' over that earth, an' now I've got a reason to stop!"

She hitched her skirts back down an' felt of her turban, slidin' it around the way it was s'posed to be.

I asked her what she was makin' an she said she planned to raise yarbs. "Isn't anythin' of more help to a woman's cookin' than a yarb garden where she can get things like parsley an' thyme an' such, fresh, she told me. "I'll be glad to show you how an' give you some starts," she finished as we reached the porch of the cabin.

"Set a spell," she said an' disappeared into the cabin. in just a little she was back carryin' a pitcher full of cool tea, which she handed to me. "I'll be right back," she said, disappearin' again. This time she came back carryin' two glasses an' a plate of cookies. We each fixed ourselves a glass of cool tea, took a cookie, an' settled back to talk.

"Where you comin' from?" she asked me, too polite to mention the package I was carryin'.

"I've been down to Wilson's Springs," I told her. "I was in need of somethin' to wear because I seem to be growin' out of what I've got. An Odd didn't get mad like I thought he would when I asked him. Instead, he took me down to Wilson's Springs to the store an' bought me a dress!" I reached down an picked up the package I had laid on the floor by my chair.

"He did!" Ansalu said, soundin' pleased. "Well, well, well. How'd that all come about?"

So, I told her about Odd sawin' wood for the Washbon's an how he figured he could get a dress out of what they owed him. I opened the package while we were talkin' an held up the dress for her to see. She looked sad an' happy at the same time.

"Oh my, November!" she said real soft, reachin' out to finger the cloth.

"Would it be askin' too much for you to put it on an let me see how you look in it?"

I was happy to oblige an went into the cabin to change. While I put on the new green cotton dress, I thought again of the beautiful blue dress that the young lady in the store was wearin'. But when I showed myself to Ansalu, I could tell by the look on her face that she thought I would do just fine. I guessed that if you didn't have somethin' as nice as that blue dress in your mind, this green cotton dress with the pretty flowers on it would do real well. But somethin' had started gnawin' at me when I saw the young lady in the store. I wanted to talk to Ansalu about it.

We sat back down on the porch an' commenced eating Ansalu's cookies.

Then I finally started to tell her about the walk down to Wilson's Springs an all the houses an' the big department store. She nodded while I talked, an' said, "You tell it good, November. That made me feel a little surer of myself," an I decided to tell her about Junior Washbon an how he made me feel.

"It was bad enough when he held on to my hand in the store. I was just glad that nobody else could see. But when he up an' followed me outside an took hold of my arm, I... I... I stopped talkin'," not able to find the right words. Ansalu looked at me real sharp.

"You what?" she asked in a voice that I knew meant she wanted me to tell her straight out.

"I felt real strange, Ansalu. I mean, I got all knotted up inside."

"Were you afraid when he touched you, November?" she asked.

"Sorta. It was funny, though, Ansalu. You know, I didn't want him to touch me, an' yet," my voice died away like I was afraid to say what I was sayin', "I didn't want him to stop, neither. Sayin' the words out loud had bothered me. I didn't know why I felt that way when Junior Washbon touched me, an' now that I had put it into words, I felt like my feelin's were shameful.

"It's all right, November," Ansalu said, gettin' up an pullin' me to my feet. An' then she put her arms around me an' hugged me tight. "It's no shame to tell your honest feelin's. An believe me, lots of people have been caught by feelin's they didn't really understand or know how they'd got 'em."

"But," I looked into her face huntin' an answer, "Why did I... like him to touch me?"

Ansalu loosened her hold on me an sat down once more. After I had settled myself into my chair, she said, "You know, November, I told you, you were comin' on to be a woman. Well, women have feelin's an needs just like men do, even though some of them won't admit it. An there are some folks who think it's real sinful for a woman to have the kind of feelin's you seem to have about that Junior Washbon. You know, to be drawn to him."

"Oh, I wasn't drawn to him...was I?"

"Sounds like it to me, November. But don't take it on about it. It was only natural. He's about the first man outside of your Paw and brothers and Odd that you've come across." An she smiled her big warm smile at me, an' I started to feel much better. "You know, November, God made women an' men different so they WOULD be drawn to each other. Ain't nothin' wrong about that. The only way there'd be somethin' wrong is if you sort of egged him on. You know what I mean, if you'd encouraged him."

"Well, I certainly didn't do that!" I said real sure.

Then I thought a few moments more, rememberin' about the young woman an' the way she looked an' carried 'erself. I sure bet that Junior Washbon wouldn't act towards her like he acted towards me.

"Ansalu!" said, not quite sure in my mind what I was startin' to ask.

"What?"

"Would you do me a favor? A real big favor?" I asked her.

"If I can," she said, lookin' like she'd like to ask a question or two before she promised.

"Well, I want you to teach me how to read an' write! An' I want to learn it all as fast as I can."

"You want me to teach you to read an' write?" Ansalu asked.

"Yep," I answered, growin' more sure with each passin' second that the way to start gettin' how I wanted to be was to learn to read an' write. "Don't you see, Ansalu? Why Junior Washbon was as nice as pie to that young lady who came to see him in the store. He'd never do her the way he did me! An I don't want any man in the whole wide world to think he doesn't have to be nice an' proper to me."

Ansalu just sat there lookin' at me and not sayin' a word.

"Ansalu," I said, leanin' close so I could watch her eyes when I asked, "Can you teach me how to be a lady?"

WIDENING HORIZONS

Once I had it in my mind that I wanted to learn to read an' write an be a lady, I couldn't wait to get started. Up til now I hadn't thought much about readin' an writin' an such, but now the idea had caught on with me, it seemed liked I'd always wanted it.

Back at Odd's cabin, I set to work with a will to make things go the best they could. I wanted Odd to agree to my goin' over to Ansalu's for her to teach me, an' so I set myself to fix him a real good supper. By the time he got home that night, I had a big pot of vegetable stew simmerin' on the stove. An I had mixed up some flour an' eggs, an' milk ready to drop into the stew to make dumplin's. I knew dumplin's were one of Odd's favorites.

I could tell he was tired the way he came in the door, an I could see how it perked him up to smell that stew cookin' away.

After he finished his third plateful of stew, he pushed himself away from the table an' groaned. "I shouldn't have et so much, November. I feel like I'm gonna bust from bein' so full"

An before I could say anythin', there comes a crashin' an' a screechin' an' a clankin' like I'd never heard before.

Odd jumped up real fast, forgettin' how full he felt. By the time I got to the cabin door, he had already hurried outside. We looked up the mountain towards where the sound had come from, but it was quiet up that way. Made me wonder if I'd really heard such noises. I looked at Odd to see what he was thinkin'.

"Sounded bad," Odd said, duckin' back into the cabin. in a little bit, he was back beside me, fixin' to light his big hangin' lantern. When he got it all lighted, he said, "Tain't dark yet, but by the time we find out what all that noise was, it's most likely to be. You comin' with me?" he asked.

I was real pleased that he'd asked me. Sometimes menfolks have a way of actin' like everythin' that seems important is men's work, an' that us women folks can't do much outside birthin' an tendin' to the cabin an gardenin' an such.

"I'm comin'," I said, hurryin' back inside the cabin. Then I grabbed a cover off the bed an' a towel from over by the cupboard. I ran back to where Odd was startin' up the hill, an' he looked at what I was carryin'.

"That's a good idea, November," he said, an started off with a will, I hurried to keep up with him, carryin' the blanket an' towel an feelin' glad that he hadn't been act in' so put out with me lately.

We climbed up the mountain towards where the highway was. It was far enough up the mountain that we never really thought much about it. There wasn't much noise from the road ever reach down as far as Odd's cabin. But that bangin' an' clankin' an' crashin' had sounded real bad, so we hurried just as fast as we could, climbin' up that hill.

It took us quite a while to get our way worked up closer to the road. As we got closer an' closer we could begin to hear somethin'.

"What's that?" I whispered to Odd.

"Sounds like the kind of radio they put in automobiles," he answered. "We'd best walk towards it," he said, hurryin' off in that direction, pushin' the brush aside so I could follow.

"Well, it wasn't long before we came upon the automobile that had made all that clankin' an bangin'. It was all smashed up an lyin' on its side against a big old oak tree. The only sign of life was that radio. It just kept playin' away like it was Sunday afternoon. Didn't seem to be anybody to turn it off.

We stopped still an' just looked. Then we began to hear another noise besides that radio that just kept playin' away. Someone was moanin' somethin' awful.

"Be carefull" I whispered to Odd as he started closer towards the wreck.

"Ain't nobody here gonna hurt me, November," he said, bendin' to look in the smashed window. He peered in there for a long time. Then he motioned to me.

"Come here, November," he said, "an bring that cover you're carryin'."

I don't mind sayin' it, I was mighty scared. I figured there'd be a lot of blood an' things would look bad an there might even be somebody dead. I had seen blood now an' then, but I hadn't ever seen somebody smashed up in an accident like this.

"Do I have to?" I asked Odd. "Look, I mean."

Odd looked at me a moment an' said, "Do your best, woman, cause the man inside here sure needs our help, an' I can't get him out without your help."

Somehow Odd an me found the strength to get that car door open. Odd pulled the man out of the wreck an' laid him on the ground. Then he fixed up a hitch like the Indians used with two poles an' a blanket slung between 'em. We managed to get the man on the blanket, an' I put the towel over a big cut on his head that seemed to be bleedin' the worst.

The man smelled of whiskey real bad. I looked at Odd to see if he noticed. From the look on his face, I could see that he did.

Odd, an' I dragged the poles with the blanket for as long as we could. I was sure glad we were goin' downhill! Then we'd stop an' rest a bit an' check to see if the man was still breathin'. We'd pull some more an' rest some more. Bit by bit, we kept at it until we finally found ourselves back in the clearin' in front of Odd's cabin.

"You go an' fix the bed, November," Odd told me. "Yell when you got it ready because I'll throw him over my shoulder an' carry him in."

It took a little bit of doin' after we got the man all settled in the bed, an' I had washed off the blood that was smeared on his face, I looked at Odd.

"What do we do now, Odd?"

"Well, there ain't no doctor around since Old Doc Brown in Wilson's Springs died, so I guess you an' me best figure out what needs doin'." First, he took off most of the man's clothes. Then he felt all over him to see if there were any broken bones. I was surprised at how gentle Odd was. He pointed to the man's leg. Sure enough, it was easy to see that somethin' was broke because his foot was restin' at an unnatural angle.

"Can you fix it?" I asked him.

"Don't know," he answered, movin' the foot ever so little while he tried to tell just what was broke in it. "But there's one thing I've learned livin' alone in these mountains," he said slow, "If you don't do for yourself, it mostly don't get done."

While I watched him, Odd went an' got two pieces of flat wood an pulled out his whittlin' knife. He whittled at 'em for a bit an then he held 'em against the man's ankle for size. He told me to go find a good-sized rag an' tear it into strips.

When everythin' was the way Odd wanted it, he showed me how to hold the man's leg real tight. Then Odd got a good hold on the man's foot an' twisted it a little this way an a little that way until he seemed satisfied. Then he set to bindin' the man's foot to one of the pieces of wood he'd whittled into size. He fixed the other one up along the ankle an' used more strips of cloth to hold it in place. It took him quite a good time to get it the way that suited him, an then he stood up an rubbed his back where he'd cramped up bendin' over so long.

"That'll have to do," he said. An there was a touch of satisfaction in his voice, so I figured he felt he had set it right.

After he had the man's foot all nicely wrapped up, an' I had sponged off his face again an put some salve on the bad cut, the man looked right comfortable, an Odd said we'd best let him sleep.

"Done all we can for him," he said, fixin' his usual place to sleep by the fire," I said I'd sit up with the man for a while case he woke up an wanted to know where he was or needed somethin'.

I wrapped myself up in an old cover out of the cupboard an' tried to get comfortable. I finally dragged one of the hickory chairs over to the table an sat with my head restin' on the tabletop. It wasn't too bad a way to be, an' I felt better knowin' I wouldn't sleep too hard in case the man needed tendin'.

I guess I must've dozed off near mornin', though, because first thing I knew, there was Odd down on his hunkers by the bed. When I went over next to him, I saw that the man's eyes were open. They didn't have a very sensible look to 'em, though. He looked at both Odd an me an seemed to try to say somethin'. I guess it was too much for him, though, because he just closed his eyes an went back to sleep.

It wasn't until goin' towards evenin' that he opened his eyes again an' said his first words to us.

"Who are you?" he asked, his voice all deep and gravelly-sounding, making me jump like a scared rabbit from where I was puttin' wood in the stove.

Odd was out fetchin' more wood, so I told him my name was November Sunshine. Then he wanted to know where he was an such things as what happened an' how he got here.

"You had an accident with your automobile an' we, Odd an me, carried you in here."

"Odd? Who's Odd?" he asked.

I was kind of tongue-tied on that one. I didn't want to tell this stranger all about how come I was livin' here in Odd's cabin, so I didn't know just what to say. Finally, I thought, "I come in to make do for Odd. It's Odd's cabin, though. I'm from over the hill away."

He seemed to take that in all right. Then he said, "I'm awful thirsty."

I figgured that must be a good sign. I remembered that whenever me or any of my brothers got sick, it was always a sure sign we were on the mend when we got thirsty. I figured he'd be gettin' hungry right along, too. So, I spread a cold biscuit with some honey an' poured him a tad of coffee. I tried to help him get himself up a bit in the bed so he could drink. Then I gave him the coffee an' the biscuit.

I watched him close to make sure he didn't eat or drink too fast an make himself sick that way. He didn't eat fast, but he kept right on goin' til he ate it all.

"I don't know when anythin' ever tasted so good," he said as he licked the honey off where it had dribbled down his fingers.

127

After he finished a second cup of coffee, he asked me to help him set up so he could take a look at his foot.

I wanted him to wait for Odd, but the man looked at me kinda funny an' said, "It's all right, I'm a doctor."

"You're a real people doctor?" I asked.

He said he was an' then smiled a bit. He said he'd been on his way to Wilson's Springs, where he was goin' to take over Doctor Brown's practice.

"But now," he said, lookin' down towards his foot, "I've got to see how much damage got done to my foot an' how long I'll be tied up."

So, I helped him sit up an' get a look at his ankle. He unwrapped the strips of cloth real careful, an' nodded with a satisfied sound when he saw how Odd had fixed the shaved-down wood along his foot.

"That Odd of yours seems to have fixed me up just fine," he said, fixin' to wrap the strips back in place. "I don't think any doctor could have made a better job than he did."

I wish Odd were here to hear the man say that.

I offered to help wrap his foot for him because he had to bend over a lot to do it, an' I could see him put his hand up to his head like it was hurtin'. So, in no time at all he was all fixed up again an' settled down in bed. He touched his head real easy-like. He asked me if I had a mirror, but I said I didn't. So, then he asked me to tell him what we'd put on his head an' I did. I told him it was just a mixture of yarbs to stop the bleedin' an such. He seemed to think over what I told him an' just lay back on the bed.

"I think it's just goin' to do fine, an I'd best leave it alone to heal," he said then.

128

So, from then on about all there was for him to do was to get well.

Odd was pleased when he came in an' saw how well the man was doin', but he got a funny look on his face when I told him the man was a doctor. He sort of shied away, if you know what I mean. Anyway, Odd began to stay outside the cabin longer an' longer. He'd always give some excuse like it was time to be gettin' wood cut or that Old Man Washbon needed him again. But I knew that he was just feelin' strange with somebody as smart an' book learned as a doctor around. I'd learned after I'd lived with him for a while that Odd wasn't much for talkin' to strangers. He seemed to have some funny idea that they were better'n him or somethin'. I knew different, but it wasn't my place to say anythin'.

The days began to drag a bit for me. The doctor didn't take much tendin', but I didn't feel I could go away for any length of time an' hunt yarbs an' greens out on the hillside. I was sad that I couldn't get to Ansalu's because I had my heart set on learnin' to read an' write. I surely was disappointed.

Then, one mornin' after Odd had left for work, the doctor called me to come over by the bed.

"You seem to lead a strange life here, November Sunshine," he said, "How'd you ever get to be here?"

I didn't know whether to tell him or not. I was thinkin' it over in my mind when he began just talkin' easy like, tellin' me all about himself.

"I'd certainly feel better if you'd call me Brad," he said, "I feel sort of unwelcome when you call me Doctor."

"But you are a doctor, I told him. I've never been so close to anybody with that much schoolin'," I told him. "It ain't fitten for me to call you by name."

129

"If I ask you to, it is," he said. He seemed to think about somethin' for a little while an then he said, "I'm goin' to tell you the truth about why I came here to the hills, November. An' the truth isn't very pretty. You can see for yourself just how fit it is for you to call me by name."

I was real fidgety about him talkin' to me like that. I sat by his bed for a long time listenin', but feelin' some better about doin' it. I could tell it was real hard for him to talk about himself. He'd sort've let his voice die out. Then he'd get a fresh start an tell me some more. I couldn't take it all in-you know, all the names an' such. But I had the feelin' that he was needin' to say the things he was sayin', so I just sat there real quiet an let him talk.

He told me how he'd been workin' too hard an' not takin' any time to do things that pleased him. An because he got tired an wore himself to a frazzle, he started to take a drink now an' then to pick himself up.

"Somehow," he said, "I started takin' just a little drink to give myself some pep. An' then," he went on so low I could scarce hear him, "those little drinks got bigger an' bigger an before I knew what was happenin' I was gettin drunk more an' more often. He stopped talkin' then an' looked as though he was about to cry. I hardly dared breathe for fear of makin' him feel worse. When he started talkin' again, his voice sounded real scornful, like he was mad at himself.

I did what no doctor should ever do," he said, soundin' ashamed. "I operated on a patient when I was drunk. He stopped talkin'.

"What happened?" I asked, unable to stop myself from breakin' into his thought.

"The patient... died," he said, barely whisperin'. "My patient, who should have lived to be a healthy young woman just about

130

your age, died because... because I was a fool. I wasn't sober enough to know how to keep her alive."

He lay back on the bed an' closed his eyes. I figured he'd gone to sleep till I saw a tear comin' out from under his eyelid. I pulled up a chair real quiet an' just sat there watchin' till I knew he was asleep. It made me feel sad to watch him.

I didn't say nothin' to Odd about what the doctor had told me about himself, but I watched real careful the next day to make sure he wasn't lettin' himself get sick or anythin. It was real strange, but I'd never stopped to think that even school taught folks sometimes worry an' fret. I guess I just thought they knew everythin' there was to know.

Sittin' there an watchin' him sleep, I could tell he was hurtin' inside.

His sleepin' was all fussy an' fretful. For a long while, he'd move around restless an uneasy in the bed. Then I could sense a sort of change comin' because he seemed to get more quiet an' peaceful. Finally, he opened his eyes.

He saw me sittin' there an' smiled. "November, you're a good person. When you're around my...my nightmare doesn't seem so bad."

"Your nightmare?"

He nodded. "Yes, I close my eyes an' go to sleep, an' then my head gets all full of awful pictures, an' I see that young girl dyin' again an..." he stopped talkin', but I knew what he meant.

"I know, sometimes when I first came here, I had bad dreams about it an about what was goin' to happen to me. I stopped talkin' real short lest I tell him more about how I come to be here than I wanted to tell.

"How'd you come here, November?" he asked.

I just shook my head. "I can't tell you," I said real low.

He looked at me for a bit an' said. "November, I'm wonderin' if maybe we could help each other. Maybe you could by the bed and we could talk about anything, or maybe you could read to me. Just somethin' to make the time pass faster for both of us."

I felt stricken. Read! "We can talk a bit if that will help," I said real fast before he got onto the readin' idea again.

"All right. We'll talk." He thought a bit. "We could talk about a book we've each read or somethin' like that," he said.

I figured I'd best tell him an get it over with.

"I can't read," I said, feelin' shamed that I had to say it out loud.

He just looked at me an then he broke into a big smile.

"That's it!" he cried. "That's what seems so strange about this place. There aren't any books or newspapers lyin' around." He looked around the cabin again. He was quiet for a bit, an then he said, "Why don't I teach you how to read, November?"

I just looked at him, not quite takin' in what he was sayin'.

"You'd teach me to read?" I asked, the memory of Ansalu plannin' to teach me fadin' in the back of my mind. "You could teach me?"

"Sure," he said. "It'll be somethin' to do till I can get on my feet again. At least I'll feel like I can do a little somethin' for you. It won't be much, compared to what you an Odd have done for me, but it will be a start."

I tried to tell him such talk was foolish cause we'd do the same for anybody in trouble, but he didn't pay me no mind. It seemed to be all settled.

Then he looked around the cabin. As he looked around he got a puzzled look on 'ns face. "Don't you have any books at all?" He asked. I knew he didn't mean to make me feel bad, but he looked so surprised not to find any books that I figured he must think we were real stupid.

Then I remembered that Odd had showed me his Mama's Bible. He had it all wrapped in an old piece of quilt an' tucked away on the top shelf of the cupboard in the kitchen.

"Sure, we got books around here," I said, an' I guess I sounded kind of huffy because the doctor looked at me real quick.

"Oh gosh, November, I didn't mean to hurt your feelin's. It's just that I'm so used to books, it seems strange not to find any here. My mother was a school teacher, an' she'd rather buy a book than food for the table."

I looked at him like thinkin' that I could sure understand how his mother had felt. Now that I was so close to learnin' to read I could hardly wait to see all the kinds of things that was in books.

Then the doctor looked at me again an' said, "Oh, we'll need some paper an' pencils or pens, too."

"Phewl," I said. "I didn't know we were goin' to need all that just to teach me to read! It's goin' to take me a few minutes to find somethin' to write on. I don't rightly think we have any paper to write on in the cabin. An...to tell the truth, Odd doesn't have any books other than his picture Bible. It was give to him by a mountain missionary back when he was a little boy. He sure does prize that book."

"Oh," the doctor said, soundin' disappointed, "I never gave it a thought that..." an then he stopped. I guess he figured he'd hurt my feelin's again.

I put my thinkin' cap on an then I remembered what we'd done back at Paw's cabin when we were wantin' to play that game where you mark down circles an crosses. So, I hurried outside an' started huntin' around till I found me a big flat piece of slate. I found a little piece of stone then an' scratched at the slate with it, pleased at the way it made marks on it.

When I showed the stones to the doctor, he seemed pleased. Then I had to decide if I was goin' to get out Odd's Bible or not. I knew Odd prized that Bible above most everythin' else, an' I wasn't rightly sure he'd like my takin' without askin' him.

But here was the doctor wantin' to teach me how to read an' write.

Me, November Sunshine.

I went over to the cupboard an got out Odd's Bible. I took utta the quilt pieces it was wrapped in an ran my hand over the fine, soft cover. It was a book to be proud of, that's for sure.

I turned an' said, "Doctor, I don't feel right about takin' Odd's Bible without his knowin' it."

"Brad," the doctor said. "My name is Brad, November, I wish you'd call me by It. Anyway, I should think Odd would be pleased to have you use his Bible to learn to read." An' then he took the Bible outta my hands an' just held it, lettin' the pages fall between his fingers an lookin' at the old pictures in it. "I can see why he's proud of this Bible, November, it's a fine book an it's been taken good care of. But don't you worry, if he says anythin', I'll just tell 'im that you didn't want to use it, but I thought he wouldn't mind."

I never was much good at tryin' to argue anyone down, an' I looked at the doctor an thought about learnin' to read. I wanted to learn to read so bad that I shushed my worry about usin' Odd's Bible an turned to the doctor, waitin' for him to start teachin' me to read.

"Here's a good place to start," he said. Pull up a chair an we'll start right at the beginnin' with the story of Adam an' Eve."

So, I pulled up my chair an' the doctor started readin' to me. At first, I just listened, but he soon had me soundin' out the words after him. I guess we were at it a long time, but it didn't seem long at all. An all of a sudden, I noticed how far down the sky the sun had gotten.

I just grabbed that Bible out of the doctor's hand, wrapped it in its quilt pieces, and popped it back in the cupboard. The doctor started to say somethin', but just then Odd came into the cabin lookin' for his supper. I hoped the doctor wouldn't say nothin' about what we were up to. I didn't think what we were doin' was wrong, but I had an awful bad feeling that Odd might not like it.

I hurried an' laid the food out on the table an sneaked a look at the doctor. He was talkin' to Odd about the mountains an' what kind of work there was to do an' how he liked it an all. Odd was answerin' him back pretty good, an' I breathed a sigh of relief.

Our lessons got to be a regular thing. Every day after breakfast, Odd started off for Wilson's Springs with a small package of lunch to keep him goin' til supper. An almost as quick as he was out of sight, I had the breakfast redded up an went to the cupboard an got out his Bible. The doctor an me were gettin' pretty far into the book, an' I was proud about all the words I was learnin'. Sittin' by the doctor's bed an readin' together had become the most important thing in my life. I didn't try to figger out why. I just knew the time I spent bendin' over that Bible an figgerin out the words an meanin's had become the center of my life. It was what I lived for. An when I made a mistake in my readin', the doctor didn't yell at me like Paw used to do when I did somethin' wrong. The doctor was so patient an' kind an' helpful that I found myself tryin' harder and harder to please 'im an bring out that glad smile on his sad face.

We used that sharp piece of stone an' that piece of slate to write with. Soon I was way past the alphabet an into makin' words an' little sentences. It was a really proud day for me when I spelled out my whole name without any mistakes. I can still hear the doctor's voice readin' it, November Sunshine Mudd.

The hours I spent learnin' were real precious to me. I stored every bit of learnin' in my head, tryin' to remember everythin' the doctor taught me. He even began teachin' me a little cipherin'. To tell it true, though, I was better with letters than I was with those numbers. Somehow, I couldn't get my sums to come out right. But when the doctor would show me where my mistakes were, I would get right at it an' make 'em right.

"You just have to keep at it, November," the doctor said to me one day when he'd been at Odd's cabin goin' into the second week. An I knew I'd do just that, keep at it. Now that I had a little taste of learnin' I kept wantin' more an' more.

"The longer you keep doin' somethin', the easier it gets," he went on. "It's...It's the same with me. Since I was brought here to Odd's cabin, I haven't had a single drink of alcohol. An it's a funny thing, but I don't even seem to crave it anymore, either."

The doctor an' I both seemed to get a lot of our lessons, an' I looked forward to my lessons to when he'd tell me about books he'd read. I liked hearin' about the people in them an' how they did all kinds of things. I couldn't figure anyone knowin' all the words it takes to make a book. I'd never heard about such things as public libraries before, an' when the doctor said there was probably a little one in Wilson's Springs, I decided then an there I'd get to see it sometime. Soon, too.

We worked on the story of Noah an' the flood an what happened to 'em all one day. I could just picture that big old boat in my mind. I tried to conjure up all the kinds of animals that I'd ever seen pictures of. The doctor told me about most of 'em. It was almost like they were next to me; he made 'em all so clear.

An' then one day Odd came home early.

It wasn't no use to try to get the Bible wrapped up an put away. He knew right away what it was the doctor was holdin'.

"What's goin' on here?" he yelled, hurryin' over to the edge of the bed. He grabbed that Bible out of the doctor's hands, lookin' for all the world like he was goin' to break into tears. But he didn't.

He just stood there holdin' that book so careful, like it was a baby or somethin'. He ran a finger real gentle over the place where it said "Holy Bible" In real gold letters. An he didn't look mad so much as he looked hurt. That made me feel worse than if he'd been mad. I didn't know what to say.

He turned to the doctor. "You... you're nothin' but a cheat!" he said, gettin' red in the face. "I take you in an make you at home, an' now you got no respect for what's mine." He looked at the Bible to make sure it wasn't torn or hurt or anythin'. When he saw it was all right, he wrapped it back up in the quilt pieces an went an put it back in the cupboard. Then he stopped lookin' sad. He was beginnin' to look mad when he turned back to me an' snapped, "What you mean showin' my Bible to a stranger?"

"Oh, Odd, the doctor's no stranger, he..."

"I needed a book to use to teach November how to read, the doctor put in, talkin' in a nice quiet voice like he was tryin' to calm Odd down.

But Odd wasn't about to be calmed down. He just seemed to get madder'n ever when he heard what the doctor said about teachin' me to read. He turned to me like he wanted to say somethin', but the words were stuck. Then he saw the slate I was usin'. He grabbed it an' threw it to the floor. He stamped his foot on it an' smashed the pieces with his boot again an' again, gettin' madder all the time. He made a funny noise an reached out his hand. I backed away, tryin' to get out of his way. But Odd was bigger an' faster'n me an' he grabbed me by the front of my dress. His look scared me so that I tried to pull away, but Odd had a real grip on me, an' the front of my pretty new green dress let out a tearin' sound that near broke my heart. It ripped from one side to the other, an' I screamed at Odd, an' he got red in the face an' started shakin' me so hard. It brought tears to my eyes.

"Stop that the doctor yelled, an' I turned away from 'em both real fast to hide myself while I tried to hold the dress together with my hands. But the dress was torn bad an' my hands were shakin', so I couldn't hold it together. I just couldn't stop the tears from pourin' down my face, an' I felt myself shakin' hard with sobs.

The doctor was strugglin', tryin' to get out of bed. His broken foot wouldn't hold 'im an' he fell back onto the covers.

"Stop that caterwallin'," Odd yelled at me. Then he turned his angry face towards the doctor an' said in a voice as cold as river water when you break through the Ice, "I should've let you die up on the hill!"

It was a terrible thing to say, an I could tell from Odd's face that the minute he said it, he felt how awful it was. He shouldn't't've said it, an' he knew it, but he was stubborn an' mad an didn't back down.

Then he went over to the cabin door an' just before he went out he turned around.

"You shouldn't oughta done it behind my back," an then he went out, shuttin' the door behind 'im.

After Odd went out, I felt like the wind was leakin' out of me. All weak an dragged out.

I helped the doctor get himself all straightened out in bed, doin' the best I could with one hand while the other tried to hold my dress together.

He looked at me a bit like he was thinkin'. Then he looked at my face an' said, "You know, November, I think Odd's jealous!"

"Jealous? Of me? Odd's got no call to be jealous of me. I b'long to 'im."

That set the doctor back some, an' he was real quiet whilst I got us some supper.

Nobody said anythin' at all when, by an' by, Odd came back in an' set himself at the table. He looked kinda sheepish an' fidgeted around in his seat. "Didn't mean to tear your dress, November," he said lookin' down at the tabletop. I knew it cost him to apologize. Odd wasn't one who believed in much apologizin'. I was still too upset to say anythin' to him.

Then he cleared' his throat like there was somethin' caught in it. He looked at the doctor an' spoke.

"I 'preciate what you was tryin' to do, doctor, what riled me up was the way you was tryin' to do it. The thing is, if you'd just talked to me about it, I could've made things plain to you from the first."

"You see, doctor, things here in the hills ain't like they be where you come from. You're just wastin' your time teachin' November how to read. It plum ain't sensible for a mountain woman to learn to read an' write. What would she want to do that for? She don't need none of that foolishness to cook an' clean an' raise kids. Ain't no call for November Sunshine to learn to read an' write." He looked at me, shakin' his head, an turned back to the doctor.

"Hell, she can't even get pregnant!"

Then he stood up an there was a fierce pride on his face when he looked at us. "There ain't gonna be no more teachin' here in this cabin," he said like he wasn't about to ever change 'is mind. "An' that's a fact!"

Then he sat down again an looked at me. "Where's my supper, woman?" he asked an I knew that he considered the subject closed.

Right then, with every bit of my being, I hated him. I could see my dream of learnin' to read wasn't goin' to amount to a hill of beans.

I thought of how I'd never had any say about anythin' in my life. Paw had always decided things for me when I was at home, an' now Odd was doin' the same thing, Bossin' me. Tellin' me what to do an what to be. It made a sour feelin' in my stomach just to think about it. I sat runnin' my fingers over where I'd tied the pieces of my dress together. It made tears come up in my eyes, but I willed 'em to go away. I wasn't goin' to let either one of 'em see me cry.

There was somethin' about me that neither Odd nor Paw had ever understood.

I'd do most anythin' to learn.

Cause someday I meant to be a lady.

MORE'N ONE WAY

The three of us were full of prickly feelin's whilst we ate the supper I fixed. Nobody dared look full in anybody else's face. We all acted like our minds was miles away. I was glad to get busy reddin' up after we ate, it gave me somethin' to do. A couple of times I had the feelin' that Odd was wantin' to say somethin'. He never managed to blurt it out, though, so whatever it was, he swallered it instead of sayin' it.

After we finally got settled down that night, the cabin was full of uneasy sounds. Even the wind comin' in through the chinks in the wall sounded different, unfriendly. And every now and then, some little night-critter scampered over the tin roof and made strange, ghostly sounds. I could hear Odd flumpin' around on his blanket over near the fire and clearin' his throat a lot. I knew he wasn't asleep. and the doctor was makin' restless sounds, too. He moved around on the bed makin' quick rooch, rooch, rooch, sounds so that I knew he wasn't asleep, neither. Everythin'd be quiet for a bit, and then I'd hear him rooch, rooch, rooch some more.

Nobody said anythin' though, and I was grateful for that. I was busy inside my head with my own thoughts. and they weren't pretty, neither. I had thoughts comin' and goin' and none of 'em seemed to fit in just right.

Before I crawled into my corner and wrapped up in and old comfort, I had turned my back on both of 'em and skinned out of my torn green dress. I felt awful sad when I remembered how proud I'd been to get it. I didn't see how I could ever fix it so I could wear it again. Then I put on the night shift, always slept in and laid green dress on the floor beside me.

I reached out a hand so I could touch the green dress and feel its softness. Tellin' it how sorry I was, it got torn and all, I guess.

It was almost like I was layin' out a person, that's how bad I felt.

All kinds of hurt thoughts chased themselves around in my head while I was lyin' there. But finally, I got to a point where I could start thinkin' ahead and stop lookin' back so much. I remembered Ansalu tellin' me one time that lookin' back at somethin' that had hurt you was foolish. She said it was like lettin' yourself be hurt all over again.

"Only way to go, November," she'd said, "Is head on. Anybody who looks and walks backward is twice as likely to fall."

I lay there in the dark, thinkin' about what Ansalu'd said, hearin' the worriesome sounds in the cabin, and wonderin' what Ansalu'd say to do now.

I couldn't quite piece everythin' together. My mind was so full of all kinds of things that nothin' seemed to fall into place.

As I wriggled around tryin' to get comfortable on that worn old quilt, I began to realize that I was makin' uneasy night sounds, too. I thought about that a bit.

You know, it's funny, but that was the first time I realized that what had happened wasn't just between Odd and the doctor. It was me, too. I guess up to then I hadn't really thought about my bein' a real part of what was happenin'. I'd sort of felt like I was the slate, and Odd and the doctor were the chalky stone that wrote on the slate. Like they were the ones who made things happen, and I was just there, lettin' it be.

But somewhere in that long, long night I came to know that it was more'n that. I'd have to answer for what happened to me. Not so much for what happened to me, but for what I did about it.

143

Once I reached that point, I was ready to go head-on like Ansalu said.

I decided that first off, no matter what, I was gonna go see her.

An I did.

"Where you goin'?" Odd asked me when he saw me fixin' to go out. I'd hunted out my old worn dress and managed to squeeze myself into it. I didn't feel very good in it, but it was all there was for me to wear.

"I'm goin' to Ansalu's," I answered, tryin' not to let my voice show how torn up I was inside.

"What for?" he asked.

"It...It ain't none of your business, I told 'im, steppin' away from "Im After what had happened the night before, I wasn't wantin' to take any chances on his rippin' this dress, too."

He just looked at me and didn't say a word. That made me feel braver and I said, "I got a right to go see Ansalu if I want. I've fixed your breakfast and wrapped up food for your lunch and fixed supper, too, right along. and now I want to tend to my own business."

An before either Odd or the doctor could say a word, I hurried out of the cabin and down that trail as fast as I could. I was a little ways from the cabin when I thought I heard Odd's voice callin', "Didn't mean to tear your dress." But when I stopped to listen better, I couldn't hear nothin' but the wind in the tallest trees.

"Maybe I just wish 'im to say that," I thought to myself as I went on.

Walkin' along through the woods on my way to Ansalu's, I began to feel some better. The big trees on either side of the path reached right up into the sky. They made a sort of cover over my head and gave me the same kind of feelin' of comfort the old black walnut tree at home usta give me. I walked along lookin' up at the trees and watchin' the birds fit in and out. Now and then a bush would slap at my legs as though to say hello, just touchin', not hurtin'.

The farther I went, the better I felt.

I knew there might be a ruckus when I got back. But for now, the peace of the woods and knowin' I was goin' to see Ansalu, was all that mattered.

Thy word, child, Ansalu cried when she opened her door to me, "but you look tattered this mornin'. She reached up and put her arms around me and held me so close I could smell the good smell of her "Not that you ain't a sight for sore eyes! It's been bout a month since I laid eyes on you".

An then I gave myself over to the warm, gentle fussin' that Ansalu always did. I could feel the soreness in my soul slippin' away while she petted and talked to me so gentle. I looked around her cabin at the rockin' chair and the braided rug and all her other welcomin' things.

"This must be what it's like to come home and see a mama who loves you," I thought. For a little bit, I felt jealous of every woman who'd had a mama to help her make it through the hard and fretful times.

But how can a body stay upset when you're busy eatin' fresh-baked ginger snaps? The kind made with real dark molasses and sprinkled with sugar on the top? The kind that fills a kitchen with a good, warm, spicy smell?

After I'd had my second glass of cool milk with lots of those ginger snaps, I was feelin' up to talkin'. and I told Ansalu about everythin', even that the doctor was teachin' me to read and write. Even though I could tell from her face she was a mite disappointed that it was him that had got to do the teachin' and not her. It wasn't like Ansalu to say nothin' about it, though.

"On, November" was what she said, real sad, fingerin' where my green dress was torn so bad. "Your new dress! Then she studied it real good, turnin' it inside and out to pull at the threads.

"You know, It's not total ruined," she said slowly. "You just leave It here with me for a little. I got a little piece of green ribbon, and I think I can pull enough threads to fix the dress up real good." Then she shrugged her shoulders a bit, "It won't look brand new, but it'll look good enough to wear."

"Would you fix it?" I asked. "I'd take it very kindly. and after we had settled about her fixin' the dress we got down to some real talkin'."

"You know, November, it wasn't right to take Odd's Bible without his leave. and there ain't no way you should ever take it to learn readin' again," she said. "But that don't mean you can't learn to read real good."

I looked at her kind, troubled face. Somethin' I had to ask. "Do you mind that I let the doctor teach me instead of my comin' over here?" I asked her.

Ansalu looked at me with a tiny smile on her face. "At first it did sting a mite when you said the doctor was teachin' you. I'd been lookin' forward to doin' the teachin'. But then my common sense took over, November. I knew that I was just feelin' a bite to my own pride." She looked at me close. "Just like I guess it took a bite to Odd's pride to find you usin' his picture Bible without a by-your-leave."

I bit my lower lip feelin' that she was chidin' me for what I'd done.

"You just stop and think about it a minute, November, I think you'll see what I mean."

"Yes'm," I said. I hadn't thought of my learnin' to read as hurlin' Odd's pride, though I had thought it might bother Ansalu some.

"But it's done," Ansalu said then. "An you were only doin' the best you could and tryin' to make do. Guess I can't fault you for that."

I began to feel better. Somehow gettin' this all out in the open made things seem a little more right. Not quite so bad and upsettin'.

"You just take all the teachin' that doctor feller can give you, November. An, if you want, you can take one of my books home with you to use," Ansalu said, pattin' the back of my hand.

I was that pleased!

After a while, I got down on my hunkers so I could see the backs of all her books on the shelf by the wood-stove, I wondered how I'd know which one to borrow.

"You know, November," Ansalu said with that kind of lift in a body's voice when they are about to share what they think is a good idea with you, "I've just thought of somethin'."

I waited for her to go on, still kneelin' in front of those books.

"It seems to me that the doctor would be knowin' lots of things about the world. You know, geography and travelin' and how people go about livin' and things like that."

I nodded, wonderin' what she was tellin' me.

"Well, November, I know that lots of folks in town get newspapers every day. and those newspapers can tell you things about the world that you didn't ever dreamed of. There are all kinds of excitin' things in newspapers."

I didn't know what she meant.

"There isn't any reason you can't walk down to Webster Springs, is there?"

"No, I guess not, I told her, puzzled by the question.

"You see, November, those people get a NEW newspaper every week. and when they get the new one, they don't need the old one anymore."

"What do they do with them?" I asked.

"Well, some people use 'em to start their fires with or to wrap up their trash. But lots of those folk just stick 'em out back on a pile or in a trash barrel."

"What's on your mind?" I asked, sensin' her excitement.

"November, what's to stop you from goin' down to Wilson's Springs now and again and collectin' some of those old newspapers that people don't want any more? She looked at me, eyes sparklin' with her idea.

"An then the doctor could use 'em to teach me all them things you were talkin' about?" I asked, feelin' a lift to my spirits. Somehow I felt like a door was openin' and I had a chance to go through it.

"I wouldn't have to pay for 'em, would 1?" I asked. "I don't have any money to spend, Ansalu."

"No, child. People would prob'ly be glad to have you take some of their old papers away."

We talked some more, and then it was time for me to go.

All the way back to Odd's cabin, I planned in my mind how I'd get down to Wilson's Springs without Odd knowin' and raisin' a fuss. I forgot to worry about the bad feelin's I'd left behind that mornin'. Time enough for that when I get there.

Odd wasn't around when I got to the cabin, so I breathed easter. I gave the book Ansalu had sent to the doctor, and he went right to readin' through it. I set myself to fixin' as good a supper as I could, fresh biscuits and all. I wanted things as peaceful as I could get them so I could go on with my learnin'.

Things was a little over-quiet at supper, and I guess Odd and the doctor were tired 'cause they both settled down to sleep soon afterwards. As soon as I had things cleared away, I got the book from where the doctor had put it and slipped it into the folds of my comforter so Odd wouldn't see it.

In the mornin' Odd looked real meaninful at the cupboard where his Bible was. He hadn't asked me a thing about my visit to Ansalu's last night, and I didn't think he would this mornin', either. He didn't have to say any words to let me know he was upset with me. But I didn't care. I knew somethin' he didn't know. I knew there was no way he was goin' to stop me from learnin' to read.

So, for the next two or three days, the doctor and me studied out of Ansalu's book. It wasn't too different from the way words came out in the Bible, but it was a lot easier to follow the story in Ansalu's book than it was followin' the stories in the Bible.

"That's because the Bible's words were all written durin' the time a king named James lived. And that was a long, long time ago, the doctor told me when I asked why they seemed different in the Bible from Ansalu's book. I kept tryin' to call the doctor by name, but I just couldn't bring myself to do it. It didn't seem right.

"How long ago?" I asked him.

"Oh, about three hundred years ago, November," he told me. "I think the Bible most people use is the King James Bible. The Bible got named for him because he paid for it to be published. If I remember rightly, James was from Scotland and became king sometime early in the sixteen-hundreds."

"Sixteen-hundreds?" I asked him, puzzled.

"Yes, November. We're livin' in the nineteen hundreds. You know, we say 1930, 1940, 1950. It's the way we number years."

"Oh, so he, James that is, lived in 1630, or 1640, or 1650?"

He laughed. But in a nice, unhurty way.

"Well, that's the general idea, November. Anyway, the people talked a lot different from the way we do now, and that's what makes readin' the Bible a little strange. But this book," he said, holdin' up Ansalu's book, "is what is called a modern novel. It's a story that somebody made up, and it's written the way people talk now."

Things ran along so smooth those three or four days that I decided I'd make a plan to go down to Wilson's Springs. I hadn't told either Odd or the doctor about my plan, and I didn't intend to.

Soon after Odd left for work the next mornin' I got myself ready to head off to Wilson's Springs. I had to be real careful not to catch up with Odd on the path down the mountain. I was feelin' excited and kinda good about what I was doin', but I wasn't ready to face Odd with what I was up to.

The doctor looked at me like he wondered what I was up to, but he didn't ask, and I didn't tell him. I just said, "I got and idea, and if it works out, I'll show you; if it don't , I won't," I said.

It wasn't as scary goin' to Wilson's Springs as when I had gone the first time with Odd. I knew what to expect this time, and it didn't seem as far, either. Almost before I knew it, I reached the point where I could see clear out over the rooftops of Wilson's Springs. I could make out the department store and figgered that was a good place to start lookin' for old newspapers. I was sure anyone as smart as Mr. Washbon would read newspapers. I wasn't keen on gettin' that close to Junior Washbon again, but I figured that if I just went around the back of the store, I wasn't very likely to run into him.

So I went around the back of the store and started lookin' for old newspapers. Paw had used some old newspapers he'd found one time to put over a broken window in our privvy once, so I knew what to look for. and sure enough! There was a big pile of old papers just crammed full of pictures and words. I picked up a great big pile of the papers, hatin' to waste a single one. But I hadn't counted on how heavy a whole pile of 'em was, so I had to put most of 'em back where I'd found 'em. Then I folded up just a couple of the papers and put 'em under my arm. I was just about to walk away when a familiar voice stopped me.

"Hello," was all he said, but it made me gnarl up somethin' fierce. I knew Junior Washbon had come from out of somewheres and was standin' there lookin' at me.

I finally made myself look at him, but it wasn't easy.

"I'm not meanin' to steal," I told him. "I just need some old newspapers, I said, tryin' to sound like I did this all the time.

"Newspapers," he said, his voice goin' uphill in s'prise. Then he sort of started over by sayin', "What in the world do you want these old newspapers for?"

I didn't know how to answer without givin' away my reason, so I just stood there lookin' at him.

"It's not that you can't have 'em, it's just that I wonder what you mean to do with 'em," he said.

An then I felt kinda mean, takin' the man's papers and not even tellin' him what for. "I need 'em to read," I told him.

"Such old ones?" he asked in surprise.

"It don't matter how old they are," I said, not wantin' to say any more.

He looked as though he was thinkin' and then he said, "Are you goin' to use these papers to practice readin'?"

I nodded. "I'm...I'm just learnin' to read," I finally admitted, thinkin' that if he laughed at me, I'd turn tall and run.

"Wait a minute," he said, hurryin' in a back door. In a little bit, he came back out carryin' two more papers.

"Here," he said, handin' them to me. "No sense in takin' those old papers, they aren't much good. Might as well take yesterday's and today's."

I started to refuse them, thinkin' he might still need 'em, but he just reached out and took the old papers and put them on the pile, leavin' me holdin' the two new ones.

Then I remembered my manners and stammered, "Much obliged." I felt like a little lad who's been caught doin' somethin' foolish by its elders.

"I can send the paper up to you each day when Odd comes home," he said in a real friendly way. But that caught me up short. I didn't want Odd to know what I was up to.

"Oh no!," I whispered, terrified.

A look came over his face, and I knew he caught on. "You don't want Odd to know about this, do you?" he asked.

I shook my head.

"Well, then, since you are a valued customer of Washbon's Department Store," he said in a funny voice so I didn't rightly know if he was mockin' me or not, "why don't I just see that you get home safely."

I didn't say anything. I didn't know what he meant.

Then he took me by my elbow and steered me over to where this big fancy automobile stood shinin' in the sunlight.

He opened the door for me and sort of pushed me inside.

"Oh, I can't," I started to say, but his look shushed me.

An then I saw Odd comin' 'round the bulldin' and I was awful glad when Junior Washbon's automobile started off real fast and whisked me away before Odd had a chance to see who was in it.

I hung on real tight. I had never been in and automobile before, and I was scared through and through. But somethin' about the man who was drivin' made me not want to tell him that, so I tried to act like I rode in automobiles every day.

After a bit, it wasn't quite so scary and I let go of my hold on the seat a bit.

It was amazin' to me how fast the thing went up the hill road. I remembered how long it had taken me to walk up and just could hardly believe how fast this automobile was takin' me. I closed my eyes and felt the air movin' by ever so nice. and then somethin' made me open 'em and when I looked, I saw we had taken a different turn somewhere. Junior Washbon had turned us off on a little old road that wasn't hardly a road at all. While I was lookin' around me, he reached over and turned a key and the car stopped makin' its runnin' noise and just stood still.

I sat and stared through the front glass at the trees. I didn't know what else to do.

I tried not to look when Junior Washbon moved over closer to me.

"Where's your new green dress?" he asked, puttin' his hand on my leg.

I figgered if I acted like I didn't notice and didn't move, he'd stop. My leg felt like it was settin' it on fire.

"Where's the new dress you just bought?" he asked again.

"It got torn," I said, tryin' to move away from him, and yet not bein' able to.

Finally, he took his hand offen my leg and put it around my shoulder. and then, 'fore I knew what he was up to, he was kissin' me.

I didn't know what to do. I'd never been kissed like that before. He held his lips on mine, and I could feel the tip of his tongue pushin' to get my lips apart.

I was scared.

But I was excited, too. Not so much at what he was doin', but at the way it was makin' me feel inside.

I finally pushed him away, and he sat back on his side, lookin' satisfied.

"Why did you do that?" I asked him in a little voice that was all I could make come out.

He didn't say anythin', so I just swallered til I could talk right.

"I saw that lady come into the store when I was there. I told him. "An I could tell that you...belong to her." He looked at me real strange, "Do you think she'd like it if she knew what you just did?"

He laughed in a funny way that wasn't funny at all.

"Prob'ly not," he agreed. "That's Eloise Bardwell, November," he said. I was taken aback that he used my given name. He must have noticed my expression because he went on, "I heard Odd call you by name. November Sunshine. It sort of seems to fit you," he finished.

"Who's Eloise Bardwell?" I had to ask.

"Her father is a minister of the First Methodist Church here in Wilson's Springs," he said. "Eloise was away at school college and she's just come back to town."

"I know about the Freewill Baptist Church," I told him. "Is it the same thing?"

"No," he said, "there are several churches in town. The First Methodist is the biggest and most important one. That's the one my father goes to."

"Oh," I said.

"A Reverend Bardwell and my father are very good friends. and they got this idea that it would be fine if Eloise and I..." he stopped talkin'.

But I understood what he was sayin'.

"You'd best let me out here and I'll get on back to the cabin," I said, fumblin' with the door latch.

He reached over me and closed the door. Then he turned on the motor and the automobile started to move again. We soon reached the road nearest Odd's cabin, and he slowed the automobile down.

"There'll be a next time," he said real soft as he brought the automobile to a stop.

I didn't dare ask him what he meant. I just pushed at the door latch until it opened, and I climbed down out of the automobile. I hurried off towards Odd's cabin, not darin' to look back.

"You forgot your papers!" he called, and I could hear a funny laugh in his voice like he was kinda proud that he'd messed my mind up so I forgot the papers.

At first I thought I'd just walk on to the cabin and leave the papers.

There was no way I wanted to face Junior Washbon again. But then I heard the automobile door open, and in a moment Junior Washbon had caught up with me and handed me those newspapers.

I took them, not darin' to look in his face. I didn't want to get my feelin's so mixed up inside again.

He didn't touch me, but he came and stood so close to me that I could feel his breath where it came in little puffs from hurryin' to catch up. I sure didn't like the way he was makin' me feel, but I couldn't seem to move.

Then he turned and hurried back to his automobile.

I watched until the automobile was long out of sight, and then I filled up my lungs with as much fresh air as I could crowd in.

Feelin' that I could handle myself again, I turned back towards the cabin.

When I came into the cabin, I saw that the doctor was sleepin'. I was glad cause if he'd been awake, I would probably've blurted out about ridin' in and automobile. and because he was so easy to talk to, it wouldn't have been easy not to tell him all the rest about Junior Washbon and all that. In a way, I would've liked to talk to the doctor about Junior Washbon and him kissin' me and all. I would've liked to ask the doctor if that's the way town men act towards womenfolk. Or was it just somethin' wrong with me?

I put the newspapers under my comforter along with Ansalu's book so Odd wouldn't see 'em. Then I went and got the pail and went on out to the well so I could get some water to make soup for supper. Odd's old pump worked real hard, and most times, I hated how hard it made me pump just to get a little water. But today, it felt good to have somethin' hard to tangle with.

I knew inside I wasn't yet done with Junior Washbon.

HALLELUIAH

It wasn't easy actin' natural outside when I was such a Jumble of feelin's inside. But I must've managed all right because neither Odd nor the doctor said anything about the way I was actin'.

I tried to go ahead with things just like they'd been before. Early on, I'd fix Odd his breakfast and somethin' to take for eatin' in the middle of the day. Then, after he'd gone off to work at the department store, the doctor and I'd pore over those newspapers.

At first, I was really taken by the pictures. There were pictures on every page, and some of 'em was really somethin' to look at. The doctor just let me look and look til I got my fill.

Then the doctor told me how newspapers were put together and all. He read off some of the big words to me and told me I'd soon learn how to read the newspaper all by myself. Didn't seem possible, but I was all for it.

By the third day after I got those newspapers, I had learned about the place where they told who died and about the back of the paper where there were lots of rows of little print. The doctor said the newspapers called 'em. classified advertisements. He said they told of things for sale and jobs for hire and houses for sale, and things like that. He said just plain people like Odd and me could put one of those advertisements in the paper. Like if Odd wanted to sell somethin', or wanted to look for work with folks, or things like that. 'Course, we'd have to pay for it.

Then I found out that all the advertisements aren't in the back of the newspaper, either. Unh-uh. Some, that people thought should be in bigger print were put on the other pages of the newspaper. Most of 'em had lines around 'em. I ask why everybody didn't have their advertisements in big print with those fancy lines around 'em, but the doctor said they cost more to put in the newspaper than the little ones on the back page.

An there was one real big advertisement that caught my eye. It was smack-dab in the middle of the second page of the paper.

"All right, November," the doctor said, spreading the newspaper on the top of the table so I could see it real good. "Now read this advertisement to me."

"Where should I start?" I asked him, puttin' off havin' to do it.

"Start with the biggest words at the top. Then you read right on down through the letters as they get smaller until you've read clear through to the bottom."

"Well, all right," I told him, leanin' down close so I could figger out the letters just right. "Re…re…vi…val, Revival. I looked to see the doctor's face to see if I was right. He nodded, so I knew I was, and went on.

"Revival."

"Yes, November, you've already read us that word. Go on!"

I breathed in real slow, tryin' to get a hold on the next letters.

"Are…are you…sa…ved?" I turned to see if I was right.

"That's good, November!" the doctor said. I felt warm and good inside.

"Only when a word has and 'ed at the end, you stick the sound onto the sounds before it. Saved, saved," he said, "showin' me how to read that word.

"If you want to… If you want to be saved, then... come to the…ta…ta…I can't figger that one out, doctor," I said, shakin' my head and wishin' I could.

"Tabernacle," he told me.

"Tabernacle?" I said, lookin' at the word real good. "I don't think I ever heard that word before. What does it mean?"

Then, the doctor explained that sometimes people call a church a tabernacle. I asked him why anybody'd want to use a real big word like that instead of a nice little one like church. He said he guessed it made 'em feel special or somethin'.

Anyway, I finally worked my way through the whole advertisement. The doctor said I did real good.

"Now read the whole thing for me from beginnin' to end," he said.

I tried to make my voice go readin' right along just as though I had been readin' advertisements for all of my life. I felt pretty proud when I reached the last row of little print without stoppin' but two times.

"That was fine!" he told me, and then he turned the newspaper over. "Now we'll see how much you comprehended."

I just looked at him, puzzled, and finally asked, "What in the world does that com-somethin' word mean?" He laughed.

"I'm sorry, November," he said; I shouldn't have used that word. To comprehend somethin' means you understand it. I want to know how much you understand the words you read. What do they mean?"

"Have you ever been to a revival, November?" he asked.

160

I told him I'd heard tell of 'em, but I'd never been to one. Paw hadn't held much with religion and church-goin', I told him. So, he told me a little about what one was like, and then we read some more, and before I knew it, it was time to start supper.

It was just a few days after that that I took a real longin' to go talk to Ansalu again. I'd come to put a lot of stock in seein' Ansalu and gettin' to talk things over with her. She was somethin' special to me. I knew things weren't always very good for her cause it was hard doin' folks washin'. Specially, when you're so little and have to carry all those heavy baskets, and knew she didn't have very much money, either, but she never did a lot of complainin'. What she did was look for the good in everythin' and keep herself real cheerful. I never saw the like.

"I'd like to go over to Ansalu's tomorrow; I told Odd that night while he was eatin'. He acted like he didn't hear me like his mind was somewhere else. And I found out directly where it was.

"I got a lot of new work down at the department store," he told the doctor and me, soundin' mighty proud as he said it. "Not just sawin' up wood like before, neither. We're goin' to build a new storeroom out back."

"That means more regular work for you!" I said, glad for him because I knew it meant a lot to Odd to have work. Odd and me didn't always get along so good, but I could never fault him for not bein' a hard worker. I had come to respect the way he managed to keep himself busy with jobs here and there.

"That's not all," he said, his lips lookin' like they was tryin' not to smile but were losin' the fight. "I'm gonna do most of the buildin'." Then he turned to me. "An I been thinkin', November, maybe it ain't such a bad idea for you to be friends with that Ansalu." He looked around the cabin and sniffed the supper that was cookin'. "Pears to me she's been teachin' you how to cook and run a house pretty good."

I felt more lighthearted about things than I had for a long spell.

It was nice seein' Odd with somethin' to feel good about. It was kind of strange, too, how when he felt good, he didn't mind for me to have a friend. I'm not quite sure why it was that way; it just was.

When I got to Ansalu's, I asked her if she'd ever been to a revival.

"Law, child, that was the prime entertainment where I came from. There isn't anythin' like a good revival to stir up your blood and make you feel good." She looked at me a moment and then asked, "Haven't you ever been to one, November?"

I felt awful foolish then. You know the kind of feelin' you get when you come to know there's a whole lot of things you don't know nothin' about? What makes it worse is that you think maybe you're the only person who doesn't know about 'em. Anyway, this was Ansalu and, so I could tell her the truth.

"No, I've never been to a revival, Ansalu," I said. "To tell the truth, I never even went to church. Paw didn't hold much with such things."

Ansalu sat straight up the way she does when she thinks things aren't right. "For heaven's sake, child," she said, "It's time we do somethin' about that!"

She bounced up out of her chair real fast and went over to her shelves. Then she took down a little bundle of cloth, and I could see it was my green dress. She brought it over and, shook it out, and held it up for me to see.

"That's beautiful," Ansalu I cried, lookin' at the careful way she had mended it. I could tell she'd taken real pains doin' it,

162

too. She'd worked that pretty green ribbon in where the biggest tear had been, and it made the dress look really special. "Why you've fixed it so it doesn't look like there was ever anythin' wrong with it." I reached out and took the dress, and held it up to myself and sort of sashayed 'round the cabin, sayin' "Thank you, thank you, oh, thank you," over and over.

"Now, you can wear that dress and you and I will make our plans to go down to one of the churches in Wilson's Springs. It's just about time you get to know a little of the world outside that cabin of Odd's," she finished. And the way she stood there with her hands on her hips, I knew she meant what she was sayin' and didn't take very kindly to my never havin' been to church.

"There's a revival comin', Ansalu," I told her. And then I showed her the advertisement in the paper. I even read it out to her.

She looked at me with a smile as big as a melon slice on her face. "Why, November! That doctor's teachin' you real good," she said. All the hard work was worth it for the way she made me feel then.

In a little bit, we sat drinkin' fresh-made berry-leaf tea, and she said, "I've never heard tell of this Brother Glen that's told about in the paper, though, November. However, I think it might be a good thing if you and I went down to Wilson's Springs to hear him."

I was so pleased I couldn't say anythin'. I wasn't at all sure what a revival was or what Brother Glen was like, but I could feel it in my bones that my world was beginnin' to change and get bigger. It was scary in a way 'cause I didn't know just what was ahead for me. But it was excitin', too. And, whatever happened, I knew I had to let it happen. I knew way down inside of me that I didn't want to spend the rest of my life just hopin' for a chance to go look into a store window now and again. The day I saw that Eloise Bardwell come into Washbon's Department Store, I started dreamin'. Oh, maybe I didn't know it just then, but I surely had. And sittin' there with Ansalu, I thought back to how pretty that Eloise was dressed, and how she walked, and how she held herself and all. Somethin' inside wanted that for me, too. I wanted to be the way she was, I wanted to be able to hold my head up with anybody!

Then Junior Washbon popped into my mind, and my dream went flyin' when I thought about how I must look to other folks. I must not count for very much if Junior Washbon had felt that free with me. I decided not to tell that part to Ansalu.

Ansalu went on talkin' about the revival and how's we could go and all that kind of thing. And I figgered if wearin' my patched dress and goin' to a revival with Ansalu would help make me like Eloise Bardwell, then that's what I was gonna do. And even though I didn't have any idea what Odd would say about it, I planned to go. I sure wasn't able to figger Odd out. Sometimes, he was nicer'n anything to me, and other times, he seemed to get mad at everythin' I did.

It was clear to me that somethin' was eatin' at his insides. But I sure didn't know what it was. I had a bad feelin' that it had somethin' to do with the way we were livin' and him goin' over to the Widder Morton's and such.

I had a lot of things to think about on my way back to Odd's cabin. I wasn't ready for what I found when I got back.

I came into the cabin like I always did and looked over to the bed where the doctor mostly spent his time. But the bed was a jumbled mess, covers every which way, and the doctor wasn't on it. More'n and more lately, he'd been gettin' out and around, but this time, things looked different. Then I saw him sittin' in a chair with all his clothes on. He wasn't wearin' that big of worn shirt of Odd's he'd been wearin' whilst he was bedded.

Now he was wearin' all his own clothes. Ceptin' the shoe for his broken foot, which was layin' on the floor next to him.

He looked different from day to night. I looked real close to see what else the difference was. It was more'n the clothes. I could see that his hair was combed and neat, and his face had been scraped clean of the beard the he'd started to grow since we'd found him.

He must've read my thoughts because he laughed and said, "Yep, it's me, November. He sounded sort of half-proud." I decided it was time for me to get out of your life and start workin' on my own. I'll send word down to Wilson's Springs Hospital to tell them I'm coming.

I felt like someone had hit me in the stomach! Havin' the doctor right close by to teach me readin' and writin' had become part of my life. He was my friend. I hadn't let myself think about his ever goin' away.

I couldn't say anythin'.

"I've been thinkin' about goin' for some time, November," he said. "I'm most grateful for all you and Odd did, and I know I can never thank you enough. But now it's time for me to go. I should've gone a long time ago," he said.

I wanted to say somethin' but couldn't find the words.

"You see, November, it's been real pleasant stayin' here with you in this cabin where life is so much simpler than it is on the outside. I've had lots of time to think about my life and the mess I made. Now, I think maybe I've got a chance to... start over again even though I'm not young anymore. I can't undo my past mistakes, but I can build a new life for myself. I haven't even had a drink of alcohol since I came here, and I think... hope my battle with booze is over. At least I'm ahead for now." He shrugged his shoulders.

"Anyway, I'll never really know til I get out there on my own and give livin' a try again." He stopped talkin' then and waited for me to say somethin'.

I just looked at him, "What about my readin' and writin'?" I asked.

"I've taught you as much as you need to be taught, November. From now on, it's just a matter of simple practicin'. Read everythin' you can lay your hands on that has printed words in it. Read labels on cans and boxes. When you go into Wilson's Springs again, read all the signs you see. Read, write, and keep goin'. There are whole new worlds hidden in books, November, and now you can take advantage of 'em."

I felt a sigh workin' its way clean up from my toes, and I couldn't talk for a little bit. I pondered what he'd been sayin', and I knew it made sense. His bein' in the cabin had been different, special. It was like the things that had been bad for him had to wait outside til he was well enough to come out and deal with 'em. And it had sort of been that way with Odd and me, too. As long as the doctor was in the cabin, there hadn't been no talk of Odd tryin' to bed me like he'd tried before. But those things were still around, just waitin' for the doctor and me to deal with 'em. They hadn't gone away. They'd just moved back a piece.

I sighed. I knew what the doctor was doin' was right, but I surely did hate to see him go.

"I guess you're right, doctor. It's about time."

"Yes," he said softly. "I know it's been awkward with me sleepin' in your's and Odd's bed. With me bein' here all the time."

"Oh, no!" I burst out, "You're all wrong! I could feel my face pinkin' up, and I was embarrassed. "It really isn't that way between Odd and me at all. I only belong to him. I ain't…" I mean, I'm not married to him." and then I told him what I hadn't wanted to say before about how come I was livin' with Odd.

"My God, November," he said when I was through. "Why didn't you tell me this before?"

"I thought it was best not to," I said. "It's done, and in a way, it turned out real good for me. I never had so much room to live in before, Paw's place was always overrunnin' with menfolks. Now I've met you, and I've learned to read and write some, and I get to see Ansalu now and again." I smiled at him. "Don't feel sorry for me, doctor, I'll make do."

Then I commenced makin' supper, and I pretended to be too busy to do much talkin'. Odd came home in a bit, lookin' real tuckered out and hungry, and was glad I had a good supper ready for him.

Whilst we were eatin', the doctor told Odd that he'd be mighty glad if Odd would talk to some people for him in Wilson's Springs the next day.

"I'll need someone with a car to come up and get me, and then I'll need help gettin' out to the car they send." He went on. "You see, Odd, I promised to take over Old Doctor Brown's practice, and people will begin thinkin' I'm never comin'. There's a house and office waitin' for me, and I need to get back to bein' a doctor again."

Odd's face kept changin' all the time the doctor was talkin'. It was somethin' like a sunrise, you know, a little smile started down low, and then it grew and grew til it was spread all over his face. It was easy to see that what the doctor was sayin' pleasured him a lot. Though, to do him fair, Odd had never complained about the doctor stayin' there to get well. That is, ceptin' that time he caught us usin' his Bible. But I reckon we had that one comin'.

Anyways, I got plum caught up in watchin' Odd. He started lookin', oh, I don't know, easier in the way he moved. You know, like he could let himself relax and not have to be on his guard all the time.

So, the next day, when Odd left for Wilson's Springs, he had a bunch of errands to do for the doctor. When he first came, the doctor had asked Odd not to tell anyone he was here or about the accident or anythin'. I had the feelin' that he wasn't sure in his mind that he really wanted to go to Wilson's Springs. Now, though, it seemed like he was right eager to go.

I was terrible sad, but I tried not to show it.

I kept as busy workin' around the cabin as I could, listenin' to the doctor talk and make plans. It wasn't even like he was really talkin' to me. He was just sort of thinkin' out loud.

"I'll have to explain to the Insurance company why I didn't let them know about the accident before this," he said, sort of talkin' to himself. "And I'll need to get a cane so I can get around til my ankle finishes mending." He went on and on, and I got the feelin' he was just tryin' to fill in the space til it was time for him to go.

Finally, he stopped talkin' and called me over to where he was sittin' in that hickory chair.

"November Sunshine," he said real solemn, "I don't know how I can ever thank you for comin' into my life; that caught me by suprise, but he just went on. "You've given me somethin' special, somethin' rare."

Nobody had ever talked like that to me before, and it made me feel sorta light and airy, I guess I liked hearin' nice things about myself, but still, I didn't feel like I really earned 'em.

"I'd almost forgotten what a truly good person is like," he said, smilin' at me. "But you nursed me back to health, both my body and my mind, November. And I've learned a lot from you."

I just stood there tryin' not to fidget; I was that moved.

Then noise outside put and end to his talkin'. In just a bit, Odd came in. I didn't know whether I was pleased or sad that he came in just then. But he did, anyway. And two other men came in right after him.

Junior Washbon! I never gave it a thought that when he went to get someone with an automobile to fetch the doctor, he might ask Junior Washbon. But it made sense, bein's Odd worked with him and all. Anyway, there he stood. I was worried about what he might say, but he was just as polite and quiet as you please.

I was grateful for that. As long as he didn't talk to me, I figgered I could just go about doin' little chores in the cabin and pretend he wasn't there.

Almost before I knew it, Junior Washbon was gone, taking the doctor with him. It was kind of hard to accept the doctor bein' gone.

Gone out of my life.

The doctor was gone out of my life. I had to say it a couple of times to myself to make it seem real.

All I had left of him was the last thing he said on his way out the door.

He took my hand in his and bent low so nobody else could hear. Then he said, "If you ever need a friend, November, you can count on me."

I thought about that and I thought about it a lot. I couldn't imagine ever havin' to call on the doctor for help, but I got the idea he was tryin' to tell me he meant to always be a friend. I felt read sad after he went, but then I got to rememberin' all he taught me about readin' and writin' and such.

And I was at rest inside.

It was time for him to move on.

An then...well, did you ever notice how when somethin' important happens to you, often somethin' else happens, too? It was like that for me. The very next day, just before Odd came back to the cabin from Wilson's Springs, Caleb came to the cabin, lookin' excited.

"Come in and set," I said to him when I saw him standin' in the doorway. "What's on your mind, Caleb?"

He didn't even wait to sit before he grabbed my hands and sort of danced me around the room.

"Guess what, November?" he said, "Paw's new woman up and left him, and he says I should come and fetch you back home to stay," he said, smilin' like he was givin' me the sun and the moon.

"To stay?" I asked, makin' time to figure this thing out.

"That's right," he said, comin' to rest on a chair where he sat like a young'un who's waitin' for a treat "Wasn't easy for Paw, but he finally lowed that he'd just as soon's have you workin' round the cabin as try to find him another woman."

I was caught by surprise and didn't expect the sinkin' feelin' that washed over me. I looked around Odd's cabin and thought about havin' made it my home, too. I just didn't know what to think, but Odd saved me worryin' it out by comin' in just then.

"What you doin' here, Caleb?" he asked, not soundin' unkindly. "Ain't seen you in a long time."

Caleb looked a bit uncomfortable at first, then he pulled himself up and said, "Paw wants November Sunshine back now, Odd."

Odd stopped, shocked still, and just looked at me and then looked at Caleb. He didn't say anythin', just dropped his gunnysack in the corner and went on outside. We could hear the sounds of him washin' up at the well, and then he came back in, shakin' drops of water offen his face and hands.

"Man sure gets dusty when he's workin' with wood," he said as though Caleb hadn't said anythin' about Paw wantin' me back. "Feels powerful good to let that cold water splash the dust outen your eyes," he said, lookin' round the cabin. I felt his eyes linger on the bed where the doctor'd been stayin'. I'd washed the bedcovers and spread 'em on the bed, all fresh-smellin' and clean.

"Food ready, November?" he asked then, still not touchin' on what Caled had said.

Caleb looked at me and shrugged his shoulders like he was askin' a question.

"Supper's all ready, Odd," I said. "You stayin'?" I asked Caleb.

"He's here, ain't he?" Odd said. "Can't send him back with and empty belly when he's goin' home empty-handed."

"But..." Caleb began.

171

"But nothin'," Odd said, patient like he was talkin' to a little tad "Your Paw and me made a deal way back, and I aim for him to keep it."

Then he looked at me as if to see what I might say.

"You see any reason why you should go back with Caleb?" he asked me.

I could tell from the look in Odd's eyes that he wasn't rightly sure what I'd say, but some kind of pride made him ask.

At first, I didn't know what to answer. I looked at Caleb with his face beamin' cause he thought I was comin' back with him. Then I looked at Odd, and I thought about how nice and quiet it was for me here and how I could get to see Ansalu and cook what I wanted and all such.

"I reckon I'm stayin'," I said then, turnin' to the stove so not to have to see either of their faces.

Supper was quiet, and when it was over, Odd filled one of the lanterns and lighted it. "Here, you'll be needin' this to get back home, I reckon I'll be by some day to pick it up." and he handed the lantern to Caleb, makin' it clear that it was time for Caleb to be on his way.

After Caleb'd gone, Odd went outside to fetch in some more wood. I stood alone in the familiar quiet of and empty cabin. I thought back over all that had happened since I first came here. I thought about how dissapointin' I must say be to Odd in some ways and what I'd heard about him goin' to see the Widder Morton. I hadn't got that all straightened out in my mind yet, but I was lookin' to pretty soon, even though thinkin' about it was bothersome. And I thought about what I'd learned in this ol' cabin. Seemed I'd learned more in the time I'd been here than I had my whole life with Paw. I thought about the readin' and the writin' and all the things I'd learned how to

172

cook. And I was beginnin' to learn about people, too. What made 'em do the things they did and such? And I found I had a proud feelin' now that I'd never had when I was back at Paw's.

I didn't quite understand all that I was thinkin' and feelin'. Most of it was still new to me. But one thing I did know was that if I had gone with Caleb, that new part of me would've stopped growin'. It would have been like makin' my life go backwards.

BROTHER GLEN

I went over to Ansalu's the next day. I didn't know how much I was goin' to try and tell her about what'd been happenin' to me and the way I was feelin'. I knew, though, that just bein' with her for a while would help me see things more clear.

"Glad to see you, November!" she welcomed me. "I was hopin' you'd come by so we could make plans for goin' to the revival."

The revival. It seemed like a long time ago that we talked about goin' to the revival, yet I knew it was only that my mind and feelin's had been so tangled. I began to feel better already. Here was somethin' new I could take in for myself.

We sat down together over a cup of fresh-brewed tea and started makin' our plans. I felt myself gettin' more and more excited as Ansalu told me about what to expect at the revival.

"I'd like to go the very first night, November," she said. "I think a body needs to be in on a revival from the very first if you're goin' to get the feel of it." She smiled. "After we go to the first one, we can decide about the others."

We planned that we'd both come back up to Ansalu's after the first revival service. It'd be too late for me to go home alone.

"I don't think there's anybody here in the hills who would want to hurt you, November, but then there's no sense in invitin' trouble, neither," she finished. All I had to do was get Odd to let me be away from the cabin overnight.

"Ask about stayin' more than one night, November, in case we want to go to all the services."

Later, when I was back at Odd's cabin, and I asked him 'bout stayin' over at Ansalu's; he looked kind of funny at first.

174

"Will you be comin' back?" he asked me, not lookin' me in the face.

"Sure," I told him. "I'll come back over early in the mornin' and fix your breakfast and somethin' for you to eat the rest of the day. He looked some better; I almost thought he looked relieved.

I asked him, then, if he wouldn't like to come along with us. He just shook his head and said he figured religion was women's business. Men had better things to do.

So early the next day, I made up enough food for Odd to eat for breakfast and for when he came home at the end of the day. Then I put on my green dress and started off for Ansalu's. I took along some of the extra bakin' I'd done. I knew we'd need to carry food for our evenin' meal and somethin' to eat when we started home afterwards. Somewhere, I got the idea that revivalin' got a body good and hungry, and it didn't seem like I should expect Ansalu to do all the feedin' of us.

So, I'd made up wheat bread and corn fritters for Odd and and extra for me to take along. I couldn't help hummin' to myself as I hurried along through the woods. Some days are like that. All the things that've been worryin' you seem to settle down inside and not be so bothersome. and then it's as if you don't sing or whistle or do somethin' to let off steam, you'll swell right up and bust with all the good feelin's you've got for a change.

Anyhow, I got to Ansalu's and we fixed the food we wanted to take. We each snitched and apple fritter "to tide us over," she said. Then she put oil in her lantern, and we finally got started. By then, the shadows were gathering in,' and it was comin' on towards evenin'.

When we got down to the valley, I asked, "Where do you s'pose the revival's to be?"

175

Ansalu shrugged her shoulders and pointed out that most people seemed to be walkin' in the same direction.

"My guess is that all we have to do is follow 'em," she said. And we did.

Sure enough, we walked a pretty good piece, with more people joinin' in as we went along. Pretty soon, we came to a big open field.

It wasn't empty anymore, but it had been. Now, in the middle of the field was a tent the like of which I'd never seen. It looked like you could put Odd's cabin and Ansalu's cabin both inside it, and there'd still be room for one or two more. It was that big. People of all kinds and shapes were pourin' into the openin' in the tent just as fast as they could get in. Ansalu took me by the hand and sort of hurried me along.

"Is this it?" I asked Ansalu. She pointed to a sign I hadn't noticed. It was propped against the side of the tent.

"Brother Glen Crabtree Brings the Word of God to Wilson's Springs!" I read out loud. I was amazed that every word had a capital letter, but I didn't have time to ask about it because Ansalu was tuggin' at my arm.

"My!" I stopped dead in my tracks. "I'd never seen so many people all together at one time!"

"C'mon, November," Ansalu whispered, "You're holdin' folks up."

Then I looked around and sure enough, when I had stopped to look around, a whole lot of folks had come to a halt behind me. I was embarrassed and hurried after Ansalu as fast as I could, hopin' folks wouldn't know I'd never been to such a thing as this before.

Ansalu went first and tugged me into a row of seats. I sat down in a hurry, wonderin' which way to look first to see all there was to see.

Wooden chairs stood in rows all the way around the tent. There must've been hundreds and hundreds of those chairs. All alike.

"Look at all the chairs!" I whispered, "They match!"

"Course they do, November," Ansalu said.

"Where'd they get so many matchin' chairs?" I asked in a whisper.

She didn't answer me, just pointed to the back of the chair in front of me.

"Williams Family Funeral Parlor," I read out. "We tuck you in for all eternity," I finished readin' the words painted on the back of the chair. Then I looked along the row, and sure enough, all the chairs had the same words painted on their backs. I leaned over the shoulder of a big, fat woman in front of me to see if the chairs in their row had the same words on their backs. They did.

"Must be a powerful, rich funeral parlor," I whispered to Ansalu. "It would sure cost a lot of money to own so many chairs."

"Oh, November!" and Ansalu looked at me with a twinkle in her eyes. "If that doesn't beat all. You know, child, all these chairs don't come from the very same place. Every funeral parlor and church around has extra chairs they lend out for special events. Like family reunions and revivals, and such."

"Oh," I said, feelin' a little foolish that I hadn't figured that out myself. But then I thought, no need to feel foolish. Even

Ansalu didn't know that until somebody told her for the first time.

I felt better.

Ansalu was sittin' in her chair lookin' around with the happiest smile on her face. I was glad we'd come.

Some of the people who were sittin' in the wooden chairs waitin' for the revival to start were busy chewin' on sandwiches or chicken legs or somethin' else they'd brought along. Seein' their food began makin' a hollow feelin' in my own stomach, and I nudged Ansalu.

"Can we eat somethin' now?" I asked her.

She smiled and said, "Sure," and reached for the package she'd tucked under her chair. My mouth watered when I thought of the wheat bread she'd spread thick with butter. Together, we had sliced up some cold ham she had fixed and made sandwiches big enough for a real hungry eater.

Which I was.

With one of those sandwiches in my hand, I had more time to look around as I ate. I figgered that was just fine. It was wonderful, sittin' there eatin' such a good sandwich and havin' all those different things to look at. I was taken with all the different kinds of people who were crowdin' into the tent. Some of them looked like me and Ansalu - hill folk. Not that we're all that different lookin' from everybody else, but our clothes weren't as citified. Most of the people from the hills wore their poor clothes with pride. You could tell time had been spent in mendin' and washin' and fixin' them to look as good as possible. And they all looked right enough. But the people from the town had a more store-bought look to 'em. Like one little girl came sort of dancin' in with a light purple dress that had a big ruffled skirt. Her mother had tied a big purple ribbon in her hair, and there was a matchin' purple ribbon around her waist. I thought she was just about the prettiest little girl there could ever be. Her mother finally pulled her into a seat on the other side of the tent, and I couldn't watch her anymore.

An the middle of the tent! It was all fixed up with a big platform that someone had built. The platform was round and didn't have anythin' on it except for one big chair all covered in red velvet that looked like a king's seat I had seen a picture of in a book. There was a tall, skinny table with a slanted top, too. I wondered what it was there for.

"What's that, Ansalu?" I whispered, pointin'.

Ansalu said, "That's where the preacher will preach from, November." It looked kind of rickety to me, but I decided to wait and see how he made out with it.

The light in the tent came from hangin' lanterns. Everywhere you looked was a lantern hangin' on a rope from the top of the tent. They looked kind of pretty all hangin' down and givin' off a soft glow like they did.

But over near the platform was somethin' I'd never seen before. It looked somethin' like a picture I'd seen once of a piano, but different.

"What's that, Ansalu?" I whispered.

"Goodness, November. I forgot how little you've had to do with the world," she said. "That's a revival organ, girl. It's made so that when the revival's all over, it can be folded up and carried to the next place it's needed."

"Will somebody play it?" I asked, strainin' to see over the fat lady's shoulder.

"You bet, November," Ansalu said. "You'll hear music like you never heard before,"

"How does it work?" I asked, wantin' to know all about everythin'.

"Well, November, the organist - that's the person who plays the organ," she explained, "plays those keys with her hands to make the notes sound out. And she pumps those two pedals down there with her feet," she said, pointin', "to make the air for it to sound. She moves those levers on each side with her knees. They make it loud or soft."

I was really puzzled. How could anyone make her hands and, feet, and knees do all those things at the same time? It seemed a wonder to me, and I sat on the edge of my chair, wattin' for somebody to come to the organ and play it.

"How does the player know what to play?" I asked.

"Oh, most revival players know lots of music by heart, November. But sometimes they bring along books of music so that they can play almost any song the preacher asks for."

I figured that even if I didn't like Brother Glen Crabtree, I was sure glad I'd come along to hear somebody play that organ.

There were a couple of other questions I wanted to ask Ansalu, but then I got to thinkin' she might be sorry she brought me if I kept askin' her questions all the time. I looked at her outa the corner of my eyes to see how she was lookin'. She looked pleased to be there, so I decided I'd chance askin' another question. But b'fore I got to ask it, everybody stopped talkin', just like that! It got real quiet, and everybody seemed to lean forward like they were expectin' something excitin'. And then a tall, thin woman dressed in a long, dark robe of some kind walked down the aisle just like the proudest woman you ever saw! She didn't look around; just walked slowly and straight to the organ and, pulled out the little bench, and sat down. I held my breath and waited. She sat there real still for a moment, and then she commenced pumpin' the pedals on the organ. You could just see the tips of her shoes goin' up and down; the robe hid the rest of her legs. And then, b'fore I was ready for it, she was playin' all over that thing! Her hands moved up, and they moved down, and her elbows moved in and out, makin' it louder or softer. And out of that little box of an organ came the biggest, most wonderful sounds I'd ever heard!

I can still remember how prickly all the excitement made the back of my neck feel.

I sat on the edge of my seat, hardly darin' to breathe whilst she played and played. I could hear some of the folks around me sort of hummin' along with her music, and the whole tent seemed to be full of the sounds she was bringin' out of that organ.

Ansalu, next to me, was as caught up in the music as I was. We sat there, hardly breathin', til the music ended. Everybody started clappin', and I clapped my hands together as hard as I could and turned to Ansalu. "Will there be any more?" I asked.

"You ain't heard nothin' yet!" Ansalu answered, and I thought I had never been so happy.

The organist played some more songs. All the time, the people in the tent were gettin' more and more caught up in the music, and some of 'em began clappin' softly in time with what she was playin'. Then she let the music fade away.

And a hush fell over the crowd. Everythin' was as still as still. I started to ask Ansalu what was happenin', but she shushed me and pointed towards the openin' in the tent where we'd all come in.

Everybody was sittin' with their eyes glued to that openin'. Quiet. You could feel their excitement bollin' under the surface as they watched.

What were they waitin' for, I wondered. I could hardly sit still; I was so excited.

And then and angel came down from the heavens and floated into that tent!

His arms were stretched wide open as though he wanted to hug everybody in the tent at the same time. His shinin' face was so full of his smile that I didn't notice hardly anythin' else. I could almost feel the power he gave off as he came slowly down the aisle, movin' his head from side to side so that everyone who saw him had to feel that he saw them too, personal.

He was dressed all in white, every bit. His suit was white, and his shirt and tie were white, too. Even the shoes were white! And his hair was like a crown. It was snow white and long and full. It sort've flowed down over his shoulders, glowin' in the light.

"Isn't he beautiful?" I heard the fat lady whisper to someone; I wanted to cry out, "Yes! Oh yes!"

I held my breath until the angel reached the platform. With a graceful movement, he stepped up and moved to the center. Then he turned around real slow so that he could see everyone, and everyone could see him.

"Is that God?" I whispered to Ansalu.

She turned a shocked face to me and said, real low, "Of course not! That's Brother Glen Crabtree."

Then Brother Crabtree raised his arms towards the top of the tent and bent his head way back so he was facin' heaven and cried out in a voice that brought goosebumps to my whole body, "Lord, help me reach the unbelievers with the truth of your word!"

Then he dropped his arms and lowered his head so he was lookin' down at the floor. He stood so quiet you couldn't even see him breathe. The tent was hushed, and even the lady at the organ seemed to be waitin' for and answer from God. She sat there with her eyes glued tight to his face, scarce movin'.

In the stillness, I could hear Brother Glen Crabtree sigh. It was a sigh like no sigh I ever heard. It started down at the tips of his sparklin' white shoes and dredged up through that entire shinin' body 'til you knew God would have to have a mighty hard heart not to give Brother Crabtree whatever he wished for.

An bit by bit, he started talkin'. Real soft and easy at first. But his words began to build up steam and get stronger and stronger. He talked about the Bible, and he opened the book that was lyin' on top of that lecture stand and read some from it and began walkin' around the platform, raisin' the Bible into the air and callin' on people to pay heed to the word of the Lord. And he got more and more worked up, and the crowd got more and more worked up right with him. Then he started thumpin' on that lecture stand and callin' to the crowd to stop their sinnin' ways and give theirselves to God.

"You cain't wait until tomorrow!" he shouted in a terrible voice.

"Tomorrow may not come!"

That scared me, and I could hear people sobbin' in the crowd and moanin' and movin' around real restless.

All of a sudden, a man jumped up from his seat and hollered, "I can't stand it no morel. I got to be forgiven for my sins!"

and went runnin' down the aisle as fast as his legs would carry him. Two men dressed in robes like the organ player stepped out to grab the man. They hugged him, and he hugged 'em back, and all the time, Brother Crabtree was callin' out.

"Look at that, folks, just look at that! Do you see the joy the Lord has brought that man? Do you see how happy askin' the Lord for forgiveness has made him? And do you see how happy It has made me?" he cried, turnin' so everybody could see his beamin' face. "An if it made ME that happy, can you dare guess how happy it made GOD!" he shouted out so loud the tent seemed to shake as people all over the tent yelled back, "Amen, Brother, Amen!"

Well, I was beginnin' to feel all wrung out, and I began to notice then that the organ player was playin' music while Brother Crabtree walked around and preached. It was the kind of music that it's hard to sit still to, and Brother Crabtree kept callin', "Now, the time is now! Come give yourself to God! Come get God's forgiveness for yourself! Don't wait, tomorrow may be too late!"

An listenin' to Brother Crabtree and that music just got more and more people cryin' and flingin' themselves into the aisle to push their way down to the platform where those two men would hug 'em and hug 'em and then everybody else down there would hug 'em and cry over 'em and yell "Praise the Lord!"

The tent seemed full to overflowin' with happy cryin' people, and every time another person went stumblin' down the aisle, it seemed to make Brother Crabtree happier and happier. It was easy to see why people wanted to make Brother Crabtree happy. He just beamed at each one and shouted, "Praise the Lord!" louder and louder. It was like they had given him a really special present. And the organ player kept pumpin' away at that ol' organ faster and faster, and before I knew what was happenin, I found myself hurryin' down that aisle.

184

I couldn't stop myself, and I couldn't even think about what I was doin'. I just knew that I had to go down that aisle and make Brother Crabteee happy and make God happy and do whatever it was they expected me to do.

An sure enough. Those two men hugged me, and a cryin' woman grabbed me to him and hugged me, moanin', "Praise God you're saved!" Then other people crowded in to hug me, and I found myself huggin' them back and sobbin' and happy and hurtin' at the same time.

I don't know how long that all lasted. I was so caught up in feelin's that I had no idea of time. But after awhile, Brother Crabtree asked us all to kneel with him, and he prayed over us for a long time. Then he got us all back on our feet and he told the crowd how blessed we were and didn't they wish they could be blessed, too? It was real quiet and hushed while Brother Crabtree walked up and stood in the middle of the platform, just lookin' at all the people, llike his heart was in all that he was sayin'. He started talkin' so quiet you had to almost stop breathin' to hear him. Everybody leaned forward in their chairs to listen.

"Go home now, brothers and sisters. Go home with your families and give thanks for what you've seen tonight. Think about it. Pray about it. Consider your own life. And when you come back tomorrow night, be ready to face your God!"

It took a while 'til everyone sort of shook himself out of the spell Brother Crabtree had made and got to movin' and talkin'. I found myself standin' right next to Brother Crabtree with people pushin' in to shake his hand and touch him. He was lookin' right at me, and I felt almost like he could see clean through me. I felt like I was caught in the power of his eyes as they looked at me real close.

"Do you give yourself to the Lord, daughter?" he asked me, his voice real gentle and carin'. "Do you truly give yourself to the Lord?"

I wasn't sure just what he meant, so I just whispered, "I think so."

He looked at me real sharp and his face changed a bit as he bent down real close. "How old are you, sister?" he asked.

I told him I was goin' for fifteen. I thought it sounded better that way than to say I was just past thirteen. He smiled and patted my head.

"I want to see you alone for a few minutes as soon as I can get away from this crowd," he said. "You've made an important decision this evenin', and I want to be sure you know what it's all about." Then he went off to talk to other folks who were waitin' to see him.

I just stood there feelin' strange and kind of like I was floatin'. He wanted to see me special! Then, someone touched my arm.

I looked around real quick, thinkin' it was Ansalu, but I couldn't see her anywhere in the crowd. But one of those men in the robes was standin' there, and I knew he was the one who touched me.

"Follow me," he said.

So I did. I figgered it was all part of my goin' down front in the revival meetin' and I had to do it. He took me out the back way and over to a great big truck thing on wheels.

"What's this?" I asked him.

"That's Brother Crabtree's Gospel Caravan," he told me. "Brother Crabtree always has it taken to any place where he's leadin' a revival. It gives him a place to be private and restore

186

hismelf," he told me. Then he went on in a sort of secret kind of voice, "You know, it takes an awful lot out of Brother Crabtree to preach the way he does." He stopped a bit and got a real serious look on his face. "Brother Crabtree is the most Godlike man I've ever met. He sure is." and then he turned and walked away, leavin' me to wait outside Brother Crabtree's Gospel Caravan.

I waited there, feelin' guilty about leavin' Ansalu, but somethin' inside me made me stay. I just had to wait for Brother Crabtree.

When Brother Crabtree came, he motioned for me to come inside his caravan with him. Oh, what a sight! It was all fixed up, soft and pretty with mirrors and lights and soft seats and a great big fluffy-lookin' bed. I'd never seen anythin' like it, and I guess I stood there with my mouth open like a ninny, tryin' to take it all in.

Brother Crabtree pointed towards one of those wonderful soft chairs. I sat down on the edge, afraid I'd spoil somethin'.

"Tell me about yourself," he said

"Well, I can't really take much time because Ansalu, she's my friend, don't know where I am, and she'll worry."

"Oh, of course," Brother Crabtree said, rubbin' his chin like he was thinkin'. "Are you comin' tomorrow night, child?" he asked me.

"I'd sure like to," I told him. "But I don't know what Ansalu plans."

He just looked at me for a bit. Then he said, "It doesn't matter what Ansalu plans, child. This is more important than Ansalu or anybody. I have a feelin' that God wants you to be here.

187

God NEEDS you to be here," he said, lookin' at me in such a way I could just feel those eyes burnin' into me.

God needed me to be at Brother Glen Crabtree's revival.

God needed me, November Sunshine, there.

I had to come.

LOVIN ARMS

"Where've you been, November?" Ansalu said, soundin' peeved at me for the first time since I'd known her. I hurried across the lot to where she stood with a few folks who'd been to the revival. When I got up closer to her, though, I could see worry on her face, and I knew she was more worried than mad.

"....and I just had to go!" I finished tellin' her about Brother Crabtree's askin' me to come see him after the revival service.

"Well," she said, still not quite done with her worry, "I sure wish you'd told me where you were goin'."

"I didn't know," I said, wishin' I could tell her how I just knew I had to go. "When Brother Crabtree sent for me, it was like... it was like I just couldn't say no, I just had to go."

Ansalu gave me a strange look like she was lookin' for answers on my face. The whole thing was new to me and had left me with a troubled feelin' somewhere inside.

"He wants to see me again tomorrow night after the service, Ansalu," I told her. "I told him I had to check with you, but he said that God intended for me to be here. I looked at her as we started walkin' towards the path up the mountain. She hadn't said much, and I wasn't at all sure of her feelin's. By now, I'd grown quite a bit taller'n Ansalu on the outside, but inside, I sure did need to know what she was thinkin'. "Will you come with me tomorrow night?" I asked her.

She thought about it, and we walked quite a piece without talkin'. Finally, she sighed and asked, "Can you get away from Odd again?"

"Oh yes, I'm sure I can. As long as I get all my chores finished and leave him somethin' to eat." We walked along quiet for a few minutes, Ansalu thinkin' and me waitin'. "That's about all he wants me for, Ansalu. I clean his cabin and keep him fed, and he doesn't.... bother me none."

She sighed again and looked at me out of the corner of her eyes. "You know, November, there've been lots of changes in your life since we got to be friends. It's been about two years now, hasn't it?" I nodded. "An sometimes I get the feelin' that you're movin' a mite too fast."

What she said made me feel uneasy. I wasn't sure what she meant.

"Hold up, November, I've got some things that need to be said and made clear between us," Ansalu said, sittin' down on an old tree stump by the path. To get her breath. I felt kinda bad because it came to me that we'd been walkin' pretty fast. It hadn't seemed so fast to me cause my legs are long and move easy. But Ansalu, bein' so short, had to move her legs a lot more'n I did.

I waited til she was ready to tell me what was on her mind.

"November, when I first met you in the woods, you weren't much more 'n a little girl. True," she said, tryin' to be fair, "you were different from most girls because of losin' your Maw and the way you were raised. But anyway, what I'm sayin' is that you sure were innocent of the ways of the world."

I had to shake my head and smile in agreement. Thinkin' back to when Ansalu came on me that day in the woods by the pond, I felt like it had been a long, long time ago.

"An then you went to live with Odd and had to keep his cabin and look after him and learn woman-stuff all at once. And you did right well," she said, smilin' at me in a way that let me know she was proud of me. "But, even though you were learnin' some things, November, you weren't learnin' much

190

about other people. You came across Junior Washbon and the doctor, and that's about all." I got a twinge inside when she mentioned Junior Washbon, but I tried not to let it show on my face. "So," she went on, "even though your body's set itself to fillin' out and your mind has spread out with readin' and writin' and thinkin', still there's a whole world of things you don't know 'bout people and how they act."

I was puzzled. "What're you sayin', Ansalu?"

"Well, it's kind of hard to find the right words for what's in my mind."

"But you got a way of takin' people just the way you sees them, November. and that's all right for some," she hurried to say lest she hurt my feelin's. "But you've got to learn not to be so... so... trustin', November."

"What do you mean, Ansalu?"

"Just that. You've got to start lookin' behind people's faces and seein' what's really in their hearts. Sometimes people aren't what they pass themselves off to be."

I had the feelin' that Ansalu was tellin' me somethin' she'd learned for herself on her way through life. I wondered what had happened to teach her that lesson. But right now, I was concerned with Brother Glen Crabtree. Was she tellin' me somethin' about him I didn't know? "I dearly want to go to revival again tomorrow night, Ansalu," I said. "Won't you go with me?"

She looked around at the tree shadows in the lantern light and fussed around, standin' up and pickin' up the lantern. I had a feelin' that she didn't want to answer me right off.

We started up the path again, but she still hadn't answered me.

"Ansalu," I asked, talkin' loud enough for her to hear me as we walked single file where the path narrowed. I felt sort of put off by what Ansalu'd been sayin' and decided not to wait for her answer about comin' the next night. "Somethin' puzzles me. Who's God?"

Ansalu stopped dead in her tracks, and I almost knocked her down. "Law, child, if you keep askin' questions like that, we'll NEVER get home! That kind of question is enough to make me lose my way for sure!" We walked some more, and she spoke over her shoulder. "God is mighty hard to explain, November. I'd 'preciate it if you'd hold that question til we get to my cabin so I can gather my wits about me when I answer it."

I told her, sure, I'd wait. We walked on just bein' quiet, not tryin' to talk anymore. I thought about Brother Glen Crabtree. I thought about him a lot.

It wasn't long until we could see Ansalu's cabin through the trees. We were inside, and Ansalu had the fire poked up and the kettle on before you could say leather britches.

When we had our cold cornbread and some hot tea all set out, we sat down across from each other at the table. I took a big bite of the cornbread because I was real hungry, and I knew we were goin' to do some pretty heavy talkin'.

"Now, about God, November," Ansalu said. "It's awful hard to tell you what God is and what He isn't."

"Why?"

"Well, lots of people have different ideas about Him." She fidgeted a bit like she was bothered some and burst out, "Darn your paw! He should've told you all this a long time ago."

"Never mind Paw," I said. "Just tell me what you think about God. Whatever you think will be good enough for me."

"Well, all right," she agreed. "It never pleasured me none to think that God was some kind of tinker or carpenter who just hung around waitin' for somebody to need his help. Sort of a heavenly handyman. That idea of God seemed kind of puny to me. But livin' here in the mountains like I do, I just looked around me real good and thought about what I saw. It finally came to me that, of course, there HAS to be a God somewhere. I mean, November, when you think that a chicken always hatches out of a chicken egg, and oak trees always have oak leaves, and things like animals and plants and people always give birth to the same kind that they are, it really boggles the mind. And I looked, and I thought, and I looked, and I thought. Then it came to me that no man or woman could make one single star, let alone the whole mess of 'em that fills the sky at night. And no man or woman could make the sun or the moon or the wind or the rain, nor day and night, neither. It just stands to reason that there has to be somethin' out there that's bigger and greater and smarter and more everythin' else than we are!"

I listened with pure pleasure to Ansalu's idea. They made me feel like I was reachin' out and touchin' the sky. It was just real recent that I'd come to do any serious thinkin', and I loved gettin' a hold of an idea I could wrestle with. You know, it's like findin' some meat still left on the bone in your soup.

"Anyways," Ansalu said then, "I figured I'd rather make the mistake of believin' in a God who just might not be real than to miss out by not believin' in a God who is ."

I had to laugh a bit when she said that. "Sounds like you sure know how to figure things out in a good way, Ansalu," I told her. "I hope I can learn to reason things out like you do. There's so much I still don't know."

Ansalu looked at me as though she was makin' up her mind about somethin'. Then she sighed again, I'd learned she always sighed when she was considerin' somethin' important. Anyways, she sighed and asked, "You really want to go to that revival tomorrow night?"

I caught my breath, "Oh yes, Ansalu, I really do."

She looked like she wasn't really likin' what she was about to say, but she was goin' to say it anyway. "All right, November, I'll go with you to the revival tomorrow night. I guess one more revival service won't do any harm."

First light, I got up and hurried over to Odd's cabin. I got busy fixin' a good breakfast and a big pot of coffee. I was so full of the revival I couldn't stand it, and I wanted to tell Odd all about how it was. But when I tried to tell him about it and that I wanted to go again, he just sort of grunted and went outside. He came back in a few minutes carryin' wood as though that's why he went. But he didn't fool me any. I knew he had wanted to think somethin' through.

"November," he said, standin' there with his arms full of wood, "I gotta speak my mind." Then he dropped the wood on the pile by the stove and turned back to me. "When I said it was all right for you to be seein' Ansalu, I didn't 'spect that she'd be fillin' your head with religion and that kind've things. What I mean is, I know I'm goin' to be spendin' more and more time down to Wilson's Springs workin' for Mr. Washbon. It took me a long while to see that someone young as you needs comp'ny. Woman comp'ny. Anyways, it's true what I said, Ansalu Williams is teachin' you good how to run a place and cook." He paused a bit and ran his hand through his hair like he was havin' a hard time sayin' what he wanted to say. Odd didn't give himself much to talkin', and I knew he had done a lot of thinkin' about what he was sayin'.

"Dang It all, November, I just didn't mean for you to go runnin' off with Ansalu all the time and learn citified ways!" His face was all screwed up as he tried to get out the right words. "I feared you're learnin' to want things that just ain't right for hill folks to want! November, you got to remember your place!"

I felt like the floor was fallin' away under me. How could I ever get Odd to see that goin' to the revival again was the most important thing in the world to me? I felt a little strange rememberin' that Ansalu hadn't really wanted to go to the revival again and that I'd had to talk her into it.

But I knew the revival was goin' to be held again, and I planned to be there.

I just had to be.

I looked at Odd and saw how stiff and awkward he was holdin' himself. I wondered if I could ever get him to see how important goin' was to me.

Then I just started talkin'. "Odd, it's really me that wants to go to the revival, not Ansalu. I just never seen nothin' like it and I'd really like to see it again. There's lots and lots of people and music and singin'..." I watched his face to see what he was thinkin'. He didn't say anythin', but he wasn't sayin' no, either. "It's like nothin' I've ever seen before, and it don't cost nothin', Odd, it's free!" I tried one more idea. "Odd, maybe you could just stay in Webster Springs after you're through workin' and go with Ansalu and me tonight!"

He looked at me, and for just a minute, I thought he might do it. Then he shook his head. "No, tain't fitten for me to go, November, but if it means that much to you, I guess it won't hurt. Not just this once."

I was so pleased to go; I promised I'd work twice as hard to get everythin' done around the cabin. And I did! It was so excitin' to think of goin' to the revival again that I hummed to myself while I worked.

I was on pins and needles til it was finally time to go, and I got started for Ansalu's cabin. "You ready?" I called out soon as her cabin came in sight.

"Sure am," she said, smilin' at me as I hurried into the clearin' where her cabin stood.

This time, our trip to Wilson's Springs seemed even shorter because I had so many things to go over in my head.

Even though we got to the revival tent early, people were already pilin' in, so we hurried to find ourselves good seats.

An just like the night before, the organ player came in and pumped the organ a bit and then began playin'. Ansalu had told me that the fancy way she played so many notes all up and down the keyboard was called revival playin'.

It sure revived me! and all around, folks were sittin' on the edge of their seats.

Then, just when everybody seemed about to bust wide open with excitement, there came Brother Glen Crabtreel. He came down the aisle a holdin' out his hands and lookin' like some sweet angel welcomin' us all back.

He talked, and he preached, and he whomped the lecture stand, and he waved his Bible in the air. And then, before anyone started comin' forward, he motioned his hands, and seven or eight men with big wooden bowls came down to the platform.

"It pains me to mention this," Brother Crabtree said, soundin' sad, "but. I have to ask you to dip into your love of God and help me pay our expenses in comin' here to Webster Springs. I always hate to mention money when we are dealin' on a higher plain, the plain of love, God's love! But it has to be, it has to be," he said, lettin' 'is voice trail off into a whisper and bowin' his head. Everybody was strainin' to hear him and he stood there with 'is head down, lookin' sad. He looked so sad that you wanted to give him everythin' you had in this world just to make him happy and smilin' again. Oh, how that man pulled at my heartstrings!

Then the men with the bowls started movin' up the aisles, passin' the bowls so that everybody could drop in however much money they had. I saw a little old lady whose clothes looked pretty tattered drop a whole dollar bill. She followed that dollar with her eyes as the bowl went down the row from hand to hand. I think she almost wished she could have gotten it back, 'cept you could tell that she was proud to have given it.

Well, you could hear the sounds of coins bein dropped into the bowls, and soon Brother Crabtree's head snapped up, and he yelled, "Stop!"

He looked around, his eyes givin' off sparks, almost, and raised his hand high over his head. "I think some of you have come here from the devil!" he shouted. "I hear the sound of COINS in our offerin' plates. Is that how you measure the love of God...with COINS?" He glared around the whole tent, not missin' anyone. "Do you think it's possible to do the work of God on just a few pennies? Do you really think so? Of course not! Doin' the work of God takes money, REAL money! Lots of money! You can't bring the Kingdom of God here to earth on nickels and dimes! If you truly want the world to be better, YOU have to PAY for it!"

He was still and serious when he stopped. No one was makin' a sound, even the little children knew better than to fuss and fret just then. All eyes were on that glowin' white figure of

197

Brother Crabtree as he slowly walked around the platform, lookin' for all the world like he'd just come from Heaven.

"Now then," he said softly, pausin' in his walkin', "I'm goin' to do what God does, give you another chancel." He pointed at the crowd, and we waited to see what he meant for us to do. "Now then!" he said again, louder this time. "Hold your hands out in front of you. Turn your palms upward, facin' Heaven! Close your eyes and pray with me that God will lay His blessin' on each and every hand held up to Him. Pray! Pray! Open yourselves to God. Oh, Father, see these hands raised to show you how much they want you to love them and forgive them for their wrongdoin'. Lay your blessin' on each and every hand, Amen." and then he just stood there, quiet.

He walked to the edge of the platform, holdin' his hand up so we could see it, and walked around the platform all the way.

"We have asked for God's blessin' for each one of you here tonight. Some of you have been blessed, and yet some of you may still be outside God's blessin'. If you think, if you hope, that you are one of God's blessed, chosen few, then use that hand that He has blessed and bring out your money to share with Him!"

I looked at Ansalu, worried and shamed. I didn't have but a couple of coins to put in the money bowls. She just smiled at me, real calm, and nodded towards the bowl comin' down my row. Quiet as I could, I laid my nickels on top of some dollar bills so they wouldn't make any noise. Other people must've done the same cause I saw some other coins in the bowl.

But we didn't hear no more coins rattlin' in the bowls after that.

It wasn't long until the men had passed those bowls to every single person in that big tent for the second time. The bowls were heaped up and runnin' over with money. Real, foldin' money! I couldn't imagine so much money. The men took their bowls up to Brother Crabtree, and he looked them over and, raised his hands closed his eyes, and said, "We surely do thank you, God, for helpin' these people to see the light!"

Then the organ player started in again, and someone yelled out, "In the Garden". I'd never heard the songs they were singin' at this revival because I'd never had anythin' to do with churches and such. But I sure did like the way the music made you feel! It was real cheerful and made me feel like I was full of sunshine. People were clappin' fit to beat all and it made me just want to get up and move around.

An after everybody seemed to work himself up by singin' just as hard as he could, Brother Crabtree commenced preachin'.

Well, I never heard anythin' like the way he preached that night. He went up one side of us and down the other. I could almost feel the heat of hell waitin' for me if I didn't do right. I'd never thought much about dyin' and what happens afterwards. But, hearin' Brother Crabtree tell how awful hell is and what'd happen if you went there made my blood run cold. I didn't know what sanctified meant, but when he talked about it, I sure wanted to get myself sanctified if it would keep me out of those awful pits of fire that Brother Crabtree was tellin' about. No way did I want to go there. No way!

So, after the service was over and the women who fainted durin' the preachin' had been revived, I told Ansalu that I meant to go to Brother Crabtree's caravan again.

"What for, November?" she asked me.

"He said he wanted to see me, Ansalu," I said. "And I want to know how to keep from goin' to hell," I told her.

So, she walked me over to Brother Crabtree's caravan, but the way she walked, I knew she didn't like doin' it. She had a funny, upset look on her face.

199

When Brother Crabtree finally came out of the tent, there was a little crowd followin' him. One big pushy-lookin' woman was hangin' onto his arm and talkin' into his face. And he was sort of listenin' to her and listenin' to a man that was talkin' just as fast over on his other side. The rest of the people were just followin' as though they were waitin' for their turns at him.

As he got near the caravan, he saw me, and Ansalu. He smiled real nice and motioned us to go on inside. In just a couple of minutes, he came hurryin' inside and closed the door real tight after him.

"What about all those people?" I asked him.

"I told 'em I was just too tired to talk any more tonight," he said.

"Anyway, they know I'll be preachin' the rest of the week. There'll be time for them later." He turned to me and smiled in a way that would warm you up in the middle of a snowstorm. "I'm glad to see you back, November Sunshine," he said. I was proud he remembered my name.

I introduced him and Ansalu and told him I had a question that really needed answerin'. When he asked me what it was, I asked him how I could get myself sanctified and not have to go to those pits.

Brother Crabtree sneaked a quick look at Ansalu and said, "I think I'm goin' to have to work with you alone, November Sunshine. I'm really pressed for time, you see, there's never enough time to do everythin' that needs done, but your salvation is important to me."

That made me feel like I was sort of special. Nobody had ever cared about my salvation before. In fact, I wasn't all that sure what my salvation was! But if Brother Crabtree was goin' to take time to work with me about it, I surely would do whatever I could to make things go right.

Ansalu commenced coughin' about then in a real fidgety way. She said we'd best start back right away if we were goin' to get home before it got too awful late.

I thought Brother Crabtree looked a mite angry for a bit, but then he smiled real quick, and I figured I'd just imagined it. "I see great things for you, November!" he said.

I like to floated up that mountain, goin' home that night and wasn't the least bit tired. But Ansalu went right to bed. She said she had some powerful thinkin' to do.

Next mornin', while we sat on her porch and drank coffee, Ansalu told me she didn't think as how we should go back to any more of Brother Crabtree's revivals.

I thought at first, she must be jokin' me, and then I saw her face was all set and determined lookin', and I knew she wasn't.

"But why not?" I asked her, wonderin' what she was thinkin' of.

"Because, November, Brother Crabtree gives me the willies."

"The willies? Brother Crabtree?" I couldn't believe what I was hearin'.

Ansalu looked at me with a sort of pityin' expression on her face. "It's hard to explain, November," she said. "I know you'll be disappointed to miss the rest of the revival, but it's a feelin' he gives me inside. I think we'd best stay away."

"Why, Ansalu!" I blurted out, "That's crazy talk! Anybody can see that Brother Crabtree must be one of the best men in God's whole world! Just look how sad he is for all the people who don't know about God and all!" I looked at Ansalu real close, hopin' that the look would leave her face.

"It's no use to try to explain to you, November, your mind is full've the revival, and organ playin' and Brother Crabtree lookin' like and Angel. You ain't in no mind to look behind what you see. But, take my word for it, child, there's somethin' about Brother Crabtree that sets my teeth on edge."

"I may not know as much as you do, Ansalu," I said, feelin' stung, "but I'm not a dummy! Brother Crabtree is a true man of God, and it's wrong of you to say he's not!" I started to get real upset at the way our talk was goin'.

"November, I've decided, and that's that. I feel like it's my fault for takin' you down there in the first place, and I'm not about to sit back and let you go again without tryin' to talk some sense into your head." Ansalu's voice was sharper than I had ever heard it. But I was feelin' more and more confused, and I wasn't about to let her spoil this revival for me.

"All right then, Ansalu, if you feel that way about it, don't go," I said, soundin' braver than I felt.

She looked right taken aback at my words. But I didn't care. I meant to go back to the revival every night if I could.

"November Sunshine, don't be so stubborn..." she started to say, but that was the wrong thing. All my anger at Paw's bossin' and my belongin' to Odd bolled up inside.

"Stubborn," I yelled, "me stubborn? Why, all you have to do is look at the way all those people come pourin' in to hear Brother Crabtree, and you got to know he's a wonderful man! I think...I think he's the most wonderful person I've ever met", and I looked right at Ansalu so she'd know just 'zactly what I meant. I could see that what I said had hurt her, but I felt she was just tryin' to spoil things for me for some reason or other.

I wasn't sure why, but I felt like bein' mean. "Maybe it's just as well if you don't go down to any more of Brother Crabtree's revivals. You probably got mad because he said he wanted to work with me alone and not you!"

It was spiteful, pure spiteful to say such a thing to Ansalu. But I was in such a state that I just didn't care.

Ansalu took a long look at me. Then she stood up as tall as she could and sort of pulled herself up straighter. Then she said to me, in a voice so cold and far-away seemin' that I felt like shivering, "So be it, November Sunshine."

She stood there just lookin' at me, and then she said, "If that's the way things are goin' to be, I can see that we'll not be seein' each other anymore."

Then she turned and went inside her cabin and closed the door.

I stood where I was, just lookin' at that closed door. The more I looked at it, the more I wanted to go bang on it and make her let me back in. But somethin' inside of me was feelin' mad and said, "Let her go."

Long after she'd gone inside, I stood there lookin' at the door. I was still on Ansalu's porch where we had been talkin', but then it came to me. I didn't belong here anymore.

I decided I'd best get over to Odd's cabin. I knew things had changed, and I felt like I'd lost somethin'. I needed a place where I could go. So I hurried over the path to Odd's cabin and made myself think about all the food I'd have to cook up for him before I could go back to the revival again that night. I didn't dare let myself think about Ansalu and what had happened 'tween us.

But no matter what had happened, I meant to go back to that revival.

I felt awful bad about Ansalu, but I knew somethin' was drawin' me back to Brother Crabtree and the revival. I didn't have no doubts about that preacher. I had never seen anyone like Brother Crabtree in my whole life, and I meant to see all of him I could. I knew he would change my life.

On the way back to Odd's cabin, I decided I'd best work out some story to tell him so he'd think I was goin' back to the revival with Ansalu. I figured he'd take a short view if he knew I wanted to go alone.

Odd was in the cabin when I got there, so I set to fixin' a bite to eat even though it was late. I just sort of mentioned that the revival was goin' on the next evenin', too.

"How long is this revival thing goin' on?" he asked me. I had figured he'd be kind of unhappy about my wantin' to go again, but he didn't seem to mind as long as I promised to fix his meals.

I didn't tell him about me and Ansalu.

Goin' alone that night wasn't too bad. The revival was just like before, somethin' really special. Afterwards, I thought about comin' up the mountain alone so I didn't hang around once the preachin' was over. I just set right off for home, walkin' as fast as I could, thinkin' about what Brother Crabtree had preached.

There was somethin' about the way Brother Crabtree talked and prayed over a body that made you feel like there wasn't anythin' you couldn't do. I'd look at Brother Crabtree and see him all shinin' in his white clothes and lookin' so grand with his white hair. I got to thinkin' there wasn't anybody like him in the whole world. Nothin' could've made me miss a night of his preachin'.

Well, come Friday, I was gettin' a little tuckered out hurryin' down the mountain and back up it every night. But so far, Odd hadn't said nothin', and I hadn't seen Ansalu, so I figured that my goin' to those revival services was the way things were meant to be. Some of the people I'd seen before had taken to noddin' and speakin' to me, and I felt like I belonged. I felt like a part of somethin' big and important.

Friday night was the biggest night of all at the revival. That tent was plum full from side to side, and people were sittin' on the ground up next to the platform. I was glad I had come early and taken a seat right up front.

When the organ player came in, she was followed by four young men. They were all wearin' the same kind of long robe that she had on, and I could tell that they were somethin' special. Sure enough, when she started to play that organ, they all stood up in a line right behind the organ. She nodded her head at 'em, and they started singin' like their lives depended on it!

Oooo-eeel, I tell you, I never heard anythin' like it in all my life. It was somethin' for a body to remember to his grave! They were all singin' the same song, but none of 'em was singin' the same notes. And instead of soundin' awful, all their notes sort of went along with each other's notes and came out wonderful. And all the time, the organ player was playin' her heart out, up and down the organ til you'd think they'd all burst open with the music they were makin'.

Honest, it made me feel like somethin' wonderful was gonna happen. Somethin' big, somethin' excitin'.

An when they finished their song, everybody in the tent commenced to clappin' and wouldn't stop until they started another song.

Then, when they finished three or four more songs, the men went and stood two on each side of the place where Brother Crabtree always stepped up to the platform.

The tent got so quiet you couldn't hear anythin' except a few people moanin' real soft. We all sat watchin' the openin' of the tent, waitin' for Brother Glen Crabtree to come.

An we waited.

An then, just when I was beginnin' to feel all torn up inside because it didn't look like he was ever goin' to come, he stepped through the openin' and stood real still with both arms raised as high as they could go. It was like everybody in the tent sighed all at once. This low, moanin' sound sort of wrapped itself around him, and he just stood there, quiet, in the middle of it.

Glory, glory!

Oh, but Brother Crabtree looked grand! He was all dressed in white, just like before, but he looked different, somehow. He was wearin' a big, long cloak that went from his shoulders all the way down to the ground. And it was made of some kind of shiny white cloth that shone back where the light hit it. When I looked at him, it was like lookin' at a big, white candle with that kind of sparkle that you see around the flame. He was so beautiful my breath caught inside me, and it almost hurt to let it out.

When Brother Crabtree started preachin', I was so full of watchin' him that I didn't really catch all the words. I just knew he was sayin' somethin' about trustin' and belongin' to the Lord and such. And somehow, in my mind, Brother Crabtree and God were all mixed up together, and it all made me feel so good that I couldn't stop the tears from comin'. I just sat there, holdin' those feelin's to myself and cryin' like a little baby while Brother Crabtree's words poured over me like warm water that's been heated to take the chill out of a body.

I was so full of my thoughts and feelin's when the revival ended that I didn't go over to Brother Crabtree's caravan like he'd said he wanted me to. I just wanted to be alone and try to think through what was happenin' to me.

It was dark when I started back up the mountain, but my mind was so full that the shadows didn't bother me. I hurried along the path, knowin' by now where the rough spots and roots were, so I didn't stumble.

Then, I began to feel like I wasn't alone. I stopped and held my lantern up high so I could see in between the trees, but I didn't see anythin'. Soon as I started walkin' again, I got the same feelin'.

Some of the good feelin's from the revival started to slip away, and I began to feel afraid. I started goin' so fast that my chest hurt where the breath went in and out so hard. But that scary feelin' was still there, eggin' me on.

"Hold it," a voice said, and I tried to run.

I was so scared and out of breath that I couldn't go much faster.

Arms went around me from the back, and I felt myself caught so I couldn't move. I tried to twist and see who had me trapped, but I couldn't. So I kicked back as hard as I could.

"Ouch! Dammit, November, stop that fightin' I won't hurt you!"

Junior Washbon! Even though I couldn't see his face, I knew who held me trapped there in the woods.

"What do you want, Junior Washbon?" I asked, tryin' to sound like I wasn't scared.

"You," he said and turned me round in his arms, still not lettin' me go.

Then he kissed me and kissed me. All over my face and my neck and down to where my green dress stopped.

I pushed and pulled and kicked his ankles and even tried to bite his tongue when he pushed it into my mouth. But nothin' seemed able to keep him from what he was doin',

And I don't know when I stopped fight in and started kissin' him back.

But I did.

And then I didn't even care that he was slippin' my clothes off bit by bit and kissin' me everywhere and makin' my head spin like I'd never get it to stop.

Part of me wanted to keep on fightin' him and bitin' and clawin' and tryin' to make him stop. But the other part of me was cryin' out to him to kiss me more.

And then, there, on the soft moss under those big mountain trees with the soft lantern light making everythin' seem unreal, Junior Washbon taught me things I'd never thought to learn.

I guess I must have sort of floated away in my mind, then. The next thing I remember is Junior Washbon kneelin' over me there on the ground sayin, "Oh God, I'm sorry, November, I'm sorry."

And then he was gone, and I was all alone, tryin' to pull my clothes back on in the lantern light, and left to deal with feelin's inside that were tearin' me apart.

A feelin' of shame took me then, and I felt weak and shaky and like I was gonna throw up. I knew I had done wrong, bad wrong.

What could I do? Where could I go? I fell to my knees, sobbin', and tried to pray, but it didn't work.

How come Brother Crabtree could make such beautiful prayers, and I couldn't say even a little one when I needed it so bad?

I stumbled up the hill to Odd's cabin, hopin' that he would be sound asleep when I got there. He was.

When I finally got myself washed up and crawled into bed, I lay there shivering like I'd never stop. I was still shivering when the first early light of dawn came peekin' in around the edge of the window.

It was a relief to be able to make myself get out of bed and be doin' somethin'; I hunted up one of Odd's old worn shirts and put it on, rollin' up the sleeves so my hands were free. Then I pushed my green dress back under the bed, figurin' I'd never feel right in it again. I started fixin' Odd's breakfast.

Odd looked pleased to see me up and cookin' so early. He looked at me wearin' his old shirt and kinda grinned at me but didn't say anythin'. The smell of coffee filled the cabin, and I hoped it would hide the way I was sure my sin had made me smell. Odd didn't seem to notice anythin' different about me.

When I reached over his shoulder to pour him a cup of coffee, he looked up at me and asked, "Is the revival over, November?"

"Not quite," I answered. "But I don't reckon I'll be goin'."

The revival seemed a long time away.

I worked extra hard around the cabin that day, tryin' to make myself forget all that had happened. I didn't know what to do.

I'd lost my best friend. I couldn't go to Ansalu and talk over what had happened with her anymore. It felt like there was a hole inside me where Ansalu had been before.

Then, towards evenin', I began to remember things that Brother Crabtree had said about God forgivin' people and things like that. and it finally came to me, I could go see Brother Crabtree and tell him what had happened and ask him to help.

Once my mind was made up, I felt some better.

When Odd came home for his supper, I told him I'd decided to go down to the Springs for the revival service. He didn't say anythin', and so I said I might stay over with Ansalu and go to the last service Sunday mornin' as well.

He thought about it and said, "Well, you ain't slighted your chores none, and since this is the tall end of it, I 'spose it won't hurt none for you to go." He gave me a look and said, "But don't forget to bake me plenty of bread before you leave."

I already had bread risin' and beans soakin', so it was easy to do what he asked.

I left for the revival feelin' like there was a stone ridin' along in my belly. I didn't know any way to get rid of that stone except to go talk to Brother Crabtree about it. I felt bad about lyin' to Odd about stayin' with Ansalu, but the way things were, I didn't know what else to tell him. Truth was, I surely missed havin' Ansalu to talk things over with. Thinkin' about Ansalu made the stone in my belly feel even heavier.

I didn't go to the revival that night. I was still wearin' Odd's old shirt and didn't want folks to see me that way. So I stood outside the tent in the shadows and just listened. I was so troubled. But I kept my thoughts fastened on Brother Crabtree, and I felt like he could help me if anybody could. I listened to how he talked and pleaded and prayed and begged people to give themselves to God. I knew he'd find it in his heart to help me get all right with God, too.

When everybody'd finally gone home, and the tent lanterns'd been blown out, and Brother Crabtree was alone in his caravan, I gathered myself together and went and stood outside his door. I had that awful kind of feelin' inside that makes you want to do a thing and get it over with and yet makes you hang back from doin' it. But I finally reached up and knocked on his door, hangin' on to the moment when I'd see Brother Crabtree's beamin face again, full of love and forgiveness.

It took a long time til I heard someone movin' around inside, and the door was opened a little bit.

When the door was opened, I felt sick with disappointment. Instead of Brother Crabtree's kind shinin' face, there stood a tired-lookin' little man with scraggly grey hair leanin' on the doorframe. I was so set back I couldn't hardly talk at all.

"November Sunshine." It was Brother Crabtree's voice, all right, the same voice that had brought tears to my eyes and set lots and lots of sinners onto what he called the 'right track in life.

I looked at that man again. and then I knew, somehow, I was lookin' at Brother Glen Crabtree. The same.... and yet different.

"Come on in, November," he was sayin', and I hadn't made any move to follow him; I was so upset. I shook myself and made myself follow him into the caravan.

At first, when he opened the door, Brother Crabtree had looked kinda tired, but now he was smilin', and he pointed towards a chair, and I sat down. Then he sat down on the chair facin' me. "What brings you here, November?" he asked.

I couldn't say anythin' just yet.

The soothin' familiar voice was makin' me feel some better, but I just didn't understand how Brother Crabtree could look like he did.

Then, he seemed to realize that I felt awkward. He looked at me for a bit and then clapped his hand on top of his head. "Oh, Lord!" he sorta said to himself, and then he laughed kind of sheepish. "I forgot I'd taken my hairpiece... off already. Please don't be upset." He pointed to the small table next to his bed. There stood a rack topped by the long, flowin', snow-white hair I had thought to see on his head.

"You see, November," he said in that soothin' voice of his, "I think a man who has been called by God to preach His word should look the best he ever can. He pointed to himself. "Take me, for instance. You can see I don't have a headful of flowin' white hair like you thought. What I DO have is just plain-lookin' tired old grey hair. Now, you ask yourself, which would win more converts for God-plain old grey hair or beautiful, snow-white hair like the angels have? Well, I can see by your face you already know the answer!"

"So, November, if I don't happen to have the kind of hair God needs for me to have, what can I do about it?" He looked at me. I couldn't seem to get any words to come out, so he went on. "Well, only one thing for a man of God to do, November. That is, get some fine wigmaker to make me a headful of the very kind of hair God forgot to give me."

"Yes," was all I could manage to say.

"My followers need me to look like I do when I'm preachin', November, but God doesn't care how I look at home." He smiled at me and I could feel the strangeness meltin' away. Now that Brother Crabtree had explained everythin', I began to feel again how thoughtful and lovin' an...good... this man was. I felt like he'd shared his own private secret with me.

I could share with him, too. While I was thinkin' how best to say things, he spoke to me.

"I was afraid you had given up on your salvation when you didn't come by for Instruction," he said.

"Oh no, Brother Crabtree, I haven't given up on my salvation. But...it's... I need your help!" I finally managed to whisper.

He reached over and, patted my hand, and said, "Of course, November. This is a big step for you. Salvation is a gift from God, but we have to be worthy of it."

I knew I wasn't worthy, still, maybe he could help me.

"I need to tell you somethin'..." I began, fighting to hold my voice from givin' out with my shame. "Somethin'... somethin' that..." I couldn't bring myself to finish with his eyes lookin' at me, so I turned my face away from him.

"What's botherin' you, November?" he asked, soundin' like he cared.

I was kinda mixed up inside, and I tried not to show my feelin's. Part of me was glad to know that Brother Crabtree was just a reg'lar man, but part of me was real disappointed to find it out, and I was havin' a hard time sayin' what I'd come to say.

"Well, then," he said, "let's get on with whatever it was that brought you here to see me tonight."

It was hard goin' at first, but he just sat there and listened and looked encouragin' and didn't say anythin'. Bit by bit, I got the whole sorry story out. I told him a little about Junior Washbon and Odd.

Brother Crabtree kept pattin' my hand.

213

"Now tell me more about Junior Washbon and the man you called Odd," he said when I stopped talkin'. So I told him all the way back to Paw's tradin' me off to Odd and everythin' that had happened since I went to live with Odd. It took me a long time to get it all out, and I was real tired when I finished. Even my heart felt tired.

Brother Crabtree just sat there and looked at me for a bit. Then he asked me how old I was.

"Goin' on fifteen," I told him.

He looked at me.

"I'm fourteen," I said, feelin' pretty silly about lyin'.

He didn't say anythin' then. But he got up and went over to a little cabinet built into the wall and pushed somethin' and a door came open. He reached inside and, took out a dark, round bottle and set it on a table. Then he reached in and pulled out two glasses. I watched while he took the top off the bottle and poured some of the stuff in it into the glasses. He moved real easy in the soft lamplight, and I found I was gettin' used to him without that white hair. I wasn't feelin' so strange anymore. The whole thing, me settin' here in Brother Crabtree's caravan, seemed real, and what had happened to me the night before was like somethin' that I'd dreamed up in a real bad dream.

"Here, November, I know you're a mite young for spirits, but considerin' all that's happened to you, I think you need some." He handed me one of the glasses and took one for himself. Then he watched 'til I took a swallow. It looked like some of Ansalu's cold tea, so I took a big gulp of it to ease my throat.

I don't know what was in that glass, but it sure wasn't cold tea! I coughed and sputtered, and finally, Brother Crabtree came over and commenced pattin' me on the back so I could stop coughin'.

214

"Take it easy, November," he said. "This is imported brandy that I keep on hand to reward myself every now and then." He smiled at me like he wasn't mad or anythin' and then poured a little more of the brown stuff into both our glasses.

"What's brandy?" I asked him.

He raised his eyebrows over the edge of his glass. When he was finished sippin' he lowered the glass and said, "Brandy is one of the finer gifts of the Lord's bountiful earth, November. It is a tonic that can make the greatest trials seem smaller if it is used right."

I was havin' a hard time followin' all his words. Somehow, even though I was only takin' little sips at a time after that first big one that made me cough, my head was beginnin' to feel like things inside were slippin' out of.

Brother Crabtree watched me, and when my head began to feel awful heavy, I leaned it down against the back of the chair and tried to fit my body into a comfortable place. He put down his glass then, and came over to me. Very gently, he took hold of my arms and slid his hands around my back. I was so tired I was hardly aware of movin' Brother Crabtree picked me up real easy. and then he laid me down on his bed and went over and turned down the lamp so the light was even softer than before.

"There, November, just relax. You're safe now. Nothin' to worry about."

I watched him, too sleepy to wonder about it when he lay down beside me on the bed.

He moved over right next to me and took hold of my hand. I didn't pull away because it felt safe to have my hand held by Brother Crabtree.

"I'm gonna get salvation," I thought to myself. That thought was comfortin'.

"Do you trust me, November?" Brother Crabtree asked.

"Oh yes," I told him.

"Do you know that I want what is best for you, dear child?" he asked.

"Yes," I answered, not sure what he meant, but feelin' like I was driftin' along beside him on my way to salvation.

"Then you must know that God was unhappy about...what happened with that man."

I felt tired and ashamed, but he just went on talkin' softly.

"There's no need to be ashamed or feel guilty, November," he said, just like he knew my thoughts. Then he started brushin' the hair back from my face real gentle. "God means for you to be forgiven."

I felt better.

"In fact, the shame belongs to the man named Junior Washbon that you told me about. He took advantage of you, November. He brought you to the ways of the flesh. He led you down the pathway of lust..."

"Uh... Brother Crabtree... I'm sorry, but I don't know all those words you're usin'."

He looked at me for a minute and then said, "Of course, November. Let me put it this way. He thought a bit and said, "To put it plain and simple, Junior Washbon did a bad thing to you."

"He did?"

"Yes, November. He took you by force."

I remembered back to the night before, lyin' with Junior Washbon on the soft moss in the woods.

"No, sir, he didn't rightly force me."

"I said he did!" Brother Crabtree said. The way he said it, I decided since he was the one in charge of salvation, I'd best not argue.

"There are some things that happen between a man and a woman, November," Brother Crabtree went on, "that are nothin' but plain, sinful lust. and yet, when the very same act takes place in another time and another place, it can be a beautiful act of love and forgiveness." He stopped talkin' and lay there next to me. I tried not to look down where his wrapper had fallen open, but I could see he didn't have anythin' on inside. It was hard to keep my eyes from lookin', but I made myself pay attention to his words and kept my eyes on his face.

"Do you understand what I'm meanin', November?" he asked me.

"I... I don't think I do," I answered.

He leaned back on his elbow and was quiet for a little bit. Then he leaned close over my face so I could feel his breath goin' in and out in quick little puffs, and I could see little sparkles in his eyes.

"What I'm tryin' to say, November," he said real soft and gentle, "is that what happened last night was wrong. Do you understand that?"

"Oh yes, Brother Crabtree, I know..." and I could feel the tears fillin' up my eyes.

217

"An what you need now is to be forgiven in the eyes of God, isn't it?"

"Oh yes," I whispered.

"I know how you can be forgiven, November," he said real soft. "I know how to fix things, so you'll be all right with God."

"You do?" I asked him, thinkin' that bein' forgiven and gettin' that mixed-up feelin' out of my heart was what I wanted most in the whole world.

"Yes, I do," he answered, lookin' straight into my eyes so close I could see little bitty pictures of myself in the black part of his eyes.

I said, real low, "I really do need to be forgiven, please."

An then I noticed that his wrapper had fallen open all the way. Brother Crabtree's hands started movin' gentle all up and down my body.

"Do you trust me, November Sunshine?" he asked so soft I had to really try to hear the words.

"I do, I do," I whispered back, givin' myself over to Brother Crabtree's hands.

"Oh, Brother Crabtree," was the last thing I remember sayin' before I got lost in Brother Crabtree's forgiveness and God and angels singin' in my head.

It was a long time later that I heard Brother Crabtree talkin' way off in another world somewhere. "You can't stay here all night," he was sayin', and I must've asked him why because he said, "No tellin' who might see you here in the mornin', November, and misunderstand."

Someone came, then, and I knew I was bein' helped back into my clothes and taken out of the caravan. It wasn't until I felt myself bein' lifted onto a cold seat that I woke up enough to ask, "Where're you takin' me?"

"Brother Crabtree said to take you home," the man who'd put me on the seat said. I looked closer at him and saw he was one of the men who passed the wooden bowls at the revival service. "Are you sober enough to tell me where you live?"

I felt ashamed at what he said, and I told him right off which road to take up the mountain.

"Where do you want me to let you off?" he asked as we rode along. Even though it was late and dark, I recognized the fork in the road where I turned off to Odd's cabin.

I was still awful tired and mixed up, but the cool fresh air was helpin'. "You can stop right here, I told him. I felt the automobile slow down and stop. I couldn't get the latch open on the door, and the man grunted a bit and then came around and opened the door for me.

"I thank you kindly for bringin' me home," I told him, tryin' to sound as polite and mannerly as I could.

"That's all right," he said. "I'm used to it; it's part of my job."

"What d'you mean, you're used to it?" I asked him.

"I mean, it's part of my job to see that all of Brother Crabtree's... converts... get home afterward."

"All of 'em?" I asked, my voice feelin' awful small and weak.

"Sure." He looked at me kind of funny and asked, "Poor kid, you didn't think you were the only one he...converted... did you?"

I guess he could tell from the look on my face that that was just what I had thought.

He just laughed softly to himself and shook his head, then he climbed back into the automobile and drove away.

I stood there on the path and tried to put things together in my head. Whatever it was, I had to drink at Brother Crabtree's sure made thinkin' come mighty hard.

I felt better after I saw the big oak tree on the path to Odd's cabin.

Somehow, my head cleared enough by the time I reached the cabin that I was able to tiptoe in without wakin' Odd. Then, without takin' off my clothes, I crawled into the bed and lay there feelin' so awful I wished I could die.

But I didn't die.

So I lay there tryin' to sort out what had gone wrong. All I'd wanted to do was to learn and better myself. My mind went back over how I'd acted every time I had seen Junior Washbon. What had I done wrong to make him think what he must have thought about me? And I thought about Brother Crabtree and the Gospel Caravan and how mixed up everythin' had gotten.

I twisted and turned in my bed, feelin' dirty and lost and awful alone. I knew deep down inside that I'd made a real mess've things. I just didn't see how it could ever be turned right.

I just lay there, waitin' out the night.

A LONG WAY BACK

Makin' myself get up and do all my chores in the mornin' was about as hard as anythin' I'd ever had to do. I wanted to stay in bed and pull the covers over my head, and not have to face anybody. My body felt awful tired because I couldn't sleep, I just tossed and fretted all night. And my head was even worse off. It was achin' with shame and worry, and there wasn't anywhere I could go that I didn't have to take my head and my worrisome thoughts with me.

It was hard to go on livin', real hard. I knew I'd made a mess of things, and makin' it worse was rememberin' that Ansalu had tried to keep me from goin' back down to that revival. I hadn't trusted her enough to heed her warnin' about Brother Campbell. How'd she ever get so wise about people?

Anyway, I'd gone against Ansalu, the best friend I'd ever had. and I'd lost her.

Somehow, I felt like I'd gone against Odd, too, but that was harder to figure out.

But worst of all, I didn't see any way of undoin' what was done. I got a pail of water and heated it and scrubbed myself so hard it made my skin all pink. But no matter how hard I scrubbed the outside, I still felt dirty inside.

Oh God.

I started gettin' up extra early mornin's since I wasn't sleepin' much anyhow and makin' Odd's favorite buttermilk biscuit. I scoured the woods for comb honey. I took pains in fixin' the table real nice.

221

I even offered to let Odd sleep in the bed and said I'd sleep on the comfort by the stove. Odd looked at me real funny when I said that. He just said he was used to it.

Anyway, I tried. I sure tried to make things feel like they had before.

I wish I could go talk to Ansalu. Ansalu has always been so kind and good to me. She'd always listened to what I said and treated me like someone special. A friend. I felt real sick when I remembered how I'd talked to her. With all my heart, I wish I'd listened to what she'd said. Just thinkin' about Ansalu made tears crowd up in my eyes.

I thought about Junior Washbon, too. I never wanted to see him again and hoped I'd never have to. What I'd done, what we'd done, was wrong. Real wrong.

But somethin' inside me kept whisperin', "You liked it."

I just couldn't understand my feelin's at all.

Brother Crabtree. I didn't want to let myself think about Brother Crabtree, but my mind kept harkin' back to him anyway. It was like when you have a tooth pulled, and you want to put your tongue in the hole to see how big it is, and yet you're afraid it'll hurt. It hurt to think about how I'd almost worshipped Brother Crabtree. I remembered how beautiful he looked when he was at the revival preachin'. If only…if only… but then my other memories of Brother Crabtree came crowdin' in, and I was sick at heart.

I felt stupid, and I knew I'd be a long time g'tting' over it.

Bitter tears just come pourin' out when I got to thinkin' back. I was cryin' for the hurt I'd done, and somehow, I was cryin' for me, too. I guess I was cryin' for the November Sunshine who didn't know what was happenin' when she went to live with Odd. My mind wandered back a long way to that awful, scary day when I follered Odd to this cabin. And I thought about the time when I had my first curse and how scared I'd been. And I made myself remember lots of things I'd done and learned.

An I thought about how different my feelin's were gettin' to be ever since Junior Washbon had held my hand in the department store.

My feelin's had started changin' a lot, then, and it seemed like I couldn't stop how my body was tellin' my head to feel. Like when Junior Washbon had taken me home and kissed me in his automobile. I didn't like to think of the way I was drawn to him then. And I wish I could die when I remembered the way I had let him be so free with me when he'd caught up with me in the woods.

Doin' my chores and tryin' to act natural was hard. But I didn't know any other way to do them to just keep on doin' what needed doin'. Sometimes, you just gotta meet things head-on.

It finally came to me that Brother Crabtree, for all his pretty white clothes and holy ways, wasn't too different from Junior Washbon.

I pondered about Junior Washbon, too. His paw owned that shiny big department store so full of all kinds of things I could never dream of havin'. I thought about how he was bound to Eloise Bardwell. "Eloise," I said her name softly to myself. Even her name was pretty and graceful like she was. And both their paws wanted 'em to be together, and they probably would be someday.. Things must seem clear and easy and good to someone like Eloise Bardwell. She was like a graceful flower. I felt like a no-nothin' weed.

I thought about my Paw, who'd traded me off for that Stevens rifle. And I'm about Odd, who'd wanted me just to cook and clean and take care of things.

I wondered if it had been Junior Washbon climbin' all over me in that cabin 'stead of Odd if I'd felt some different. And about Odd havin' to sleep on the floor near the stove…

Shame flooded over me when I thought that way. I knew it wasn't right…

But I couldn't help myself. Why had Junior Washbon done what he had to me when he had someone like Eloise Bardwell?

An Brother, Glen Crabtree. What about him? He had a big caravan and lots of people who worked for him. and there were so many women, hundreds of them, who'd hung on every word he preached and who follered him with their eyes like they could almost eat him up. Why had he bothered with me? Salvation? I couldn't help thinkin' that Brother Crabtree's salvation wasn't too different from what Junior Washbon'd wanted.

I knew now they had both used me. I felt ashamed and worthless.

Lyin' in bed one night, I looked over at Odd lyin' in the firelight from the stove, and I wondered why it'd been so hard for him to lie with me. I had hated the gruntin' and sweatin' and thumpin'. I'd hated it, and for a time, I'd hated him, too. I couldn't find any answers to give my heart peace.

Then, one night at the supper table, Odd turned to me and asked, "How come you ain't asked to go to Ansalu's cabin lately, November?"

He took me by surprise, and I didn't have an answer. I hadn't figured that Odd paid any mind to what I did so long's his food was ready for him when he was ready for it. I couldn't find any way to answer him.

I studied out about Ansalu that night lyin' in bed. I wondered if I'd ever be able to go over to her cabin again. I felt real sad when I remembered how happy it used to make both her and me when I'd come for a visit. And I thought of all the spice cookies we'd eaten and cornbread, and even fried cakes that she'd made up special for one of my visits. What made me sad was to think I might never go there and see her anymore. Ansalu, whose body was little but whose heart was as big as the whole mountain.

I knew I was bein' punished. There wasn't any way I could ever be able to face Ansalu after all I'd done.

Things went on that way for about two months, Odd scarce talkin' and me just doin' my chores without half thinkin'.

Finally, one day, Odd said, "Peers, to me, its 'bout time for you to get another dress, November."

I looked down at myself. I really hadn't paid much attention to how I looked. I'd washed out my green dress and went on wearin' it. and when that dress was out on a bush dryin', I'd wear that old shirt've Odds I found. It didn't matter much to me how I looked.

"This dress'll do, Odd," I said. I wasn't expectin' the look that came on his face when I said that. He looked almost disappointed.

"I just thought..." he said.

"That's all right," I told him. "I 'preciate your kind offer, but I ain't got anywheres to go in a new dress."

It was about a week later when he said, "Whyn't you go down to the Springs with me tomorrow, November? I got enough credit now to buy you a new dress, even nicer than that one was."

I didn't say anything', I just shook my head, no.

"Well, I need a pair of new shoes," he said, holdin' up his foot so I could see where he had worn plum through the bottoms. I felt bad that I hadn't noticed how much he needed new shoes. I looked at the rest of his clothes and saw how worn they were. I tried to imagine how he'd look to other people.

Here was a chance to make things a little righter. "All right," I said slowly. "I'll go down to the Springs with you, Odd, but not to buy me a new dress. I'm goin' to see that you get some new pants and a new shirt or two. As I was sayin', all that I began to feel some better. Sort of like if I gave up gettin' a new dress, then Odd could have new clothes.

It was hard not to let Odd see how much the thought of goin' to Washbon's Department Store upset me. Gettin' ready to go tore me up inside somethin' dreadful. I hadn't been down the mountain since that awful night several months before when Brother Crabtree's man had brought me home in his automobile. I tried not to think about that when we passed the oak tree at the side've the path where I had gotten outta the car. That was just about the same place where I'd met up with Junior Washbon the night he'd caught me, too.

I was sure glad that old oak tree couldn't talk.

I began to get a real sick feelin' in my stomach when we got closer to Wilson's Springs. It was hard to keep myself from shivverin' when we finally got near the department store. I sure hoped Junior Washbon was off tendin' to business somewhere else. But I knew I daren't let Odd see the way I

226

was feelin, so I just put my head up high and follered him into the store.

Old Man Washbon saw us right off and came over to see what Odd wanted. I was surprised at how nice he talked to Odd and all. Odd was as good as any of his customers.

It didn't take long at all to get Odd some new clothes to work in. Gettin' shoes that fit took a mite longer. Specially since Odd had to buy some socks before Mr. Washbon could let him try on the shoes. Some kind of a sanity rule or somethin', he said.

Whilst we were in the store, I couldn't help sneakin' a look at the racks of brand new dresses. It made me feel a little sad when I caught a look at myself in that big mirror they keep so people can see themselves in what they plan to buy. I didn't look like much.

We were only in the store a little bit, and Junior Washbon never did come around. I was breathin' a little better by the time we started home.

Walkin' up the hill, Odd reached in the bag Mr. Washbon'd put his new things in and pulled out the socks. He said that was only the second pair of socks he'd ever had, and he was lookin' forward to wearin' 'em with his new shoes.

Them other socks sure made wearin' my shoes a lot nicer.

I'd never thought he might like socks to wear inside his shoes. Paw and my brothers never had 'em, and I'd just thought wearin' shoes without 'em was the way things were.

After Odd told me about the socks, he didn't have much to say, and we walked along real quiet.

An then, when we were just about up to the big oak tree, here comes Ansalu down the path from her side of the mountain right towards us.

I stopped, shook still, and looked for a tree to hide behind. But she looked me square in the face and said, "November," sort of holdin' her voice back. You know, stiff and too polite. The way that makes you know somethin' is wrong? Then she turned to Odd and said, "You must be Odd. I be Ansalu."

At first, I thought she was goin' right on by. Then she stopped in the path like she was thinkin' things over. She turned to me and said, "Pears to me, you and me've got things to talk over, November."

I guess I stood there for a long time cause Odd finally nudged me and said, "Ain't you gonna answer her, November?"

I had to swaller real good before my voice would work. "If you say we got things to talk over, I'll take your word for it." Inside, my heart was bangin' and flutterin', and it was all I could do to keep from runnin' off. All the time Odd was lookin' at me real curious.

"Then we'd best do it," she said without another word and went on her way down the path.

All the rest of the way back to the cabin, I wondered just what Ansalu had in mind and what I should do. Odd didn't say a word. It was clear he meant for me to make up my own mind. He always was one for mindin' his own business.

Well, after about a week, I couldn't stand it anymore. So, one day, I baked up extra cornbread put fresh honeycomb in a little bowl, and covered it with a damp cloth. There was plenty of cornbread and honey left for Odd, so I didn't mind takin' some with me. Then I told Odd I was fixin' to go to Ansalu's. He didn't say anythin', but he did somethin' real strange. He smiled at me like he was pleased about somethin'.

I started over to Ansalu's, but I didn't hurry along like I'd used to do. I wasn't sure in my mind just what she wanted to talk about, and I was still feelin' pretty bad about myself.

When I was still a ways from her porch, Ansalu came to the door and stood waitin'. I almost called out to her like I'd used to do, but I held back. I had it in my mind not to tell Ansalu about all that'd happened. I had learned a couple of real hurtin' lessons in these last months. One of 'em was that you have to own up for everythin' you do. Isn't anybody but yourself you can lay blame on when you do somethin' wrong.

Another lesson I'd learned was that if you don't take care of friendships, they wither up and go away. I knew I hadn't taken care of my friendship with Ansalu, and now I was afraid I'd lost it.

I follered her inside and sat down.

Ansalu went and got a plateful of ginger cookies. Then she poured us each a cupful of mint tea. I could smell the nice smell of mint hangin' over the whole cabin. It was nice to smell.

We sat and ate and drank our tea, and sort of fidgeted around in our chairs.

Finally, I couldn't stand it any longer, and I burst out, "What's on your mind to say to me, Ansalu? If it's that you think I've been a fool, you don't have to tell me. I already know."

She just looked at me a bit, and then she commenced smilin'. Her smile started kind of shy-like, but it grew til it covered her whole face.

I was beginnin' to feel some better.

"I know, November. I think we've both been foolish more than once in our lifetime. If a person weren't goin' to have any fools for friends, he'd get mighty lonesome."

An then somehow we was talkin' just like we used to do. It felt so good I felt like cryin', both from mad at myself and for relief that we were sittin' here together like friends again.

"How was the rest of the revival, November?" Ansalu asked.

She caught me off balance. "How'd you know I went?" I asked her.

"I saw you goin' down once, November, and Mrs. Johnson over to Beely Way said she saw you two other times. So I figured you went to just about all of Brother Crabtree's preachin' services.

I just nodded. I couldn't think of anythin' to say.

"I'm sorry I tried to talk you out of goin', November, it's clear to me those revivals meant a whole lot to you. I should have trusted your judgment instead of bein' so bossy about doin' things my way."

I wished I could tell her the whole story then, but I didn't think I ought to. I just didn't want to take a chance on ruinin' the good feelin's that were startin'up tween us again. I just sat there, feelin' awkward and not really knowin' what to say. I didn't want to chance gettin' Ansalu upset with me again. I'd come to know only too well how much she mattered to me.

"I missed you, Ansalu," I blurted out.

She smiled real big and said, "Could you use a hug, November?" I ran into her arms and grabbed ahold of her like I'd never let go. My eyes started to tear up, and I tried to wipe 'em so she wouldn't notice.

"Oh, Ansalu," I said when we sort've let go of each other. "I was afraid you'd never want to be my friend again."

"November," she said, holdin' my hand while she talked, "this you've gotta understand. I always loved you, even when we weren't speakin'. It was just that for a while, I didn't LIKE you very much!"

When I had stopped cryin', I asked, "What in the world can I do, Ansalu?"

"Do?"

"Yes. How can I make things right? I've… I've done some things I hadn't ought to've done. I........can't even tell you, Ansalu."

She looked at me for a bit. "I guess you'll have to decide what to do and when's the best time to do it, November. No one else knows what's makin' you feel so bad, what's in your heart. Maybe it'll never be the right time to share what's inside you, child. Maybe it's best to keep it all to yourself. Keepin' somethin' hurtful inside is mighty uncomfortable, November, but at least you don't hurt anyone else with what's already done. Seems to me that when somethin' is already over and done, there isn't much good that can come out of passin' it aroun' for everybody to know."

Even though I felt filled up with shame, I had to smile at the way Ansalu talked. And when I thought over what she was sayin', it had a way of makin' real good sense.

She hadn't done those things to me, I had let them happen.

No reason why I should dump my feelin's onto her.

I stood up and said it was time for me to get back to Odd's cabin.

231

"I was glad to have a chance to meet Odd, November. I got the feelin' that mostly he's awful shy." Then she asked, "Do you have to go already?"

"Reckon I do, I told her. "I've got a piece of meat that's a mite tough, and I want to cook it good and long before supper." I started to walk towards the door. Then I turned and faced her. "Anyway, Ansalu, I was so upset about comin' to see you today that I left a lot of my chores undone. Oh, I meant to do them, of course, but somehow, I just couldn't get my mind to settle down to any one thing. And now that we got to talkin' and things are gettin' better between us again, I guess I want to go home and think over all we've said. For some reason, Ansalu, I'm all of a sudden dreadful tired."

She smiled at me and said, "Nerves can do that to you, November. When you worry about somethin', and it finally gets taken care of, settled, you feel sort of let down. And that often makes you feel tuckered out." I left soon after.

"Did you have a nice visit?" Odd asked me when I came in. I wasn't used to his askin' me bout such things, but I told him all about how good it felt to be friends with Ansalu again.

"I really missed seein' her," I said.

A couple of days later, didn't Ansalu Williams come visitin' me at Odd's cabin! She hadn't ever done that before, and I wondered what was on her mind. As soon as she settled in, I made us some tea and spread honey on what was left of the breakfast biscuits. Ansalu settled back in one of the hickory chairs and looked at me.

"I been thinkin," she said. "Somethin' that wasn't good came between us and nearly spoiled our friendship. Neither one of us was at fault, yet both of us were. I wasn't understandin' at all of what you needed and wanted. And you were too quick to jump when I spoke. And now I want to say that I hope the

232

bad feelin's are all over, and we can be friends like we used to be."

I just looked at her, thinkin' how nice she always was to me and wonderin' how she could stand bein' around me after the things I'd done.

"Anyways, I got an idea, November," she said.

"What is it?" I asked.

"Well, remember when we were goin' to the revival, November?"

"Oh yes, I remembered all too well!"

"You kept wantin' to go back and hear Brother Crabtree, and I said maybe we could go down to a reglar church in Webster Springs sometime."

I nodded, rememberin'.

"It occurred to me that there wasn't nothin' to stop us from goin' down this very Sunday." She looked at me, her face all lit up from thinkin' her idea would make me real happy. I didn't have the heart to tell her that the very last thing I wanted just then was any more preachin' and religion.

But she must've read some of what was in my mind because she said, "It won't be at all like the revival, November. I promise you that!" She shook her head. "It will be real different and a lot more peaceful and healin'."

While she waited for my answer, I could see the light just fadin' out of her face. She had wanted to please. It tore at my heart, and I couldn't stand hurtin' her any more than I already had. "That will be just fine, Ansalu," I finally managed to say, soundin' like I meant it.

We made plans to go down to Wilson's Springs on Sunday and go to the service at a regular church. After we made the plans, Ansalu said she'd best get on home now cause she had things to do.

Later, when I told Odd what she'd said about goin' to church in Wilson's Springs, he didn't seem to mind at all if I went along with Ansalu. He'd taken to smokin' a pipe lately, and he was sittin' out on the porch, fillin' the air with the good smell of sweet tobacco, when I asked him. I guess he'd seen some of the men smokin' pipes down in Wilson's Springs and thought he'd like to give it a try. It wasn't one of those corn cob things, it was a real honest-to-goodness pipe. He seemed to take to it, too. Most every day, when he came home from work, he'd fill up his pipe with tobacco and smoke whilst he waited for me to put his supper on the table. It seemed to take the edge off his tiredness.

Anyway, he seemed to think a bit after sayin' I could go, and then he said, "Just don't get to be a Bible-thumpin' hell-fire and brimstone tee-tote-ler. I guess I looked like I didn't get his meanin', for he went on, "Only things I remember 'bout my Granmaw was her always wearin' a black dress with a white collar and hergettin' all worked up and yellin' about gettin' saved and not drinkin'. Made my Paw so mad he hauled me home one time when she was yappin' at him, and we never did go back to see my Granmaw again."

I told him I wasn't gonna get to be anythin' like that, and he said it was all right then if I went to church. "I ain't about to put up with no woman tellin' me how to act in my own place," he finished.

And that was all he said about it.

Before I left to meet Ansalu on Sunday mornin', I set out all the food for Odd's noon meal. Ansalu had said we'd best not be late for the church service, so I'd got and early start. I'd washed my green dress and smoothed it out so il looked passable, and washed my hair and taken a bath. I was feelin' some better than I'd been feelin' for a long time. The grease on the beans showed me they were fixed just the way Odd liked them. I was glad because I didn't always get them just right.

I met Ansalu down her cabin, where our two paths came together on the way to the valley. When I saw her all fixed up so nice and fresh-lookin' in a blue dress with a white collar and a fresh white turban on her head, I felt ashamed of my green dress, even though it was clean. But Ansalu seemed to know what was botherin' me and went all the way back to her cabin and fetched me a pretty yella shawl to wear over it. I turned this way and that with that shawl over my shoulders. I'd never seen anything like it, it was so pretty. It had tassels, and when I moved, they moved too. Ansalu declared that I looked. Just fine, and we started off again.

I didn't care much which church Ansalu picked out for us to go to. So when we got to Wilson's Springs, I just let her lead the way. We came to a big white clapboard church with a steeple on top of its roof. I could see a big bell in the steeple and hoped they'd ring it so I could hear how it sounded.

Anyhow, we went inside just like we belonged there. Some people standin' near the door smiled and gave us each a folded paper. Ansalu said it was a program to tell us what was going to happen in the service. Then we went and sat down, and I spent a lot of time just lookin' around.

An would you believe it? There was Eloise Bardwell. I was glad I was sittin' where I could see her cause I hoped to watch what she did and maybe learn somethin'. She was sittin' up front with a bunch of people in long black robes like the bowl passers from the revival. Ansalu whispered that they were the choir. Eloise sat in the second row, and I wondered just what they were goin' to do.

235

A woman was playin' the organ real soft, and people kept comin' in and takin' seats. It wasn't real peppy music like at the revival, but it made me feel just as good in a different kind of way. It was all sure a lot different from Brother Crabtree's revival. At the revival, I'd got a feelin' of hurry up and do somethin', even if I wasn't sure what. Here in this church, though, I felt more comfortable, sorta peaceful, like Ansalu had said. I watched the way colored glass windows threw rainbows over the church and the people. and I just filled myself up, listen in' no to the organ, and thought, "This won't be too bad."

Eloise kept lookin' over towards the side of the church. I raised myself up in my seat and poked my head around the man in front of me. I could see where Eloise was lookin'. Junior Washbon was sittin' there with Old Man Washbon and some lady, I figgered she must be his Maw. He looked like butter wouldn't melt in his mouth, sittin' there so still and all made me feel funny inside.

The church service got started. To tell the truth, at first, I was sorta. Disappointed. It wasn't nothin' like the revival, and people didn't sit on the edge of their seats to see what would happen next. It was more like everythin' was all planned out and had been all planned out for a long time. I had the feelin' that things hadn't ever changed very much in that church. I didn't know if that was good or not.

It got a little better when the choir sang. They all stood up at one time and looked kind of snappy about it. And then the organ player waved her hand at 'em and commenced playin'. It wasn't fancy playin' like at the revival, but it was passable. And there were lots more people in the choir than in that singin' group at the revival, so they made a lot more noise. It got so I could tell the men's and women's voices apart. I liked the way they didn't all sing the same notes. Some of the men's voices were real low, and they gave a nice sound to the whole thing. In all, I liked it.

But I sure didn't care much for Reverend Bardwell's preachin'! He said his words like each one was heavier'n a rock. And he took so long between some of them that I wanted to help him get them out. I wished he'd dance around and thump the lecture stand like Brother Glen Crabtree had. The old man in the front row who kept noddin' off sure wouldn't've been able to sleep if Brother Crabtree had been preachin'.

Brother Crabtree.

I let my mind wander and thought back to all that had happened, and I wanted to get up and run right out of that church. How could I have thought Brother Crabtree's preachin' was so good when... when I'd found out what kind of a man he was? I tried real hard to like the Reverend Bardwell's preachin' after that.

When Ansalu and me were goin' out the door after the preachin' and prayin' were all over, I ran right into Eloise Bardwell as she came out of a small room off to the side of the church.

"Oh my gosh, I'm sorry!" I said, hopin' I hadn't bumped her too hard.

"Don't apologize," she said, smilin' at me like I was someone she knew and liked.

She had such a nice smile. Not like Ansalu's, though, different. Eloise Bardwell's smile was more like she knew she was doin' it. Ansalu's smile acted like it came on before she knew about it.

But it was all right, Eloise's smile seemed to fit her.

That's the way a lady smiles, I told myself.

"I asked," Elotse Bardwell was speakin' to me, and I had been so busy with my thoughts I hadn't heard, "Where are you from?"

"Oh," I said, catchin' myself. "I'm from up the mountain."

"Have you ever been here to church before?" she asked me, lookin' at me real close.

"No, Ma'am, this is my first time, I told her."

"I feel as though I've seen you somewhere before," she went on. I didn't know whether to tell her or not.

"I... I saw you one day in Washbon's Department Store," I finally said. "I didn't think you saw me, though."

"Of course!" she said, breakin' into her smile again. "I remember now!"

"Yes, I did see you. I envied you the way you looked."

I was struck dumb! Eloise Bardwell had envied me in that Light of dress I'd been wearin'!

"For the law's sake, why?" I had to ask.

"Oh, I don't know if I can explain it exactly. But you looked like you belonged on the mountain. You looked so free and graceful an... untroubled," she finished.

I couldn't believe what I was hearin'. There was no way I could've said a word if my life had depended on it. My mouth felt like it was all stuck together. All I could do was just stand there.

Just then, Ansalu came up to us, and we moved on past Eloise Bardwell and out through the big church door, and I was glad we did.

I walked along, quiet, not payin' much attention to where I was goin'. I just sort of trailed along after Ansalu.

"November, is somethin' wrong?" she asked, pullin' me over under the shade of a tree and lookin' close at me.

"No, Ansalu, nothin's wrong, I just have a lot to think about," I told her. She seemed to think I meant about the preacher's talkin', and that seemed to satisfy her.

"I've planned a suprise, November," she said, her eyes sparklin'.

"A suprise? For me?"

"Yep. I'm goin' to take you to a real ice cream store and buy you a dish of ice cream." She watched my face while she talked. I didn't disappoint her, either, and I didn't have to pretend to be excited.

"Oh my gosh, Ansalul, you shouldn't spend your money like that for me!" I told her. I had no idea how much money it cost to buy ice cream in a real ice cream store. The only ice cream I'd ever had was twice when Paw was given some milk with cream in it by a neighbor. He'd hunted out an old ice cream churn that he'd found where somebody'd thrown it away. He sent one of the boys down to the creek to sand it down real good and get the rust off. Then he put the cream off the milk and some sugar into the churn and packed the whole thing with salt. I had to help turn the crank for what seemed like an awful long time.

But I could still remember how good that ice cream tasted! Raspberries were ripe the first time he made ice cream, and Caleb'd picked us enough to put on it. The second time he made it, we didn't have fruit, but he let us dribble honey over it. I thought about that ice cream a long time after we'd had it.

And now, I had a chance to eat some real store-bought ice cream in an ice cream store. I truly didn't want Ansalu to spend all her money, but I dearly wanted to have that dish of ice cream. I followed her into a place with a big glass window in it, with the words Ice Cream Parlor written in gold right across it. There was a big green awning over the window to shade folks inside, and it looked like the most wonderful place ever.

"Don't you worry none about the money, November," she said as we sat down at a little white Iron table. "I just dipped into my lard can full've coins and decided we needed a real treat. So, you best just hush up and enjoy," she told me.

And did I ever!

I nearly went crazy sittin' on that pretty little white iron chair studyin' all the flavors they had printed on a big slate board back of the counter. I asked Ansalu about every one of 'em, too.

"What's vanilla?" I wanted to know. And she tried to explain it to me. "Know about chocolate," I said proudly. "I had some chocolate candy once when the ladies of the Freewill Baptist Church put a bagful in with the clothes they sent up at Christmastime." My mouth watered just thinkin' about chocolate.

"But what's maple walnut, Ansalu?" I asked. I was glad the doctor had taught me to read, and it was kind of proud-makin' to read off the names of the ice cream like I'd been readin' ice cream flavors all my life. Then I wanted to know about cherry strawberry, and rainbow, which was the last one of their flavors.

It was a hard choice to make. I finally gave in to my memory of that chocolate I'd had and asked for a dish of chocolate ice cream.

I wasn't sorry after I tasted it, either.

The ice cream was so creamy and smooth and cold that I didn't have to even swallow it. It slid right down my throat all by itself. I scraped every bit of that ice cream out of my dish. And when Ansalu wasn't lookin', I ran my finger around the inside of the dish and licked it off.

When we left the ice cream store and started our walk up the mountain, I put out my tongue and ran it around my lips, just imaginin' I could still taste that chocolate ice cream.

"That surely was a fine treat, Ansalu," I said from my heart. "I don't know when I've had such a nice time since I first got this green dress." I looked down at myself as I walked along followin' Ansalu and tried to remember how the dress had looked when it was brand new, fresh from the department store.

I was sure glad I'd had the loan of Ansalu's yella shawl.

We walked alongside each other up the hill, Ansalu hummin' one of the hymns they'd played in church. In time, Ansalu turned off towards her cabin, and I went on to Odd's.

Then everything washed over me and made me sort of dread comin' back. It was like all my troubles were waitin' right there for me. I wondered what it would be like just to walk and walk and never come back.

But I guessed I didn't feel much like runnin' away.

NO WAY OUT

I looked around at the cabin I'd been livin' in for a couple of years and wondered if I'd ever really feel at home here. Oh, Odd was decent enough to me, and I didn't mind the work. And it sure was nice not to have all the noise and ruckus I'd had back with Paw and my brothers.

But still, and all, this was Odd's cabin; it wasn't mine. And no one had asked me if I wanted to come here. I'd been told.

It gave me a funny feelin' that I was somethin' like a dandelion seed. You know what I mean, they're all soft and fuzzy and don't have any roots. And they just blow every which way when the wind is blowin'. You can find dandelion seeds caught in bushes or floatin' on mountain creeks. They just don't seem to belong anywhere special.

If you've ever just lived from one day to the next, you know how it was for me then. As I watched the sun come up in the mornin' after another restless night, I just hoped I could make it clear through 'til sunset. I tried not to look ahead and wonder what life was goin' to be like for me in the years to come. I didn't hope for much. I knew I couldn't expect much, either.

Sometimes, when I was feelin' real low, I'd get to wonderin' what life was all about anyway. I hadn't started out to hurt anybody. I hadn't even asked for very much. All I wanted was to be somebody that people would look at and say "Howdy" to when we passed. I wanted to be a lady.

That didn't seem like an awful lot to ask. At least, I didn't think so. But I guessed that God if there be one, must have decided that I was tryin' to be too uppity or somethin. Leastways, it didn't look like I'd ever be anythin' but what I was now.

242

Life with Odd went on from day to day. I didn't feel any better about the things I'd done, but I'd sort of learned not to worry over it anymore. It didn't do any good at all to keep lookin' back.

I don't know when I started feelin' peaked.

It sometimes seemed like it took all I could make myself do to get through my chores. At first, I figured I was just off my feed. I sure wasn't very hungry. I almost wished for some of Paw's moonshine. Paw used to tell us, kids, to take a big seller of it when we were feelin' poorly. It most generally helped.

But this was different. I didn't really ache or hurt or nothin'. I just plain didn't feel good. My head hurt like I'd been sewin' and mendin' without enough lamplight. I'd boil up a cup of sassafras tea. Sometimes it would help, and sometimes it wouldn't.

Then I started pukin'.

I'd no more'n get set at the table when, no matter how hungry I'd been, the smell of that food would just make my stomach twist and knot and want to empty everythin' out.

Odd got tired of my runnin' outside to throw up at most every meal.

"Can't you stop doin' that, November?" he asked. "Seems to me you must be doin' somethin' to make yourself sick like that."

He didn't like it because it sort of spoiled his meal to hear me retchin' outside in the yard. Said it put him off eatin'.

I did what I could to stop gettin' sick, but nothin' seemed to work.

243

An then one mornin' I was sicker'n a dog. I felt like I was throwin' up my toenails. I finally stopped bein' sick and just lay down on the cool, worn wood of Odd's porch and let my stomach calm down. Lyin' there, I couldn't help but notice how loose my dress was fittin' me. It made me wonder what was wrong with me. I thought back to when I'd had my first curse and had thought was dyin'. I sure had been scared then. I was almost that scared now.

I remembered how much better I'd felt after I'd talked to Ansalu when I had my first curse. She had told me that what was happenin' to my body was like it was s'posed to do, and it wasn't anythin' wrong. She'd been kind and understandin' and gentle. I began to cry when I thought of how safe Ansalu had made me feel then. And how alone and awful I felt now.

I brushed away my tears and made up my mind.

Now was the time to tell Ansalu what had happened.

I fixed things so I could go to Ansalu's cabin the next day. When I told Odd what I was fixin' to do, he said he was glad.

"Maybe she's got some remedy that'll make you stop bein' so sick." I think he was plum tired of hearin' me puke.

Early the next mornin', I fixed Odd's food and redded up the cabin. I didn't take time to fix any cornbread or biscuits to take along. To tell the truth, I didn't feel like eatin' anything anyway. I just went.

I felt real tuckered out by the time I reached Ansalu's place. She came out on the porch when she heard me comin'.

"HI, November," she called out. "Did you come for a visit?" she asked.

"Yes. I came to sit awhile like old times," I told her, glad to see that old warmin' smile spread itself on her face. But when

244

she took in how thin I'd gotten and how draggy I was, she began to get a worried look.

I don't know why it took me so long to get around sharin' my troubles with Ansalu. It just did. Thinkin' about it later, I guessed I was afraid she'd be upset with me. I'd done an awful lot of foolish things. But she'd always been one to praise me, and now I guess I was afraid I might see disappointment in her eyes.

Now, sittin' there with Ansalu, all that didn't seem to matter much anymore; I knew, just watchin' her fix tea, that I should've come to her long before this. I knew she was goin' to understand.

But it was hard to get started. There was so awful much to tell.

She just sat quiet, waitin' for me to find the right words.

"Ansalu," I began, "I've got a real sorry tale to tell you."

"Figured you might," she said, waitin.'

"It's not nice," I warned her, lookin' to see how she took it.

"I'm willin' to listen."

"Well then, it's about me and Junior Washbon," I began.

An somehow, once I got started, I got the whole thing out. I didn't save back anythin', either. Just told it all like it happened. Even to the part that shamed me most, the part where I really didn't hate what he did to me.

Ansalu was real quiet when I finished, and I couldn't bring myself to look into her face.

Neither of us said anythin' for a bit. Then Ansalu said, real gentle, "Is that all, November Sunshine?"

245

When she put the Sunshine to my name, I knew she was treatin' this real serious.

I sighed.

"Not quite," I said, hatin' to get started on the Brother Glen Crabtree part of the whole mess. I guess I hated that part so much because I had a feelin' that, by rights, she could say, "I told you not to go back down there! And even though I had it comin', I knew I didn't want her to say it. I felt myself sigh real deep.

Bit by bit, I got through the whole story. Ansalu only spoke once. That was when I told her about Brother Crabtee givin' me brandy when I was in his caravan.

"The scoundrel Ansalu said then, soundin' like she wanted to pitch into him or do somethin' to him. Men like him should be drummed out of town!"

But other than that, she was quiet til I got to the end of the whole sorry tale.

Then she did somethin' I'll always remember. She didn't say a word, just stood up and came over to where I was sittin'. She took my hands real gentle and sort of lifted me out of my chair. She put her arms around me and held me tight and warm in her arms. and even though my head was a good space higher than hers, she gave me the feelin' that she was stronger than I was and would look after me.

I wanted to stand there with our arms round each other, just rockin' together in such a comfortin' way until the day I died. I could just begin to feel the warmth of her goodness creepin' into the cold places inside me that I thought would never warm up. Then she began sort of croonin' and patted my back for a little while.

And then my stomach started heavin', and I broke away and ran outside. I just made it out to the yard when I began to throw up again.

Ansalu came and stood in the doorway watchin' me. I couldn't pay much attention to her; I was too busy losing my mornin' biscuit.

By the time I stopped heavin', Ansalu was standin' by my side and wipin' my face with a soft, wet cloth.

"Well, November, it's no wonder you threw up like that. You've been carryin' the weight of the world on your back for some time now. And you don't have to do that anymore, November, things that happened weren't your fault, not directly. I had a bad feelin' about that Brother Crabtree from the start."

She led me inside and over to her rockin' chair. I sat down feelin' tired Ansalu went on, "Never did trust a man that was too good lookin'," she said in a peppery voice. "Time has taught me that men who make themselves out to be so great with all their smooth talk and fancy clothes are usually out to flimflam other people into doin' what they want 'em to do. No matter who gets hurt."

I couldn't help wonderin' how Ansalu had gotten so smart. She knew an awful lot about things I'd never dreamed of.

"I wish I'd listened to you and not gone back to the revival," I told 'er, feelin' sorrowful that I hadn't. "Iffen, I'd done like you said; I wouldn't feel so bad now."

I watched Ansalu's face to see if she was put out with me. But she had a faraway look, and I could tell she was thinkin' back to somethin' in 'er own life. "A body can't always see the rocks in a road when the road bends this way and that, November," she finally said. "An you musn't be too hard on yourself. You didn't do anythin' that lots of other girls before you haven't done. And for less reason!" she said. Then she paused and added, "Not that that makes it right, of course," and smiled at me, takin' the bite out of 'er words.

"You know, Ansalu, I feel much better after tellin' all this to you. I sure hated not bein' able to talk with you and all. I was afraid you'd be so upset with me you wouldn't want to be friends anymore."

She turned and looked at me with 'er mouth hangin' open.

"Why November Sunshine!" she cried, "don't you know that friends aren't like that? Not real friends, I mean. Real friends care about you and what happens to you. They love you warts and all!" she finished. I had to laugh out loud.

"Thank you, Ansalu, I feel so much better. Maybe now I won't throw up so much and feel sick all the time."

Ansalu sat up real straight.

"Tell me about that, November," she said, her voice real sharp

So I told 'er about not carin' to eat very much because everythin' I put in my stomach seemed to come back up later.

After I'd explained about my not feelin' good and she had asked me a whole lot of questions, she leaned forward in 'en chair and took hold of my hand. She rubbed the back of my hand and looked into my face like she had somethin' to say; she wasn't wantin' much to talk about.

"November, you ain't sick, child," she said in a real gentle kind of voice.

"Oh yes, I am, Ansalur; I told 'er, I really am."

248

"No, November, you only THINK you're sick," she insisted, "what you really are, November, is with child."

"I'm what?"

"With child, November, I mean, you're goin to have a baby," she explained.

I just looked at 'er, not really takin' in what she was sayin'.

"But I CAN'T have a baby," I said. "I'm not ready to have any babies yet?"

She just looked at me and shook 'er head, "I'm sorry, November," she said, "But that's 'zactly what I think is wrong with you,"

"But… you mean… when Odd?" I couldn't finish.

"No, November," she said, real serious soundin', "I'm pretty sure that it isn't Odd who started that baby in your stomach."

"But who else could it be?" I started to ask.

But I didn't finish, I knew.

The baby inside me, still just part of a bad dream, belonged to Junior Washbon. Or, the thought washed over me like a bad feelin'; it might belong to Brother Glen Crabtree!

The truth of what was happenin' was just too much. I couldn't seem to move or talk or even think. All I knew was that I couldn't let go of Ansalu's hand. I held on tight, real tight, and waited for the nightmare to go away.

"Are you all right, child?" Ansalu asked me. Then I noticed she had moved closer and was usin' her other hand to stroke the hair back from my forehead, just like a soft summer wind will do.

"I'll be all right, I tried to tell 'er. But inside, I wasn't sure at all that I'd ever be all right again. I couldn't have a baby! I wasn't ready for a baby! Are not that way, not that way! Oh God! Inside, I was filled with screamin' sounds tryin' to get out and be heard."

"Let's walk out in back, and I'll show you how my yarb garden is comin', November," Ansalu said softly. At first, I wanted to tell 'er I didn't care about 'er old yarb garden, but then I found it was a relief to think about somethin' else besides the baby and the mess I was in.

I follered 'er from one plant to another while she told me all kinds of things about what you could do with each different yarb and how it would grow and all.

After a while, the screams inside died down somewhat, and I found I could think and talk again.

"I'm better now, Ansalu. I'm about as much better as I'll ever be, I guess."

We went back inside, and Ansalu poured me another cup've her good tea. Whilst I sipped it, feelin' the warmness spreadin' into my stomach and warmin' me, I began to think of all the things I'd need to know about havin' a baby.

"Ohhh!" I moaned, wonderin' where it would ever end up. I'd had no idea that night on the mountain path with Junior Washbon that this could happen. And I certainly'd never thought anythin' like this when I went to Brother Crabtree's caravan. "Oh my," I whispered, "On, my, on my."

Ansalu just patted my hand.

I wish I could die," I whispered. But Ansalu heard.

"No, you don't," she hollered at me. And I mean hollered!

She jumped up out of 'er chair as mad as a wet hen. "Don't you EVER let me hear you talk like that again, November Sunshine!" she said, 'er voice comin' down a little from where it'd started.

I couldn't look at 'er for the way I felt about myself.

Then Ansalu came over and stood in front of me. "Look at me, November Sunshine!" she said. I turned my eyes up in 'er direction. "No, I mean, really look at me!" she said again, leavin' no doubt that she meant it.

I lifted my head and looked at 'er right on. She was standin' in front of me lookin' like she was fit to burst, and she started waggin' her pointy finger at me when she began talkin'.

"Now you just listen to me, young woman. I'm not goin' to stand by and watch you feel sorry for yourself and ruin your life, I'm just not!"

I wondered what she was aimin' at.

"There's somethin' you've gotta learn about yourself, and learn it fast"

"What's that?" I asked.

"It's that you got it in you to be a survivor! If you fall apart over this thing that's happenin' to you, it'll be because you let yourself fall apart. Do you understand me? Survivors are people who hang on when everybody else peters out!"

"But, Ansalu, I'm goin to have a baby!" I said, tryin' not to blubber. "It's not like I fell and broke my leg or somethin',"

"I know about havin' babies, November. Didn't I have two of my own who died back when they were little from the wastin' away sickness? Don't tell me nothin about havin babies! You aren't the first girl wh's ever managed to get 'erself in a family

251

way, and you won't be the last." She looked at me with such fire comin' from 'er eyes that I thought she'd almost burn me up if I dared to argue with 'er. So just kept my peace and listened.

"Now, November, I'm gonna tell you somthin' and give you some advice, and you'd best take it! First off, I already said you can be a survivor, and I mean it. Why, November Sunshine, you're stronger than all those men put together! Not even if you rolled Odd and Junior Washbon and Brother Glen Crabtree all together would they be as strong as you. You think any of those men could stand up to what you've already stood up to in your short life? Bein' raised by a passle of brothers who weren't much older'n you in the first place. And a Paw who didn't give a tinker's dam about his only girl baby. All he cared about was that he figgered you'd killed your Maw gettin' born. Such stupid thinkin'!" She shook 'er head like she was mad clear through. "Anythin' you learned, you had to learn almost by yourself. I remember how scared you were that day I first came across you in the woods. Your Paw hadn't even thought to tell you about the curse, and there you were, bleedin', sure you were gonna die."

Ansalu reached out and patted my back real gentle. "Which of those men do you think could survive bein' traded off for a measly rifle? Not a one of 'em, I'll bet! They'd all turn mewly and weak and curl right up and die havin' to put up with what you've already had to put up with."

"Now, don't you know, girl, you already ARE a survivor. All you gotta do is dredge up some of that spizz that got you this far, and you're all set. Pshaw! It won't be hard for you to have that baby. I'll be right here to tell you things you need to know as you go along. and your body doesn't need to be told, it already knows everythin' there is to makin' babies. You and me together are gonna see this thing through."

She stopped talkin' and walked over to the door and stood there like she was thinkin'. Then she turned to me and said, "You know, November, there isn't any reason why we can't go down to Wilson's Springs and see that doctor feller who stayed with you and Odd back a place. I hear tell he's set up his office, and folks seem to like 'is doctorin. He can tell you anythin' you might need to know first off."

I started to say no; I didn't want to see the doctor. Havin' him see me like this, well. I just didn't want to do it.

Ansalu leaned over and put 'er face right near mine. "Do you under-stand what I've been sayin', November?"

I signed and said I did. Ansalu seemed satisfied.

Then she went over and poured 'erself another cup of tea and sat down. She looked at me and said, "Now you just sit there real quiet whilst I do some heavy thinkin'."

I did, and she did.

By the time she put down 'er tea cup, empty, she seemed to've gotten through whatever heavy thinkin' it was she wanted to do. She sat up real straight in 'er chair and started talkin'.

"November, I've been thinkin' what you should do. There ain't no doubt in my mind that you're goin to have a baby, and there ain't much of any way to get out of that. That's a fact, and people can't go round just willy-nilly changin' facts. So, there you are, number one, you're goin' to have a baby."

"I already know that Ansalu," I said, just a shade annoyed. "You don't have to tell me that!"

"Don't get upset, November; I'm just goin' through the whole thing so you know what kind of choices you got."

"Choices? What do you mean by choices?"

"That's what I'm gettin' at, November. Sometimes, folks forget they got choices. We've got to look at the way things are real close to see what choices you got. And the way I see it, you don't have any choice about havin' the baby. That's a fact."

"An?" I tried to hurry 'er on.

"And now we'll look at your choices. You got at least three that I can see so far. Maybe four. Maybe we'll find some more choices while we're talkin'."

"What choices do you think I have, Ansalu?" I asked 'er. I was gettin' curious about what she meant..

"Well, child, you got three men in your life at this point. Any one of 'em gives you a choice. First, you could say that Junior Washbon fathered your baby. You don't know for sure that he did, but you don't know for sure that he didn't, either. So you could just up and say that Junior Washbon gave you this baby."

I looked at Ansalu, all upset, but she didn't pay me no mind and just went right on ahead.

"An then you might just as easy say that Brother Glen Crabtree gave you this baby. and you don't know iffen he did or iffen he didn't. It really don't matter. It's whatever you say. And the third choice is Odd. You could say that Odd is the paw of your baby An, just like Junior Washbon and Brother Crabtree, you don't know for sure whether he did or he didn't!"

"Those are my choices?" I croaked.

"Well, for a start. You got the choice not to say anythin' about it and just have the baby by yourself . And the third choice is Odd. You could say that Odd is the paw of your baby, and just like Junior Washbon and Brother Crabtree, you don't know for sure whether he did or he didn't. Also, remember, folks will talk. They'd talk somethin' terrible, November, but you could live through it".

I thought of how life would be for me havin' a fatherless baby, and the whole idea scared me, so I started to cry.

"Wait now, November, time for the water works later if you need 'em. What you gotta think about is, do you want to say that one of those men is the father of your baby? If you do, you can hold out for any one of them to marry you or pay you enough right along to live on!" She finished, soundin' proud of herself for gettin' it all said.

"Well, Ansalu," I said, laughin' a little in spite of now bad I felt, "I sure do admire the way you get to the bottom of a problem and set a body onto her choices. I shook my head in wonder, thinkin' about what she'd said and tryin' to imagine how things'd be. "Do you think I could go down there to Washbon's Department Store and tell Junior Washbon that he's goin' to be the father of my baby? I know that Eloise Bardwell is fixin' to marry Junior Washbon some day. You've seen her, Ansalu. She's a real pretty lady and has had a lot of schoolin' and has a real importan' paw and all. What do you think Junior Washbon would say to my tellin' him he has to marry me? How do you think he'd feel about givin' up Eloise Bardwell? He just plum wouldn't do it, Ansalu." I felt sure about what I was sayin' and stopped talkin'.

"On November, I don't intend that you should marry him. I'm only just sayin' that if you decide he's the one who fathered your baby, then he ought to own up to it and see that you're cared for and all that."

"It wouldn't work, Ansallu, and you don't think I'd ever hear of marryin' Brother Glen Crabtee, do you?" I knew I'd never want to do that after all, I had found out about him from the man who drove me up the hill that night. "An I know held not be about marryin' me, either, I thought some more about what

Ansalu had said were my choices. Odd "An, as for Odd, well, I've been livin in his cabin quite a while now, and he don't look to me for you know," I said, still shy about talkin about such things. "Anyway, he's never once offered to have the words said over us by a preacher."

"Well, November, you have plenty of time to think things over. You're gain to have to figure out which one of them you want to call the father, though, cause everybody knows that a woman can't start a baby all by herself. There has to be a man in it somewhere!" She stood up and started puttin' the tea things away. "I guess we've talked enough about this for now," she said. "Seems to me the next thing is to go down to the Springs and see that doctor, you know what did you say his name was, November?"

"He said his name was Brad Fletcher. He wanted me to call him by his name, but it didn't seem fittin' to call a man with all that schoolin' by his first name." I smiled as I thought of the month or so that the doctor'd stayed with Odd and me and taught me how to read. His automobile had long since been hauled away, and all his things were gone. But I could still remember the gift he'd given me. The gift of readin' and writin'. I felt good thinkin' about it. "He sure was good to me, Ansalu."

"Of course, and don't forget, you were good to him, too. Don't forget that. After all, you and Odd prob'ly saved his life. If you hadn't carried him down from the woods when he was hurt, he'd have died, right!!!!! There. And no one would've known a thing about it 'til somebody finally found his automobile all smashed up on the mountain."

"But, Ansalu, it makes me feel funny to think of him. Seein' me, you know, undressed"

"Well, you'll just have to get over that, November. After all, he's a doctor, and he's seen lots and lots of men and women

256

without their clothes on. That's the only way a doctor can figure out what's wrong and how to cure a body. You won't be a mite more than just another patient when he's lookin' to see now you be." She thought a bit. "Peers to me, he'll be happy to make sure that everythin' is all right with you while you're carryin' the baby, too."

I thought about goin' to see the doctor and how I hadn't seen him since the day he left Odd's cabin. I wondered if I'd be able to deal with him as a doctor. But since I'd never been to a doctor in my whole life, I didn't have any idea what to expect. I just shrugged my shoulders and said I'd do what she wanted. It was for sure I'd need help havin' the baby, I didn't know a thing about havin' one, and I sure couldn't remember when I was one. So, I guessed that Ansalu was right. I might as well go see Doctor Brad.

Before I left Ansalu's, we made plans to go down to Wilson's Springs next time I came over.

I decided it was best not to tell Odd anythin' about where I was goin' or why. He'd been strange enough about the doctor, and I didn't want him to say I shouldn't go. It wasn't time to make up my mind about my choices yet.

I lay in the bed thinkin' long into the night. I must've gone to sleep sometime, though, because I had a real scary dream. I couldn't remember much of it when I finally woke up, but it sort've hung over me like a grey cloud most of the day.

While I was doin' my chores around the cabin, I put my mind to what Ansalu had said. She had made me a little restless with all her talk, but now today, lookin' back, I could see what she was almin' at. And she was right. I had to decide sooner or later who to claim the baby's paw so that the baby could be cared for. But I wasn't ready to make that choice yet. I had to do a lot more thinkin' about what each choice would mean to me and the baby. What would happen between Eloise

Bardwell and Junior Washbon if it got out that some girl up the mountain was havin' Junior Washbon's baby? I knew I didn't owe Junior Washbon or Eloise Bardwell anythin'. Still and all, Eloise Bardwell had been nice to me, and it was her I wanted most to be like. I didn't fool myself into thinking people in Wilson's Springs would care a hoot about what happened to me. How could they? They didn't even know who I was. But I remembered what Eloise Bardwell had said about my bein' free. She'd know she'd care. And she'd probably be real hurt, too. Maybe not for me, but that Junior Washbon had given somebody else his baby.

And then I thought about Brother Crabtree. I had felt so special when he was teachin' me after the revival each night. He had told me about my soul, "Immortal soul," he'd called it. I still didn't know just what he meant, but he'd said the soul was real important, and I had one. But then I remembered about that drink he gave me and how dizzy I'd got from it. I couldn't remember much else about that night, but I remembered how ashamed I'd felt being hauled home like I was just some throwaway stuff he needed to get rid of. I thought about how the automobile driver'd let slip that there'd been other girls like me, lots of 'em. I knew Brother Crabtree would never hold still for me to say the baby was his'n and that he oughta do right by me.

That brought my thinkin' up to Odd. and that was a hard nut to crack. Odd was the one I was sure wasn't the baby's father. Oh, it was all such a puzzle! I got to thinkin' that if I said Odd was the baby's paw, that would mean I'd be tied to him from there on in, and I'd never get away. It would mean I'd spend all my days here in this little cabin, and I'd never, never, get to be somebody; I'd just never get to be a lady.

Some choices, I thought.

I tried to put the whole thing out of my mind. But it was like if you burn your hand or arm or leg. You can try to put it out

258

of your mind so it doesn't bother you so much, but it's a pain that just won't go away. And it was like that about the baby. Knowin' I was goin to have a baby was right there in my mind all the time. It just would't go away.

I started makin' dough for tomorrow's bread. And the more I thought about the mess I was in, the harder I pounded that dough. It'll probably be the best wheat bread I've ever baked, I thought, havin' to laugh some at myself standin' there poundin' the bejabers outta that dough.

When I sat down for a cup of warmed-up coffee at midday, I decided I'd best see if I couldn't begin to make some food stay down. I could tell from the way my clothes fitted me that I was gettin' some thinner. Ansalu had said it was important for the baby that I eat regularly. I crumbled a biscuit into a bowl and heated a little milk on the stove. Then I poured the warm milk over the biscuit and spooned it in that way. I'd never done that before. Ansalu had said people fed biscuits and warm milk to sick people and old ones who didn't have any teeth. I was suprized at how good it tasted, better than I expected. I was pleased when it stayed down and didn't make me sick.

Workin' around, I couldn't help! Think how Ansalu had called me a survivor. I had asked her what a survivor was, and she'd said it was somebody who managed to get along in spite of trouble. Like if your biscuits don't rise, you pour honey over 'em and call 'em flapjacks. Anyway, knowin' that the thought I was one, a survivor, made me feel like I wasn't maybe all that bad. Ansalud said Junior Washbon and Brother Crabtree'd taken advantage of me. It would be nice to think that. But in my heart, I knew better. I hadn't really felt all that bad about what was happenin' to me when it was happenin', I'd have to remember that to my shame forever.

It was about two weeks later that I felt up to takin' another walk over to Ansalu's. I washed myself real good and put on the clothes I'd washed out the night before. I didn't want to go to Wilson's Springs to see the doctor lookin' like I couldn't take care of myself. It would be bad enough havin' him know I was havin' a baby, and I wasn't even married or nothin'. I didn't want any more shame than that.

Ansalu was glad to see me and said today was just fine for goin' to the doctor's. She also said she had a little money put by to pay for our visit.

"Do you have to pay to see a doctor?" I asked.

"Of course, November, where do you think he gets money to live on?"

She shook her head at my not knowin', but she told me not to worry about that just now. That'd take care of itself. I didn't see how it would, but together, we started off down the trail.

"What will he do to me?" I asked her, catchin' up so I could hear her answer. Truth is, she wasn't walkin' all that fast; I was just walkin' extra slow, not wantin' to get there.

I don't know for sure, November. But for starters, he'll put a thing around your arm and take your blood pressure."

"What's that?"

"It tells him how fast your heart is beatin' and if your blood is movin' like it ought to be."

"What happens if it's not?"

"He'll give you some medicine."

"I'm not gonna take no medicine," I blurted, meanin' it. "I had some tonic Paw gave me once when I got sick, and it like to killed me!"

"Oh, November, this is different medicine. Mostly, doctor's give out pills that you just pop in your mouth and swallow with a drink of water"

"Oh, I felt some better about it, but I hoped I wouldn't need any medicine."

Then Ansalu made our trip seem shorter by tellin' me some of the different things the doctor might do to make sure I was all right. None of 'em sounded real bad except for the one where he puts a needle in your arm and takes out blood.

"I've heard tell of night creatures that sucks out peoples blood," I said to Ansalu. I didn't like the sound of that one at all.

"For pity's sake!" Ansalu said, stoppin' right there on the path and turnin' to look at me. "If you aren't something, then she told me how the doctor just took a tiny little bit of blood and examined it. She said it didn't hurt hardly at all, and I wasn't to make a fuss about it if he stuck me with his needle.

"I won't shame you, Ansalu, I promise," I said. "It was just that everythin' was comin' so fast, and I didn't feel ready just ye'!"

When we got down to Wilson's Springs, Ansalu asked a boy on the street where the doctor's office was, and we went there.

NOTHIN' STAYS THE SAME

It wasn't as bad havin' Doctor Brad check me as I was afraid it was goin' to be. He seemed real glad to see me when Ansalu and I got to his office. But once he knew I needed him to help me as a doctor, he sorta changed. I mean, he acted like I was a customer in a store. Sort of like he wasn't treatin' a friend now, but what Ansalu later told me was what they call his professional manner. She said good doctors had to do that lest their patients get too embarrassed. He showed me where to go and take off my clothes and put on some kind of backwards shirt thing. I had a hard time holdin' it together in the back so part of me wouldn't stick out, but I managed. Then I climbed up on a big table he had there that seemed awful cold on my back where the shirt thing came apart. I felt the goosebumps poppin' out and scooched around some to warm myself up. Doctor Brad started pokin' and proddin' at me and ask if it hurt and things like that. All the time, he didn't look at my face at all, and it was like he didn't know it was me.

Then, after he was finished pokin' and askin' questions, he told me to put my clothes back on and went out of the room. I did and went where Ansalu and Doctor Brad were waitin' for me. It was funny. When I came in with my clothes on, he acted like the old Doctor Brad again.

"Well, November," he said when I was all settled into a chair, "Ansalu was right; you most certainly are goin' to have a baby. His face was smilin', but his eyes seemed sad. He just looked at me that way for a bit, and I didn't know what else was comin'.

"How do you feel about havin' a baby, November? You're still quite young to start a family."

"Oh, this baby ain't my family!" I burst out. I hadn't meant to say that. It just came out.

Then I didn't know what to say, but Doctor Brad just waved his hand in the air like it was all right not to say anythin' more. It seemed to me, sittin' there in his office with those papers with little round gold things and fancy printin' on 'em on the wall sayin' he was a doctor, that he must know just about everythin' there was to know. I figured since he stayed in the cabin with Odd and me for such a long while that, he must know the baby wasn't Odd's. I guess he thought it best not to ask me where the baby was comin' from. Or who.

"November," he said in a comfortin' kind of voice, "things in life don't always work out the way we plan for 'em to. And you had a rougher start than most. He smiled to show he wasn't holdin' nothin' against me. "So, however, this happened, you're startin' a baby; I mean, that's your business. I just want you to know that I'm your friend, and I'll always be. I'll do whatever I can to help you get through what's ahead for you, and I don't want you to worry about havin' this baby. Things will work out.

I couldn't stop the tears from comin' to my eyes. Thinkin' how good Ansalu was bein' to me and now Doctor Brad. Somethin' down inside me was beginnin' to warm up like the sun was shinin' on it, and I wasn't so scared anymore.

Then Doctor Brad started tellin' me all the things I was 'sposed to eat and do and told Ansalu that she should check up on me now and again.

When we were leavin' the office, Ansalu made like she was goin' to take some money out of her little drawstring bag, but she stopped when Doctor Brad gave her a look like he didn't want her to and shook his head.

"We're friends," was all he said.

Later, she said, "It would have been and insult to try and pay that man, November. It didn't take two eyes to see that he's a good friend, and friends don't do things for each other for pay."

I thought about that a couple of minutes as we walked along the street, I wasn't payin' much attention to where we were goin', and when I looked up, I was s'urpized to find we were outside the ice cream parlor!

Ansalu gave me a little push inside. "Seems to me, November, since I already counted that money as spent that we ought to spend some of it. and I can't think of a better place than right here!" I began to feel even better! We looked around and found us seats in a little stall over by a window. She called it a booth when I asked her what it was. Sittin' in the booth made you feel like you were closed off in a special little world of your own. I liked the feelin' a lot.

"I'm goin' to have chocolate again, I told her. "I've been thinkin' right along that if I even came here again, I'd have me another dish of that chocolate Ice cream."

"There's enough money for two scoops this time," Ansalu said. "You can pick one of chocolate and one of somethin' else if you want."

"Are you sure?" I asked, not wantin' to use up too much of her money. She nodded and smiled at me, and I started to read the list up on the wall. "Ansalu, that makes it even harder to choose!" I said I studied the list of flavors up on the wall for a bit, havin' a hard time decidin' which to take, so busy in choosin' that I forgot for a bit about the baby and my worry. Then, right in the middle of thinkin' I'd have vanilla, I remembered, and the feelin' of worry washed over me, and 1 stopped studyin' the flavors of ice cream; I saw Ansalu lookin' at me with a worried look on her face. And decided I'd best brighten up, or it'd spoil her treat.

"Wish ALL my worries were like choosin' which flavor of ice cream I want," I said, lookin' back at the list on the wall.

Ansalu laughed out loud right there in the ice cream parlor. "You see, November," she said, " I TOLD you... you were a survivor. That's the way you need to accept things when you can't change somethin' bad, find some way to laugh about it. It's like takin' the sting out of a bee bite. After you laugh about it, when the sting is gone, it don't hurt so much."

She was right.

I up and ordered two scoops of chocolate!

It was late the next week when I got over to Ansalu's cabin again. Odd was beginnin' to take longer gettin' himself shaved and dressed and off to work in the mornin', so it made my chores take longer. I had begun to notice that Odd was takin' a lot more pains with himself, too. Sometimes, he even heated up extra water and took a bath in the metal tub. And he'd sharpened up his straight razor and scraped every bit of chin hair off each mornin'. And when his shoe lace tore, he knotted it together real careful and tucked the knot underneath where it wouldn't show.

I didn't ask him why he was gettin' more particular about himself, but I wondered about it. I put it down to his workin' more and more at Washbon's Department Store, which is what he was doin'.

Anyway, I finally got over to Ansalu's.

"We've got to begin gettin' things together for the baby, November," she said to me. Then she held up a piece she was knittin', and I could see that it was the littlest cap you ever could make.

"Is that for the baby?" I asked.

"It certainly isn't for Odd!" she laughed. Then she showed me a box she had that was just full of real soft yarns.

"I decided to rip out a couple of old sweaters of Will's," she said. "Then I bleached out the yarn and used berries to dye it."

I was so pleased! 1 knelt down before the box and just fingered that yarn. How good that would feel to a little baby, I thought. How warm and nice that soft yarn would make him feel. Him? Oh my, would the baby be a girl or a boy? I pondered. There wasn't any way to know beforehand, I guessed.

And for the first time, I began to think of the baby as real. Up to now, the baby had just been a worry. Suddenly, that yarn and the tiny cap Ansalu was knittin' for it made the baby a real thing. It was goin' to be a livin' and breathin' thing. A boy or a girl. A real person.

"Can I tell if it'll be a boy or a girl?" I asked Ansalu.

"There's no way of tellin' yet," she told me. "Some say you can tell later on by the way you carry the baby."

"You mean carry it in my arms?"

"No, November. When the baby grows bigger inside your stomach, it will make your stomach pooch way out. And some folks say the way it pooches out shows if it's a boy baby or a girl baby. If you stick out more at the top, it's goin' to be a boy." She was still for a minute. "Or is it the other way round?" she asked herself. Then she shook her head. "Oh well, it doesn't really matter yet. We'll ask Doctor Brad by and by if he can tell."

I had a worry. "Won't Odd find out about the baby if he sees me makin' such things?" I asked.

"Oh, I don't mean for you to take 'em home yet," she said. "I figure you can come over here whenever you can find the time, and we'll work on 'em here."

That seemed like a mighty good idea to me. I never had done any real sewin', and I'd never learned to knit. All's I'd ever sewed was patches on my brother's pants and the hem in that curtain I'd put up over the chink in my window back in Paw's cabin. But Ansalu said she'd show me how to make things for the baby, so I was content.

Thinkin' of Paw's cabin made me remember all the different scraps of material in the pretty box Lem had made for me so long ago. I decided I'd try to get word to Caleb to bring me the box if it was still around the cabin, someplace. Knowin' Paw, it probably was. He never was one to clean up and throw things away.

Goin' to Ansalu's cabin became the center of my world. She was teachin' me how to sew in neat little stitches, and once, we walked down to Wilson's Springs for more thread and some pretty new ribbons. And it was a proud day for me when I could hold up the prettiest little wrapper for a baby you ever did see. I could hardly believe I'd made it myself!

 Deep down inside, though, I knew I still hadn't solved my problem. It was sittin' there, heavy.

Finally, one day, Ansalu laid down her knittin' and looked at me real hard.

"November, we've got to talk," she said.

I put down my sewin' slow; I was afraid of what was comin'.

"You can't put off decidin' about the baby's paw any longer, child," she said. "In just a little bit, you're goin' to start showin', and then it will be too late to make up your mind.

You've got to be thinkin' on it now, while you still have the choice."

I sighed. "I know, Ansalu, and I've been worryin' it over and over in my mind; I wouldn't feel right about facin' Junior Washbon with bein' the father. Even if he might be!" I tried to explain, "It's just that I've been thinkin' how people would feel if I said the baby's paw was Junior Washbon." I hurried on, "Oh, not about me, Ansalu; I reckon I could live with whatever they'd dish out. But it's just that a baby seems awful small and can't take care of itself. And if I were to tell that its paw was Junior Washbon, everybody would know that and call the baby a bastard; I was near tears. "An Ansalu, I don't want this poor little baby to be nobody's bastard! I might be poor and just hill-folk, but nobody in Paw's cabin was ever in a place to be called a bastard, and I can't do that to this baby, neither."

Ansalu just nodded.

"An the same goes for namin' Brother Crabtree. You and I already know he's the kind of man who'd try to weasel out of anythin' he didn't like. You knew it 'fore I did. What kind of a paw would he make for my baby? He sure wouldn't marry me, and my baby would still be called a bastard."

Ansalu nodded again.

"So, I've just about made up my mind," I said firmly. "An I'm not sure how it's all goin' to work out, but I've got to give it a try."

"Can you tell me what you're goin' to do?" Ansalu asked.

"I'll try, although I don't have everythin' all worked out yet," I told her. I laid down my sewin'. Explainin' what I had in mind would take all my wits. I took a deep breath. Ansalu hitched her chair a little closer to listen.

"Well, I've thought, and I've thought," I began, "and there ain't no way I'm goin' to choose to name either Junior Washbon or Brother Crabtree as this baby's paw. None. So that leaves me with Odd." I had to take another deep breath to go on. This was hard goin'. "Now I know Odd ain't as easy a man as those other two, but he'll have to do. Anyways, everybody knows I've been livin' in his cabin for a long time now. He doesn't have much schoolin', but he's pretty smart in the ways of the woods and all. And he's doin' fine at Washbon's Store and keeps a right smart of food and money comin' in. and lately he's been keepin' himself clean and right nice lookin'. He's not given to drinkin' a lot like my Paw was, neither.

"I know Odd ain't never goin to be much more'n he is right now. But I can live with that. I don't have any time to look around and find any other choices. Since it can't be Junior Washbon and it can't be Brother Crabtree, it just has to be Odd. I'm gonna have to tell Odd that he's the father of this here, baby."

Ansalu was quiet for a bit, then she asked, "But, November, you said Odd hasn't been near you that way for a long time. Won't he know that there's no way this baby could be his?"

"I figured on that, too, Ansalu. And this is the part I don't like very much," I told her. "I'm goin… I'm goin… to have to trick him."

"Trick him? How're you gonna do that?"

I wished I didn't have to say, but I owed it to Ansalu to be honest. "I know a lot more about makin' babies than I did before," I said. "An lookin' back on what happened between us nights when I first came to his cabin, I see now that Odd didn't know all that much more than I did." I stopped talkin' and shook my head at those memories. "He likes to wear himself to a frazzle," was all I wanted to say about that.

"So," I went on, "now the next part is up to me. I've gotta ... gotta ... Oh, Ansalur, I cried. "I don't think I can do it!"

"I think I knew what you got on your mind, November, but you'd best spell it all out for me."

"Thinkin' about all that bumpin' and pawin' stuff again nearly makes me want to die, Ansalu, but I've gotta do it. There's no other way. I've gotta make Odd try again so that I can tell him the baby is his."

"Oh, November," Ansalu said, takin' me in her arms like she often did when she knew I was upset.

"It'll be all right, Ansalu. I'll make do some way."

I didn't know how, but I'd figure out some way to make myself more temptin' to Odd. I had to make him come into my bed again. and I knew someway I had to help him do a better job of this man and woman stuff with me than we'd done before. And there wasn't any time to waste.

For the next few days I watched Odd real close, lookin' for some way to make him want me again. Bein' with child had made my breasts swell up, and I was beginnin' to swell over the top of my dress just like Sara had done. I remembered how Len'd moaned and groaned pawin' her that time in the woods, and even though it made me feel all knotted up inside, I knew I had to get Odd to do the same thing to me.

But the right time just didn't seem to come.

I waited, and I watched. I was beginnin' to be afraid the right time might never come. I knew I had to take things into my own hands.

I hoped for it to rain. There's somethin' about bein' in a snug cabin with a warm fire and soft lantern light that makes you feel easy inside. So I waited for the first rain. I watched the sky for clouds and kept hopin'. And then one mornin', I woke to the sound of rain fallin' on the tin roof overhead. I smiled to myself.

Today, I was goin' to make everythin' all right. I didn't think about all that meant I'd have to do and all, I just thought about gettin' the baby a paw.

Somewhere durin' all this worrisome time, I had come to believe that things are only right or only wrong when people say they are. You know what I mean? I mean, like, it's not right to lie. People always say it ain't right to lie to other people. And that's so. But if somebody is awful sick and they look like they're dyin', then it seems to me it's all right to tell a lie. It's all right to say, "Oh, Sister Lucy, you're lookin' much better today. It won't be long til you're up and around again."

You see, sometimes a lie is a lie, and sometimes it isn't. I figure it's only a lie when it's hurtin' somebody.

So I had figured out that what I was goin' to do with Odd wasn't really bad. I had it figured out that it might please Odd if I made him like all that roochin' around together in bed. Leastways, it seemed to me that that's what men seemed to want from us women. So, I wouldn't be takin' anythin' away from Odd if I gave him pleasure, would I? and besides, it'd be gettin' a paw for my baby. And that was good, wasn't it?

So I cleaned that cabin to a fare-thee-well after Odd went off to work. I cleaned it til it looked and smelled real nice and fresh. and I put bread to bakin' because Odd liked to come home and smell the place full of bread smell. I fixed and extra good supper and had it simmerin' away on the back of the stove.

Finally, just on toward dark, Odd came home from work. Usually, I just nodded when he came in or started puttin' his supper on the table.

But tonight, I had a plan.

Soon's, he came in the cabin door; I took his wet hat from him and shook the water offen it. Some of the water splashed on top of the wood stove and danced and sizzled on the hot tron top, makin' a real friendly sound.

Then I went over to him, lettin' worry show on my face and helped him take off his wet jacket. I hung it careful over the back of a chair so it'd dry out by the stove.

Then, and this part was hard, I went over to him and, reached up and started unbuttoning his shirt.

"I can do that, November," he said, pullin' back.

But I didn't stop. "Let me help you, Odd," I said real soft and went on unbuttonin' his wet shirt. He just stood there wonderin' at me. I reached up and slipped the shirt off his shoulders, lettin' my fingers sort of slide down over his skin. I was surprised at how nice and smooth it felt to do that.

The next part was harder. I reached down and unbuttoned the top of his pants. I almost couldn't bring myself to do that at first, but Odd stood real still as though he didn't know what was goin' to happen. The one button caught on a thread, and I couldn't manage it.

"Here," he said and opened it himself.

While he was gettin' that button open, I reached up and unbuttoned my dress and let it fall to the floor.

I'm a little 'shamed to say it, but I didn't have anythin' on under that dress.

I just stood there naked and felt Odd lookin' and lookin' at me.

I don't know who moved first, but before you knew it, we were both on that bed, a feelin' and a touchin', and Odd was makin' the same kind of moanin' sounds Lem had made over Sara.

It wasn't as bad as I'd thought it'd be.

Not near.

I had to help Odd just a little; he was kinda shy about gettin' himself into me. But he managed.

And after it was all over, I lay back just thinkin'.

It's done.

It hadn't been as hard as I'd been afraid it'd be. That made what I was plannin' a lot easier.

Odd went right off to sleep. After a while, I climbed out of bed to take the supper off the stove. Just because he didn't want it right now wasn't any reason to let it go to waste. I figured to let him sleep a little and then wake him up to eat.

I thought about takin' the comforter over to the corner near the stove, but I decided against it. I had gotten used to the bed, I told myself. Might as well sleep there.

I was feelin' sort of shamed and yet sort of proud of myself when I went over to Ansalu's a couple of days later.

"I got me a paw for my baby," I told her.

She just looked at me and didn't say anythin'. After a bit, when she'd fixed us both tea, she sat down next to me and said, "Are you all right, November?"

I knew what she meant. "Oh, yes, Ansalu, everythin' is goin' just fine."

"I mean," she said real clear, "that I know you didn't like what you were goin' to have to do."

"It's not to worry, Ansalu; I figured everythin' out just fine. And now Odd is goin'to be my baby's paw. Even though he don't know it yet!" I added.

We didn't say any more about it, and I was just as glad I hadn't really allowed myself to think about what had happened between Odd and me on that rainy night. And then Odd made it happen again two nights later.

Sometimes I'd have to deal with my feelin's, but not just yet. Not yet.

So I had a new heart for my sewin' and Ansalu, and I made a whole bunch of clothes and things for the baby. Sometimes, I'd suggest that Ansalu come over to Odd's cabin instead of my always goin' over to Ansalu's. I said she could leave just before Odd'd come back, and he wouldn't know. But she said it gave her pleasure to have me come over there, and besides, we didn't want to take a chance on Odd comin' home early.

I was feelin' more at peace than I had been for a long time. Odd said. "One day, that Brother Crabtree was preachin' over at Gauley Bridge. He wondered if I was fixin' to go." I told him, "I guessed I'd had enough revivalin'."

He didn't say much, just sort of smiled.

An I decided somethin'. I decided that I'd best get Odd to sleep in my bed more regular. So I made it my business to sort of let him see me, accidental like, without my clothes on every now and then. I'd act like I hadn't meant it to happen or like I didn't know he was anywhere around. and it always worked. I could see his body g'tting' all excited and next thing, he'd be in my bed again.

I began to feel safer and safer. Ansalu said it was 'bout time to tell him.

Then one day Odd came home from Wilson's Springs lookin' like he was about to burst.

"Gotta tell you, November, gotta tell you," he said, tossin' his hat on a chair and throwin' his jacket after it.

274

"What you gotta tell me, Odd?" I asked.

"I had a talk with Junior Washbon last week, November," he said.

"Junior said he liked my work. He'd never said it before. But for some time now I've been feelin' his eyes on me while I was workin' out back of the store. Anyways," he hurried on, "he said he had a plan for me."

I felt a little pinch inside me when I thought of Junior Washbon havin' a plan for Odd. Looked like he and me were both usin' Odd and makin' plans for him. I didn't feel too proud.

"So today Old Man Washbon called me to his office, November."

I was caught up by this turn, and I wondered what was comin'.

"Yep, he sent a clerk to bring me to his office and he told me to take a seat and I sat down just like like..." he was caught for words.

"Just like any business man?" I asked.

"Yes, that's about it. He made me sit down just as though I were important. November. First time he ever did that!"

I waited.

"An then he said somethin' about Junior tellin' him how good a job I was doin', and that Junior had given him and idea." He paused, thinkin' back in pleasure over his visit to Old Man Washbon's office.

I tried to nudge his thinkin'. "Then what, Odd?"

"Then he told me that he was thinkin' about openin' a new job at the store. He said business had been good and he was fixin' to make the store bigger, and it just made good sense to open a new job. He said he's goin' to have a man who won't do anythin' except take care of the bulldin's and keep 'em painted and in good repair. He says he plans to build a lot more onto the store, and takin' care of all the buildin's will be mighty important." Odd paused to look at me and let that all sink in.

"And, November, he wants me to be that man! Old Man Washbon asked me to be the man who takes care of his store property! He says I'll be in charge. I'll be in charge of all the buildin's for the Washbon Department Store." He stopped, lost in the good feelin's that he was filled with.

I was mighty pleased to see Odd so happy. For just a little bit, I couldn't help wonderin' if Junior Washbon had somehow guessed about the baby. But I pushed that thought away. Wasn't no way he could know. This was somethin' Odd had done for himself.

I was real glad for Odd and asked him all kinds of questions.

"When will the new job start, Odd?"

"Oh, it'll start right off next week, November. The Washbon's are already at work on the plans for their new buildin', and they said they want me to be there from the beginnin'. I'm to wear different clothes, too, November."

I could see his eyes shinin' as he told me how Old Man Washbon told him that in his new job, he should have nicer clothes to wear. "He said, from now on, anythin' I buy at the department store won't cost as much, November. He said I can buy anythin' they've got for just about what it cost them to get it."

He looked real pleased with himself, and I started to set supper on the table, thinkin' that life sure did go off on unexpected side roads now and again.

THE CHOICE

It took some doin', but things were goin' along pretty well for a bit. I went down to Wilson's Springs with Odd when he went to get some new clothes. You know, to wear on his job at Washbon's Department Store. Goin' down, he was almost like a little kid; he just wanted to fly down that path! 1 had to keep slowin' him down, or he'd have left me way behind.

When we got to the department store, he wanted me to come in with him and help him pick out what was right. I backed off from goin' in with him. I hadn't seen Junior Washbon to talk to since, well... since that night on the path. And my stomach pure knotted up at the idea of facin' him if he should come by while Odd and I were pickin' out Odd's clothes. But lookin' at how excited and proud Odd was, I just couldn't spoil things for him. I went into the store with him. I thought about what I'd learned from Ansalu, so I held my head as high as ever I could. And I didn't once look down. I had on my green dress, and I knew it was gettin' awful shabby, but I'd fixed at it so it wasn't but a little too tight, and Ansalu'd given me her shawl to keep, so I was wearin' that, too, and I felt pretty good about how I looked.

But I thought I'd die if Junior Washbon came by and could tell I was gettin' on towards havin' a baby, I remembered his eyes and I figure he'd know right away that the baby on the way was his.

Things worked out all right, though. Junior Washbon did come by while Odd was pickin' out which kind of pants would be best for him to get. But Junior Washbon only nodded hello to me and then started talkin' to Odd.

"If you want somethin' that is practical and still looks good, Odd, why don't you get yourself a pair or two of these?" he asked, holdin' up some grey pants from a big pile on the table.

"I've got some of these myself to wear when I'm doin' outside work."

Well, hearin' that Junior Washbon himself wore those grey pants set Odd up higher'n a cloud, I could tell from his face come hell or high water he was gonna have a pair of those grey pants.

"Do you think it's the kind of pants your Paw wants me to wear?" he asked.

"Sure do," Junior said, smilin'. Then he took us to a rack that had shirts made out of the same kind of grey material. He looked at the little tags inside the collars and picked one out and gave it to Odd. "This one looks like it ought to fit you," he said. Then he motioned to the little changin' room and said, "Maybe you'd better try things on, Odd. Nothin' like tryin' somethin' on to be sure you got the right fit."

Odd smiled kind of sheepish, I could see he had some doubts about undressin' in that little place with the curtain around it. But he didn't want to look foolish in front of Junior Washbon, so he just took the clothes and went inside.

As soon as Odd pulled the curtain and shut himself off, Junior Washbon moved over close to me. He was so close I could get the smell of him and see where he'd shaved himself. He smelled like no man I'd ever come across before. There was a kinda sweet smell about him. Almost like the smell of spices when you're bakin' with 'em. And I was too proud to move away from him. I didn't want him to guess what a bunch of jangles I was inside just from seein' him again and bein' this close.

He didn't say a word, just leaned himself against the door frame and looked at me in a way that made me feel like he could see right on through.

Seein' him made me feel terrible inside and started me rememberin' things that were best forgotten. But it made me surer than ever that I never wanted to name him as father to my baby. I wanted all that behind me.

By then, we could hear Odd makin' sounds like he was about finished in the little room, and Junior Washbon stepped back from me just as cool as you please.

"Lovely weather we're havin'," he said just as Odd pushed back the curtain.

An then Odd was back, and I could breathe easier.

Well, Odd and Junior talked about the clothes and that Odd oughta get two pairs of pants and two shirts.

"It's cheaper in the long run," Junior said, "what with the discount and all." Then they talked about payin' for 'em and everythin' and I could see that the two men seemed to get along pretty good. I already knew that Odd kinda looked up to Junior Washbon.

It made me feel uneasy inside.

"While we're here, November," Odd said, comin' back to where I was waitin' for him, "I want you should pick out a dress for yourself." Then he stopped a bit and looked at me, "No," he went on, "I want you should pick out two dresses for yourself. Get one for workin' around the cabin and in the garden that you can wash real easy. And get one for good, too. If I'm goin' to be in charge of the department store bulldin's we'll most likely be comin' to town more'n we do now. You oughta have a dress just special for that. For when you want to be fixed up nice."

It plum took my breath away to hear him talkin' so. Two dresses! I'd never thought to hear Odd say anythin' like that, and somethin' inside felt real warm and good.

Then Junior Washbon said, "Why, that makes good sense, Odd. Every woman needs more than one dress."

I didn't know quite how to take Junior Washbon, so I just looked at Odd But I saw by his face that he really wanted me to pick out two dresses, so I turned to the racks of dresses wonderin' which ones to pick. This time, though, I knew more about buyin' a dress, and I didn't feel as flustered as when I bought the green one. I went up and down lookin' at all those pretty new dresses and tryin' to picture myself in them. There were two I liked special, but the one cost too much, so I didn't want to mention it to Odd. I didn't want him buyin' me somethin' like that. I didn't want to be beholden to him.

I tried the other one on. It hung nice and full from the top to the bottom. I figured that even when my stomach got real big with the baby, I could still wear that dress. And it was made out of some kind of cotton material that looked like it would wash real good without fadin' a whole lot. It was a dress that would give me a lot of wear, and I told Odd I'd like to have it.

He was pleased with it, too.

There was the one other dress that I liked even better. But, like I said, it cost too much. It was made out of some kind of nice material that hung real soft and full and swished when you moved your hand. And it was blue. A beautiful blue. It was every bit as pretty as the dress that Eloise Bardwell had worn that day so long ago when I first came to Wilson's Springs.

I truly wished for that dress, imaginin' that I'd look almost as nice as Eloise Bardwell had looked in the blue dress she'd worn. But I was still feelin' guilty for what I was doin' to Odd, so there wasn't no way I'd ask him to buy it for me.

I wouldn't take but the one dress. It upset Odd a little bit, but when he saw I meant it, he said, "Well enough," and just got the one I'd tried on.

Things were startin' to move pretty fast for me.

Odd got started in his new job and came home nights lookin' like things were goin' pretty good. He'd walk off proud in the mornin' wearin' his new clothes and come home at night lookin' like he was right satisfied with himself. Sometimes he got home later than he was used to, and I had a hard time keepin' the supper warm and tasty. But he always had some kind of tale to tell me about somethin' interestin' that'd happened at the store, and he seemed to like it that I sat long at the table with him, and just let him tell whatever it was.

Seein' Odd so happy and doin' so well just made me feel more and more troubled in my mind. I knew that pretty soon now I'd be startin' to show. I could feel my stomach swellin' up, and even with my new full dress on, I had to be careful not to let myself pooch out. I was real careful not to let Odd see me without my clothes on anymore, I didn't want him knowin' yet.

But I knew I had to do somethin' pretty soon about tellin' Odd about the baby I'd stew about it and get real upset and promise myself that I'd tell him when he got home that night. And then he'd come home lookin' tired and proud and somehow I just couldn't do it.

At first, I'd just thought about gettin' a paw for my baby.

That was the most important thing, right?

But I hadn't counted on how I'd feel about tellin' Odd. You see, at first I guess I just thought of him as bein' there. I mean, I didn't really think about him goin' on bein' the baby's paw and how he'd feel and all that. and I'd come to see that Odd was a lot smarter than I'd first thought. He was just real quiet.

About speakin' his thoughts and feelin's. And now that he had a real job that he could take some pride in, he was beginnin' to share more and more of his thoughts and ideas with me. I could begin to see things about him I'd never seen before.

Like how he really felt responsible about the buildin's at the store and would sometimes walk down to Wilson's Springs on a Sunday afternoon when the store was closed.

"Just checkin'," he'd say, "Just checkin'."

And it scared me. It scared me 'cause I wasn't sure that he was goin' to hold still and let me fool him into thinkin' the baby was his. The more I thought about it, the less I was sure I wanted to.

But it was sure time to do somethin' about the baby. I just didn't know what. I wanted to go over and talk to Ansalu about it. I dearly wanted to go see that welcomin' cabin and rock in her rockin' chair. And I wanted to see if she'd made any more things for the baby. But since I'd set myself to trickin' Odd the way I was, I hadn't gone over to Ansalu's. I wasn't really proud of what I was doin', even though I didn't know any other way to handle things. It wasn't but a couple of weeks since I'd seen her, but it seemed forever. The more I thought about talkin' it over with Ansalu, the worse I felt. I could remember how bad I'd felt when she and I were on the outs with each other. I'd felt so alone, like part of me'd stopped livin'. And now that we were friends again, I didn't want to take a chance on spollin' things. I didn't know how'd she take to my trickin' Odd the way I was. She wasn't much on trickin'. She believed in sayin' things straight out.

I wanted Ansalu to think good of me.

An yet I needed Ansalu's help. I was all caught up in my own feelin's, feelin' ashamed and guilty and purely miserable.

282

Nights I didn't sleep well, and daytimes, I just walked the floor, pacin' off my misery. I didn't know what to do. I hadn't counted on feelin' this way. And it was tearin' me apart inside. Bein' a kid and livin' with Paw and all the boys hadn't always been so good, but it sure was a lot easier than gettin' to be a woman and havin' to take charge of myself.

One side of me was kinda proud about how I was gettin' a paw for my baby. No matter what I had done, it didn't seem fair that my baby should have to pay for it.

So... makin' sure the baby would have a paw and a name folks wouldn't point a finger at was good. But on the other hand, bad as I needed a paw for the baby, I was beginnin' to feel awful about trickin' Odd into bein' that paw.

I didn't know why that bothered me so much, but it sure did.

There just didn't seem to be any way to turn.

I guessed I'd better go see Ansalu.

NO WAY OUT

"Oh, Ansalu, I just don't know what to do." I stopped talkin' and just sat there, waitin' for her to tell me what to do. Ever since I'd finally gotten up the courage to come see Ansalu, I'd felt kind of relieved. Like believin' that Ansalu'd tell me what to do to make everythin' right.

Ansalu had that way about her. I don't mean she could really make everythin' she set her hand to come out right. But she had a way that made you feel good about whatever it was you had to do. Like it was all right to be you.

Anyway, once I'd started talkin', I hadn't stopped 'til I ran down. And now I was waitin' to see what she'd say. Ansalu just sat rockin' back and forth in her chair and studyin' over what I'd said.

"A conscience can be a terrible thing to have, November," she said at last. "People without consciences have a much easier time of it. They can do most anythin', and so long as they're happy, nothin' bothers them. But it didn't work out that way with you." She looked at me and shook her head. "You turned out to be one of them folks who cares about other people and tries to be decent and honest." She shook her head and sort of sighed a little. "An now you've got a Jim-dandy of a problem to solve. I don't know how you can work it out, November, but it's somethin' you got to do all by yourself."

"But, Ansalu!" I began…

"No, November, there ain't no way I can't help you with this one. You see, girl, even though I wish I could help, you're the one who's trapped inside with your conscience and your heart. You're the only one can figure out what will make that conscience feel all right."

Then she got up and went over to her sink. "An now," she went on, "I've got to get busy and finish this washin' if I ever expect to get paid for it. I promised to have it back by tomorrow mornin' and there's a lot yet to do."

I felt bad about havin' taken her time and was tempted to offer to help 'er, but I knew she was too proud to accept help with the work that brought in her money. Ansalu'd found several families who needed help with their washings, so she washed for them. I don't 'spose it paid much, but she was a real fine person and proud to be able to earn her own way. So I heaved myself out of the chair and said good-bye and started home. I hadn't got the answers I'd come for, and somehow I felt more mixed up than ever. I guess I hadn't realized how much I was countin' on Ansalu comin' up with and answer for me. She'd listened real hard and thought things over and then said it was my worry and I'd have to work it out.

What she'd said about my havin' a conscience set me back a bit. I hadn't thought of all the upset inside me as bein' a conscience. That took some gettin' used to.

Well, I got back to the cabin and started fixin' Odd's supper. He'd be comin' along right soon, and I wanted to have things ready and hot for him.

After he came home and washed up and was sittin' at the table, I just stood behind where I usually sat and looked at him. I was nervous and fidgety.

"Ain't you eatin', November?" he asked.

"Uh, not just yet," I told him. I had to do it. I had to tell him now. And somethin' inside knew I had to tell him the truth. I wanted to be standin' up so I could hold on to the back of the chair for strength.

"Odd," I started, havin' a hard time gettin' my voice to come out right. "I've got somethin' I gotta tell you and I don't know how to do it."

He looked up, surprised and stopped eatin', his fork halfway to his mouth.

I tried to keep my eyes on that fork so I wouldn't have to watch his face. But it didn't work.

"Odd," I blurted out, "I'm goin' to have a baby."

He looked at me and his mouth fell open. Then a smile started in his eyes and spread all over his face.

"Why, November?" he finally said, "That's....that's..."

An I stopped him right there. I wanted to let him go on believin' it was his...I truly did. But I couldn't.

"It ain't yours, Odd."

He sat there real still, the smile dyin' away and a hurt look creepin' into his eyes.

"I'm not just sure whose baby it is, either," I told him, wantin' to get the worst of it over with.

"What d'ya mean you don't know whose baby it is?" he said, the hurt look changin' to anger. "Are you tellin' me that you been sleepin' with other men besides me?" he asked, gettin' to his feet and glarin' across the table at me.

I didn't know how to answer him.

"What you been up to, November?" he asked in such a tone that I knew I'd best find and answer.

"It's.... It's a long story, Odd. I don't mean for this all to happen. It was...somethin' I couldn't help...it was..." I didn't know how to finish.

"How long've you known you was goin' to have a baby?" he demanded.

"For about two months, Odd," I told him, my voice was so low it was like I was whisperin'. I was afraid of what he'd say.

He just looked at me, kind of startled at first, then his face got all tightened up and he started to talk through his clenched teeth. I knew he was fierce upset. "You knew all along that you was goin' to have this baby ... and you were goin' to make me think I was its paw?"

He slammed away from the table and yanked open the cabin door. Then he turned, his hand still on the door. "You...you just been foolin' me with all your soft talk and lovin' and stuff. You just wanted to make me think it was my baby. And all the time you been off foolin' around with Lord knows how many men. and I thought you were gettin' to like me pretty good. What a God-dam fool I was! You ain't doin' nothin' but usin' mel You ain't got no feelin's for me at all!"

He stamped out through the door and stopped on the porch, raisin' his fist and smashin' it against the cabin wall. "November Sunshine Mudd, you ain't nothin' but...you ain't nothin' but a tramp. You ain't no better than my Maw was when she run off on my Pawl." and then he disappeared into the darkness of the night.

I hadn't known about his Maw runnin' off on his Paw.

The cabin never felt so quiet and lonely.

An cold.

I sat down at the table, afraid my legs wouldn't hold me up anymore. I looked at all the food on the table, gettin' cold now, and was afraid I might throw up. I was too churned up inside to think or even cry, so I started gatherin' the plates together and scraped all the food onto one. Then I made myself get up from the table and take the food over to the door. I stood a bit and listened into the night, but I didn't hear any sound of Odd comin' back. So I went down the steps and scraped all the food into a wooden bowl that was sittin' on the ground. I knew that pretty soon the raccoon who feasted on our scraps would make a real good meal out of all there was for him tonight.

Thinkin' about the 'coon kept my mind off my troubles.

Then I went back into the cabin and sat down, tryin' to work things through.

I did the best I could, thinkin' back over what Odd had yelled at me, and I felt pretty shamed of myself. I had hurt him real bad, and now I had to figure out some way to begin to put things right. If I could.

I looked at the old spring-wound clock on the shelf and saw that it was just about time to go to bed. But I knew that if I went to bed now I'd just lie there and toss and turn and feel bad.

Then it came into my mind to do somethin' real nice for Odd in case he took it into his mind to come home after a bit. Somethin' special.

I had some buttermilk, and part of a box of cocoa, and a couple of eggs. I had everythin' I needed to make Odd's favorite chocolate cake. I even had some sugar left in my big mason jar so I could make him a White Mountain Icin'.

White Mountain icin' was somethin' I had learned from Ansalu, and Odd loved it. You had to beat and beat and beat

288

it whilst it was cookin' on the stove. I didn't make it very often, either, because it took so long and cost so much to make. But when you got it done, it was all fluffy and sugary and sweet, and it heaped way up on top of a cake.

Now I figured, bakin' Odd a chocolate cake and makin' White Mountain icin' was just exactly what I ought to do.

Well, I thought it all out, gettin' the things I needed out of the cupboard and puttin' them on the counter to work with. Then I remembered, I'd best build up the fire. It was comin' on towards spring, and we didn't keep a big fire in the stove most times. It was easier just to build a little one when I went to cook a meal. Otherwise, the cabin got too hot inside, and if you left the doors open, the flies and things came in.

But I'd need a big fire to bake a cake and make White Mountain icin', so I decided I'd best bring in quite a bit of wood.

I looked around for the lantern, but I guessed Odd had taken it with him cause it wasn't on the nail where it always hung.

I lit a coal-oil lamp and stood it on the floor in the open doorway.

Then I started out to gather the wood. The sooner I got the wood in and built up the fire, the sooner I could start on the cake.

There was a knot in my stomach that wouldn't let me be. I was mad at myself for not tellin' Odd a long time ago what'd happened to me, but it didn't do any good to think about that now.

It was hard to see the steps goin' down in the dark. The lamp didn't throw much of a glow. But I was real careful and hung on to the rallin' Odd had built, good and tight. I made my way down to the woodpile. I knew I should only carry two or three pieces of wood cause they were big and rough, and heavy. But the thought of havin' to make my way out here again in the dark didn't sit well. So I picked up as much wood as I could carry. I loaded myself up good and started back to the cabin.

I walked pretty slow cause my load was heavy and I wanted to be sure and step true. I didn't have any trouble findin' the steps and makin' my way up them, either. I took the steps one at a time, countin' them off in my mind like I'd counted them hundreds of times. I touched each one careful with my foot 'cause I couldn't see them in the dark over the top of my wood. I felt careful all the way up the steps to the top, and stood there puffin' a bit.

Then I stepped out onto the porch.

It wasn't there!

Just that quick, I knew I'd stepped wrong, and with a horrible sickenin' lurch, I felt myself fallin' off into the darkness, bangin' and crashin', the wood peltin' down on top of me and boundin' off in every direction into the night. My arms and legs seemed to have a mind of their own, twistin' and turnin', pullin' my body along, me and the wood smashin' our way down.

I hit the ground with a thud that drove the breath clean out of me. All I knew then was that somethin' was wrong, bad wrong.

An then pain washed over me, and the darkness swallered me up.

TIME HAS A WAY OF PASSIN'

Black, real black.

An then the black started to lighten up a little, and bit by bit I began to remember. As my head began to clear I could tell that my leg was twisted under my body. Real unnatural. I moved to try and get it straight, and the pain was so sharp it caught my breath. And even though there wasn't anyone to hear, I screamed, "Help, help!" as loud as I could.

Then I just lay there listenin' to the echo of my cries fadin' away over the mountain.

Nothin' but Inky dark all around.

I was so scared I could feel my heart poundin' like it was tryin' to get out of me.

I knew there wasn't a soul anywhere around to help me. But I couldn't just stay out there on the ground with my leg twisted up so bad. Slowly, I pushed with my arms, tryin' to get myself turned around so I wouldn't be restin' on that twisted leg. It was real slow and hurt dreadful, but I could feel the weight beginnin' to ease off my bad leg.

An then a new pain began tearin' at me. A pain down deep inside.

I stopped tryin' to move and held myself as still as I could, hopin' the new pain would go away. But it throbbed and pushed and felt as though all my insides were drainin' away. The pain caught my breath and I could feel it leakin' out in low moans between my teeth where I clenched 'em tight together. I tried to will the pain away, but it had a fierce hold on me and just wouldn't let go.

My baby! Was my baby tryin' to come so soon?

I touched myself fearfully, dreadin' what I'd feel.

My hand came away wet and sticky, and even though it was too dark to see, I knew what covered my hand.

Blood.

Then the pains grew worse and I couldn't fight 'em anymore. I couldn't even stop the blackness as it swallowed me up.

"November."

Way off in some dream, a voice was callin' me to wake.

Go away, voice. Go away.

"November Sunshine! What happened? Open your eyes, November, talk to me."

I couldn't.

Somehow, I knew it was Odd's voice talkin' to me. But part of me remembered that he was mad at me. He'd gone away. Odd was mad at me. I couldn't face him. I felt myself slipping away.

I hid then, hid in the blackness of the pains and felt someone touchin' me, movin' me. It hurt. Oh God, how it hurt!

I wanted to cry, "Leave me alone!" But no words came out.

Blackness.

I just seemed to float in and out of the blackness, too weak, too hurtin', to make any sense.

An then after floatin' in that darkness for a long time, I finally opened my eyes and saw, truly saw, where I was.

It took awhile, comin' up from all that blackness, to know the soft light of a small oil lamp and the friendly warmth of a wood stove's fire. I moved my head and saw Odd, sittin' on a hickory chair, hitched up close to the bed. His head was bent with tiredness and sleep. I wondered how long he'd been there.

"Odd," I tried to speak his name, but nothin' came out.

He must've sensed my wakin', though, because he jerked his head and leaned over me.

"November! Are you awake, November?" he asked.

"I'm sorry," was all I could manage. But I don't think he heard me. I had wanted to tell him how very sorry I was for so many things, but I had no way to tell him because the pain was takin' over again, and my eyes just wouldn't stay open.

Sometime later, I felt somethin' cool bein' laid on my face. Oh, how nice that felt! By then my body felt as though it was burnin' up and I had thrown off my covers, restless and muddled in my mind.

I knew someone was talkin' and tellin' me somethin', but I couldn't make any sense out of the words. I let myself drift off into the darkness again.

I must've been driftin' a long time, not makin' any sense at all.

"November. Can you hear me, November?"

It was Ansalu's voice comin' soft and sweet as a balm out of the darkness. "November, you've got to make yourself wake up, girl," she urged, brushin' the hair back from my face and gentiin' me.

I tried. Oh, how I tried. I could feel Ansalu's hand holdin' mine and squeezin' as though she was tryin' to help me. and bit by bit, the blackness faded away and the brightness of a sunny day took over.

When I first opened my eyes, I had to shut them just as quick. The sun was so clear and bright that it hurt my eyes and made them sting.

I tried to say "Ansalu," but no sounds came out. Then I closed my eyes again to rest them from the sun, and drifted back to sleep, feelin' safer, somehow.

The next mornin' I woke to the sounds of Ansalu hummin' as she worked round her cabin.

"Mornin'," I said, though it came out in a sort of croak and startled Ansalu so she came runnin' to the bed.

She was all over smiles when she felt my face and said, "Good! That fever's done left and your skin nice and cool to the touch. Are you feelin' better, November?"

"Yes..I think so," I answered. I moved a bit, little by little, testin' to see if those awful pains were real or part of a nightmare.

"Don't try to move too much, November," Ansalu cautioned me. "Your legs are not in a splint, and you don't want to jar anythin' loose. We set it best we could, but you were lyin' so still we just wrapped it tight. Should hold lest you try walkin' or some such foolishness!" she said. I knew she was tryin' to sound cheery.

"Don't fret, Ansalu, I don't feel up to movin' very much," I said.

Then Ansalu went and got me some milk toast and fed me just like I was a baby. To tell the truth, I relished bein' taken care of that way. The milk toast tasted so good. I could tell she'd toasted some've her own baked bread over the stove, and then covered it with warm milk and a tad of honey. I could feel the warmth and goodness as it spread itself all the way down.

After I'd finished the milk toast, I felt more like talkin'. Maybe now was the time to ask some questions.

"Ansalu," I began, "I wish you'd set me straight on some things."

She looked a little strange at first, but she went and dragged the rocker over to the bed and sat down facin' me.

"What do you want to know, November?"

"Well, I want to know about a lot of things. But first, what happened to me when I fell? Why was I bleedin'?"

She just looked at me and seemed to put off answerin'.

"Well, first, November, why don't you let me tell you about Odd?"

"Odd?" A faint memory of him sittin' by the bed floated into my mind, but it floated away again before I could get hold of it. "What about Odd?"

"Well, it was Odd who found you and brought you here."

"He did? How did he get me all the way to your place with a broken leg?"

Ansalu shook her head like she wondered her, too. "I tell you, November, I could hear him yellin' clear across the mountain when he brought you. I went rushin' to the door and peered out, but I couldn't see a thing at first. Then I saw a little bit of light a wigglin' off in the distance, and I figured that to be Odd."

She looked at me and patted the back of my hand.

295

"I didn't know what he was up to, just kept yelll' and comin' and tellin' me to get things ready." She paused, rememberin', "But I didn't have any idea what it was he wanted me to get ready!" She sighed. "An he was comin' so fast that pretty soon I could see he was carryin' somethin' big, and then in a bit I saw it was you!"

I must've made some sound, then, because she bent down close and asked, "Are you all right, November?"

I nodded and said, "Go on"

"Well, I went flyin' down the path with my lantern to see what he was carryin' you for and you looked so pitiful it near broke my heart! Odd'd wrapped you up best he could in a cover, and he must've broken his broom cause he'd used the handle to your broken leg so it wouldn't hang loose and hurt you more." She stopped, shakin' her head from side to side as though seein' that sight again. I just don't know where he got the strength to carry you all that way."

"Well, we got you inside, then, and he laid you down on my bed, November, and you've been here ever since."

I lay there thinkin'. It came to me how far it was from Odd's cabin to Ansalu's. Had Odd really carried me all that way by himself? How in the world had he managed? I'd gotten to be a pretty big woman, and I certainly hadn't been able to help him any. I looked at Ansalu and she must've read my question in my eyes.

"Yep. Odd carried you all the way here by himself. Without once stoppin' she added. "I've thought about it over and over again since that night, and I can't see any way he did it. But he did!"

I lay there in Ansalu's bed, just thinkin' back over what she'd said. I wasn't able to put it together, yet, and when I thought about it, I wanted to be good and clear in my mind.

"What happened then?" I asked.

"Well, Odd hung over the bed like a mother bird whilst I checked you out and made you as comfortable as I could. Was no way we could get the doctor up here that late at night, so we had to make do."

She stopped talkin', then, and moved her chair back from the bed.

"That's enough for now, November. Won't do to get your mind so riled up, it takes away from your body's healin'." She spoke so firm that I knew she meant what she was sayin'. I wouldn't get any more by askin' questions right now.

Anyway, I was feelin' awful tired, and the thought of just closin' my eyes and tryin' to sort my thoughts out made me feel peaceful.

For a while, I tried to make some sense out of what Ansalu'd told me. I mean, mad as he was at me, how come Odd'd carried me all the way over here to Ansalu's that way? I tried to picture him strugglin' along with me just like a big old rag doll in his arms, and I knew it was and awful load. I went to sleep wonderin'.

Next time I woke up, I had that heavy feelin' that bad dreams, lots and lots of bad dreams, leave you with. I didn't let myself remember the dreams, I didn't feel I could deal with them. I just lay there tryin' not to think about them. I thought about the baby, and how scared I'd been about it at first. But now I wasn't so scared anymore, and thinkin' about it filled my thoughts and helped push back the bad dreams.

"Oh, you're awake," Ansalu said after a bit, comin' to check on me. "I just about thought you'd sleep forever. But it's good you got a good sleep. Isn't anythin' that equals a real good sleep for settin' the body back to rights." She fussed around the bed then, straightenin' the covers and such. "Do you want a bite of breakfast, November?" she asked me.

I was surprised to find that I was truly hungry. and the idea of some of Ansalu's cookin' suited me just fine:

"I sure am, Ansalu," I told her, "don't know why I'm so hungry this mornin' I lay back to wait til she fetched me somethin' to eat.

Ansalu looked at me for a few moments as if makin' up her mind about somethin'. "Well," she finally said, "you've been sleepin' for the best part of two days," she said, turnin' back to her kitchen.

I lay there takin' that all in. Two days! How could a body lose two whole days and not know it? I didn't fret long, though, because in just a little bit while Ansalu was back with a steamin' bowl and a little pitcher of milk. Before I could ask any questions, she was feedin' me some fresh-cooked oats and milk, and I just let myself stop thinkin' and enjoy them.

When the oats were nearly gone, she seemed willin' to just sit on there by the bed for a bit.

"I got some questions," I said.

"Empty your mouth first, November. You've gotta eat all your food to get your strength up. Then we'll talk," she said, spoontr' in another mouthful. I didn't have any trouble at all eatin' every bit of the oatmeal she'd made me, either.

"All right now, November, let's hear what's on your mind," she finally said after she'd rinsed out my empty bowl.

"Well, I'm still mixed up about gettin' here," I said. "I remember goin' outside to get some wood so I could do some bakin'. I wanted to bake a chocolate cake for Odd," I explained. "An the light wasn't good so...so 1 fell," I told her, wishin' I could hide from the mem'ry. "Then," I made myself go on because I needed to get things straight in my own mind. "Then I guess I don't remember anythin' at all. "Cept, somewhere in my mem'ry I think I woke up and Odd was sittin' by the bed. But that's just a little mem'ry and I'm not sure it isn't just a dream."

I looked at Ansalu hopin' she could tell me which it was.

"I guess you might've done just that, November. From what Odd told me when he brought you here, he found you lyin' in back of his cabin by the steps, all twisted up and big chunks of wood all over the place. Said he thought you were dead, and he grabbed you up and carried you in where there was light so he could see better. He could tell, then, that you were still alive, so I guess he put you right into bed and did what he could to make you comfortable. Then he just sat by the bed and waited. And waited. And when you didn't wake up, he began to get real scared that somethin' was bad wrong, and he wrapped you up and headed over here."

Ansalu had an approvin' look on her face as she told me this. I could tell that she and Odd had hit it off, and she thought he'd done just right.

"An then, first light in the mornin', Odd went off to Wilson's Springs to bring back the doctor."

"Doctor Brad was here?"

"Sure was, November. But you weren't in much way to pay him notice." She smiled at me. "He looked you over real good and checked where Odd'd set your broken leg. He said Odd sure knows a lot about settin' broken bones! Anyway, he says

299

you're goin' to be all right. He says all you need now is lots of time to get yourself all healed up. He'll be back again tomorrow, too."

I thought about what she'd told me. And I thought about why I'd gone out in the dark to get wood. And I remembered what I'd done to make Odd so mad at me and how he went stormin' out of the cabin and all. I felt dreadful.

"I don't know why Odd did that for me," I said real low.

"What're you talkin about?" Ansalu asked, leanin' over to hear me better.

"I mean, Odd hates me, Ansalu."

"What makes you think he hates you?" she asked.

An best I could, I made myself tell Ansalu what had happened and the hurtful things we'd both said and how he thought I'd been trickin' him about the baby and all.

"He thinks I'm no good and that I just used him to try and get a paw for my baby. He thinks I went around layin' with other men, Ansalu." I was quiet, thinkin' back over the last months. "An the worst of it is, he's right. He's right in everythin'."

"On, November, Ansalu said softly, pattin' the back of my hand like she was wont to do when she thought I needed gentlin'. "You're bein' too hard on yourself."

"No, Ansalu, it's true. I did everythin' wrong. But at least I didn't tell him about Junior Washbon. That'd just about kill him, workin' at the store like he does. It's all my fault. I didn't listen to you when you tried to tell me about your feelin's about Brother Crabtree and the revivals and all. And if I'd just listened to you, none of this would've happened."

"November, we all do the best we can at the time. That's what you did, what you thought was the best thing at the time."

"But I spoiled everythin', Ansalu. "I wanted so bad to learn everythin' and do everythin' and get to be somebody who mattered, and I messed it all up. And then, when I found I was makin' a baby, I got so scared and set out to get a paw for the baby, and I didn't even once stop and think how Odd'd feel. Not once." I couldn't talk anymore then, I felt all choked up with tears.

Ansalu busied herself doin' somethin' in the kitchen for a bit to let me get myself all together. Then she came back and sat by the bed.

"I don't know what to do, Ansalu, I can't go back and live in Odd's cabin no more."

She didn't say anythin', just patted my hand.

"Oh, Ansalu, I just can't go back, there's been too many bad words between us. I can't go back there knowin' how Odd feels about me. He truly hates me, Ansalu, he does."

She thought a bit, then she said, "No, November, I don't think it's that Odd hates you." She had a real serious look on her face. "I think it's just that when there are bad hurtin' words and bad feelin's between two people, it isn't easy to be kindly towards each other. It takes a bit for the hurt to die down. But you've gotta remember that it was Odd who brought you up here, and Odd who went for Doctor Brad." She thought a minute and went on, "True, Odd didn't have much to say. But he did what he thought he had to. He did it, and that's for sure."

"Don't count that too high, Ansalu. You know that's the way us hill folk have to do things. There's nobody else to do for us. We have to do for each other." She just looked at my face real sad, while I talked.

301

"November, there isn't any way you can make yourself forget the hurtful things between you and Odd. Once they're in your mind, they sorta stick there. Best you can do is learn to live with them. In time, things'll get easier."

I thought about what she'd said and wondered if I ever would learn to live with what Odd had called me. What made it worse was that I figured he was right about me. I wasn't any good, I felt so bad, I turned away from Ansalu.

"Well," I said at last, takin' a deep breath to steady myself. "I guess I'd best stop thinkin' about what's over and done and start riggerin' out what to do about the baby. The baby. The thought of my little baby so snug down under my heart sort've made me want to take hold of things again. I had a lot of thinkin' and plannin' to do.

Ansalu'd turned her back on me while I was talkin'. She'd never turned her back on me before. I was puzzled.

"What's the matter, Ansalu?" But she wouldn't turn around. "Are you hidin' somethin' from me?"

She turned around real slow and came and took hold of both my hands. Then she sighed like it hurt her to breathe.

"That awful pain you were havin', November," she said more gentle than I'd ever heard her talk. "Do you remember it?"

I told her it was like a nightmare that I didn't want to remember. It was long and scary, and not all the pieces came together in my mind.

"That's because you kept passin' out on us, November. I didn't think you'd remember it."

I nodded, waitin'.

"Well, when you were havin' all that pain, the pain that made you cry out, well, well," she stopped, tears wellin' up in her eyes and lookin' away again.

I waited, fearin' what was ahead.

"You...you lost your baby, November," she said in a whisper so low I could scarce hear. "Poor little thing was all mixed up, and it couldn't wait to get itself born."

I didn't know I was cryin' til I put my hands up over my eyes and felt the tears runnin' down my face.

Poor little baby, poor little thing, I thought. You never did have a fair chance at things. First, you got started in a mama not ready for you, and then you didn't have no daddy. "It's not fair! I cried out, reachin' out blindly for Ansalu and the comfort of her arms.

I don't know how long she sat there on the bed holdin' me in her arms and lettin' me cry. She patted my back and rocked me back and forth and cried along with me.

An then I found I was cryin' for more than that little lost baby. I was cryin' for all the bad times and sad times and sorry times. I was cryin' for Odd and what I'd done to him, and I was cryin' for me, too.

I cried and cried like the well would never run dry.

I must've cried myself to sleep, because when I looked again, the sun was near down and the room had a soft twilight glow. Ansalu laid me back on my pillows and covered me up. She was sittin', rockin' real quiet, watchin' me as I woke up.

"Are you feelin' any better, November?" she asked.

303

I knew she was hopin' I was, so I said, "Yes," even though the hurt was still as strong inside and I didn't think I'd ever feel happy about myself again.

There just didn't seem to be anythin' I could do right.

Well, Ansalu set herself to fix us some supper. She always had a way of goin' about things so that whatever she did, it seemed the best thing to do. I didn't feel the least bit hungry when supper was ready, but Ansalu made me eat a bite or two. She said I needed to eat to build up my strength. I didn't much care about my strength. Or anythin' else.

An then, later, when she was fixin' to go to bed, I got my courage together and asked, "Are you sure, Ansalu? About the baby, I mean?" She looked at me and sighed, real sad. "I'm sure, November. That's what Doctor Brad said happened." She thought a moment, and then went on, "But, November, he said you're goin' to be all right. I mean, you'll be able to have another baby when the time is right."

That made me feel real cold, like winter icicles had filled me up inside, I couldn't bear to think of me ever startin' and carryin' another baby. No way would I ever take a chance on havin' so much sadness and pain inside again. The pain, the hurts to my body, those I could learn to live with. But the hurt in my heart? I never wanted to feel such hurt and loss again.

I lay real still, just lookin' at the cellin' and tryin' not to think.

"It'll be all right, November, honest, Ansalu said softly, leanin' over the bed. "I know the pain you're feelin' now is awful bad, but it will get easier to live with by and by."

I remembered then, Ansalu had lost a child once, too.

304

I looked at her out of the corner of my eye. I could see some of the old pain on her face even now. But, somehow, she had learned to live with it.

Oh Lord.

It would be hard. Awful hard.

Could I do it?

LIVIN' TAKES TIME

I just lay there on my back, thinkin'. Ansalu went off and busied herself, leavin' me alone. My mind skittered from one thing to another. It was easier fillin' it up with bits and pieces of memories than it was thinkin' about now. I remembered how my brothers used to tease me and how I'd turn to Lem for comfort when I was little. and I remembered the first time I'd tried to make cornbread. All my brothers had taken just one look at that cornbread on the table and told Paw they weren't hungry. He was upset at them 'til he tasted that cornbread. He got him a mouthful and started to chew, then he went over to the door and spat it all out. Next, he got his jug, took the cork out, and swallowed as though he had a ten-year drought inside him. It was funny to think about now, but I'd been mighty put out about it then. My mind slipped from that to when I made buttermilk biscuits so light that my brothers, Paul and Righteous'd fought over the last one. Ansalud taught me how to make those biscuits. I guessed, thinkin' back, thanks to Ansalu's patience, I'd learned a lot about cookin' in between makin' the cornbread and the biscuits.

Then I stopped myself thinkin' about when I was livin' with Paw because some of the hurt things started takin' over. I turned and looked out the window at the beautiful sky with clouds so fluffy you'd think somebody had painted them on a piece of bright blue cloth.

I lay there a long while just lookin' at the little bowl Ansalu had filled with dirt and put by the window. There was just one little leaf stuck in the middle of the bowl. And when I asked Ansalu why just that one little leaf was stuck in that bowl of dirt she'd told me.

"Well, in the long hours I was sittin' by your bed wattin' for you to wake up, I saw that leaf that was broken off my African Violet plant lyin' on the floor under the bed. I guess that when

306

Odd had carried you into the cabin that night, somehow, a leaf got broken off my favorite plant. So, while I was waitin' for you to get some better, I filled that bowl with dirt and watered it and planted that leaf. You just wait, November, and you'll soon see why."

She didn't say anymore, so I tried to think of reasons while I lay there. It helped keep my troubled thoughts away.

An so the day passed. And the evenin'. I pretty much managed to keep from thinkin' about my troubles. But then I fell into a worrisome sleep, filled with awful torment in dreams. It's hard to keep the bad thoughts away when you're asleep.

When the sun finally began to lighten up the sky next mornin', I felt like I hadn't had any rest at all. I don't know when I've ever been so glad to see it was day again. It's much easier to push the nightmares away when the sky's crystal bright with mornin' sun. Doctor Brad came like Ansalu'd said he would. He spoke real cheerful and I knew he was tryin' to make me feel better, so I acted as cheerful back at him as I could. He gave Arisalu a tonic to give me and said it was just a matter of time.

An each day slid slow into another, and the pain in my heart was still hard to bear.

Then one day I sat up in bed and called Ansalu over.

"I guess I'd best get started doin' somethin', I can't just stay here in your bed forever," I told her.

She looked stern. "November, you can't get up for another two or three weeks. You've got to give your body and that leg time to heal. Anyway, it's plum nice to have you for company. Helps give meanin' to my days. I get awful lonesome now that my will is gone."

"Two or three weeks! Oh, Ansalu, I can't stay in bed that long! What would I do? I'm already so beholden to you..."

She shut my mouth with her hand and sparks flew from her eyes. "Don't you ever mention bein' beholden again, November Sunshine. I ain't forgettin' that you were the very first person hereabouts to make me feel at home here in this part of the hills. And you and me have been good friends for a long time now. So, don't you ever mention beholden again!"

I was shocked by her seemin' so vexed with me, and sat there, silent.

She went off and made some tea, and I could see her busy with the kettle and cups and such. She seemed to be makin' more noise gettin' that tea ready than I'd ever heard her do. I guessed she was workin' off her feelins'.

Sure enough, by the time she carried the tea things back on her old brass tray she'd calmed down and was smilin' at me. I felt so much better to see her smile that I took a cup of tea and drank it right off, even though I wasn't the least bit thirsty, and I burned my tongue doin' it.

After she'd finished her cup of tea, she perked up and said, "I've got somethin' to talk over with you, November."

I just waited.

"Remember how you liked this rug when you first saw it?" she asked, pointin' at the big braided rug on her floor.

I said, "I sure did."

"Well," she said, beginnin' to sound real excited by what she was sayin'.

"I thought about how much you liked it and that gave me and idea. Soon after you were here that time, I went down to Wilson's Springs and talked to the lady who runs that nice store over near the Baptist Church. I asked her if she thought she might ever want a braided rug or two to sell in her store, and she was that tickled! She said people from the city are always passin' through Wilson's Springs sight-seein' and such.

They stop in her store and ask for things made here in the mountains that they can buy. She said they call them native crafts or some such, and pay good money for them."

Ansalu stopped to look at my face and see how this was soundin' to me. She was so fired up with her idea that she sort of pulled my feelin's along with hers. She could tell by my face I was int'rested.

"Anyway," she went on, "it wasn't the right time for me to make anything for her store back then, but I'm wonderin' if now wouldn't be a good time. I thought, maybe, that is you might like to learn how to make braided rugs, too. And then you and me could both make rugs and sell them down to Wilson's Springs."

I was nearly blown over by the idea, imagine! Me, November Sunshine, makin' somethin' so fine that somebody would pay real money for it and take it to use in their home!

"Do you think I could?" I asked.

"Of course," Ansalu reached over and squeezed my hand. "I can teach you how in no time, November."

"But where are we goin' to get enough material, Ansalu?"

"Oh, that part's easy, November. I already got lots of old clothes and scraps of material out in my lean-to. I get them from the ladies I do washin' for. They save their old things for me." She looked at me real proud to have and answer all ready for that question.

I ran the idea through my head real slow, lookin' for anythin' wrong with it. It slid by just as easy as pie. There wasn't any reason at all, as far as I could see, why Ansalu and me couldn't have a go at rug makin'.

"I'll be glad to do it I told her, excited by the idea in spite of all the pain and hurtin' I'd been dealin' with.

An then it broke all over me. All of a sudden, I realized that for the first time in my whole life, I was makin' a choice about my life for myself. Nobody was tellin' me what I had to do. I was free to say yes or no. Whatever I wanted! It was a wonderful feelin', for sure, but it was a bit scary, too. what if I chose wrong?

I looked at Ansalu, and the worry slipped away. "How could doin' somethin' I wanted to do so badly with someone as wonderful to me as Ansalu always was, be wrong?"

"Oh, November!" Ansalu cried, huggin' me as best she could whilst I sat there in bed. "You don't know how happy that makes me!"

"Do you really think we can make them good enough to get real money for them ?" I asked.

"Of course, November. and I don't mind tellin' you that it will be fun doin' it with you workin' here besides me to chat with and help make the workin' time go faster."

"I'll like that too, Ansalu." I looked at her kind face, "It will help keep my mind from thinkin'… thinkin…" I stopped. But Ansalu knew. She understood.

So, we began to talk about makin' rugs and Ansalu told me how we do it and what we needed and all that. and then she asked me if I'd be all right to stay alone for a while the next day, and she'd go see if any of her ladies had saved any more clothes and scraps for her.

"Of course I can stay alone," I told her, scared inside about it, but not wantin' to spoil her pleasure.

An the next day she bustled about real early, gettin' me cleaned up and the bed fixed and settin' out food for me to eat. When she had the breakfast all redded up she looked around the cabin and said, "I really ought to dust and sweep out 'fore I go, but I'm so anxious to see what they've saved that I don't believe I'll bother cleanin' any more. She grinned happily at me and moved a little table over near the bed. Then she put some bread and fruit on the table. "That's in case it takes me longer than I figure and I'm not back by midday," she said.

After she took one more look around and came and felt my forehead to make certain I didn't have a fever, she hurried out the door, hummin' a song to herself.

At first, after she left, I felt the loneliness of the cabin as though it was real and heavy and sittin' on my shoulders. I told myself that was foolish. I had to learn to be alone, I couldn't expect to stay with Ansalu forever.

The day looked awful long ahead of me, so I figured out a way to fill up the time. I thought about colors. I thought about all the colors I liked best and how I could put them into rugs and make them look like flowers in a garden. I closed my eyes and tried to picture those rugs, lookin' so bright and cheery and fine. I dreamed up one rug after another, and found myself beginnin' to look forward to really learnin' how to make them.

When the sun was overhead, I ate some of the bread and fruit and settled myself for a nap.

An then, before too long, Ansalu was back. and she carried a great big bundle in her arms.

"Look at this she cried, happy as a lark, untyin' the bundle and dumpin' the bits of material all over the bed. There were blues and greens and reds and yellows and plaids and flowered material. There were more kinds and colors of cloth than I had ever thought there could be.

"It's like a rainbow," I said, laughin' in spite of myself.

Ansalu looked at me when I laughed. I knew hearin' me laugh'd made her happy, but when I stopped laughin' the pain rushed back in all the harder as though I hadn't any right to laugh.

"We'll start first thing tomorrow," she said, pretendin' she hadn't seen the tears start again. and when she turned away for a minute, I brushed away the tears and made myself talk as happy as I could.

Well, we both woke up early in the mornin'. I'd been wakin' up right early ever since the accident. Bein' awake was safer

311

than bein' asleep and havin' nightmares. Ansalu, though, woke up early because of the rugs.

We hurried through breakfast and then Ansalu set herself to teachin' me how to make braided rugs. She was patient, ever so patient, and showed me how to choose my colors and cut the cloth into strips. She didn't ever lose her patience with me, even when my cuttin' got crooked and I spoiled a real nice piece of cloth. Then she showed me how to hold my hands and braid the strips together. She had to show me some parts over and over 'til I got them right.

We worked that way for a long time.

Then Ansalu stopped what she was doin' and looked at me with a funny look on her face.

"November," she said real solemn like. "I've got somethin' to tell you"

I wondered what it was, somethin' inside me knotting up at how serious she looked. She finally went on.

"While I was out collectin' these pieces of material yesterday, I just happened to meet up with Odd."

I sat there in bed, shaken. Odd! I felt like I was being swamped with all kinds of mixed-up feelin's.

Since I'd told her about the trouble between Odd and me we hadn't either one of us mentioned his name.

But now she stood up tall as she could and looked me straight in the eye. In a voice that showed me she wouldn't take at all kindly to my arguin' about it, she said, "I think the two of you need to talk."

Talk! The thought of havin' to face Odd after the awful trickin' I'd done to him and the mean things he'd said to me made me feel sick. There was no way I wanted to talk to Odd!

But Ansalu went right on, she wasn't givin' in to my feelin's at all.

"He'll be comin' by here, November."

NOW WHAT?

I looked at Ansalu, not believin' what she'd just said. She was lettin' Odd come by her place when she knew how I felt!

"No call to get upset, November," she said quietly, like you soothe and upset child. "We got to passin' the time of day, and he asked how you're doin'. He seemed quite concerned. Then he asked if I thought he could stop by and see you. He wondered if that'd be all right."

"What did you tell him?" I asked, afraid I already knew.

She took a deep breath and said, "I said I thought that would be fittin'." she answered. She looked me straight. In the eyes, and said, "Specially since he's the one who found you and carried you over here and went for the doctor and all."

I didn't dare argue.

"He's comin' by this evenin'," she said, actin' like it just occurred to her to tell me.

"Oh no, Ansalul so soon? That's awful!" I cried.

"Why is it awful?" she wanted to know.

"Well, just because it is!" I cried, breakin' into tears.

The rest of the day my stomach felt like there was a knot inside, and my head hurt, and I felt hot and cold by turns. Ansalu said it was nerves. I didn't know what it was, but I wished Odd wasn't comin'. I just felt I wasn't ready to face him. Not now or ever.

An then it was suppertime, and he'd be comin' soon, and I couldn't eat a bite of the supper Ansalu set down in front of me.

An before I knew it, he was standin' in the doorway.

"Hello, Ansalu, November," he said, stoppin' just inside the cabin door.

I made myself look at him and saw that he was brushed and polished to a fare-thee-well. I'd never seen Odd get himself so fixed up, and I tried to look him over real good without him noticin' me doin' it. Then I caught him studyin' me, and we both looked away.

"I've got to see about waterin' my plants, Ansalu said as calm as you please!

I knew she'd already watered her plants and just wanted to leave me and Odd alone. "Do you have to do it now? I asked her.

She got my meanin' clear, I knew, but she pretended she hadn't. "Of course!" she said, just as perky as you please. Then she went outside, closin' the cabin door behind her.

It sure was quiet.

"Well," both Odd and me said at the same time. And then it was quiet again. "Come on in," I said at last, and he did.

It was quiet again.

"You're lookin' some better, November," Odd said standin' beside the bed. That was worse'n ever. He's so tall I had to bend way back to look up at his face, and that bothered me. Made me feel small and like a little kid about to be yelled at again.

"Uh, you could sit down," I said, motionin' him to sit in Ansalu's rocker there by the bed. He did. He sort of had to fold up his long legs because I'd forgotten how low Ansalu's rocker is to allow for her short legs, but neither one of us mentioned it.

"You look good too, Odd," I said into the silence.

An then we sat there sort of stupid, neither one of us havin' the right thing to say. The longer I sat, the more I got thinkin' back over things, and then I burst out, "How come you never came up to see how I was doin'?

The minute I said it, I knew it was stupid, too.

He looked sort of startled at how mad I guess I sounded. Then he hitched the chair closer and faced me.

"Well, November," he said, soundin' like he was about to say somethin' he knew I wouldn't like but meant to say it anyway, "I wasn't just sure if I wanted to see you again." Then he paused for a bit, and I could tell he was thinkin'. "Things weren't too good between us before… before…"

I nodded and sighed real deep. "I know, Odd, I know."

Well, we sat there kind of dumb again, and I wished he'd go.

Then Odd took a deep breath and his face got a funny look to it, and he said, "That was a real hurtin' way you told me about well about the baby." he stopped, lookin' sort of embarrassed and hurt, both.

I didn't know what to say.

"You mighta known I'd be proud if I had helped make the baby. But just about the time you let me get feelin' kinda proud, you ups and tells me it wasn't me what made it."

By the time he finished, his face had taken on a real sad look. I felt awful that I hadn't thought any more than I had about his havin' feelin's.

"I didn't mean to hurt you, Odd," I said, and then I didn't know how to go on. I sat silent for a little bit, and then I tried again. "Things weren't like you thought. I mean, I wasn't off with a bunch of different men or anythin'. But you see, I had to have a paw for the baby, and I didn't want to tell you about now I' shamed myself, so I just didn't know what to do."

"What d'you mean, shamed yourself?" he asked.

I swallowed, my mouth felt so dry, and I couldn't get any words to come out.

"Aren't you goin' to tell me, November?" he asked.

I thought it over.

"I guess you have a right to know," I said slowly, tryin' to think of a way to explain how I got a baby without tellin' him about Junior Washbon and spotlin' things for him down at the Washbon store.

He sat there, lookin' hard at my face.

"It was… it was that preacher at the revival, Odd. Ansalu didn't want me to go back after the first time, but I thought the whole thing was so wonderful and excitin' with the music and all that I went back anyway."

"What happened?"

"I stayed after the service and went to his caravan, an... well, he..." I turned away from him, I just couldn't finish.

"You mean he… he took you, November?" Odd asked, anger makin' his voice real sharp and cold

I just nodded my head.

"An then he went galavantin' off, leavin' you to face things alone?"

Odd got to his feet and started pacin' the floor, over to the stove, back to the chair, over to the stove, back again. His steps were heavy, and I could tell he was really upset.

"It's over, Odd. Can't do anythin' about it anymore. It don't matter now, anyways." Then I made myself say it, even though it came out only as a whisper, "The baby's gone Dead." I could feel the tears tricklin' down my face.

Odd stopped his pacin' and stood by the bed, lookin' at me. "I should've known it must be somethin' like that," he said, his voice low and sad. "I shouldn't have gotten so mad and not let you explain or anythin'."

We sat there, dumb again, but this time, I felt better because the part I told him had been true, and now it was out in the open. And I felt better than I had in some time because I'd managed to tell him without mentionin' Junior Washbon and takin' away his pride in workin' at the Washbon store.

I owed him that much.

Then Odd's face brightened up.

"Wanted to tell you how things are goin' with me, November, not sure why, but it looks like things are beginnin' to change for me."

"Change?" I asked him, curious.

"Yep. First off, things have been goin' good, real good, down at Washbon's department store."

I just waited.

"Old Man Washbon said he's real pleased with my work. He said he'd be glad if I would think about movin' closer to the store. He's got it in mind for me to take on more responsibility around the place. You know, seein' that the buildings are kept painted and în good repair, and things like that, I've been in charge of takin' care of the bulldin's right along, but now he says he wants to pay me to check the place out every night and open it up in the mornin'. Says he's willin' to pay for me to have a telephone so he can call me or I can call him whenever I need to. You know, sometimes a shipment is comin' in real early, or people need to pick up somethin' special. Anyway, I guess he's goin' to pay me quite a bit more money," he said with a grin.

I looked at Odd while he talked, and couldn't help seein' how much prouder he was holdin' himself and how much easier he could talk about somethin' that was so important to him.

"That's wonderful, Odd," I told him, really meanin' it, too

He grinned at me, "Yep, it is, isn't it, November?" He paused, shakin' his head like it all surprised him, and then went on, "Well, anyway, I've been sort of lookin' around Wilson's Springs and thinkin' how scared I used to be to go down there with all those strangers, but it isn't that way no more why, shucks, November, I can't walk down the street in the Springs now without somebody sayin' "Hello," or "How you be?" He nodded at me like he was tryin' to make me see it like he did.

"I got to thinkin', November, it's and awful long walk all the way down from my cabin to the store, and some days I like to think I almost can't make it back up the hill at the end of the day. Well, I've been passin' a right nice little place for sale on Cherry Creek. He looked at me to see if I knew where he meant. "You know, you take the road up the mountain just a little ways til you get to the first right fork? Well, the place is just up the fork a real short way. It's not real big, but it's white clapboard and it's got a nice white fence clear around the

318

property and cherry trees and grape vines growin' in the yard. I heard the folks who live there might be lookin' to sell, so I went 'round to talk with them. They're willin' to dicker. It's got runnin' water in it and all. I already know that Bill Waters, who lives up in back of me, wants to buy my place for his son who's gettin' married."

I guess I was sittin' there with my mouth open, Odd was movin' so fast in what he was tellin' me. I almost couldn't believe what I was hearin'. "But, do you think you'll like livin' that close to the Springs, Odd?" I asked.

He shrugged. "Can't hurt to try," he said. "It'll sure be a lot easier than walkin' up that mountain after workin' all day. Anyway," he went on, a sheepish grin on his face, "to tell the truth, I've kind of gotten to like it around Wilson's Springs. Things are happenin' all the while and there's lots of people and places to get to know. And you know, November, it's not so lonely as it is livin' way up the mountain like I do."

Thinkin' of Odd bein' part of Wilson's Springs and the people there was just about too much, I thought back to the strange, shy man who'd taken me with him to his cabin up the mountain from Paw's a couple of years back. I looked at him now. How come I hadn't noticed what was happenin' to him before?

"So," he was sayin', and I realized I'd missed what he'd just said, "I'm wonderin' what you want me to do with your things up in the cabin, November?"

When what he was askin' sank in, it took my breath away. I just hadn't stopped to think about what would happen after I left Ansalu's. Odd had a place to go, a job to do.

I had neither.

I saw he was lookin' at me, wattin' for and answer.

319

"Well ... I don't really have all that many things .... " I said, and then I just ran out of words and sat there starin' at him, feelin' like I didn't have anything solid to grab onto. Like I was fallin' into a hole.

I looked down so Odd wouldn't see how scared I was feelin' after what he'd said, and a bit of color in one of Ansalu's rug scraps that was still lyin' on my cover caught my eye. Right away, I began to feel better.

"I'm glad, truly glad, that things are goin' well for you, odd," I managed to say. "I think my life is goin' to be changin', too." I told him.

He looked at me, suprized.

"Looks like Ansalu and me are goin' into the rug-makin' business. We're fixin' to make rugs like that one there on the floor. Ansalu has a shop in Wilson's Springs where the lady said people travelin' through town are always askin' for such to buy." I felt better, tellin' it.

Odd's face brightened as he looked at me. "That's good, November. And I thought he sounded like he really meant it.

"Uh, November," he said, shiftin' from one foot to the other like he used to do, so I knew that what he was goin' to say was costin' him "I gotta say somethin' and clear things a bit between us it's about when… when I got you from your Paw and you came to live with me" He faced at me, but his eyelids were lowered and I couldn't read what was in his eyes. "I never did feel right about takin' you in trade for that Stevens rifle your Paw wanted so bad. I knew it wasn't the right thing to do, but… well… at the time." He stopped and swallowed and went on. "You see, November, I was terrible lonesome up there in that cabin by myself. But I just couldn't seem to get the hang of talkin' to a woman. Felt like I was swallowin' my tongue whenever I'd try. But I'd seen you workin' in your

Paw's garden, and I got to thinkin', heck, she's only a kid, and I wouldn't have to be scared talkin' to her. It was about then that your Paw told me he wanted my Stevens rifle and offered to trade you for it. I don't know if you remember, but I came to your cabin a year or so before you came home with me. Anyway, when I got to see you up close, I knew you were just too young. But then later, when he offered to trade again, I could see you were on your way to becomin' a woman."

Odd looked at me shyly, "An you were gettin' right pretty about then."

He stopped, embarrassed. "Well, you know what happened. Your Paw in me traded and you came home with me."

I felt so strange, hearin' Odd talk about his feelin's like this. In all the time I'd been with him at his cabin, I never knew he'd had such derp thoughts. I sure never knew he thought I was pretty. Hearin' him was almost like I was evesdroppin' on somebody's private thinkin'.

"Then, after you came and I saw how scared you seemed but how hard you worked anyway, I thought I'd put and end to the bargain I'd made with your Paw. Even let him keep the rifle. But then I'd get to thinkin' how lonely I'd be with you gone, that I just didn't say anythin' at all. November, it was sure nice havin' you around to talk to and fix up things, and take away the empty feelin's.

I could almost feel the hurt and anger I'd felt when I first came to live with Odd, meltin' away. Things were movin' so fast now, and I just wasn't ready for them. I wasn't ready to think of Odd as somebody who'd been caught in his own loneliness and fear. Somebody who'd been willing to make that horrible trade just to try and keep the coldness out of his own life. I was gettin' so mixed up I didn't know how I truly felt."

"Anyway," he went on after he took a long breath, "I know I shouldn't have treated you like a thing. I had no right." He looked at me, his face tight with the effort of what he was sayin', his voice droppin' so low I could scarcely hear, "So I guess I can't blame you for whatever it was you did or said, November."

We were both silent, and there was somethin' new in the way we looked at each other. It was as though, for the first time, I could look at Odd and see him like a person, if that makes any sense to you. Somethin' like when you go to draw a picture of a ball with a pencil, it's just one line and flat and still. But a real ball isn't flat, it's round and it rolls and bounces and is a joyful thing. Well, it's like I'd only ever seen Odd as a flat pencil line. I'd never realized that there was much more to him than that.

I looked at this man here by my bed and thought about how different things might have been. But, they weren't. Things were just what they were, full of pain and sorry things and hurts that would take a long time to get over.

"I guess you didn't mean to hurt me, Odd, any more than I set out to bring hurt to you. I was just wantin' to learn everything and do everything 1 had never gotten to do. And I didn't rightly know how, and got myself into and awful mess. Then, when I was needin' a paw for the baby, I didn't know what else I could do but what I did." I stopped. There were no more words.

Odd folded himself back into Ansalu's chair, and this time the silence was easter.

"Anybody want a cup of hot tea and a mess of fresh ginger cookies?" she asked.

Odd brightened up, and havin' Ansalu there made me feel better, too.

322

Odd helped her find a place for the tray she'd brought and went to the other room to get another chair. When he got back with the chair, Ansalu was sittin' in the rockin' chair, arrangin' her best teapot and her good cups on the little table by the bed. In the middle of the table sat that rose-covered plate, heaped with ginger cookies.

Ansalu started pouring in the tea, but Odd couldn't wait. He reached out and snitched a cookie and popped the whole thing into his mouth.

"Ummmmm!" he moaned, rollin' his eyes up towards the ceiling, "If that don't taste good!"

Ansalu reached out and pushed the plate closer to him so he could reach the cookies easier. You could see she was tickled that he liked them so much.

"Help yourself, Odd," she said. "I've baked lots and you can take some home with you if you want." She smiled at him like they were becomin' friends. "It's nice to have a man to feed again," she said.

Well, in no time we emptied the plate of cookies and drank up all the tea, and Ansalu went to the kitchen for more.

Odd stood up and said, "Well, I'd best be gettin' home."

I just sat there, waitin'.

"You know, November, I'm feelin' much better about some things," Odd said watchin' me while he talked. "I'm feelin' good about my work at the store and about movin' down to Cherry Creek. An, I'm feelin' better about… about…".

"The way things are 'tween us," I finished for him.

"Yep. That's so. I know things take time, November, and that you and me both got new things to do and new ways to go, but I'd like…" he stopped again.

But this time I didn't finish for him. What he wanted to say, he'd have to say himself.

I just waited.

He took another long breath, and started again. "I guess what I'd like to say, November Sunshine, is that I'd like, I mean I hope, well." His voice trailed out and he closed his eyes a bit like he was tryin' to build up strength or somethin' "I mean," he finally said, "I'd like it if you'd let me come callin' and maybe you'd go out walkin' some with me. When you're feelin' better, that is, you know, like, can we maybe be friends?"

I looked at Odd, needin' and answer, aware that I was seein' him different than I'd ever seen him before, and feelin' all right about it. I thought about what he'd just asked me, and I thought about the wonderful plans Ansalu and I were makin', and for the first time in my whole life, I was beginnin' to feel like a whole person, somebody who counted.

My thoughts began tumblin' around in my head so fast I didn't know just what it was I really wanted to say. There wasn't anybody to say what was in my mind but me. Mixed up, I turned away from Odd and looked out the window.

Sittin' on the windowsill in the soft light, I saw the bowl of dirt with that African Violet leaf of Ansalu's. And there, growin' up along the stem of that poor, broken leaf, were two tiny new leaves. They were pushin' up from the moist earth, green and fresh and strong. I thought about how the leaf had gotten knocked off Ansalu's plant and how careful she'd planted it in that little bowl. And now, what had been just a broken leaf was growin' and sendin' out new leaves of its own.

And somewhere, deep down inside me, like that little African Violet leaf, somethin' fresh and good was beginnin' to come to life again.

That's when I knew.

I'd been hurt, and I'd done some things right and some things wrong, and I'd been in an awful mess. But now it was like I could see ahead a little, and I knew there would be lots of things to do, and I'd have choices to make, and whatever happened to me, I was gonna be all right.

It was easy then to make a choice. I turned back to Odd because I knew now what to say to him about us bein' friends.

"I think I'd like that very much, Odd," I said.

www.ingramcontent.com/pod-product-compliance
Lightning Source LLC
Chambersburg PA
CBHW070212260626
47160CB00002B/529